NO LONGER PROPERTY OF
SEATTLE
W9-CTP-864

"A novel full of heart and verve. Strikers, spies, propagandists, anarchists, immigrants, suffragettes, and provocateurs—schemers and dreamers all—converge in this portrait of turbulent pre–World War I San Francisco. Part political drama, part family mystery, *The Blast* is vividly imagined, a quintessentially American story of power and corruption, solidarity and sabotage."
—Cara Hoffman, author of *Running*

"*The Blast* is quite simply a tour de force. Matthews brings to life a lost world of radicalism, in a riveting story that ripples out across multiple continents, with the entanglements of the personal and the political squarely in his sights. He has a keen ear for the passions, large and small, that impel women and men to take matters into their own hands. This is a novel for our troubled times."
—Sasha Lilley, author of *Catastrophism*

"In this immersive novel, Joseph Matthews transports us to San Francisco at the dawn of its modern age: a restive town of immigrants and *arrivistes*, robber barons, and political radicals, where suffragettes and anarchists and Wobblies all fought to shape the city's future. In a taut narrative that's also a delight, this is essential reading about how and why what happens in that city has so often shaped America."
—Joshua Jelly-Schapiro, author of *Names of New York*

"Joseph Matthews's gripping novel pulls back San Francisco's curtain of fog to explore what was America's most radical city. The novel's characters are entwined with the labor-left-anarchist-immigrant cultural stew that made the city so dynamic, all against the backdrop of revolutions in Mexico and Ireland, labor and women's rights struggles on both sides of the Atlantic, and the 1916 Preparedness Day bombing, a response to big capital's exhortations for the US to enter World War I, seeking to grow their fortunes and quash labor unions while wrapping themselves in that most cursed of refuges, 'patriotism.'"
—Peter Cole, author of *Wobblies on the Waterfront*

"A compelling and affecting novel, vividly bringing to life a complex and tumultuous chapter in the history of American class conflict."
—Kenyon Zimmer, author of *Immigrants against the State*

"Joseph Matthews has done it again. With masterful storytelling, *The Blast* takes a deep dive into the ferment of San Francisco before World War I, revealing the complex racial, ethnic, gender, and class dynamics of a militant and multifaceted opposition movement pitted against the Bay Area's burgeoning plutocracy and its apparatus of repression. A compelling glimpse of what might have been and, perhaps more importantly, why it isn't."
—Ward Churchill, author of *Wielding Words Like Weapons*

THE BLAST

a novel

Joseph Matthews

Also by Joseph Matthews

Everyone Has Their Reasons

The Lawyer Who Blew Up His Desk

Shades of Resistance

Afflicted Powers: Capital and Spectacle in a New Age of War
(with I. Boal, T.J. Clark and M. Watts)

The Blast
© Joseph Matthews
This edition © 2022 PM Press

All rights reserved. Except for brief quotations in critical publications or reviews, no part of this book may be reproduced, used, or stored in any information retrieval system, or transmitted in any form or by any means, electronic, mechanical, photocopying, recording, or otherwise in any manner without prior written permission from the publisher.

ISBN: 978–1–62963–910–9 (paperback)
ISBN: 978–1–62963–911–6 (hardcover)
ISBN: 978–1–62963–921–5 (ebook)

Library of Congress Control Number: 2021936604

Cover by John Yates / stealworks.com
Interior design by briandesign

Cover photo: A portion of the *Gruppo Anarchico Volontá*, San Francisco, 1916, *Archivio Centrale dello Stato, Ministero della Cultura*, Rome.

10 9 8 7 6 5 4 3 2 1

PM Press
PO Box 23912
Oakland, CA 94623
www.pmpress.org

Printed in the USA.

for Sanjyot and Jesse

1

"Those hands."

Emerging from a reverie about early days with Jamey, Kate realized that her hand was running back and forth through the deep maroon velvet of the seat, and once again she marveled at finding herself in this private compartment of a first-class car, just five days out of Boston, yet, remarkably, on the new Transcontinental Express, only one more until she would reach San Francisco. Marveled, but was also discomfited: by the car's fulsome gilt-and-purple splendor, by the steam-heated air as soft as the carpet, by the porters in their crisp white jackets bringing her fresh towels each morning and asking whether Madam would be taking breakfast in the dining car, and was there anything Madam needed. Asking her, Kate Jameson. Though despite all the years married and widowed with that surname, to herself—abetted by unrelenting subtle and not-so-subtle reminders from the Jamesons, notwithstanding their ironic decision to call her Katherine—she was still and always would be just Katie Carey from South Boston. A "Southie." How did she get here? And tomorrow, San Francisco. Again. After so long.

Images from that city, from her months there with Jamey and Maggie, now flitted behind her eyes as if on a cinema celluloid that keeps skipping off its sprockets, each street or building or room making a tantalizing appearance then sputtering away before she can quite manage to bring it into focus. Well, no surprise, she consoled herself, it had been fifteen years now. And anyway, after the great quake and fire a decade ago, how much of the rebuilt city would she even recognize? She bent her head, shook it slightly, and again caught sight of her hand splayed there on the compartment's velvet seat cushion.

"Those hands," Jamey would say now and again, the words and his slightly awestruck expression coming always as a surprise to her, he'd be staring at them, her hands, captured by them, then slowly he'd look up at her with sweet crinkling eyes.

"Ah, Jamey," she said aloud, granting herself permission for thoughts that, in all the years since he'd been gone, she had struggled against so mightily. Especially while Maggie was still at home. Because to think of him too often or too intensely would have been to risk speaking of him. And that was closely guarded against, except ever so briefly and in a deliberately vague if always adulatory way intended to shut down quickly the rare direct foray about him from Maggie. Part of the long-held evasion. A conspiracy of silence concocted—in the very first days after Jamey's death—between Kate and her family, the Careys, to shield the little girl Maggie, at the time only six years old. Insisted on, too, by the Jamesons. To protect their name. But in truth also for Kate herself. To wall herself off. From such pain—and incomprehension—that could not otherwise be managed. And such anger. Silence as a way to carry on. For Maggie, yes. And for herself.

It was not the sight or feel of Kate's own hands, though, but sense-memories of his—her husband's hands, those surgeon's hands—that now rushed through her blood and flushed her cheeks. Since Maggie left home more than a year ago, Kate had begun allowing thoughts of Jamey to reemerge, slowly, slowly. But as she neared San Francisco, echoes and images from her time with him there had begun to tumble over one another, ungovernable, unstoppable. Like falling down stairs. She'd feared this, or perhaps hoped for it, when she'd accepted this strange job, this "expedition" as she'd come to think of it. But already she was finding that knowing this might happen and experiencing it were very different things, and the closer she got to San Francisco the more agitated she became.

Because, also, what if she really did manage to find Maggie there? Which after all was part of why she'd agreed to go. That, and because for the first time she'd be escaping, at least for a while, the years-long suffocations of her life-after-Jamey in Boston. And yes, also for the seemingly exorbitant expense monies and the hefty pay, more than five times what she was then earning at her law firm clerking job, and even greater multiples more than what she and Maggie had lived on for most of the years after Jamey had died. For that matter, far more than when he'd been alive, with money so far down the list of things he'd cared about. Which had only added to the Jameson family's chagrin over his marriage to this young Carey girl, this Southie, whom they blamed for expecting, for demanding, nothing more of him. But without an actual address for Maggie or even a wisp of other information—just the note card that arrived over a month ago: "Dearest Mother. Doing fine. San Francisco. Don't know why. Much love, Your Maggie"—Kate knew it was extremely long odds to find her. If she was even still there.

Maggie. Whose notes to Kate, all as brief as this latest, had arrived in Boston every month or so, from different spots on the map, always moving, always west. Maggie. Who seemed almost casual in this minimal contact with her mother. Who could have no way of knowing the surge of joy and longing that Kate felt each time she saw even just such few words sloping across a card in her daughter's lovely flowing hand. Maggie. Hands. How would Kate begin, finally, to speak to her about Jamey? When Maggie left Boston, fled the years-long silence and its penumbra there, Kate understood that she'd waited too long to speak to her about Jamey and vowed to hold back from her no more. But how to go about it, after all this time? And in truth, what could Kate tell her? Because how much, how deeply, did Kate herself understand?

Despite the first-class compartment's luxurious steam heat, Kate found herself shivering. She rose to pull from the overhead rack the costly traveling valise she'd bought with just a sliver of the first hefty installment of expense money Lansing's Bureau of Secret Intelligence—U-1, as the new State Department group referred to itself—had handed her at the end of the often puzzling week she'd spent with them in Washington receiving instructions and an overview of the major San Francisco characters in whom Lansing was particularly interested. Against her chill she now pulled from the bag a large silk shawl—another new purchase—and also dug out the leather-bound notebook she'd bought to help with her duties. She'd been tasked with traveling back to Washington after three months in San Francisco, to give a detailed report to Lansing on her findings there, then to return west if Lansing believed there was more she might learn. It had also been arranged for her to send back secure dispatches from California, if she felt there was particular information that should not wait until she returned east; such messages would be handled by the San Francisco office of the federal government's recently expanded Bureau of Investigation. About the need for two different bureaus—one Intelligence, one Investigation; one secret, one not—the U-1 people had briefly and not very successfully explained to her. Nor had Lansing himself been able to convince her, despite his emphasis on her connections to and in San Francisco, of her suitability for the project, since she was utterly without experience in such matters.

Lansing and his Washington men had been grimly serious while preparing her; after all, the underlying question—whether the nation should join the Great War in Europe—was of almost incalculable gravity. And as part of advising President Wilson on the matter, Lansing needed to know the extent to which Washington could depend on the industrial barons of California—particularly in oil, armaments, rail, shipping, and shipbuilding—to support the war effort if it came to that: they and their enterprises would not only need to facilitate defense of the West Coast against possible German incursions through Mexico but also mobilize on a massive scale to help provide the nation with ships and arms that were in desperately short supply. Hesitation or half-heartedness on their part, let alone resistance, could prove disastrous.

Notwithstanding the monumental decision to be made, several times Lansing had reassured Kate that he had no particular expectations for her time in San Francisco; it was just that the far coast was a mostly uncharted land to the eastern political class, and even if only a few bits of information, or the tenor of a few key characters' feelings about the war, emerged from her foray there, that would be well worth the effort and cost of her project. And indeed, during her time in Washington Kate came to realize that the monies to be spent on her venture, which seemed to her so extravagant, were utterly trivial to Lansing's bureau. Nonetheless, during her Washington preparations, some of the Bureau men had failed to hide their disdain for her mission; toward the end of her time there, she'd even overheard one of them referring to her as "Lansing's folly." And the barb had stuck.

Given all her uncertainty and disquiet about the expedition, plus the expectation that she provide an extensive report when she returned, Kate had decided she would make a contemporaneous written record of her interactions and impressions. So, the notebook. Now she opened it on her lap and—to begin limbering herself for the task of putting thoughts to paper, as well as to distract herself from runaway images of Jamey and Maggie—began writing what came to mind.

Neutral. About Europe's Great War and all. And about the people I will meet in San Francisco. Such a Washington kind of word.

Part of why they chose me. So they said. That I was something like neutral. Familiar with both sides, one of Lansing's men put it, but attached to neither.

Such a short-thinking notion, that a person who's not partial about something should be the best person to report about it. And short-thinking about me. They know so little about me, Lansing and his men. The insides of me. So how could they possibly decide such a thing? From what bits of me they think they know? Balancing what against what? That Lansing once knew Jamey, at university, when they were barely more than boys? And knew that many Jamesons had been military men? That Jamey too had joined the Jameson line of officers? And fought a war?

But no, never fought. And not truly a soldier. A surgeon to soldiers is far from the same. And left it before his time. Which they also know.

Both sides, that Lansing man said of me. Which means what? That the Jamesons are one thing, the Careys so much another? True enough. But also that having known the young Jamey, and his family, means Lansing believes he knew the older Jamey, my Jamey, too? And so thinks he also knows how Jamey must have schooled me, his wife, his Carey wife?

Because who did truly know him, Jamey? In the end, not even me. That I must say to you, Maggie, admit to you. Nor of course could you yourself have had more than an inkling of your father's angels and demons, still so young you were when he died. Which is something I want finally to talk with you about. The blank spots. The dark spots. At least, as much as we can. Before you left home, I'd never gathered the courage. Forgive me. This too I hope. That you can forgive. If not your father, at least me. When we talk again. When I find you. If I find you.

Kate felt a tightness gripping her neck and put down her pencil. Maggie. Again. So quickly she had returned to thoughts of Maggie. Though she savored every memory of her daughter, the recollections and imaginings now sent her spinning.

A porter tapped at the door, announced that the dining cars had opened for supper. Which for Kate, on this fraught, befuddling journey, meant the separate first-class dining car, with its shining silver and perfect linens and rarefied food the likes of which she never saw in Boston except on those few holiday occasions each year when she and Maggie were allowed the grace of the Jamesons' table.

Up to now on this journey, Kate's dining car orders had all been very modest, the kinds of things she was comfortable with, consonant with her sense of self. Tonight though, she decided, she would order the very best that the first-class car had on offer. U-1 was paying.

2

Blue had been gone from San Francisco for nearly three years. First, just heading vaguely east, after a while he'd heard tell of the great Paterson, New Jersey, silk workers' strike—with so much of its energy coming from hell-bent Italian immigrant radicals like those he'd grown up with—and eventually got himself there. But too late: the strike, already crumbling, soon collapsed. So he'd kept moving, crossing over for the first time to the Old World: Dublin; Liverpool; London. Serious, adrenaline-rich times in each. But Dublin had become untenable for him after the lockout disaster in early '14, then England insufferable once the jingoist bellowing had overwhelmed all the voices opposing Britain's leap into the Great War slaughter at the same time it drowned out the suffragettes, including a small, especially militant band with whom he'd become enmeshed. But anyway, by then he'd had enough of being the Yank. No, not the Yank, exactly, which mostly he'd been called with teasing affection in both Ireland and England, but simply an outsider—notwithstanding the embraces he'd enjoyed, comradely and otherwise—and finally he'd been overcome by a hunger for home. Despite no longer having anyone there to welcome him back. At least, not anyone close. And knowing that the last place he'd actually called home, a boardinghouse along the city's northern edge, was gone, razed along with the rest of that particular shoreline's down-market buildings to make room for San Francisco's recent gorge of self-aggrandizement, the Panama-Pacific Exposition—its massive spectacle lasting all of 1915, which he was glad not to have witnessed— and for the grid of upscale Golden Gate–facing homes that were to follow in its place. But now, after a year of small-time prizefights and other odd-job scuffling on his way back west across the country, here he was, just a ferry ride across the bay from San Francisco, where he'd been born and raised. And battered. And bereaved.

It was time. Past time. He was elated.

Dozens of travelers from the Oakland train depot were making their way the hundred or so yards over to the ferry dock, some of them followed by porters pulling handcarts loaded with baggage from the long passenger train that had just arrived. Blue, who'd come in on a boxcar from Nevada in the middle of the previous night—carrying a bedroll, a small satchel, several days growth of beard, and a bruised and swollen left eye and cheek courtesy of a final cash-gathering boxing match—had been woken by the bustling of the newly arrived train travelers and now roused himself from the nest he'd made against a pile of folded fishing nets, eager to board the morning's first ferry across to San Francisco.

He was content to hold himself back as the crowd jostled between the shed where the ferry tickets were sold and the boarding dock: he was a man of the people, he'd been known to explain, just not too many of them at any one time. When the crowd thinned, Blue went over and bought a ticket and as he turned back had to avoid colliding with a tall, imposingly bulky middle-aged man in a finely made tweed waistcoat suit. The man was striding toward the dock at the head of a procession that included, next in line, a woman in a feathered hat and a satin dress over heavy petticoats, all of which seemed to Blue decidedly incommodious for either train or ferry travel, three small children in natty outfits who were bouncing and boistering as if they were squirrels who'd just been freed from long confinement, and a very young slight woman in low-end versions of the other woman's hat and dress—minus the feathers and most of the petticoats—who was struggling to corral the children and keep them moving forward. Bringing up the rear were two stocky, square-jawed, denim-clad porters from the train depot, pulling a cartload of travel valises and a large trunk.

Not until he'd grimly overseen the arrival of his family onto the dock did the big man in tweed realize that the porters had stopped at the dock's edge and were unloading the baggage there. The man rumbled back across to them, his expression struggling to maintain dignity amid his choler at his children, at the hapless au pair girl, at the porters, the crowded dock, the whole lot.

"The ferry."

"Carters, bub, not stevedores," one of the porters answered matter-of-factly. "This is it."

"What good do they do me here?"

"Not for us to say, is it?"

The big man fumed but after a moment's hesitation it was clear that the porters were not going to budge and that, since one of them had his foot placed firmly on the trunk, the man had no viable option but to pay them. With a grunt, he reached into his pocket and picked out their fee. They turned and left without another word or glance.

People were now being allowed onto the ferry. The big man looked around and spotted Blue leaning against a nearby piling.

"Say there. Want a bit of extra cash?"

"Musha," Blue replied with one of the language tics he'd picked up from his Irish immigrant father and from his immersion during adolescence in the boxing world of San Francisco's South of the Slot, a heavily Irish-inflected district of the city. Tics that had been shaken loose and burnished during his recent time in Dublin, and in London during intimate months with an Irish music hall performer. "Why, d'ya have too much of it?"

When Blue followed the remark with neither movement nor expression indicating that he might agree to carry the bags despite his wisecrack, the man turned back toward his family.

"Moira!" he called, but the au pair girl was occupied trying to herd the three children and did not hear. Or seemed not to hear.

"Moira!" he called again, louder, and the girl's head shot up with something approaching terror on her face. She looked beseechingly at the children's mother, who gave a long-suffering nod. Moira hitched up her long dress as if transporting rather than wearing it and scuttled over to the big man and the pile of baggage.

"You'll be getting these on board, if you please," the man grumbled while trying to maintain the appearance of composure. "Carefully."

The man picked up one end of the big trunk and began hauling it across the dock toward the ferry, leaving the slight girl to face the other three pieces of baggage. She struggled to carry and drag and push them along with the moving crowd, finally managing them to edge of the boarding ramp. But getting them up the incline was proving more than she could handle, and the largest suitcase almost toppled into the water. Trailing behind her, Blue grabbed onto the endangered case and hauled it up the ramp; the girl was now able to lug the remaining two bags onboard, though not without her hat falling over her eyes so that she had to choose between putting down the bags to fix the hat or moving forward blind. Blue gave her a steadying hand as she stumbled the bags onto the ferry and dropped them just past the entryway. She and Blue were the last ones aboard; a crewman closed the ferry railing, and within moments they were underway.

Grateful but flustered, the girl straightened her hat and murmured thanks to Blue, who replied with a well-practiced but nonetheless sincere—at least in this instance—smile of charm, then noticed the big man glowering at him. In response, Blue nudged the top of the upright largest case, thudding it heavily onto the deck. The big man now made his way over, his face turning dark; as he neared, the girl took a step back.

Blue boxed mostly as a middleweight, though for some good money bouts—and for the rough-and-tumble small town fights he'd taken while returning west the past year—neither he nor the fight promoters worried about such niceties, and he'd often taken on much larger men. So the looming presence now of this big man caused him no distress. Blue faced him with legs set apart not only in a clear statement of his physical readiness but also, along with his clothes, ragged satchel, and general unkemptness, in a defiant display of his class position. In truth, though, he wasn't looking for a scrap with the man: he'd never felt the need to declare war over every minor border incursion, and he'd been in so many real fights—inflicting and suffering their very real consequences—that he made it a point to avoid the sort of casual bluster that might lead to fists over a meaningless affront or asperity. Yet here he was, despite himself, picking a ridiculous quarrel with this inconsequential man: without realizing it, the ragged edge of his emotions, on the occasion of returning to San Francisco, had been rubbing him raw.

The big man, towering with menace as he approached, appeared to be considering something to say to Blue. Or to do. But as he neared, he apparently also considered potential outcomes, and that other people on the deck, including his family, were watching. He stopped, tight-lipped, a few feet in front of Blue, just beyond arm's reach.

Blue glanced at the au pair girl, then across to where the man's wife stood with the children, then back at the man.

"Well now, not one but two!" Blue said with faux admiration, looking back and forth between the girl and the woman, then stepped easily forward, nodding, and gently squeezed the man's shoulder in an exaggerated gesture of confidentiality and congratulations. "And both beauties. You're a most fortunate man."

It took a moment for the man to realize something of what Blue might be suggesting.

"I have no truck with you, sir. You needn't be offensive."

"Needn't," Blue repeated, then thought for a moment. "Arrah, you could be right, so. 'Need,' as opposed to 'want.' But a close question, I think. And a very personal one, wouldn't you say? I mean, for you to have decided about me so quickly?"

Now the big man looked puzzled as well as chagrined. Shaking his head as if to create distance from Blue's oddness, he grabbed the large case and, followed by the au pair with the other two bags, crossed the deck to where his family waited to go inside the ferry's housing.

Relieved that the encounter had stopped short of farce despite his foolish provocation, Blue now settled himself against the rail. He turned his attention across the bay but was caught by the presence of a woman standing a few feet away. She was looking not exactly at him but more generally in the direction of his pas de deux with the big man, wearing the expression of a disinterested but mildly entertained spectator.

This prompted Blue to conduct what he'd admit was a shallow, but contend was nonetheless a remarkably reliable, well-practiced instant class and character assessment, which included a read of her clothes—a smart, muted, well-tailored woman's equivalent of a man's business suit—and of her accoutrements—a high-end, seemingly new valise and an equally posh new travel trunk. There was something curious about her, though, something that did not quite fit the picture otherwise conjured for Blue by her outfit and gear: something in her face and carriage that was both self-aware and weary, a combination of aspects not normally observed, in Blue's experience, in women who could afford such a well-turned ensemble. She was about forty, he guessed, not striking but quietly handsome: a very pale, angular, V-shaped face under a big pile of auburn hair, her body erect but with a casualness to her posture that suggested she paid it little attention. About forty meant she was maybe ten years older than he was. In recent years, Blue increasingly had found that particular vector of difference to be a positive thing, and he turned to her.

"Sure there are only two sides, you know," he said.

"To what, exactly?"

"To anything."

She looked into his face for a moment, then gave off a small "Hm," which seemed friendly but the more complex judgments of which—if there were any, Blue had to concede to himself—he couldn't read.

"I'll place that in mind," she said, then gathered herself and unhurriedly settled onto a railing bench a few steps further away, a move which put her trunk and valise between herself and Blue.

In the course of his recent years' wanderings, Blue had come to favor the company of women. Perhaps in part as an outfall from adoration of his mother following her death, which, three years before, was one of the reasons Blue had put distance between himself and San Francisco. His mother, who had fought so tenaciously to maintain both food on the table and dignity while raising Blue and his fractious older brother mostly on her own, and then entirely so after the boys' father had walked out on them the final time, and who had long struggled but ultimately failed to hold herself together after Blue's brother had gone off to the Philippines war and got himself killed. But this preference also arose from his particular experiences in the two years he'd been overseas: in Dublin, during the citywide lockout, among the factory women and the theater women and the other brave Church-defying women of the Kiddies Scheme; and later in England among the suffragettes, many of whom looked, in their dress and comportment, not unlike this woman on the ferry. He had enjoyed the arms of one of them, yes, but much more markedly the comradely companionship of many, with their fervidness and honesty unmarred by the bravado and brutishness and other male nonsense Blue had been accustomed to in his San Francisco youth and young manhood, and from which, with these women of varied backgrounds, he'd found a large measure of relief. And now here on the ferry was this maturely attractive, intriguingly self-possessed woman about to spend the next hour or so just a few feet away from him. And who would also be landing in San Francisco.

But maybe, Blue considered, the woman had a purpose when she put herself on the other side of her baggage from him. In London, he'd suffered once from an accusation—made by someone in the small sub-rosa group of suffrage militants with which he'd become con-nected—that, on a particular occasion, his banter had amounted to ill-disguised flirting; she'd made the remark to a knot of three other of these women, with Blue off to the side but clearly within hearing. It had seemed a mild enough, even slightly comic, reproof—particularly when measured against the seriousness of their joint endeavors—and at first he had simply put it down to cross-cultural misunderstanding. And anyway, he'd later considered, wasn't accusing him of flirting, with him in obvious earshot, a kind of flirting itself? Nonetheless it had bothered him. Though he'd sensed that it might be partly good as well as bad to be thought of as having flirted, he'd had to consider that it might instead be only bad and, in either case, he didn't know *how* bad. And if it was only a lightly weighted charge, that itself nettled him: to be thought of as frivolous; a dallier; insubstantial. In the end, he'd been considerably irked by not being able to settle on exactly what it meant. He'd also disliked the distance it created, however slight, between him and the women among whom the aspersion had been spoken. And though he didn't believe he'd ever made a false promise to a woman, or told a tactical lie—at least not of any great import—the accusation of having been a flirt had led him to vow to himself never to be seen as an importuner or a bother.

He also wanted to avoid now some deflating exchange with the woman on the ferry that might dampen his home-returning high spirits, which had been lifted even further by the brief rush of confrontation with the big man in the suit and by the frisson—despite being carefully limited by his current resolve in such matters—with the au pair girl.

So the woman at the railing he left to herself and turned his attention to the outline of San Francisco across the water, trying to pick out recognizable bits of urban landscape as the ferry slowly approached: Telegraph Hill on the city's northeast corner, its stone quarry on the hillside that directly faced the ferry's route, with ramshackle wooden houses scattered across the top and down the other visible slopes, and the steep streets of his boyhood base in the North Beach neighborhood just over the far side; Rincon Hill and the central docks, and the jive joints of the Barbary Coast's Terrific Street just behind; Potrero Hill toward the south, with its large ironworks and coal yards; and Butchertown further south still, home to ship repair yards and slaughterhouses, and to his old friend Elijah.

He strained to see the northeast rim of the city, the piers and the bright red and orange lateen sails of the Sicilian *felucca* fishing boats at the edge of North Beach and, further along, the wide cove of Harbor View and the phantom shadows of its workmen's community where he'd been living when last in the city, now flattened to make way for the previous year's mammoth Panama-Pacific Exposition—in the official city demolition notices, posted on the various small workshop buildings, boardinghouses, and cheap eateries and taverns, the only word invariably spelled with a capital letter had been *Progress*. But the ferry was still too far away for him to make out details, and the angle was wrong, and Goat Island smack in the way, and, in contrast to the clear stretch of water directly ahead of the ferry, a smooth white milk-spill of fog was pouring into the bay through the Golden Gate, hugging the water and sliding eastward from the Pacific as if pulled by an invisible thread—the sight of it after his three years away as pleasingly familiar as the sudden appearance of a childhood chum—and just grazing the city's north shore, blocking any view of it, or of the Gate, or of the hills on the other side, except for the top of majestic Mount Tamalpais, its deep green wooded crown looming above the fog line.

When the ferry was about halfway across the bay, Blue thought he noticed the woman on the bench watching him. But when he turned to face her she neither looked directly at him nor changed her expression, which was concentrated, almost grave. On the other hand, neither did she look away. Blue took it under advisement.

~

In fact, Kate was not watching the scruffy young man at the railing. Though for a few moments she'd been mildly intrigued by him: his unorthodox verbal sallies against the imposing paterfamilias, his playful articulateness seemingly at odds with his rough appearance, and his familiar Irish-American lilt, reminiscent of her childhood in Southie but without the awful Boston flatness pressing the life out of it. No, Kate was not fully immune to the attractions or attentions of men. Just substantially inoculated against them. For several years following Jamey's death she'd been nearly incapable of engaging in even the simplest personal encounter with a man, let alone anything even hinting at intimacy. And later, when her emotional barriers had begun to slacken, the world threw up new, insuperable walls: being a widow with a child but no money drastically curtailed both her time and energy for anything outside work and home, and just as emphatically reduced the number of men who'd be interested. And this was not just any world. This was Boston. So her higher education and marriage to a Jameson all but removed her from the sight lines of the men of Southie, where she'd grown up a Carey and where those family connections might otherwise have produced at least a trickle of suitors for the young widow. Particularly if she'd moved back to the old neighborhood and accepted her family's help with daily life, especially the raising of Maggie. Which she hadn't. Especially the raising of Maggie. At the same time, though, this Carey bloodline tainted her prospects with the higher social strata that her marriage to Jamey and her truncated stint attending law school had introduced her to. This was especially true among the men at the big law office where she'd been working as a higher-skilled, though not higher-paid, clerk. The Jameson connection—their family business concerns were among the law firm's most substantial clients—had got her in the door there for her initial job interview, but the Jamesons had also sent along a back-channel dossier of her personal history. And in Boston, history was everything. So, the men at the firm kept their distance. And the Jamesons themselves, while self-satisfied to have helped her find work to support herself and her child—their grandchild—certainly made no effort to assist with the interpersonal interests of their former daughter-in-law. Which, after Jamey's death, is how they referred to her: former.

But now she had embarked on this strange project for Lansing and his U-1 Bureau, which, among other things, was freeing her for a while from the constraints of her Boston life. And San Francisco, she recalled from her time there, was a kind of liberated zone compared to Boston. In San Francisco, it seemed that what you did with yourself counted for as much as where and what you'd emerged from, since for so many people in that young, tumultuous city, the "where" and "what" were not only far away but also hazy with the distance.

Lansing. Whose hiring of the Boston law firm on some big government admiralty matter had brought Kate to his attention. And for whom her convoluted history—most notably her marriage to his old university acquaintance Jamey and her connection through him to San Francisco—had given him the idea for what he'd admitted to her was an unusual undertaking. Moreover, the Jameson family's resentments about Kate had no effect on Lansing's consideration of her: he was sufficiently higher than even they were on the social ladder, and had much more important things on his plate, so that such matters were of no consequence to him. Kate's experience with and comfort level among the lawyers and clients of the big firm, plus her intelligence and bearing, obvious when he'd interviewed her, had clinched the matter.

So, as she neared San Francisco Kate felt herself off the leash, given liberty by Lansing to make her own way there. The there that was not Boston. Still, while the rough-edged fellow at the railing had been momentarily of interest—a forthright charm; seemingly bright, or anyway clever; and a pleasing face, at least from what she could see notwithstanding an unruly mop of black hair straggling over his fore-head, several days' growth of beard, and a swollen cheek and eye—she had too much else on her mind to give in to random conversation. A too much that included what she'd actually been staring at when Blue thought she might be looking at him: over his shoulder, beyond and above the fog, the top of Angel Island. Where she'd first seen Jamey again after his return from the Philippines; where the army had kept him in quarantine for three months—Had it truly been concern about his physical illness, as they said, though that turned out to be only a mild case of malaria and not something contagious? Or had they recognized the deeper malady?—and had only allowed Kate to visit, across a wide table, without touching, once a week; and where, when first she'd set eyes on him again, she'd understood that he was not the same man who'd left Boston a year and a half before.

The boat from Oakland tied up behind the massive arch-windowed, clock-towered Ferry Building. Because both Kate and Blue had spent the entire cross-bay ride out on the deck close to the ferry's board-ing gate, they wound up next to each other at the head of the crowd waiting to move down the ramp.

"Seems like we're going the same way," Blue found himself breach-ing his self-imposed silence toward her.

The remark was delivered so casually, almost diffidently, that Kate was not put off by its facetiousness. She briefly glanced at him, up and down: "Well, anything's possible, I suppose."

Blue self-consciously passed fingertips over his swollen cheek, then looked down at his decidedly soiled jacket. "Ah. But a clean heart."

Kate smiled a bit but said nothing more and turned back toward the gate.

"Anyway," Blue surprised himself by continuing, "book by its cover and all."

She didn't respond.

"Especially since I'm *under*cover, so I am," he half-whispered.

For a moment Kate didn't react. Then slowly she turned back toward him and stared, her mouth opening but no sound emerging. She had assumed her first contact would be at the Bureau of Investigation office. Why hadn't they told her she'd be met by someone before that? Why here, on the ferry, before she'd even arrived in the city? And why someone, well, like this? What was she supposed to do or say to this person? Or not? She felt her cheeks flush from the sudden confirmation of the fear she'd had all along that, despite her training in Washington and her assurance from Lansing that he expected no particular results, she was completely out of her depth.

Blue thought that his jokiness had been obvious but her expression made him wonder. "For the Swiss crown," he added and, just to make sure, hunched his shoulders and furrowed his brow in mock intensity.

Realizing now that he was just wagging, and that her work for U-1 had not, in fact, begun prematurely, Kate's insides did a series of rapid, wrenching emotional somersaults. First, from shock to embarrassment. Then to anger, which frequently follows embarrassment and which, as it so often does, played out in misdirections: at this man, who'd been nothing worse than mistakenly chummy; at Lansing, for having coaxed and suborned her into this position; at Maggie, for having unwittingly tugged her toward this place; at the Jamesons, for all they'd put her through, and for being who they were; and at Jamey, always at Jamey, for having wrenched away so much love, so much everything. But also anger at herself—in the end, all of it rolled together, at herself—because of what she felt must somehow have been her shortcomings with all of them.

After a moment composing herself, she managed to get past the anger and make a final emotional turn, into cautious bemusement.

"Crown, eh?" she said, "Sorry, but Switzerland doesn't..."

"Shhh!" Blue wagged a finger for silence.

This got a small laugh from her, but the gate opened just then, and the crowd immediately surged behind them, nudging them down the ramp. Relieved, Kate moved along ahead of Blue and did not look back.

∽

The passengers disembarked up some steps into the Ferry Building's second floor while their baggage moved through below. They then crossed to a stairway that led down to the building's arched main entrance and out to East Street, the wide boulevard that stretched along the waterfront in each direction.

Although he'd been pointing for almost a year toward this moment, this return, Blue still didn't know exactly where he intended to go once he went out through the archway. In part, this was how he always approached things, disdaining set plans and waiting to size up a situation before deciding where to put down his next step. But in this instance it was also that he'd not yet been able to imagine what the next version of his life here would be. And so didn't know how it should begin. There was no home to go to, nor family any longer, by which to seek grounding. So, despite not having to wait for any bags to be carried in from the ferry, as did many of the other passengers who were now idling near the entryway, he lingered behind them, leaning against a back wall and staring out through the portal into the city's fog-wisped morning light.

Kate's emergence from the crowd, to take charge of her arriving valise and trunk, caught Blue's attention and lifted him out of his trance. She paid the man who'd brought the bags on a handcart, then spoke with two scrawny teenage boys whom the man had called over from the entrance and who were now circling the big trunk as if it were a hibernating bear they needed to move without waking.

Blue sidled up. "Would you be searching for a hand?"

"I think I have all the hands I need, thank you."

The two boys eyed Blue warily, worried he might be trying to horn in on their little hauling business.

"I'll hail you a taxi, M'am?" one of the boys asked.

"No, I don't think so. It's just a few blocks along Market Street, right, the hotel? Second Street? I could use the walk. If you'll just bring these along."

The boys dragged the trunk and valise out to the street and hoisted them onto a three-wheeled cart hooked to the back of a bicycle.

"Market Street," Blue said toward Kate, but without looking at her directly. "Now how was I knowing we'd be going the same way?" He moved along parallel to her as they headed out the archway but kept a bit of distance, not wanting to put any pressure on the situation, particularly since he really didn't know whether he was acting out of actual interest or merely the habit of interest.

The archway opened directly onto the foot of Market Street, the city's main commercial thoroughfare, and the little group emerged into a noisy welter of streetcars and autos and delivery trucks and horse wagons and baggage carts and hawkers and newspaper boys and scores of ferry travelers moving in all directions. The bicycle cart boys pushed out into the throng but Kate and Blue both stopped short at startling sounds that shocked above the street clamor: furious shouts and breaking glass from fifty yards or so south along East Street. Looking that way, they saw two rows of police, one line down the middle of the wide waterfront boulevard and a shorter line perpendicular to it, facing them at the foot of Market Street and keeping people from moving any further in that direction. All of them holding wooden truncheons at the ready. On the water side of the longer police line, in front of the first pier south of the Ferry Building where a large steam freighter was berthed, a crowd of two or three hundred men was seething, the distinctive round white flat caps of the longshoremen's union on almost every head. Across the road, buffered by the police line, was another crowd—white union caps notably absent—of perhaps a quarter that size. The shouts, and a few hand-propelled bottles and other makeshift missiles, were being hurled from the dockside over the heads of the police toward the group on the landward side.

Blue moved a few steps in that direction, craning to get a better look, then abruptly turned his head and shoulders a few degrees away from the crowds and stopped short, stiffening, staring intently. Kate followed his gaze to the street corner. Standing there just behind the second blocking row of police, in a space cleared of pedestrians, were three men: two of them, dressed in baggy shapeless suits, were listening to the third—an enormous block of a man with a bull neck and square head whose preternaturally pale face was partly shrouded by the wide brim of a slouch hat—as he gestured toward the crowds in front of the pier.

Kate saw Blue gather himself, tightening the satchel and bedroll under his arm, readying to head for the fray. He took a quick look back at her.

"I didn't think we were going the same way," she said flatly, then turned and began to follow the bicycle boys out into the city.

"Second and Market, ay?" Blue called after her. "But how about a name?"

Kate slowed a bit, turned, and heard herself say "Jameson," then immediately worried for having done so and turned away again.

Blue smiled, not expecting to have won the prize. "Grand! And what would be a first name?"

She took a few more steps into the bustle of the intersection. "Mrs.," she called back over her shoulder, and kept going.

3

Belle Lavin's creaking twelve-room hulk on Mission Street was as much meeting ground as boardinghouse and, over the years, had survived many a serious threat: the 1906 great quake and the citywide conflagration that followed; a cockeyed original wood-frame construction that had allowed Belle to buy the place cheap but which, exacerbated by the quake, gave a slight but unsettling tilt to two of the corner rooms, which newcomers might not notice right away but longer-term residents knew to avoid; a trumped-up attempt by police to tie Belle to the deadly 1910 Los Angeles bombing of the *Times* newspaper building and her resulting temporary flight underground (actually, just down the street to a friend's house, within eyeshot of her own place and well-protected by neighborhood loyalties); her penchant for caring less about a boarder's ability to pay than about the person's life story and politics (there were socialists, Wobblies, syndicalists, anarchists— "Which stripe?" Belle would be sure to press, but only for purposes of future late-night arguments, since she welcomed any variety—and undifferentiated working stiffs); and the occasional, sometimes window-rattling rows resulting from Belle's inconsistent position on in-house romance: a full-bodied woman of middle age but not middling appetites, Belle allowed herself as many lovers as she could muster, but there was raucous hell to pay for any man who dallied—under her roof, that is—with both Belle *and* someone else.

Still, when she wanted to, she could be "civilian," as she put it, such as when she'd sit in the morning sun that flooded the house's large communal dining room, visiting with one or another woman friend and drinking tea from the delicate porcelain pot and two cups she'd been left in lieu of rent by a Japanese anarchist who'd brought with him for a several-month stay in San Francisco only a single change of shirt and trousers, a photo of his wife, a battered copy of Kropotkin's *The Conquest of Bread*, which he was translating into Japanese, and this proper tea set. Within a year of returning to Japan he'd been put to a firing squad: something about trying to overthrow the emperor and abolish the throne.

On this particular late spring morning it was Lily Bratz, MD, who sat at the big table drinking tea with Belle. Dr. B, as most of her friends and patients affectionately called her, was a tiny woman with cropped white hair over a face that was startlingly severe when at rest, which was rarely, and wildly variegated—consoling, mirthful, impishly ironic, accusingly tart—when not. Despite her relatively privileged position as a physician in the Ukraine, she had fled pogroms there in the early 1890s and eventually reached California where for several years she'd labored long and hard—existing on miniscule amounts of food and sleep—doing double shifts in fruit and fish canning factories, and briefly in a Barbary Coast dancehall-cum-brothel, until she'd saved enough money to get herself recertified at medical school in San Francisco. She'd then opened a practice in which, not unlike Belle, she was less diligent and effective at collecting fees than she was at providing treatment and comfort. Many of her patients were women she'd informally ministered to when she'd labored beside them in the canneries and the saloon, as well as other working-class women, some of them "in trouble" and others seeking an effective way—legally prohibited, though easily available to women of means—to avoid it, whom the network of factory and dancehall women referred to Dr. B.

Belle and Lily were reminiscing that morning about the Japanese anarchist—Lily had given him a cot in the front room of her flat after she'd learned of their mutual adoration of Kropotkin, and that for months he'd been taking up a room at Belle's without being able to pay her for it—when a woman in her early twenties clattered through the house's front door and into the large entry hall, stopping when she saw the two women through the dining room's open double doorway.

"Meg, girl. Get yourself in here," Belle called. The young woman's distracted, harried expression softened at the sight of the two older women. She managed a wan smile as she shuffled into the dining room, sat down at the table, and unburdened herself of a hefty sheaf of large papers enclosed in a cardboard folder.

Except for the neatly aligned and carefully protected papers, everything about her was disheveled: thick chestnut hair failing to signal clearly whether it was meant to be corralled on her head rather than swirling around it; a flowered summer frock that wrapped uneasily, as if it were buttoned askew, around her thin angular frame; a pair of tattered rough denim trousers beneath the dress, the bizarre combination suggesting that maybe a second person was hiding under there; and a pair of work boots splattered with several colors of paint.

Lily smiled indulgently at the picture of chaos and exasperation Meg presented, then leaned over and gave her a grandmotherly kiss on the forehead. Meg nodded in thanks that, without needing to explain herself, she was appreciated by the older woman.

"Cuppa tea, m'girl?" asked Belle, who had become protectively fond of Meg during the two months earlier in the year when the young woman had stayed at the boardinghouse.

"No, thanks, I'll just sit for a minute."

"So, you will tell me, what have you there?" Lily asked, nodding toward the sheaf of papers. Despite her diminutive size, Lily's voice was deep and gravelly, with an underlying throat rumble like that of a resting jungle cat. With latent kindness behind her somewhat stilted syntax and her thoughtful if often curious word choices, Lily's speech could mesmerize, and often brought forth heartfelt replies from even the most reticent of her patients and the most cynical of her friends. Moreover, the effect of Lily's hypnotic presence did not seem to abate over time. Meg, for one, had remained fully in its throes since the moment she'd met Lily several months earlier, soon after Meg had arrived in the city, when she'd immediately allowed Lily to take her in hand and lead her to safe haven at Belle's place. So, despite having not the least inclination to discuss the matter, Meg now found herself opening her grievance for Lily's inspection.

"Well, what am I always slogging around?"

Meg took from a stack in the folder a large printed handbill that announced a "Workers' Picnic" to be held at a campground south of the city, proceeds to benefit striking dockworkers. The text was supported by a bold, brightly colored painting, taking up three-fourths of the poster, which depicted in dynamic, flowing execution a Woman of the People in bygone European dress—bright blue jacket over loose white shirt, dark green apron over long skirt—standing on a barricade of broken paving stones in the midst of a fiery street battle, her uplifted right arm defiantly brandishing a red banner, her left hand holding a burning torch, her wild hair streaming, and her head raised in a shout to her comrades, to the enemy, to history.

"Hey," Belle said, "it's a grabber."

"Yeah, well, thanks." Meg's response was barely half-hearted.

"That is Paris?" Lily asked. "The Revolution?"

"Paris, yah. But later. The Commune. Your doing, Dr. B."

Lily raised a querying eyebrow.

"Louise Michel group," Meg said by way of explanation. "The women... at the *Volontá* rooms."

"*Gruppo Volontá?*" Belle put in with, for her, a rare touch of alarm. "The North Beach lads? They're a bit... Well, they tend to, uh... get their Italian on, don't they?"

Lily laughed. "Ah now, Belle, maybe your Irish is showing."

Belle glowered. "No flags, no nations, Lily. You know me so."

Lily tilted her head in a calming gesture. "Yes, Belle, of course." She smiled, and Belle's face showed in reply that she immediately relented with her old friend. "Anyway," Lily continued, "I think most of what the *Volontá* lads get on, as you say it, is just their *anarchismo*. But however... I mean, it's wrong... All right, yes, certainly they are lively, no doubt. Their intents are, yes, maybe the fiercest in this town. But I can tell you that these men have been most excellent with me and the clinic. Translating things into Italian, medical advices and other such, and passing them round the neighborhood... the *Volontá* rooms are just down the street from the clinic, you know? Often too they bring food for the families who come in to see us. And never any interfering with the women. Never."

"Yeah, okay," Belle replied a bit impatiently and turned back to Meg, "but what've they got to do with your picture here?"

"Well, this women's bunch that Lily told me about, the Louise Michel group? The *Volontás* give over their meeting room to them every Friday night. Mostly Italian, some Spanish and French women, Mexican, Portuguese. Laundry and bakery workers, a lot of them, and the sausage and cigar works. The canneries. And a few from the dancehalls."

"Yeah, yeah," Belle said. "I get around some, you know?"

"Okay, yes, sorry. So anyway, I've dropped by there a few times now. I like the women. And they seem to like me well enough too. So a few weeks ago I happened to ask where their name came from, and they told me all about Louise Michel and the Paris Commune and all that, and showed me some of the *Volontás'* books and pamphlets about it. Though mostly they were in Italian, so... And well, it was all amazing to me, the Commune, and its women, and what the different kinds of anarchists were about... Yah, yah, Belle, you know all this, I realize, and probably everyone else around here does too. But not me. Sorry to disappoint you. Anyway, when Treat asked me last week to do another drawing, for this poster here... my own work can wait, can't it, he has no trouble with that... I decided to do 'Louise at the Barricades.' And instead of just a drawing, I wound up doing a full-on painting that Treat said he'd be able to print onto the poster. Turned out pretty well, I suppose. If you like that sort of thing."

"First of all," Belle replied sternly, "just 'cause I think you have things to learn ain't at all the same as being disappointed. You never disappoint me. Let's get that straight. Leastwise not yet. And what do you mean, 'If you like that sort of thing'?" Belle indicated the image on the poster. "What should I like better? The new Europe stuff? People with eyeballs where their ears oughta be?"

~

When she'd arrived in San Francisco a few months before—alone, and with little more than her youth, a sketchbook, a general feistiness, and a few self-preservation skills she'd picked up on her travels—the first paid labor Meg found was in the all-female work brigade at one of the northern waterfront fish canneries. As with many other worksites in San Francisco that winter, the cannery had been embroiled in a labor fight, which Meg unwittingly walked smack into the middle of. The strikers' complaints went beyond the usual: not just a recent cut in the already pitiful pay rate and a workday stretched to twelve hours but also a system whereby workers were laid off and called back in unpredictable spasms, depending on when the factory decided it wanted them, which meant that workers had to show up at the cannery every day before dawn even though they might go for weeks without getting "hired" on, and if hired might be laid off again, with no notice, a day or two later. Moreover, the work was cold, wet, filthy and dangerous, with no help for the many women made sick or injured. On top of that, and most galling of all, was widespread abuse by the foremen, not itself unusual in a nonunion factory but which in this place took particularly egregious forms because all the workers were women: a constant spew of lewd remarks, frequent gropings, and demands for sexual favors in exchange for better work assignments or, given the at-will hiring system, for any work at all.

Adding to the cannery women's travails was their invisibility to—the willful blindness of—the city's traditional labor unions. The women had no specific skills, the labor leaders would say when pressed, and did not fit any particular craft or trade union, so their requests to the central labor council for some sort of recognition and, thereby, support in their fight against the cannery owners were ignored. They were not truly workers, the mainstream unions said; they were just women who sometimes took on work.

So the women at this particular cannery picked up the cudgel on their own and, to everyone's surprise—including most of the women themselves—went out on strike shortly after Meg began working there. Meg herself knew nothing of unions, factory wars, strikes and lockouts, or much else in the world of paid labor. But the righteousness of the women's cause was obvious to her after only a few weeks of spotty work in the cannery, during which she was repeatedly set upon by two lecherous foremen at the same time she found that her pittance of pay barely covered the rent for a shared closet alcove, referred to unblinkingly by the landlord as a room, and the cost of sporadic minimal meals. And she had only herself to worry about, unlike many of the other women there who had children to house, clothe and feed. Meg was also mightily impressed by the women's energy and spirit of resistance, despite exhaustion from their labors, as embodied by one woman's speech, consisting of no more than three extremely well-formed sentences, hollered from atop a wooden packing crate to the assembled workers outside the cannery the night the strike was called. "No... more... fucking... with us!" the woman—wiry, wild-haired, thirtyish, wearing flappy trousers and a denim work jacket—bellowed the double entendre toward the lighted windows of the factory management's upper story offices, then turned back to the cannery women: "Now... they can go... fuck... themselves!" The women cheered wildly. But the speaker wasn't quite finished. She turned and pointed to a representative of the labor council, lingering at the back of the crowd, who had showed up earlier to tell them they had no official sanction for a strike: "And you, you suck-ass shit-for-a-heart, FUCK... YOU... TOO!"

That was it, all the organizing the women needed: they were out on the picket line the following morning. And it was all the convincing—in language both startling and exhilarating to her—that Meg needed to join them.

It turned out that the vernacularly proficient orator was a former cannery worker named Rebecca—she called herself Reb—who was now allied with the local branch of the Wobblies, the Industrial Workers of the World. In recent years these San Francisco Wobblies had formed what they called a "mixed" union local, which included many categories of workers shunned by the city's traditional trade unions: Latins, a term of disdain and exclusion when used by employers and mainstream unions but embraced proudly by the members of this Wobbly local, which included people of Italian, Spanish, Basque, French and Mexican heritage, immigrants and US-born alike, many of them highly skilled but forced by employer and union ethnic line-drawing to do only low-paid unskilled labor; Blacks, many of whose families had been in the city since shortly after the Civil War but who had never been allowed into most of the traditional trade unions; and Asians, including a few Japanese Americans and Filipino Americans and a handful of second- and third-generation ethnic Chinese young men who had braved the hostile reception of the outside world, not to mention their own families' disapprobation, by consorting with people beyond the city's tightly hemmed Chinatown.

The Wobblies opposed the self-segregation of organized labor into individual craft unions—carpenters, metalworkers, seamen, long-shoremen, etc.—through which, the Wobblies believed, labor was too often divided against itself. On the other hand, Wobblies were always ready to lend their bodies to any of these unions or to any other workers who were actively engaged in battles with their employers. So the first morning of the women's cannery strike the Wobblies sent a dozen members, from the mixed local's headquarters in nearby North Beach, down to the waterfront to join the women on the picket line. They meant to offer corporal support to the women, particularly if, as often happened, private enforcers hired by the factory owners got nastily physical with the strikers when bringing in scab replacement workers. But the cannery women, while glad for the Wobblies' appearance, decided to handle any confrontation themselves, consigning the Wobbly men to holding picket signs and yelling encouragement from the sidelines.

Local police ranks were filled with working-class lads, many of whose families had deep union roots in this heavily union town. So in general street cops tended not to intervene in labor confrontations unless and until things turned particularly violent or destructive. Which this one soon did. Bloody fights broke out between the strik-ing women and the private security thugs who tried to bludgeon a path for the scabs to pass through the picket lines. And after one of the scab women got thrown off a wharf into the bay, the police finally stepped in to break it up. When it was all over for the day, the cops hadn't arrested any of the scabs or security men, but neither had they arrested any of the women strikers. The only person they'd hauled off—at the insistence of their supervising captain—was one of the cheerleading Wobblies, charging him with inciting a riot: despite sympathy for traditional unions among the cops' rank and file, the police brass had serious antipathy toward the more radical Wobblies; moreover, in the case of this particular strike by the cannery women, the police captain on site simply couldn't get it into his head that there'd been no male behind it all.

A number of strikers had been badly beaten up in the melee, and Meg found herself tending to the wounded. This was not a fully conscious decision, and certainly not from a sense of vocation, which she had decidedly rejected the year before by walking away, right on the verge of taking a diploma, from her two years of nursing school. But she felt lost in the confusion following the picket line battle, and binding wounds was at least some way she knew how to be helpful. Reb, the fiery orator from the night before, had also been a fiery fighter against the scabs and security men that morning, and she came out of the scrum with a heavily bleeding scalp. Meg was able to stanch the blood for her, clean the wound with a bit of bay water she confidently directed someone to fetch, and with a scarf created a makeshift bandage which kept enough pressure on the wound that Reb was able to walk, gingerly, without bleeding too much more. Reb, who'd become a nurse after her stint in the canneries, liked this girl's assertiveness and resourcefulness, particularly appreciating the efficacy of the jaunty headband. So when her first few steps were tottering, she accepted Meg's proffered arm, as well as her contention that Reb should have her injuries properly treated. Another woman managed to hail a taxi, and Meg and Reb climbed in.

Reb directed the taxi into nearby North Beach where it stopped in front of a multilevel dark wood modernist building with a small sign that said Telegraph Hill Neighborhood House. Meg helped Reb struggle up some stairs into a lovely shaded inner courtyard, then up another flight and into a large sunlit room with high windows, a handwritten paper by its open door saying simply "Dispensary." There, two older women were tending to a couple of children in what was some sort of makeshift medical clinic: an examining table, a small cot, four simple wooden chairs along one wall, two cabinets with a thin array of medical supplies and medicines, a chicken wire cool box with some fruit and bread, and a sink. The dispensary women moved quickly when Reb, whom Meg had thus far managed to keep upright, buckled to the floor. They nudged Reb onto the table, told the children to return later, and began to treat her wounds. One of the dispensary women was a nurse who volunteered at this clinic two mornings a week. The other was the doctor who ran the clinic: Lily Bratz—Dr. B.

~

"I thought Treat was gonna give you some workshop space. For your painting. Wasn't that part of your... arrangement?"

Meg hesitated before replying. Lily looked away, clearly annoyed at Belle for having broached the subject of Meg and Treat: though Lily had the uncanny ability to get people to talk to her when it seemed necessary, she believed—by both inclination and profession—in being otherwise unobtrusive about people's personal lives. No such reticence by Belle. She wanted to know as much as she could, about anyone: you could never tell, she contended, what might come in handy someday. And in this case, she had a special interest, having been the person who'd introduced Meg—at the time still brand-new to the town and its characters—to Treat during a gathering at the boardinghouse, then doubted herself for it when, just a couple of weeks later, Meg moved out of Belle's to live with Treat at his printing workshop.

"Space. Yah." Meg finally said. "The old greenhouse shed out back. It's fine, plenty of light. But then, he's always asking me to do drawings for the pamphlets and posters and newsletters he prints for all the groups. Then going around distributing... like today," she indicated the posters on the table. "And more drawings, and a few paintings, for some of his full-pay customers. Plus deliveries. I mean, I have to help pay the bills, right? That's also part of our... whatever. So, space, yeah. But time?... Among other things."

Belle raised her brow at this last remark, but a quick cautionary look from Lily stopped her from whatever she might have asked Meg next.

There was a commotion in the hallway. The women looked out to see a group of four men roistering just inside the front door. With claps on the others' backs, two of the men, boarders there, peeled off and went up the main stairway. One of the remaining two—a very short, lean, bouncy man in his early twenties, with pale freckled skin and spiky red hair—spotted the women in the dining room and headed toward them, tugging along the fourth man, who held a satchel and bedroll under his arm. Blue.

"Warren. What kind of devilment you been into now?"

There was dried blood all down Warren Billings's shirt and jacket, with a nasty gash across his forehead, and an obviously recent rent in the shoulder of Blue's jacket. A strong smell of beer came into the room with them.

"Hey, how about some mercies, Belle, will ya?" Billings complained. "I just come home from the wars!" He turned to the other two women. "Hiya, Meg. Dr. B."

"Warren," Lily nodded to him and smiled, but Meg's scowl did not change and she said nothing. Billings didn't seem to notice; he rocked back and forth on the balls of his feet, in constant motion though technically stationary, like mercury loosed from a thermometer. His boyish face was dominated by a crooked sort-of-grin comprised of one-half amazement at the dizzying variety the world kept spinning out in front of him, and the other half a smoldering, unremitting anger at much of that variety's content.

"Oh," he remembered that Blue was with him, "this fella here's back from even bigger wars. And put in some hellish licks this mornin', down the docks."

"Baldino, is that you?" Lily was peering at Blue.

Blue smiled, rubbing his sweat-stained whiskers with a skinned and swollen hand. "The very same, so I am. Been a long time, Dr. B. And I must say, you're looking mighty."

"Ahah, that tells me this really is you," she shook her head in mock disapproval, then smiled warmly at him.

"You know this bo?" Belle asked Lily.

"Oh, yes. For a long time. A North Beach boy. Everyone in the neighborhood knows Baldino. But you were gone for some years now, yes?"

Blue nodded, then offered a handshake to Belle. "Blue Cavanaugh," he introduced himself.

"Ah," Belle said, "it's a name I might have heard now and again, a while back."

"And yours for sure, Belle," Blue replied with respect.

"So," Belle glanced at Blue's bedroll and satchel, "you want to be stashing here?"

"Told him if he does," Billings put in, "he can be hearin' all about Mexico and joinin' up with Villa. I already started fillin' him in."

"So I can smell." Belle said.

"Come on, now," Billings pleaded, "we had us a rough go at it this mornin'. It was some serious wildness down there. Had to recuperate ourselves a bit."

Blue turned to Meg, whom he'd been peeking at sideways. "And how are *we* at all?"

She looked him over. "So, another hero, eh?"

Blue's eyes widened. "Was it something I haven't had a chance to say?"

"Baldino, this is Meg," Lily interceded. "Meg Carey."

"Aren't you meant to bark before you bite?" Blue said to Meg with a mix of interest and mild irritation.

"Actually, you haven't seen either, yet."

"I don't know should I be worryin' or hopin'."

"Hey, what's with you, Meg?" Billings challenged her testiness.

Meg pursed her lips and frowned. "Yes, beg your pardon," she addressed Blue perfunctorily. "Pleased to meet you, I'm sure. But, I'm sorry... Blue? Is that a name? And Baldino? Um...?"

"Ah, it's a long story. But if you've got the time, so." He managed to summon a bit of charm in the form of a small smile, though without much conviction: he was still too distracted, too troubled, by what he'd seen that morning at the docks.

"Time," Meg mumbled to herself. "Which reminds me," she turned to Belle while getting up and indicating the sheaf of posters. "Can I put one of these up in the hallway?"

"Of course, girl. Anywhere you'd like."

Meg thanked her, touched Lily's hand, and went to put up the poster without another word or glance at either of the two men. Blue, on the other hand, watched Meg's back for a couple of beats. Belle noticed.

"Warren, why don't you take him upstairs," Belle said. "Number eight's empty." She looked over at Meg, then turned back to Blue. "A room—that'll be what you *can* have," she said, her eyes grinning. At most other times, Blue would have appreciated the jab. This time, it barely registered.

4

The story of Blue's name and the story of what had so dispirited him at the morning's dockside brawl were part of the same longer tale.

He was the second child of immigrant parents: mother Sicilian, father Irish. Blue's mother Maricchia had named him Baldo. Not having had the chance with her firstborn, she'd wanted, through the naming, to provide her second son with an explicit connection to her Sicilianness. And since the child's heavy-drinking father Michael Cavanaugh, by that time only sporadically participating in family life, couldn't be found when she went into labor, there was no one to stop her.

Growing up in the city's heavily Italian North Beach neighborhood, little Baldo was called Baldino by his mother, his older brother, and their neighborhood friends. By seven or eight years old, though, Baldo had begun to venture out of North Beach on the coattails of older brother Declan—an occasional, not very competent petty thief who was at least savvy enough not to steal in his own neighborhood—and a bit later through forays into the world of boxing, the skills for which, including the ability not to show that a blow from an opponent, or a father, hurt as much as it did, were among the very few things Baldo and Declan were left by Michael Cavanaugh when he abandoned the family—Baldo was twelve, Declan fifteen—for good. Once outside Little Italy, however, Baldo found that too many people took pleasure in changing his diminutive from Baldino to Baldy. Which he very much did not appreciate.

It was boxing that gave him a chance to shake off the nickname for something more amenable. By the age of fourteen, Baldo had become just about the best fighter of anyone near his age in the entire city. His older brother had continued the father's schooling of Baldo in fisticuffs, and later Baldo had been adopted by a training gym South of the Slot, a downscale district of warehouses, small factories, machine shops, and flophouses just south of the city's main commercial district along Market Street. His embrace by Flaherty's gym, which like the gym's neighborhood was heavily Irish, was an early example of how easily Baldo Cavanaugh moved back and forth between the two worlds of his parents' ethnicities.

San Francisco was a boxing town. There were gyms all over, and many had programs for junior fighters, so there was no shortage of competition for him. He made quite a name for himself during his early teens, easily dominating the score of fights that Flaherty lined up for him, to the extent that he'd even gotten attention in the newspapers, and this success helped boost the gym's reputation, which translated into new paying members. Flaherty was duly appreciative, rewarding young Baldo with little side jobs—helping to train other young boxers, making an occasional political or police payoff delivery, accompanying an out-of-town promoter or other noteworthy visitor to a protected house of iniquity run by one of Flaherty's associates—for which Baldo was compensated well beyond what most kids his age could earn and also far better than what would have come from continuing as an accomplice in his older brother's petty larcenies.

But along about age fifteen, Baldo Cavanaugh met his match. His name was Elijah DuPree. Elijah's people were originally from Louisiana but for three generations had lived in Butchertown, the farthest southeastern district of San Francisco where the waterfront slaughterhouses sloughed their bloody runoff into the bay. As with Baldo, Elijah's father had abandoned the family when Elijah was a boy and, also like his North Beach counterpart, Elijah had matured under the tutelage of an older brother, Isaiah. They also shared something else, Baldo and Elijah, which wound up bringing them together across neighborhood and racial lines: both of them could fight like hell.

They first met each other in the ring during a small tournament where each entrant fought four others for one round each. Baldo and Elijah had been much superior to all the other boys, but neither had outshone the other when they met head-to-head. This was a first for Baldo, and for Elijah as well. They fought again two months later in a larger tournament, in which each of them had two three-round bouts in the morning and another in the afternoon before they wound up meeting each other in the evening finale. Despite the soft, oversize gloves junior fighters wore, they delivered pretty nasty beatings to each other and fought to a draw that neither of them was happy with.

They next met a half-year later, when both boys were sixteen, as a preliminary exhibition to a professional card of fights at the big Mechanics Pavilion down by City Hall. The boys went five rounds against each other, and when it was over they were both bloodied and battered, and again the bout was declared a draw. After the fight, they sat on opposite sides of a dank basement dressing room, glaring at each other and not speaking as they slowly began putting on their street clothes. An adult fighter for an upcoming bout came in, decided that Baldo was in his way, and roughly pushed him aside. When Baldo complained and pushed back, the older man took a swing at him; Baldo ducked under it and got in a good punch to the man's ribs. The enraged man now grabbed Baldo and, outweighing him by nearly a hundred pounds, wrestled him to the ground and started beating him. At this, Elijah jumped up, said "Hey!" and gave the man a kidney shot. The man now turned on Elijah, dragged him to the ground and began pounding on him. Baldo jumped on the man's back, and together he and Elijah got in some good licks. The commotion soon brought in another man who, rather than mediate, immediately grabbed Elijah from behind and started whacking him. The two boys acquitted themselves pretty well at first but eventually began to take quite a hammering from the much larger adults until several other people came in and broke it up.

When it was all over, Baldo's gym boss Flaherty, along with Elijah's older brother Isaiah, took the boys upstairs to a small washroom where they could clean themselves and finish getting dressed. Flaherty looked at the bruises on Baldo's swollen face—from a combination of the basement fight on top of the official bout against Elijah— and told him, "Boy, they turned you black and blue." Then he looked over at Elijah, who was equally bruised and swollen. "And you'd be blue if you wasn't black." Then Flaherty looked from one boy to the other and started laughing: "Yup, that's who you two are, all right: Black and Blue." Hesitatingly, the boys smiled at this linking of them by name after they'd supported each other in the basement melee. "All right, come on, Mister Blue," Flaherty said. "Let's get out of here." Flaherty again called him by that name when he saw him at the gym the next day. And it stuck. It took some getting used to, but in the end Blue was glad of it: it was a damn sight better than Baldy.

When Blue had headed over to the longshoremen's street battle near the Ferry Building immediately upon his arrival back in the city, he wasn't particularly looking to get involved: he was exhausted from his overnight boxcar ride in from Nevada, sore over every inch of his body from his twenty-two round prize fight there the night before, and needed to get himself settled somewhere so he could figure out what he was going to do with himself next. About which he had no idea. Also, he had no connection to the longshoremen, an insular bunch who were powerful enough on their own not to need much support from the more independent, and to a large extent more extreme, radical types with whom Blue had associated in the years before he'd left the city, or any call for the very specific kind of technical assistance at which Blue was adept. On the other hand, they were union workers in a battle, and that was enough for Blue at least to take a look. Which, at first, was all he'd done.

He'd made his way around the line of cops and over to the edge of the pier in front of which the longshoremen were massed. Finding an old man who seemed to be holding himself back from the fray but whose loyalties were clearly evinced by his well-worn white stevedore's cap, Blue asked where he might stash his satchel and bedroll. After giving Blue a quick once-over, the man indicated the near north corner of the pier. Blue came upon a dozen or so wooden staves that looked as if they'd been collected for ready access behind a stack of shipping pallets, watched over by another old man with an equally venerable union cap sitting back to front on a cane chair, and by a trio of scrawny ten- or twelve-year-old boys lurking behind and trying to look tough.

Blue left his gear there under the old man's protection and headed back out but didn't immediately join the crowd. Instead, he climbed up on a packing crate at the edge of the pier wall: as was his wont, he first looked to identify where strengths and weaknesses were. It was during this reconnoiter that he spotted Warren Billings, with his shock of red hair, standing at the near edge of the massed longshoremen, alternating between catcalls at the scabs across the road and wary glances at the line of police. Blue didn't know Billings, but knew of him from three years before, knew his face and reputation: shooting off part of your own thumb during a drunken episode at a strike-riven shoe factory with a mini-revolver you never got out of your pocket, and managing with the same single bullet to also hit a security guard's toe, will get you that kind of notice. At least in the circles Blue had frequented.

Billings was about ten years younger than Blue. He had arrived in San Francisco a few months before Blue had left it, having separated the year before from his large, shambolic, benighted family in New York. In particular, Billings had fled from a long stretch of servitude to his policeman brother-in-law—Billings's father had died when Warren was two—who had enforced his punishing authority over Billings not only with beatings but also with a setup fake arrest, assisted by his police brethren, which placed Billings under an entirely bogus "parole" in the brother-in-law's custody. The experience formed in Billings an attitude toward the police that would be repeatedly confirmed and expanded during his time in San Francisco and would last for a lifetime.

Billings had left New York and set off bumming around the country. By the time he reached the Pacific Northwest a year later, though, cravings for a sense of belonging were reaching parity with the wanderlust inspired by his nineteen-year-old's romantic vision of the social and political upheavals sweeping the world. So once he got to San Francisco and stumbled into its large, well-entrenched radical labor cohort, he decided to stick around, enjoying the almost family-like comradeship while gathering information and contacts, he hoped, that would propel him toward Mexico and Pancho Villa's revolution. It was now three years later but, he told Blue later that morning without the faintest touch of irony, he was still on his way to Mexico.

When Billings first arrived in San Francisco, he'd gone looking for work as a shoe cutter, the best-paying lawful skill he possessed. Someone told him of a particular shoe factory that was hiring, but when he got there he discovered that the workers were on strike and the hiring was of scabs. He loudly refused to cross the pickets. One of the strikers, an IWW man, heard Billings and took him around the corner for a chat. Would he like to work in the factory anyway, but on the right side? Billings was excited by the prospect of engaging in his first labor battle and was keen when, taken to the home of a free-range radical named Tom Mooney who was helping in the strike, he heard the Wobbly's idea: since Billings was new in town and the factory bosses and their Pinkerton security men didn't know him, he could go to work there and act as a union spy, reporting on what the company was doing and how it was faring. For the plan to work, though, it would also have to remain a secret from most of the strikers, since the majority were not Wobblies and might have a company informant among them. This would make it even more dangerous for Billings, since he'd be at risk not only from the Pinkerton agents if they learned of his true colors but also from the strikers themselves who would see him as a scab. The notion of being such a double agent thrilled the teenager—spiced even more by the little popgun pistol he was given for protection—and he jumped at the chance.

Unfortunately, a few weeks into the job Billings also jumped at another chance, the rogue offer from a couple of strikers for him to act as a saboteur. They paid him—he'd accepted the money rather than reveal his undercover role—to bring some whiskey into the factory after hours, with which he got the two security guards drunk, then unlocked a door so that a handful of strikers could sneak in and ruin hundreds of pairs of finished shoes. With the sabotage trail so clearly leading straight to Billings, the next morning when he showed up for work he was immediately pounced on by three company detectives, and during the course of the beating the soon-to-be-notorious pistol went off. He ended up not only badly battered and thumb-maimed but also arrested. Once the striking workers were told by the Wobblies that Billings wasn't truly a scab, though, their union came to his legal defense, the charge of assault was dismissed—the sight of scrawny five-foot-four teenager Billings next to the three huge detectives made patently absurd the charge that he'd been the one to attack them—and his reputation as a fearless young labor man, albeit something of a loose cannon and fuck-up, was made.

Already knowing a patchy version of these events helped Blue to chauffer the garrulous Billings quickly over his telling of the shoe factory story as they sat in a saloon recovering from the dockside battle. Billings became circumspect, though, in describing to Blue certain events of the next labor battle he'd been involved in after the shoe factory fiasco and from which he hadn't escaped so fortunately. In the months just before Blue had left the city three years before, electrical workers all over the northern half of the state had embarked on what was to become a long strike against Pacific Gas and Electric, the giant power company. Through Tom Mooney, with whom Billings had gone to live after the thumb-shooting episode, Billings had become involved in this strike and particularly in one of its most significant tactics, the damaging of power lines, which occasionally included the dynamiting of electrical towers. Blue now perked up his attention which, until then, had been focused far more on a lingering image from the morning's dock fight than on Billings's rapid-fire prattling. Billings offered few details of his involvement in events from the power strike, and instead told Blue simply that in the fall of '13 he'd been caught carrying several sticks of dynamite in a suitcase of which, he maintained, he'd only been an unknowing, unwitting courier, that he'd been set up by some power company detective whose actual target had been Mooney, and that he—Billings—had wound up doing a year in Folsom Prison because of it.

It was the mention of Mooney, whose path Blue had crossed many times, and of dynamite, with which Blue was well acquainted, that kept him around the saloon for another round of the local steam beer—rather than Billings's blather, which had now turned to his plans for joining Pancho Villa in Mexico—and that nudged Blue past the exhaustion and sense of anticlimax that had overwhelmed him after the fracas by the pier and toward Belle Lavin's boardinghouse, at Billings's side.

Exhaustion and anticlimax. But also, from the pier, a blindside of deep distress.

From his packing crate perch behind the massed longshoremen, Blue had seen a very large but otherwise standard-issue labor confrontation: picketing strikers bracing to repel an attempt by a troop of scab workers and company-hired security men to enter the pier building and reach the docked ship; and police taking up a position between them, making a lukewarm effort to keep the two sides apart and waiting to pick up the pieces once it was all over—shepherding ambulances, if needed, and making a few arrests if knives or firearms had been used.

After a couple of minutes Blue saw the intensity suddenly ratchet up. A contingent of company security men began moving between a double cordon of police, trying to wedge their way into and through the crowd of longshoremen and onto the pier. Blue watched these developments without much interest, though, having seen the same dance many times before and certain that in this case the striking stevedores so far outnumbered the security men and scabs that the skirmish would be over quickly.

But something wasn't right. The security men seemed in no hurry to make a breakthrough, instead allowing the longshoremen to easily block the path, and appeared more intent on starting scuffles than in actually getting the scabs to the pier. Blue also noticed that there were only a half dozen or so men being escorted, not much help to the company even if they did manage to get to the ship. Perhaps, Blue thought, this was just a way for the security men to test their tactics. Or maybe it was some sort of symbolic effort, intended to let the union and the public know that the shipowners were willing to do battle, even if not in full force this particular morning. Or... something else was going on. Which Blue, from his vantage point at the far edge of the pier, soon spotted: an unmarked ferry-style boat making its way around the end of the pier from the south, its arrival—on the north, opposite side from where the cargo ship was berthed—blocked from street view by the pier building itself. This ferry chugged toward a small landing platform, and Blue could see that the boat was packed with thirty or forty men in work clothes. Some of them were holding the lading spikes that were part of a stevedore's work gear, and all of them were pushing up against the aft railing in anxiety to get off the boat, onto the landing and into a door that had been opened for them on the side of the pier.

It was taking some time for the ferry to maneuver on the rough bay waters into the tight spot intended for smaller boats, and while it did, Blue galvanized himself. The only person he recognized in the crowd of strikers was Billings, and he shouted the young man's name. Eventually Billings heard and turned to see Blue, whose violent gestures toward the side of the pier caught enough of his interest that he peeled away from the crowd and came to investigate. At the same time, Blue climbed down from the packing crate and headed along the narrow pathway on the north side of the pier building.

It took only a couple of moments for Billings to see and understand what Blue had: these were scab stevedores on this ferry, being brought in surreptitiously to sneak onto the pier in order to work the big ship while the company's detectives engaged in a diversionary skirmish out front. Blue barked "Get help!" at which Billings nodded and sprinted back toward the crowd out front. It apparently took some convincing for Billings to get some of the stevedores to break away from the main group, during which time the ferry was tying up to the little annex landing. A dozen or so union men finally came rushing up with Billings, and when they reached Blue and saw the ferry, nothing needed to be said. They charged down the narrow walkway alongside the pier just as the scab workers were getting off the ferry, and all hell broke loose.

Once the fighting began, Blue didn't notice much of what went on around him. He picked out a security guard among the large group trying to get into the pier building and jumped between him and the pier door. The man was big but slow, with no skills to take on Blue unless he could grab onto him and wrestle him down, which Blue's quick series of blows and sidesteps made impossible. The man collapsed on the ground, which blocked the path of several scabs immediately behind him and shifted their expressions from anxious determination to doubting dismay. But proper boxing skills only go so far, a brawl is a brawl, and the next thing Blue knew someone had jumped him from behind. He managed to wrench himself away, the shoulder seam of his jacket taking the biggest loss, and immediately found himself grappling with two other men—scabs or security men he could no longer tell—whom he finally managed to drive off when he got his arms free, though not before taking a fair number of blows from fists and elbows and knees. It was at that moment that he noticed Billings leaning against the pier wall, pressing his jacket sleeve against a heavily bleeding forehead but watching Blue's efforts and, despite the awkward pose, nodding in appreciation.

The fight now began to change shape. There were too many scabs and security men on the walkway for the smaller group of longshoremen to control, though some of the scabs were driven back onto the ferry. A couple of longshoremen started to follow but were stopped by a security man on the boat deck who raised a shotgun at them. The largest group of scabs made it into the pier building where armed security guards stood ready to defend the property. A middle group of scabs and strikers continued to fight on the landing and walkway, Blue among them, and some serious damage between the two sides continued there for another minute or two, with several people getting knocked into the bay. Eventually, two guards from the pier building came out and threatened the union men with shotguns, forcing Blue and those strikers still fighting to back down the walkway, helping along those of their comrades who had taken the worst of it.

Further out along the walkway, on the far side of the guards and a knot of injured scabs, a single two-man fight carried on. One man was on top of the other on the ground, delivering a rain of nasty blows. A security guard took a step in their direction but then stopped and did nothing while the man on top continued to pummel the other, who now lay curled up, his arms covering his head and its white stevedore cap. Blue and the strikers kept backing up along the walkway. Several guards were blocking Blue's view of the two men on the ground, and the punching man's back was turned toward Blue. For a moment, though, the man on top picked up his head and glanced behind him.

Blue wasn't entirely certain. He only got a quick glimpse of the man, from thirty yards away. Also, it had been years since Blue had last seen him, and for years before that only rarely, since the man had become a father and no longer spent much time with his younger brother, whom Blue had also seen so much less of after their relationship had torn nearly to the breaking point. But as he toted up all the reasons why he couldn't be sure, in his sorrowed heart Blue knew who it was, this waterfront scab: Isaiah, the older brother of Blue's erstwhile boxing opponent, teenage partner-in-mischief, and for years closest friend, Elijah DuPree.

5

"We've received almost nothing from Washington, Mrs. Jameson. Only a request to provide you with assistance. Which, I'm afraid, has been nearly impossible to prepare for. Since we have no clear sense of your... Well, what it is you're meant to be doing here."

"Mm," Kate said. "Neither do I."

Alton Breyer—a sturdy little man in his fifties, whose pale face and dark eyes under dark, hooded brows were as blank as his voice—was experienced at his trade: years with the Secret Service; now with the fledgling Bureau of Investigation. So his expression didn't change at Kate's reply. However, a faint rise in his color told her, even before her own consideration of the words she'd blurted, that this was not the best of responses.

But she'd needed to let go. After not being permitted any mention of the matter during the several weeks in Boston after she'd been recruited by Lansing or later after she returned to Boston following her week of preparations in Washington, she was relieved to finally speak with someone who at least knew the pretenses under which she'd come to San Francisco. And yet here in her first moments with Breyer, her only official support in the city, all she'd done was admit just how befuddled she felt. He made no reply to her remark. But given his position as head of the Bureau's local office, and the flush that had appeared behind his otherwise noncommittal professional mien, she had a pretty good idea that it didn't make him happy.

∽

That had been pretty much the sum total of Kate's first visit to Breyer's office: letting him know she'd settled in at the Palace Hotel, the city's finest; a brief, perfunctory exchange about her travel on the new cross-country express; Breyer's tepid declaration that the Bureau was available to assist her; and Kate's awkward remark. She'd intended to ask Breyer's advice, perhaps even assistance, about trying to locate Maggie. But after her clumsy comment, she decided to hold her tongue about this unofficial matter, hoping that her next visit might offer a more propitious moment to raise it.

Now, three days later, she was sitting in her room at the Palace, grander than any other room where she'd ever spent the night in all of her forty-two years. It was almost dawn and she hadn't yet slept, but she wanted to make some notes while it was all still fresh: the night's high society costume gala, her first foray into the world of San Francisco's elites to which her Jameson name gave entry and about which Lansing wanted her to report.

What a strange lot. Or just strange to me? Maybe that's how the uppers here always carry on. Not in Boston. Not the Jamesons and their kind. Though how would I know, since I never got to see them when they loosed themselves? If they ever did. Only those horrible stiff holiday suppers at the Brookline house. And on Grandmother Jameson's birthday. Jamey never seemed to mind. But then, Jamey knew who he was, around them. Whatever else he became, he never had to doubt that he was still one of them. But he never seemed to notice how they looked at me, spoke to me. Head in the clouds, you were, Jamey. Would you have noticed if you could have seen them in later days? After you were gone? When it was just Maggie and me? How each visit everyone in the family was already there at the big house, settled in, before we arrived. As if Maggie and I had been invited for a different, later hour. How they spoke of family things, of gatherings, occasions, that Maggie and I knew nothing about. How no one ever offered to bring us to the house in their motor cars. Or take us home. Which meant having to leave early, always the first to go, for the long trolley ride home. Two different trolleys. I didn't really mind, the leaving early. Getting out of there. Those airless rooms. But Maggie? Did she mind? Always having to go when everyone else was still there. Did she notice?

Well, the party here, and the people—

—Spreckels. Sugar king. High on Lansing's list. His mansion, the party. Invitation said charity for "those fallen in Europe's war." But no sides mentioned. Mrs. Spreckels said something about the poor people of Belgium. Old man Spreckels frowned.
—Matson. Shipping. On Lansing's list. Made a nasty remark about Rolph, the mayor, who wasn't there.
—Schoen. Ironworks. German born? (Ask Breyer.)
—Mullally. On the list. Likes to charm. Seems the easiest way in for me. Ugh.

~

The Spreckels mansion, site of the gala, was a massive neoclassical stone and marble confection looking out over the bay and the Golden Gate from atop the city's northernmost hill, with large, high-ceiling, tall-window room after room on the second main level converging on a vast mirrored ballroom; bayside terraces in the rear lorded it over the hillside and flatlands below. The place was staggering enough on its own, but add the boisterous society crowd in its array of masks and bizarre party costumes and Kate felt as if she'd been dropped into some sort of Devil's rout from one of the old paintings the nuns had shown to terrify her and the other children in catechism class.

Kate's invitation to the society event had been waiting for her at the hotel when she'd arrived in the city four days before. The letters of introduction sent weeks earlier to San Francisco by her erstwhile father-in-law, at Lansing's behest and no doubt crafted by Lansing's U-1 men, had proved—from the evidence of the waiting invitation and the close attention she received at the party—extremely effective. A significant part of Kate's work the past several years at the Boston law firm, once they'd recognized the extent of her talents, had been to draft and edit legal briefs and correspondence for the several partners whose seniority had been achieved through deal-making skills or family connections but without any legal acumen or facility with written language. So Kate knew a nuanced piece of writing when she saw it. Given copies of the introduction letters before her departure from Boston, she'd been highly impressed by them. And as she reread them several times on the train coming across country, her admiration for their subtleties had grown. One letter was addressed to a distant, low-ranking cousin of a Jameson in-law whose class credentials had nonetheless been sufficient some years before to allow him to insinuate himself into a San Francisco social elite much newer and more permeable than Boston's. The other letter was to someone well-placed in the upper echelons of the Pacific coast commercial world whose shipping company had been engaged not only with one of the Jameson businesses but also with Lansing before he'd joined the government, and who, therefore, would know well the enormous power—including the awarding of huge government contracts—that Lansing now wielded as Secretary of State. The letters had been models of understated temptation: treasured daughter-in-law Katherine, they explained, was traveling to San Francisco to consider relocating there, a place she'd once known and loved, and thereby to establish a Jameson family beachhead; legally trained Katherine would also, the letters vaguely suggested, be familiarizing herself with the West Coast business climate for potential Jameson investments; and—the clincher—these Jameson interests carried the Lansing imprimatur, though exactly what or how was never stated, the Lansing name being casually dropped rather than explicitly wielded. Those who offered Katherine their hospitality, the letters concluded, would be appreciated by quite a few people—an image as large as the readers' imaginations—on the nation's other, weightier shore.

In the mansion's vast entrance hall, Kate was given a half-mask to wear, as were those other party guests who arrived in formal evening clothes rather than costume. Apparently her hosts had been prepared for the fact that she'd be on unfamiliar ground, because she was immediately taken in hand by someone who appeared to be waiting for her, a voluble woman of an age and physical appearance made difficult to discern by a green half-mask and cap and a red voluminous round costume which, taken together, Kate finally surmised must have represented some kind of vegetable or fruit. The woman whisked Kate up a grand staircase and into the throng; the first knot of revelers they joined included a man costumed as a hunchback, another as a lion, and a woman in blackface and a wig of tightly curled hair, dressed as a child's raggedy doll.

"Ahh, Annabelle," the Lion addressed Kate's companion, "I always thought you were quite the tomato."

"Richard," the Tomato replied, "You probably expect I'm flattered. But king of the jungle you're not. More like a big… well…" She turned to Kate: "Wonderful, isn't it? How charity brings out the best in people? Oh, but let me present you. Dears, this is Katherine Jameson. Of the Boston Jamesons."

Polite smiles and introductions. None of the people's names registered with Kate, which meant that none of them was on Lansing's list of main interest. The Tomato then led Kate through several more such groups, at every stop making introductions, but none of them rang any bells for Kate. After a while, Kate recognized that her mask allowed her the appearance of paying attention to conversation while her eyes could actually roam over the larger crowd: well over a hundred people in just this large salon, or whatever it was, and in the next-door ballroom, with others spilling into rooms Kate could glimpse through the crowds on the ballroom's far side, plus a steady stream continuing up the main staircase. The sight of all these costumed or masked and evening-dressed bodies reveling amid the mansion's baroque furnishings, gilded mirrors and lush draperies was truly astounding to Kate—Katie Carey from Southie—and, when next she was spoken to, she realized that her open mouth might have been giving away something of her amazement.

"Yes, you must find us a bit provincial after Boston," a cultured deep Southern drawl came from just over her shoulder.

Kate turned to see a tall, lean, middle-aged man with unusually long swept-back black hair above a handsome fine-featured face—neither masked nor painted, one of very few such in this gathering.

He was wearing some sort of military officer's formal dress uniform. Complete with plumed hat and saber.

"And Washington as well?" he continued. "Or have I just imagined that?"

Kate was taken aback by mention of Washington, since her only experience of it had been during the weeklong training with the U-1 people. How could this man have known? But before coming to the party she had reread the introduction letters, with their vague references to Lansing and, flashing back to them now, she guessed that one of these was probably the man's source for connecting her to Lansing's name and, thus, to Washington. This allowed her to compose herself. Though how had he seen one of the letters? Or had he only heard reference to her? And by whom?

"No, actually," she replied, looking around at the welter of masks and costumes, "this reminds me quite a bit of Washington."

"Ah, Thorny," the Tomato reacted to the new uniformed arrival, "this is Katherine Jameson. Or did you already know? Anyway, Mrs. Jameson this is Thornwell Mullally."

Mullally gave an old-fashioned bend at the waist.

"But be careful," the Tomato continued to Kate, "he's quite the mover."

The little group laughed.

"You see," Mullally explained, "I am. . . involved with United Railroads. 'A mover.' I'm afraid that passes for local humor."

"Well," the Tomato said, "that wasn't *all* I meant."

The banter was interrupted by music striking up in the ballroom. The group broke up and moved with many others in the salon toward the open double doorway. Kate held back, glad finally to be separated from the Tomato. Mullally lingered with her. One of the army of servers passed by with a tray of champagne; Mullally took a glass and one for Kate.

"I hope you'll find things of some interest here, Mrs. Jameson," Mullally said with a shade less formality now in his syrupy vowels. "Things may not be quite as well-ordered as in the East. But then, that allows us a bit more. . . freedom of association."

"Association. Well, that is something of why I'm here."

"Ah. 'Something of'…" Mullally smiled and took a sip of his drink. "I'm intrigued."

An attractive thirtyish woman in a rather indeterminate gauzy outfit—perhaps representing a sylvan spirit but certainly well-representing herself—sidled up to Mullally.

"Thorny, aren't you joining?" she said, ignoring Kate and taking Mullally by the elbow, tilting her head toward the ballroom music.

Mullally looked at the woman for a moment: "I suppose otherwise you might think me remiss, Victoria?" The woman looked somewhat puzzled: whether at Mullally's hint of sarcasm, or simply at his vocabulary, Kate couldn't tell. "Will you excuse me?" he said to Kate, gave a little bow and moved off with the gauzy woman toward the ballroom.

Kate headed in the other direction. Noticing a French door ajar, she slipped out onto a wide veranda. It was a great relief to get away from the crowd, with its social clamor and visual assaults; Kate took off her mask, another relief. But the light through the glass doors seemed harsh, so she headed toward the shadows between two balustrades, found a broad staircase, and wandered down. On the next level was another veranda skirting the entire rear of the mansion. It was quieter down here away from the party, and Kate strolled along, marveling at the view of the moon-glittered bay far below. Toward the middle of the wide building she came upon a brightly lit room from which loud, brutish voices reached through closed glass doors. Kate stopped in the shadows and peered inside.

The room was very large, perhaps half of the great ballroom directly above it. Thirty or so men—Kate saw no women—were standing around the walls, spectating. Another dozen were sitting in high-back gilded chairs surrounding a construction that took up the entire middle of the floor, a raised platform with ropes tied around four corner posts: a makeshift boxing ring. Kate was surprised enough by the ring but astonished by what was going on inside it. To a raucous combination of cheers and catcalls from the formal-dressed or costumed spectators, two large men were pummeling each other. But instead of normal boxing attire, the men were wearing chin-tied caps with floppy strips of thick red cloth on top, and body suits to their knees entirely covered with feathers, a few of which flew off when a solid blow was struck, occasioning a surge in the spectators' cheering and jeering.

"We must have some sort of connection."

Kate jumped. It was Mullally, moving from the shadows behind her.

"Mr. Mullally..."

"Thornwell, please... I'm sorry to have startled you."

"Actually, I was already..." she turned toward the lighted room. Mullally's eyes followed.

"Ah, yes," he said, "I imagine this could be a bit... unexpected. But it's not unusual here. Several of us are keen on boxing, you see, and we sometimes put on exhibitions at various functions... among friends. Livens up things. I myself maintain a gymnasium near our railroad's carbarn, in the central city. Several of our workmen are quite top-notch fighters. We allow them a certain amount of... leeway at their jobs. In order to keep up their training. These two, in fact, come from that very stable."

"Well, the boxing, yes... But..."

"Ah. The outfits, the feathers. That is certainly... You see the gentleman with the large mustache, sitting down, with the stick?"

A man in evening clothes was seated in an armchair, gesturing toward the boxers with a gold-handled cane.

"That's William Matson. Captain Matson"

"Captain?"

"Yes. Of the seas. A man of considerable interests. Not least of which is his Pacific shipping fleet. This is a bit of a tale..."

"No, please," Kate said, "I'm here to learn."

"Hm. So you are." The tone of this reply was a bit off from his narrative voice, but Kate could not read his face in the shadows, and he quickly resumed his story. "Well, as you may have heard, there is more than a little... unpleasantness these days between the shipowners and the stevedores."

Kate nodded. Not only had she briefly seen the confrontation near the Ferry Building when she'd first arrived in the city but she'd been reading about the ongoing furious waterfront battles in the daily newspapers, all of which she'd been devouring in an effort to pick up local knowledge.

"And they've been costing the owners quite a bit, these strikes. Pushed into it by all the agitators in this town." Kate sensed a whiff of anger working its way into Mullally's otherwise calm, slow drawl. "Willing replacement workers, men just trying to make a living to support their families, they're being blocked from getting to the ships. And the police failing to protect our... well. So the owners have been making use of private security firms. To... manage things. But they can only do so much, without the force of law behind them."

Mullally stopped, perhaps sensing from the sound of his own voice that his equanimity was slipping. He stared at Kate for a moment, as if wondering whether this lesson in local politics was worth the effort. But Kate's face told him nothing: one of the skills she'd mastered while working in the Boston law office was to listen to males blather away without betraying any part of her true feelings about what they said or how they said it.

"But... the feathers?" Kate put in.

"Yes. Yes, it may seem otherwise, but actually I am getting to that. So, about our security men... Well, Captain Matson there, and several others, they called on the mayor, Mr. Rolph... Do you know of him? Sunny Jim Rolph, friend to all and sundry?... Anyway, they brought to the mayor a simple solution: just deputize the private detectives, who'd then enforce the law. But Sunny Jim refused... despite the substantial support these gentlemen had given to his election. He claimed that such a move would make him too many enemies among his otherwise adoring public. A decision which ensured that Sunny Jim now has rather more... important enemies."

Several loud bellows from the room drew Kate's attention; one of the boxers had landed heavy blows, sending the other down, feathers flying. She turned back to Mullally.

"Do you think," she said with some discomfort, "we might...?"

"Yes, certainly." They moved along the veranda, away from the boxing room, and settled against a balustrade several yards away.

"So, the feathers," Mullally continued. "The mayor, you see, considers himself something of a showman. And one of his crowd-pleasers is to hold cockfights of a Sunday afternoon inside... if you can imagine this... inside his home, some rambling wooden place, over there somewhere," Mullally gestured vaguely with his hand, "and invites members of his public to watch. Of course, true cockfights are illegal, so Sunny Jim has leather guards made to cover the cocks' beaks, and... finally, you see, we've arrived at our destination... tiny boxing gloves to tie over their feet. Which means the birds can't actually harm each other. But they're allowed to keep trying until one or both of the pathetic creatures collapses of exhaustion. In a heap of feathers. So according to Sunny Jim, it's not really a cockfight, it's a boxing match. Well, several gentlemen here want to remind Rolph of how he's now regarded by... people of standing. So they find various ways to mock him. As with this boxing here, with the feathers. Of course, Sunny Jim isn't invited to see it. But word will trickle down. With perhaps a photograph on one of the society pages. And someone will be sure to remind him of it, with a laugh at his expense, at some function or other."

"Seems like an awful lot of trouble," Kate put in, "just for a taunt."

"Yes, well, actually it's not. Not for these gentlemen. Getting the fighters, you see, I was happy to oblige. As for arranging the ring, well, they have no shortage of... people. Or, I suppose, of feathers. Although that was something of a surprise. Even to me."

One of the doors of a room at the end of the veranda opened, with light and a bit of smoke emerging.

"Ah," Mullally brightened, somewhat theatrically Kate thought. "Some of the very gentlemen, I'd venture."

He steered her along the veranda until they had a view through the open doorway. The room was smaller than the others she'd seen, though still substantial, and instead of mirrors and baroque gilding it was paneled in dark wood, with row upon row of perfectly matched, perfectly aligned leather-bound books in recessed shelves taking up much of the wall space. The furniture, too, was different: a massive flattop polished wood desk and a large table of similar wood, and plump chairs and sofas of burgundy leather. Arrayed on them comfortably, casually even, were a dozen or so white-haired men wearing formal evening clothes; most held drinks and several were smoking cigars. In one part of the room four women in evening gowns sat together chatting. A couple of party masks sat on the table, but none of the men or women wore a costume. On a pedestal behind the women was a large bronze statue, of which Kate could see only the top part: a woman's head, with wings towering above her naked torso and outstretched, fist-clenched arms; she seemed to be howling.

One of the men got up and moved to a decanter on the table, refilling his glass and offering it around in a sweeping gesture; Kate could see no household help or party servers, unlike in the other rooms which had been swarming with them.

"That's Frank Drum," Mullally indicated the man with the decanter, "the one with all the energy." They were still far enough away from the door that they could speak quietly without being overheard, but neither could they hear what was being said inside. Mullally seemed to expect some recognition from Kate for his remark, but she had none to offer.

"My apologies," Mullally drawled, "Occasionally I descend into the local humor: '... the one with all the energy.' You see, Mr. Drum is Pacific Gas and Electric. The power company."

"Ah."

"Well, and other... concerns. And there's our host, Adolph. The rather portly fellow. In the wheelchair."

"Oh, yes," Kate's interest was piqued, "the sugar man."

Adolph Spreckels's vast fortune, she knew from Lansing, included not only his sugar empire but also massive shipping and shipbuilding enterprises and huge tracts of land in both California and Hawaii. His father was German-born, and Adolph had been educated, for a time, in the old country. The combination of this Teutonic background plus the strategic significance of his holdings had landed him high on Lansing's list of interest.

"Oh, and many other things. Ships. Iron. Rail."

"And you a railroad man yourself."

"Yes. You recall. Or did you already know? Though I also serve as something of a liaison, for people with… related interests. And other concerns which… affect the public good… Ah, and there's Alma. Mrs. Spreckels."

An extremely tall, statuesque woman in her thirties, dressed and bejeweled even more elaborately than the other, older women around her, stood up and pointed out to her companions something about the bronze bust behind her.

"Such an… extraordinary woman," Mullally said in a way that Kate was unable to parse. "And her *Genius of War.*"

"Excuse me?"

"Oh, I'm sorry. The sculpture. It has an official title, something French, I don't recall, but here we call it *The Genius of War.* One of Alma's favorites."

"Quite an array," Kate's eyes flicked back to the room upstairs, "the people you know."

"Well… they all play a part."

"I hope you don't find that I'm speaking out of turn. It's just that, as a newcomer, I'm at something of a disadvantage."

"On the contrary. I am at your service."

"Well, I appreciate it. You've… helped. Already I have a better sense of things. For example, what it is *you* do."

"Oh?"

Kate indicated the people in the room in front of them: "You're with them."

Mullally hesitated, then smiled slightly and tilted his head toward her in appreciation.

"Perhaps you'd like to join them?" He indicated that they'd go in together.

"Do you suppose we could?" Kate then hesitated for a moment, looking at Mullally's military uniform. "But would you be…? I mean, none of them is in costume."

"Ah. This. No," he said, "this isn't a costume."

6

The Barleycorn Vegetarian Café occupied the street level of a four-floor wood frame and clapboard building on Market Street that had been hastily thrown up soon after the '06 quake and that now, only ten years later, seemed shabby and bygone in the shadow of the massively larger stone and cement office buildings, department stores and hotels that had gone up around it. Blue was about to go in the café's front entrance when he was nearly bashed into by someone rushing toward the door from the other direction. It was the young woman—again carrying a stack of oversize papers—he'd seen at Belle Lavin's rooming house a week before. With the mnemonic help of the leaflet stack, Blue remembered her immediately. But Meg took a moment to place him, which was not surprising since he now presented a significantly different picture than on that earlier occasion: gone were the swollen cheek and eye, the sweat-matted growth of beard, the filthy jacket with the shoulder torn in the waterfront skirmish, and the overall layer of grime he'd accumulated during the final boxcar leg of his return to San Francisco. He also smiled, which he hadn't at all in the few minutes they'd passed together that morning at Belle's.

"You always come with a side dish?" Blue nodded toward the papers she held.

"A side dish... And what would that make me?"

"Arrah, I didn't mean..."

"Oh. Well, then... So what did you mean? If you know."

"Seems we've got ourselves on the wrong foot again."

"Yeah," Meg conceded, letting her shoulders slump, "it's been a long day." Her eyes darted inside the café. "And getting longer."

"All right so. What say we start over." He dipped his head then raised it again, widening his eyes as if he'd just now seen her. "Ah, sure and behold. And how's herself?"

"Which version?"

"Whichever suits you."

"Suits me? There's something different... Well, how about a short version. Stretched thin. Feeling old, at twenty-two. And you? I hear you moved out of Belle's."

"You asked?" Blue enjoyed the idea but tried to keep a straight face.

Meg showed no reaction. "Just part of the general rumble around there," she said flatly. "Most everything's common knowledge at Belle's."

"Maybe that's why I moved."

"So, you've got things to hide." Meg's voice took on a tinge of affect, hinting at pleasure in perhaps having snagged an advantage in their to-and-fro.

Blue's mouth turned down at the corners. "There's a difference, so, between hiding things and just keeping some things to yourself."

Meg showed the palm of her free hand and tilted back her head, indicating that she hadn't meant to touch a nerve. They were silent for a moment, peering at one another as they stood in the recessed entryway. From Meg's expression, Blue sensed that his remark had made her curious, though he hadn't intended that. He hadn't intended anything, in fact had surprised himself with the serious turn he'd suddenly taken. Surprised, too, that he found himself glad of it. He couldn't have said why he'd responded this way—not only suddenly changing his tone but also beginning to contradict the very "keeping things to yourself" he'd just claimed—nor why it pleased him to have done so. Just something about this harried, contentious young woman, whose name, he hoped she hadn't figured out, he was still scraping his mind to recall.

The café door opened and a huge, florid man—with nearly shoulder-length, swept-back white hair, wearing a vast pinstripe suit that might have been stylish if there hadn't been so much of it, even more than required by the enormous body underneath it—squeezed his way out. The procedure was complicated by a big burlap sack he carried, heavy with clacking metal inside.

"Ahh, if it isn't the glorious Margaretta!" the man beamed.

Blue latched onto the name and, after a few moments, was able to winnow it down to Meg.

"Hullo C.V.," she replied with friendly resignation. "More health for the masses?" she nodded toward the burlap sack.

"Yes, indeed... and who have we here?" he immediately pivoted to Blue. "A face I think I once knew."

"So it is, C.V. Been quite a while. But your man here," Blue indicated the sack, "might be something I don't know. Last time I saw you was in a courtroom."

Indeed, Cornelius V. Clay was, among other things, a lawyer. But for years he'd maintained no office and disdained anything close to an actual law practice, limiting the use of his legal license and talents to occasional appearances on behalf of an eclectic, unpredictable selection of freethinkers and political outlaws: he'd appeared at Emma Goldman's side a few years earlier when she'd been arrested in San Francisco for "inciting to riot" and "outraging public decency" following a speech that had ranged through anarchism, pacifism and birth control; had defended the proprietor of the city's Liberty Bookshop after his arrest, following a complaint by a nearby church, for displaying in the shop's window "obscene and lascivious" material, which consisted of a staged photograph of a priest running down a Paris street hauling on his shoulder a flailing nun, legs emerging from under her habit, which celebrated the 1905 French law separating church and state and was captioned, with a French *bon mot* of the time, "Get out priest, and take your sister with you!"; and had helped represent local labor radical Tom Mooney after his arrest three years earlier for conspiracy to blow up electrical towers near the edge of the bay, despite the fact that no explosives had been found—during an unsanctioned search of his fishing skiff by power company private detectives—among Mooney's gear.

Recently, however, C.V. had become dedicated to—many said obsessed with; hence the slight exasperation in Meg's greeting of him—the flogging of peanut paste and its health benefits to all and sundry or, in his own sui generis locution, "spreading groundnut elixir over the unenlightened polis." The burlap sack he carried was crammed with tins of the stuff, which he'd first discovered while he was drying out, from a deeper-than-usual dive into alcohol, at a high-end sanitarium in the wooded countryside north of the city. In addition to becoming both a vegetarian and a teetotaler—the combination of which had helped him drop from some astronomical figure to a relatively svelte three hundred pounds—during his stay, he'd discovered peanut paste there and became determined to pry it away from the confines of exclusive health spas and to make it a central part of The People's diet. He contended that the nut paste was particularly delicious if eaten in a manner of his own creation, which was to spread it generously on a thin slice of soda bread, or the local sourdough, add a dash of salt, and top it with a light layer of mashed fruit. You could even, he boldly suggested, cover it all with another thin slice of bread to make what might fairly be called a sandwich.

So smitten was C.V. with this revolutionary new comestible that he'd put considerable time and energy into building a small paste-making workshop in which—ignoring neighbors' complaints about the "foreign" smell—two acolytes roasted, ground, and tinned the nuts, while C.V. himself roamed the city engaging in peanut paste proselytizing. One of his major customers was the Barleycorn, which displayed a small pyramid of the tins for sale and which, after a substantial number of customer-rejected trials, found a place for the paste on its menu—despite C.V.'s complaint about the addition of sugar and flour, which he referred to as "insalubrious adulteration"—by making dessert cookies out of it. The café's proprietors had gone to these great lengths to use and sell the paste not so much because they shared C.V.'s culinary-political opinion of the stuff but because they were always looking for something to perk up what seemed to be, in the considered opinion of their far too irregular dining clientele, an otherwise pallid menu. In addition, they were beholden to C.V. for his crucial financial infusion to the Barleycorn at its inception several years earlier when one of the original backers, the local writer, radical and vegetarian Jack London—who offered up the café's name, at the time finishing his own Barleycorn-titled work—had experienced a sudden conversion to a diet centered on raw meat and had buggered off to Hawaii or the South Seas or some such place with barely a farewell and, more importantly, without having delivered a promised bank draft.

"Ah," C.V. perked up at Blue's mention of the burlap sack, "let me enlighten you, my boy."

Blue had no idea what was in the sack or the lecture it would inspire, but from years past he recalled C.V.'s general propensity for extreme long-windedness.

"No doubt I could use enlightening, C.V.," Blue said, "but there's a gathering about to get underway." He nodded toward the café's interior.

"Ah yes, right you are. But we'll catch up soon, I hope. You can find me here many an hour. As you can the marvelous Margaretta here, brightening the premises with her vibrant persona and the painterly fruits of her vision!"

As he and Meg retreated a few steps to allow C.V. to squeeze by with his sack, Blue registered this vague piece of data about being able to find Meg at the café.

"Coming or going?" said a voice from down the street. Approaching was a tall, sandy-haired, fair-skinned man of about Blue's age, carrying under one arm a stack of papers like the one Meg was holding. As the man's face came into the light of the café windows, Blue could see that he was smiling brightly, almost beaming, at Meg. Blue could also see, to some annoyance, that the man was strikingly handsome.

"You done in there already?" the man continued to Meg in a solicitous voice, barely glancing at Blue.

"No, actually, I haven't made it inside yet."

"Which would be my doing," Blue put in.

"And who are you meant to be?" the man asked brusquely, looking at Blue but without turning his body away from Meg.

Blue did not, would not, answer right away, letting the man's slightly hostile tone linger in the air between them.

"This is Blue Cavanaugh, Treat," Meg intervened. "I met him over at Belle Lavin's the other day."

"Oh, Billings's new playmate, eh?"

"What, does someone keep a chart?" Blue looked from one to the other.

"What's that supposed to mean?" Treat scowled.

"Seems you've got yourself on the wrong foot again," Meg said to Blue, attempting to lighten things.

"Better than underfoot," Blue replied, not exactly to either of them.

After an awkward moment, Meg said, "Well, this is Michael Treat. We're... I mean, his printshop... where I stay."

"Yes, she does," Treat said, not to Blue but to Meg, smiling again. "So you're coming to the meeting?" he addressed Blue directly now, suddenly chummy. "Call me Treat. Everyone does. Shall we?"

∼

A decade after their separate arrivals as children at Ellis Island in the early 1890s, Maysie Wolf and Ike Meadows—whose more consonant-packed Pale of Settlement names had been transformed into Wolf and Meadows by port of entry immigration officers—discovered each other within Chicago's Yiddishkeit milieu. When they met, Maysie was fifteen, wiry, high-spirited. Ike was eight years older, small, slight, and soft-spoken. A year later they decided on marriage (the curious terms of which, initially a matter purely between the two of them, caused quite a furor upon being exposed to public consideration years later in San Francisco). Faced with their families' disapproval, they lit out on their own: first to New York, where over the course of two years they engaged with the forceful but deeply sectarian European-flavored anarchist communities there; then out west, where they'd heard of and hoped to join a less dogmatic and more permeable radical milieu.

Maysie and Ike reached San Francisco two years after the earthquake and quickly connected with San Francisco's antinomian bohemia, staying briefly at Belle Lavin's and then sharing a house in the North Beach neighborhood with several immigrant Italian syndicalists. But Ike couldn't find work in his trade as a printer, and Maysie, young as she was, had no real trade, so they struggled to make ends meet by hopscotching from one odd job to another. After a rough and not very promising year, they decided to try the Russian River countryside north of the city where a number of radical types were in the midst of a back-to-the land phase, ridding themselves of modernist trappings and trying their hands, often in communalist formats, at older, "purer" crafts: truck garden fruit and vegetable farming, woodworking, winemaking, chicken ranching, and such. Lifelong city boy Ike bounced around uncomfortably from farm to orchard to lumberyard doing occasional labor while Maysie found steady work as a cook at the upscale, woodsy health spa sanitarium where C.V. Clay happened to be drying out. The job introduced her and Ike not only to C.V. but also to vegetarianism, the combination of which in turn had connected them with Jack London and to the idea of opening a vegetarian restaurant back in the city.

After a year, Ike returned to San Francisco—in part to begin investigating what it might take to open the restaurant he and Maysie envisioned, but in equal part just to get away from the alien countryside—where, with C.V.'s help, he found work at a printshop that did many of the pamphlets, leaflets, journals and such that were being churned out by the city's many radical political and labor groups. He took the cheapest possible boardinghouse room and saved as much pay as possible to help fund the putative café. Maysie did the same up at the Russian River sanitarium resort, her saving bolstered by a free bed in an empty shack on the property and by the food she pilfered from the spa's kitchen.

Soon, though, Ike and Maysie realized that, even with their current Spartan living regimes, at the rate they were going it would take years to put together enough money to start the restaurant. So they spoke about it to C.V. He in turn called on his friend London, who promised to help get the place started. Maysie immediately left the spa kitchen, moved back to the city, and began looking with Ike for a suitable commercial space. Maysie and Ike also had another small piece of mixed fortune: after many struggling years, the man whom Ike worked for decided to give up his bustling but always financially strapped little printshop, selling the equipment and lease to Ike for the small amount Ike had managed to save to start the café. This meant that Maysie and Ike would now be operating—if and when they got the café going—not one but two enterprises, based on business experience that consisted entirely of one six-month stint running a corner cigar and magazine shop on the Lower East Side of New York, a bumbling venture that had succeeded only in hastening their decision to head west.

Arriving back in San Francisco from the countryside, Maysie rented a room in the flat of Lily Bratz, another in the Bay Area's small but passionate claque of vegetarians; Dr. B even promised to put a little money into the café venture. Taking this room, however, meant that Maysie and Ike were now paying for two living spaces, which put extra pressure on their funds to run the printshop and to get the restaurant underway. But Maysie insisted.

~

Fewer than a dozen people were gathered in chairs next to a makeshift two-tier scaffolding against the café's rear wall, which was bare except for some vague chalk lines and a few seemingly random patches of color; paint tins, brushes and drop cloths were pushed aside on one end of the scaffold's lower rung. The square room was quite large—about fifty feet each side—and the few paying customers that evening were scattered among tables near the street windows on the café's far opposite side from the scaffold. Still, those gathered against the rear wall kept their voices down and their faces turned away from the street.

The meeting had been called by Tom Mooney, a short, thick-necked, stocky man, frequently pugnacious but just as often charming—albeit blarney-tainted—who brought tremendous energy to any room. He was an iron molder by trade, with forearms to prove it, but his true calling was not so much laboring as organizing others who labored. His political praxis had always played long odds: he'd helped in Eugene Debs's 1908 Socialist Party campaign for president; produced an ambitious if short-lived Wobbly-flavored newsletter called *The Revolt*; and, along with his young satellite Warren Billings, had been heavily engaged behind the scenes with the electrical and gas workers during their long strike against the mammoth power companies three years before. The power company struggle had resulted in Mooney's arrest and trial, plus two retrials, for conspiracy to blow up electrical towers. Ultimately he'd been acquitted, but the nature of the charges against him had led the established labor unions and the central labor council to hold him at a distance.

Mooney's current target, and the subject of the evening's meeting at the Barleycorn, was United Railroads, which over the years had gobbled up competing local companies until it had cornered nearly the entirety of the city's substantial rail system. Although Mooney had no direct connection to rail or trolley workers, he nonetheless chose URR, as the company was known, as the focus of his efforts. Its chairman, Thornwell Mullally, ran URR like the near monopoly it was: as the company expanded to become the city's largest nonunion employer, Mullally sabotaged all attempts to organize its workers; he hired professional boxers—who trained at Mullally's gym near the trolley carbarn—as assistant conductors and yard security but whose real duties were to act as worker-control spies and enforcers; and he served as conduit and fixer among the various barons of industry who made up a violently anti-labor cabal which held puppet strings to the Chamber of Commerce and to several city hall insiders. For Mooney, Mullally was not merely powerful but also a conspicuous symbol of power.

URR was also San Francisco industry's beacon of violent strike-breaking. From 1902 through 1907, the Carmen's Union had repeatedly called strikes at URR, seeking not only union recognition and bargaining for a decent wage but also safety improvements: accidents were rife in the car yard and maintenance shop and along rail lines under construction or repair, but the company refused to address dangerous practices and workers received no compensation whatsoever for their injuries. The strikes culminated in 1907 when URR brought in a large contingent of scab workers and housed them in the barb-wired carbarns. On a day that came to be known as Bloody Tuesday, the company rolled out half a dozen cars manned with armed guards and drove them through a crowd of pickets outside. The crowd attempted to block the tracks, and the guards on the cars, along with others inside the carbarns, opened fire. When the chaos ended, two men lay dead, twenty others wounded.

The strike dragged on for months, with frequent skirmishes between strikers and armed URR enforcers. Over time, URR managed to hire a full complement of nonunion replacement workers and eventually the strike shuddered to a halt. By the end, six strikers had been killed and hundreds of others injured, the supporting labor council had lost several hundred thousand dollars in strike funds, and the Carmen's Union disbanded. Ever since, the URR strike had remained painfully stuck in the craw of San Francisco's radical labor cohort.

But now, almost ten years later, Mooney believed that Mullally and his company were vulnerable, that a combination of tides had turned against them. A few years before, URR's owners, then led by Mullally's uncle Patrick Calhoun, had been exposed for bribing the city's Board of Supervisors in an attempt to stop a measure that would have forced many of the city's rail power lines to be put underground, a very expensive proposition for URR. Calhoun had been kicked out in disgrace, replaced by Mullally, and public outrage was such that voters approved a massive bond measure to begin construction of a publicly owned municipal railway system. As that municipal system slowly got up and running, it increasingly encroached on URR's territory and profits—URR's trams and "Muni's" trams were now running side by side on parallel competing tracks along Market Street, the city's main commercial thoroughfare—as well as providing alternative employment for disgruntled or fired URR workers. Also impinging on URR was a new jitney cab venture, among the leaders of which was Mooney's friend Izzy Weinberg; the jitneys offered five-cent rides in six-passenger motor cars along Market Street and some of the city's other main routes that were also served by URR.

Most of all, Mooney decided to target URR because he believed that if a strong labor union could entrench itself in the transport system, it could wield enormous power not only on behalf of its own members but for all the city's workers. Mooney understood that a transport system was the blood flow of big business—the larger the enterprise, the more dependent it was on the unfettered movement of materiel, people and product—and that the capacity to shut it down was the capacity to paralyze a city's entire commercial body. In part, Mooney knew this because he had carefully followed from afar how Irish tram and rail workers had brought Dublin to a standstill three years earlier, which in turn had led to a pitched, months-long citywide battle between labor and capital, and to a near general strike.

Mooney had heard from Billings and others that Blue—whom Mooney knew from the shadows of the 1913 power company strike—was back in San Francisco, and that he'd been in Dublin during the transport strike there. So Mooney got word to him, asking Blue to join them at the Barleycorn meeting, to lend an authoritative voice about the centrality of the Dublin tram workers to the foundation-shaking events there. Blue wasn't crazy about the idea, being constitution-ally unsuited for the long slog of organizing: no patience, a quick temper, an ungovernable mouth. But on this occasion, because of his old friendship with Mooney, he'd managed to overcome his near allergic aversion to organizational meetings.

"Fuck me," Mooney grumbled as he emerged from the café's rear kitchen area and saw the gathering's small size and, more importantly to him, composition: of the few people there, only two were URR workers. The others were Rena Mooney, who was Tom's better half in many senses, politically dedicated but also levelheaded and, through the music lessons she gave at her studio further along Market Street, a regular breadwinner, which Tom most definitely was not; the café's owner Maysie Wolf (husband Ike was bustling between kitchen and customers); Warren Billings, who would show up to a meeting on Mars if called by Mooney but who'd have nothing to offer the group other than unbridled enthusiasm for action of any kind; Izzy Weinberg of the jitney operators association, an interested party to be sure but not one who had any influence within the URR workforce; Meg and Treat, who likewise had no purchase among the URR workers, though their creation and distribution of flyers and pamphlets could be crucial if Mooney could get organizing efforts off the ground; and Blue, there to act as witness regarding the momentous transport strike in Dublin in which he'd tangentially participated.

Blue knew that he'd be able to speak with passion, if asked, about how the tram drivers of Dublin had begun the great strike there and how, despite the railroad owners' enormous power, and in the face of virulent opposition to the strike by the police and by the overweening Catholic Church, they'd brought the city to a near standstill. As he sat there listening to Mooney begin speaking, however, Blue realized that he had not thought about what he'd say, if asked, about the Dublin strike's outcome: after months of struggle and deprivation for the workers and their families, in the immediate, practical sense—notwithstanding its arguably lasting symbolic value—it had been an unmitigated failure.

Mooney was never one to be deterred by facts on the ground, so despite the poor turnout of URR workers he began enthusiastically to deliver a status report that could only be described as mixed, at best. He opened with his ace: approval from the national Amalgamated Association of Street Railway Employees to organize a union at URR. However, after listening to Mooney declaim about this approval—including extra articulation of the word "national" that seemed to seek some response from the URR men—the two rail workers wanted to know more concretely what such approval meant. This forced Mooney to reveal the rest of his hand: that he'd received from the association only token funds and no other organizing support, and that he'd not yet generated any interest, let alone backing, from San Francisco's powerful but often conservative, cautious central labor council.

In their turn, the two URR workers surprised Mooney by being upbeat. They reported that although URR had threatened to fire anyone attempting to "foment" a union, or even being seen talking to "Thomas Mooney, known dynamiter"—the two workers had shucked their uniforms before coming to this meeting, entered through a rear alley door, and carefully kept their faces turned away from the café's street windows—they believed there was considerable support for a union among URR workers, though they had to be very careful about voicing it: the company had a slew of informants on its payroll. The workers knew who most of them were by the fact that they did little work—many spending more time in Mullally's boxing gym than on their shifts—and didn't bother to hide their special status; indeed, it seemed to be part of URR's strategy to make clear to the workers that they were being monitored. But apparently there were also other, hidden, informants: a couple of women in the URR clerical offices had reported to their fellow workers that the pay for certain employees was, for unaccounted reasons, much higher than for others doing the same jobs.

Hearing about official sanction from the national union office would give a boost to the URR workers, the two men told the gathering, and they mooted the idea of Mooney calling a mass nighttime organizing meeting. This would allow large numbers of URR workers to show up anonymously—which would be easier, they said, if workers from other unions also turned out to provide cover—and to listen to Mooney there without actually engaging with him in company-prohibited direct contact. Mooney immediately took to the idea, and told the two men that he'd make the arrangements and let them know where and when, but only on relatively short notice, so that Mullally couldn't find some way to sabotage the event. He also told the two workers that he would have a flyer produced on equally short notice— he glanced at Treat, who nodded his agreement; Meg scrunched her mouth in contemplation of yet another rush job—to spread the word for other union workers to show up in support.

Before winding up, Mooney wanted to tell the gathering one final thing.

"Swanson." He said the single word and let it sink in for a moment. Of those at the meeting who'd been involved over the past few years in San Francisco radical labor politics—Blue, Maysie, Billings, and Izzy Weinberg—the name got their immediate attention. However, for the edification of Meg and Treat, both relative newcomers to the scene, and most of all for the two URR workers, Mooney explained. Martin Swanson had been an operative for the Burns Detective Agency who'd left his job in 1913 to work exclusively for the power companies and then engaged throughout the state in the companies' bitter, violent struggle with labor in which Mooney and Billings had been deeply—and Blue glancingly—involved. It had been Swanson who had used an inside provocateur to set up the teenage Billings—Mooney had been the actual target—to act as an unknowing dynamite courier, ostensibly for the striking electrical workers. And it had been Swanson and his private detectives, in another setup during the same power company strike, who had Mooney arrested and three times unsuccessfully prosecuted for conspiring to blow up electrical towers.

Now, Mooney told the group, Swanson had opened his own detective agency called the Public Utilities Protection Bureau, its only clients being United Railroads and the Sierra and San Francisco Power Company, which was a subsidiary of URR and supplied the railway with its electricity. Mooney was certain he'd spotted men tailing him in recent weeks; he had no doubt they belonged to Swanson. He hadn't spotted Swanson himself lately—"the big ugly Scando son of a bitch"—but he described Swanson to the group so they might recognize him: a very large, broad-shouldered, flat-faced man with almost translucent pale skin whose square head seemed to sit directly on his torso, and who liked to give himself the extra sinister touch of a wide-brimmed slouch hat pulled low over his forehead. Mooney concluded the meeting with a warning that, given the rats working inside URR, plus Swanson and his goons, everyone involved in the organizing effort should at all times be aware of their surroundings, refuse discussion with anyone they don't know well and avoid moving about the city alone.

Blue squirmed through the meeting. His feelings about—as distinct from his belief in—strikes had taken a beating by what he'd experienced in Paterson and then in Dublin: massive and massively supported walkouts that had ended in massive failures. Masking those feelings in a speech about Dublin to this Barleycorn gathering would have left him with a bad taste, so he was relieved that Mooney hadn't called on him for a cheerleading, and thus necessarily somewhat duplicitous, history lesson. He found himself in good spirits when the meeting broke up and now wanted to get reacquainted with Mooney, whom he hadn't yet spoken with in person since returning to the city.

But the two URR men immediately went into a huddle with Mooney, so Blue had to wait. He said hello to Warren Billings, whom he hadn't seen since Blue had moved out of Belle Lavin's, then he drifted over to the edge of the scaffold where Meg was talking with Maysie. Meg was gesturing at the wall, the two of them looking up at it. Treat was leaning against a table behind the two women, as if waiting for them to finish.

"I don't want to say I can see it," Maysie was telling Meg as she linked arms with the younger woman, "but I can imagine it."

Maysie turned toward whoever was closest, which happened to be Blue, and said of Meg: "No end of passion, this one." Over Maysie's shoulder, Blue saw Treat flinch.

"So this is yourself, is it?" Blue asked Meg, indicating the painting gear and whatever was happening on the wall.

"Yeah," she said wearily, "when I get the chance." A stack of leaflets sat on the edge of the table beside her, like a silently reproaching duenna.

"As long as she needs," Maysie put in. "So," Maysie continued to Blue, extending a hand to shake, "what brings you back among the living?"

Blue knew Maysie and Ike from years before, though not very well. The café had opened and become a radical meeting spot a year or so before Blue left the city, but his impatience with the endless sectarian arguments that went on across its tables, plus his general avoidance of meetings, meant that he'd rarely appeared there. And when he had, he'd always made sure to eat something in North Beach beforehand—maybe *osso bucco* from the unofficial kitchen at the rear of the Ancora bar or sautéed calamari from the Colombo Ristorante. He wasn't alone among the radical milieu in avoiding the place. Many rough-edged labor militants thought of vegetarianism as fey, etiolating, even possibly a subversive threat to radical energies. And not a few others were simply confounded by it: when, early in the café's existence, Blue had mentioned to a North Beach anarchist friend that the Barleycorn catered not only to vegetarians but also to fruitarians, the friend had furrowed his brows, thought for a moment, then replied, "Huh. Well, that's all right, I knew a Huguenot once." Still, Blue had liked Ike and Maysie from the first, not least their highly unconventional marriage, and was glad to see them again.

"Couldn't stay away from your cooking," he said, and they shared a grin. "And how are we at all?"

"Well," Maysie said, "there's no shortage of action hereabouts," she glanced around the café and laughed, "just of customers."

"And the printshop? Ike still chasing there, too?"

"Nah, we couldn't stay ahead of the bills. And what with the café and all. So we sold it up to Treat here. And he's soldiering on. Does all the devil's work…" she indicated the political leaflets in his hands, "and makes a living too. Don't know how he does it… Well," she turned toward Meg and smiled, "I know *some* of how he does it."

Mention of his name, or maybe the reference to Meg, seemed to nudge Treat into motion.

"Getting late, yeah?" he said to Meg. "I mean, for you, getting to the Palace…"

"Late," she repeated flatly. "I suppose."

She gave Maysie a hug, then Blue a nod—in a way, as he chose to read it, that recognized the gesture's inadequacy but also asked him to understand that the situation permitted nothing more—and with Treat at her side moved toward the door, waving goodbye to Rena Mooney.

Maysie went off to help Ike with the café's customers and Blue turned his attention back to Mooney, who was still engaged with the two URR workers. As he waited, his eye was caught by Meg and Treat on the sidewalk in front of the café, framed by one of the windows. Their conversation seemed calm but Blue saw—or thought he saw—something a bit off, the physical space between them oddly wide as they spoke to each other.

The two workers finally wound up their parlay with Mooney and moved through the kitchen door to leave through the back alley. Blue sidled up to Mooney with a wide smile. Mooney opened his arms.

"Ah, a most essential fellow," Mooney said and the two men heartily embraced.

Blue had intended to see if Mooney had time for a pint and a chat. But as they disengaged from their bear hug, Blue again saw Meg and Treat through the window. He couldn't make out their faces, but there seemed something sad in their movements: Treat shook his head slightly, lowering his chin, then slowly turned and walked away; Meg looked after him for a couple of moments, then moved off in the other direction.

"So, when can I see you, Tom? Shall I come to your place? Soon enough, for certain. And you're lookin' grand!"

Blue pumped Mooney's hand, then hurried out the door.

7

When they moved back from the countryside to open the Barleycorn, the reason Maysie lived apart from Ike was their marriage contract. An actual written contract—which teenage firebrand Maysie had insisted on back in Chicago, and the politically sensitive and desperately in love Ike had reluctantly agreed to before they, loosely, tied the knot—drawn up according to Maysie's instructions by a lawyer acquaintance of Ike and signed before a puzzled but compliant notary. Neither Maysie nor Ike believed in official, state-sanctioned marriage. But young as she was, Maysie had already seen enough of what happened to most bohemian women who lived in "free love" coupledom: the same roles and the same power imbalances as in marriage, but without the counterweight of societal legitimacy. So she decided instead on a sort-of-binding personal partnership—though she and Ike would refer to themselves as married—under terms of her own devising. And one of those terms was that after five years the partnership would automatically end, after which Maysie and Ike perforce would separate. Only after another six months, the contract read, would they be free to recombine, if they so chose, in whatever shape suited them. Or not.

The five years had run out shortly after Ike returned to San Francisco, while Maysie was still up in the countryside, working. So when she came back to the city, she'd moved in with Lily Bratz rather than with Ike. During this contractually dictated partition, Maysie and Ike opened the Barleycorn and took over the printshop, working together twelve, fourteen, sometimes sixteen hours a day. But stayed in separate rooms at night. To the extent that anyone was curious about this, Ike and Maysie simply said that they were looking for the right place—a word that allowed for both literal and metaphorical meanings—for themselves. But in any case, there were many other nontraditional living and sleeping arrangements within the antinomian stew in which Ike and Maysie floated, so no one probed. When the six-month contractual separation time was up, and with barely any mention of it between them, Ike and Maysie took a small flat together and resumed their conjugal life without anyone else particularly noticing.

And their curious sort-of-marital path would have remained a purely private matter had it not been for an after-hours Barleycorn conversation a year or so later in which Ike offered their contractual wedlock as an exemplar. Marriage, or anything else as puny as the relations between just two people, was not usually a subject of conversation at the café; late-night denizens there tended to argue Big Things. But on that particular night the difficulties of someone's personal life had intruded, leading to a discussion of how couples of radical persuasion might maintain relative independence while forging something more than a merely ephemeral bond. And Ike—who unlike C.V. Clay had found, rather than abandoned, a taste for the local grape during his time in the wine-producing countryside—had become lubricated enough to describe to the table his and Maysie's matrimonial odyssey, which at that point seemed to him a safely distant piece of social and political, more than personal, history.

The little group at the table had been impressed by and admiring of the tale and of Ike's somewhat prideful relating of it (in which he had notably failed to mention that it had been Maysie's idea entirely, and that he had only reluctantly agreed). One of the people at the table, Harry Schnell, proprietor of the radical Liberty Bookshop—over the entryway to which was painted Cicero's late-life dictum *otium cum dignitate* (idleness with dignity)—was particularly intrigued by Ike's story. Harry was an ascetic. Partly by political choice: the first time he saw the bookshop's starkly monastic little back room, where Harry lived, Blue made some startled remark to which Harry retorted, "If you don't care about buyin' shit, you don't have to eat so much shit chasin' after it." But also by financial necessity: on another occasion Blue found Harry boiling a single small, unidentifiable root in a battered little pan on his hotplate and said, "Not much of a lunch, Harry, a bit of neep or whatever it is," and Harry replied, "Oh, the turnip? That's not lunch. That'll be dinner. Lunch is the broth." Not surprisingly, given his peculiarities, Harry had no intimate personal life of his own. Nonetheless, he was a tireless critic of the state's involvement in matters of individual conduct—he'd been known to appear at public events dressed only in the skimpiest of loin cloths, in order to test the state's prevailing notion of "decency," a test which on several occasions the police had physically informed him he'd failed—and he left the Barleycorn that night inspired by the tale of Maysie and Ike's arrangement. So much so that he wrote about it in an effusive article for the little newsletter he printed and distributed at the bookstore.

Unfortunately for Maysie and Ike, however, the story didn't stop there. It was picked up by one of the city's major newspapers, which spread it over a full page, including curated statements of outrage from a list of churchmen, civic leaders and society ladies who called Maysie, among other things, a "girl on a five-year lease" and their contract a "parchment of shame." The rest of the city's newspapers soon also ran with the story, reporting not only on Ike and Maysie's pact itself but also on the thunderous sermons on the subject being delivered at churches around the city, which called down Heaven's wrath against this Godless woman, this brazen hussy—Maysie took the brunt of their outrage—whose campaign of sin threatened to destroy the very institutions of hearth and home. Maysie was all of twenty-two years old.

Eventually the commotion dissipated and the story of Ike and Maysie's marriage passed into the mists of local legend, lingering mostly among the circles that frequented the Barleycorn and similar centers of radical peculiarity, such as Belle Lavin's boardinghouse. Which is where Meg heard the story from Belle.

Meg had met Maysie at the boardinghouse and, though Maysie was infinitely more worldly than Meg, she was only a few years older and the two had immediately formed a sisterly bond: soon after they met, Maysie invited Meg to create a mural on the back wall of the Barleycorn, and Meg looked to Maysie for instruction on the characters and ways of the city. So when Belle told Meg the story of Maysie's contract with Ike, Meg took it to heart. Which was exactly what Belle had hoped. Belle was concerned about Meg's rash decision to go to live with Treat, since Meg had known him only a few weeks and, even more importantly Belle thought, since Meg still knew so little about herself.

A mandatory separation date wasn't the only part of the Ike and Maysie marriage contract that caught Meg's attention. Although this other aspect had not made it into the newspapers and thus into general circulation, Belle knew of it and included it in the packet of wisdom she offered Meg when Meg left the boardinghouse to go live with Treat. At age sixteen, when Maysie had forged the marriage contract, she knew she didn't want to become a teenage mother, not least because she'd seen how motherhood had forced so many women to abandon their activism and indeed most of their worldliness. And while Maysie would later be introduced to birth control through anarchist circles in New York and later in San Francisco, the sixteen-year-old was not yet literate on the subject when she drew up the contract: not only effective birth control devices themselves but even just information about them was illegal under the federal Comstock Laws, and both were generally out of reach for everyone except the well-to-do. So Maysie included a chastity clause: for the first year of the marriage, she and Ike would have no sex, though they'd engaged in it happily enough quite a few times before the marriage. This would also be a test, Maysie felt, of her and Ike's true devotion to one another. Ike, on the other hand, had no doubts about his devotion. He worried instead about his sanity. He signed anyway.

Taking all this under advisement, soon after Meg went to live with Treat she insisted on instituting a version of the Ike and Maysie contract. She set a date of one year living together, after which they would have to separate for a minimum of six months. She also declared that after the first month, this year together would be abstinent. At least, with each other.

Lily Bratz, along with Belle, had become one of Meg's unofficial godmothers and had given Meg access to proper, if under-the-table, birth control—the devices sold as "hygienic products" in pharmacies, such as the "womb supporter" and the thick rubber "thumb guard," were notoriously cumbersome, ill-fitting, and unreliable—so as a practical matter Meg wasn't as concerned as Maysie had been, in her original contract, about the contraceptive need for abstinence. Still, Meg felt that taking sex with Treat out of the equation for a while would provide her with a measure of breathing space. The sex she'd had with Treat before this self-imposed restraint had been by far the best she'd experienced, though comparisons were from an extremely limited sample: awkward fumbling with a neighbor boy, finished almost as soon as it began, as a going-away gift to herself the night before she left home, to mark her self-liberation; a silent contorted scrum with a fellow young drifter in a dark compartment of a nearly empty night train, an encounter which, in retrospect, she realized she'd observed more than participated in; and a literal tumble in the hay with a wiry, rasp-handed young sheep rancher she'd met at a county fair in the Pacific Northwest and with whom she'd drunk enough homemade liquor that neither one of them could remember much, after the fact, about how things had gone. Treat, on the other hand, had been tender, patient, and lovely to look at and feel during their lovemaking in the weeks before she instituted the contract. She'd liked it very much.

But there was something about Treat. Something that had made Meg cautious and was the impetus for her latching on to the notion of Maysie's contract. She'd included the abstinence clause not as a test of Treat's devotion but out of concern that giving in to her own physical desire for him might keep her from sorting out what this something was about him that made her uneasy. Even in their brief time together certain things had disquieted her. She'd noticed, for example, that he had the habit of saying this thing or that not because it was what needed to be said but because it seemed to allow him to avoid saying something else. There was also a general blank receptiveness about him, a one-directionality, that offered no markers of his inner life. Which she assumed must be there. And contain a heart.

She wasn't actually able to articulate any of this to herself: she was too young and inexperienced of the world. But she felt it.

There was also the fact that Belle Lavin had never warmed to Treat. Belle hadn't offered any particular reasons, and on the surface Meg dismissed it as just another of Belle's arbitrary likes and dislikes. Still, somewhere in the back reaches of Meg's own ambivalence about Treat, Belle's judgment counted.

~

Blue had left high school without finishing. In his early teens, boxing and the various side jobs given to him by Flaherty the gym owner had increasingly challenged Blue's attention to formal education. Still, he'd kept at it until the fall of 1900. When he was sixteen. When the news about Declan reached the little North Beach flat that Blue shared with his mother. Declan, dead in the Philippines war. His big brother Declan.

His brother had flirted with minor criminality throughout his youth, leaving school at the age of thirteen. He'd wanted to make his own way, Declan had, make his own money, get away from his father's drunken beatings which, as the older son, he'd suffered worse, more frequent versions of than did younger brother Baldo. And by fifteen or so, Declan had become firmly entrenched in a life of petty-to-middling crime. Which is how he ended up in the Philippines.

He'd been caught by security guards during a warehouse burglary. When the guards started to administer on-the-spot punishment, Declan—a boxer, though not as talented as his younger brother—had inflicted some serious damage on them. So he'd had to face a judge—who just the year before had sentenced him to three months in a juvenile workhouse for a similar bungled heist—not only for the burglary but also for grievous bodily injury to the guards. He had just turned eighteen, so serious adult jail time, likely a stretch in Folsom or San Quentin prison, was in his immediate future.

It was the army that saved him. Temporarily.

There was never a shortage of volunteers for the army's officer corps: "good families," especially from the East Coast and the Old South, had long sent a steady stream of boarding school and university boys into the military as officers, and there was a surge of these would-be heroes following the brief, relatively bloodless "glory" of the Spanish-American War. But getting enough grist-for-the-mill grunt soldiers was a struggle, and the army had recently focused on local jails as particularly compliant recruitment sites. Enlistment sergeants across the country developed pipelines with local police departments, which notified the recruiters anytime a boy who fit a fairly generous profile—eighteen to twenty-five, not too much education, preferably a rowdy whose mild to moderate violence had landed him in trouble—wound up in their clutches. Then the deal was simple: enlist in the army, have the charges dropped and walk out of jail. Judges were happy to oblige—it meant not only wiping a case off the court's docket but also shipping a troublemaker out of town—and a chosen boy, usually poor and without prospects, was further tempted by the promise of square meals, a paycheck, the shine of a uniform, and the idea, however notional, that he was wanted.

In Declan's case, though, the balance sheet hadn't been so simple. He was certainly a battler, but he was also an inveterate thief. And most worrying, the police thought, was the fact that on the two occasions when he'd been caught—as well as on numerous other burglaries the cops believed he'd gotten away with—he'd used explosive devices to break into the shops and warehouse buildings he was robbing. Rather than scaring away the army recruiters, though, Declan's use of explosives piqued their interest. They talked to him in the jail, and once he understood that they might get him out of the mess he was in, he told them about his dynamiting skills. Michael Cavanaugh, Declan and Blue's father, had been a wizard with explosives, fuses and timing devices, much sought after by the burgeoning region's many mining, oil and gas and construction firms. And over the years the father had passed on much of his knowledge to his two sons. After Declan gave the army men a brief description of his skills and their source, the recruiters confirmed with a local mining firm about the technical talents of the father, Michael Cavanaugh, and returned to offer Declan not only a get-out-of-jail pass but the purportedly elevated position of sapper in the army's engineering corps. Declan quickly accepted and almost as quickly—after only a month's training—found himself in the jungles of the Philippines, in the midst of a war he didn't understand, pitted against Filipino independence fighters struggling against the United States army's attempt to "pacify" the islands following the recent ouster of the Spanish, the previous colonizers, in the Spanish-American War. Two months later he was dead. The letter delivered to his mother in San Francisco did not say what he was doing when he'd been killed, or how it had happened. Only that he'd died "nobly," while serving his country.

Blue's mother Maricchia was shattered by her elder son's death. She had managed, just, to hold herself together over the several years since her husband had left, taking with him not only the income he'd brought in but also her status in the neighborhood as a married woman. The paltry pay she got for her work at a cigar factory during those years was supplemented by money Declan and Blue brought in from their late-night endeavors—Maricchia asked for no details—and by the vegetables she was allotted for her work with fellow Sicilians at their communally tended truck farm on the southern outskirts of the city. There were also occasional neighborhood contributions of fish and milk and cheese to *la vedova*—"the widow"—and her boys, and frequent donations from a local baker who would call to Baldo whenever he'd pass and hand him warm *focaccia* straight out of the wood-fired oven, even though this baker was Ligurian and church-going, whereas Maricchia and her boys were neither. Of course, Maricchia wasn't actually a widow, at least as far as anyone knew, but she was considered as such by many of the materially supportive but socially judgmental neighbors: "Well, what could you expect," it was said, "of a mixed marriage like that?" Maricchia bore it all in silence; Declan bore it by drinking; Blue, by beating the crap out everyone he met in the boxing ring.

Once Declan was gone, the teenage Blue was on his own supporting himself and his mother. Fortunately, when he turned sixteen he started getting paid aboveboard for boxing matches, and the gym owner Flaherty obliged with more side work, too. But when he wasn't working, boxing, or training to box, Blue was at home as much as possible. By that time Maricchia's poor health had forced her to quit the cigar factory—as a Sicilian, she'd never been given one of the slightly better paid jobs as a roller, which the Genovese owners and foremen gave to the Lucchesi and other Ligurian women, but was consigned instead to the cutting room, where years of inhaling tobacco shards had left her lungs in ruin—and the only work she was able to manage was a bit of mending she took in at home. She no longer went to help out at the truck farm. She stopped visiting with neighbors. For the most part, she stopped leaving the little apartment at all. She hardly ate, unless Blue fixed her something and sat with her. She didn't say much, unless Blue coaxed her to speak of her childhood in Sicily. Didn't move much, unless Blue went with her down the three flights of stairs and out for a short walk. The only time she smiled was when Blue read to her.

Work for Flaherty; training and boxing matches; occasional forays of minor criminality; and close care of his mother. Other things had to go. School was one of them.

But not reading. Nor his affection for and facility with language. His mixed parentage meant that he'd grown up, in heavily Italian North Beach, "natively" speaking English, Italian and Sicilian. He found early on that his articulateness in the three languages, especially his ability to translate the other two into fluent unaccented English, made him a valued member of the neighborhood—and later for the district's many Italian anarchists and syndicalists, who needed trusted translations of a vibrant flow of papers and journals and declarations— and served him well as he worked for Flaherty in various corners of the city. He also discovered that lively, flexible use of language in general opened doors for him more easily than did the limited burglary skills and tools his brother had left him.

So, from early on, reading, reading and reading. Anything he could get his hands on. The North Beach district of Blue's youth was flooded with local, national and international broadsheets, newspapers and pamphlets in both English and Italian, and numerous places where he could read free copies: the local branch of the public library for the more respectable papers, and politically sectarian storefront social groups for the more scandalous and subversive journals. In his adolescence he also discovered the city's several radical bookshops, in a couple of which he was allowed to sit undisturbed to pore over papers and journals. And in one of them, the proprietor allowed young Blue to take home pamphlets and books without charge from the shop's rental collection. The political slant of these bookshops and neighborhood groups meant that the particular papers and pamphlets the youngster inhaled tended to deepen a thoroughly left-wing perspective initiated in him by the overall political tenor of working-class life in the city of the time and, in particular, in immigrant-heavy North Beach.

The neighborhood library also had a good collection of books in Italian. So, during his teenage years following Declan's death, and into his twenties, when Blue spent so much time at home with his mother, he was able to continue his education despite having dropped out of school, filling many hours reading variegated volumes of history and literature in both languages, some to himself, some out loud in Italian to his mother.

His education continued in other ways, too: Lotte Backstrom, a newcomer to the city who lived just across the rear alleyway, had a merchant seaman husband who was away for months at a time and who apparently was no bargain when at home, either. At age sixteen, Blue found that the initial enticement of Swedish meatballs wasn't the only thing on offer if he quietly made his way up Lotte's rickety back staircase late at night.

The fact that he always had a book with him, and would read in any quiet moment, was one of the several things that had endeared Blue to the theater women whose paths he'd crossed in Dublin in '13 and '14, and to a particular one of the group of suffragette women in London with whom he'd engaged after Dublin. In fact, the parting gift he'd been given, by the London woman with whom he'd been most intimate, on his departure from England in early '15 was a book: the novel *Howards End*. He'd read it as he'd made his way back across the Atlantic and the States to San Francisco, savoring it even more after he was able to laugh at himself for having wondered, in the first several chapters, when Howard would appear. Though he'd been unsympathetic at first to the dithering of the novel's rich people, and irritated by the residual costiveness of its pallid bohemians as they purported to separate themselves from the anxious middle classes, he soon settled down to appreciate the book's examination of human foibles across a spectrum of social positions. And more than once he'd marveled at the acuteness of the author's specific perceptions, one of which in particular had stayed with him: the most unsuccessful life, the author wrote, "is not that of a man who is taken unprepared, but of him who has prepared and is never taken." Blue had copied it onto a scrap of paper next to a line another suffragette close companion in England had introduced him to: "The tygers of wrath are wiser than the horses of instruction." Given his antipathy toward the Church, which had been so much inflamed by his recent experiences in Dublin, Blue had particularly liked the fact that this latter sentiment came from a work called the *Proverbs of Hell.*

Blue had been captivated by each of these lines not because they introduced him to notions he'd never considered but rather because they confirmed sensibilities he'd always deeply felt but never seen expressed. "If your juices tell you something," he'd later frame these sentiments himself, "it's true."

So, Blue: believed in the moment; in the verities of his gut; believed that caution was the same coin as surrender, and that its only purchase was emptiness.

Before he'd left San Francisco three years earlier, Blue had heard a bit about Ike and Maysie's marriage contract, though it hadn't held much interest for him. And he had no idea that what he saw of Meg and Treat through the café window that night of Mooney's meeting—their slight distance from each other, their strain—was both the reason for and result of Meg's version of the contract. All he knew was that he'd become intrigued by the young woman, had heard her living arrangement with Treat spoken of in ambiguous terms and, through the café window, had noticed the space between them. So, in the moment, he'd reacted: he left Mooney standing there without engaging in the reunion conversation that he'd intended and that Mooney was clearly expecting, went straight out the café door without farewells to Ike, Maysie or Billings, and quickened down Market Street after her.

"We're going the same way, are we?" he said, coming up behind her.

Meg looked at him as he came abreast but didn't slow down—she was striding at a good clip—or turn to face him.

"Apparently," she said without inflection, stepping into Market Street amid the welter of trams and jitneys and carts and cars, and crossing to Kearney, which passed close by the central commercial and hotel district of Union Square and carried on past Chinatown to the Barbary Coast and North Beach.

"You're late, is it?"

She slowed. "Late? For what?"

"Sure I couldn't say. It's just that the fella back there, he mentioned something about it. The Palladium or some such."

"Oh. The Palace. Yes, well... he worries a lot. The fella."

They walked along in silence for several strides.

"So... Are you terrible great with him?"

She stopped. "And why would you want to know that?"

Blue was caught off guard. He hadn't planned on being so direct with her. And to the extent he might have expected a reply, it would have been some sort of fluster on her part, or a deflection, not a retort that turned the tables on him.

"Arrah... I meant nothing by it. Just, ah, trying to get the lay of the land again. Being away so long and all."

"Well, if you meant nothing by it, there's not much point in answering, is there." She resumed walking. Left silent in her wake, after a moment he caught up with her.

"The Palace? You mean, the posh hotel?"

She glanced at him and gave out a slight coughing laugh but kept striding along. "Not hardly. The Barbary Palace. On Broadway." She seemed to wait for a response but Blue didn't know the place, so none was forthcoming. "I work there," she added. "A few nights."

They walked a bit in silence.

"So, it's new, this Palace? I was knowing the Broadway territory, once upon a time."

"New? Doesn't feel like it. But yeah, a year or so, they tell me. From when they choked down on all the actual Barbary places. Some of the owners just moved a few blocks outside the official Barbary zone and opened the same sort of joints, with new names. The guy who runs the Palace used to have the Hotsy, down on Pacific. Someplace you would have known, the Hotsy?"

She'd done it again: put him on his heels with a response that both probed and mildly provoked. He didn't like being knocked off balance. But he found himself liking her more for having managed it.

So, how to answer? Indeed Blue had known many of the places in the Barbary Coast, the city's special district of bars and dancehalls and jive joints, famous since Gold Rush days for various forms of iniquity. And he also knew that in preparation for the giant world's fair-like Panama-Pacific Expo of the year before—intended to demonstrate the city's regeneration after the '06 earthquake and to showcase it as the post–Panama Canal gateway to the Pacific—the local authorities had enacted a series of laws intended to protect the tens of thousands of Expo visitors and the city's new reputation, from the fistfights, pocket picking, drunk rolling, lewd dancing, general licentiousness and, most especially, open prostitution that the Barbary Coast places were known for. The most draconian of these laws forbade women from working in any place where alcohol was served within the specific twelve-square-block area officially identified as the Barbary Coast. This killed off many Coast businesses, and put a lot of women out of work. A few places struggled on with taxi dancing but without alcohol, or with music and alcohol but no women servers, performers or taxi dancers. And a number of other places simply pulled up stakes and moved to a different part of town, including—as Blue now learned—the Hotsy-turned-Palace, where Meg was headed.

Through his late teens and into his twenties Blue had been a fairly regular visitor to the Barbary Coast but mostly to its so-called Black and Tan clubs: music halls, a couple of them Black-owned, where bands showcased jazzy music and the latest swing dances, and where Black and White locals were able to mix without self-consciousness or censure. He'd been particularly partial to Lew Purcell's So Different

Club at the edge of Pacific Avenue—the Barbary Coast's main drag, referred to by its self-promoters as Terrific Street—and to the club's house musicians, the Sid LeProtti Band. Blue had forged something of a bond with Sid, the band's piano player and leader, when they'd laughingly discovered that they were both products of mixed Italian parentage: Blue was startled one night when brown-skinned Sid joked with a club patron in fluent Italian, and Sid was equally surprised when the guy he knew only as Cavanaugh joined in the banter. Blue particularly liked Purcell's because it was a place where he and his boxing rival-turned-tightest friend Elijah DuPree could comfortably unwind together after an evening's training. Blue and Elijah dancing and cutting up in the wee hours at Purcell's: not something Blue had thought about in quite a while.

He realized that he'd drifted away for a moment and hadn't replied to Meg about the Hotsy. It had been one of the seedier Coast destinations, Blue knew, though he'd never been inside; his aversion to over-liquored men—a legacy from his heavy-drinking father—plus his ability to find female companionship on his own meant that places like the Hotsy had no appeal for him. But now he took care what he said about it to Meg: he'd been friends with women who, before the clampdown, had worked in various capacities in similar Coast joints and perhaps even in the Hotsy itself—he wasn't sure, the women moved around quite a bit from club to club, to provide "new faces" to each place but also to escape the depredations of the clubs' owners and managers and bartenders, which tended to increase with familiar- ity—and he didn't know how much of the Hotsy's unsavory backroom arrangements continued in its new Palace incarnation. Nor did he know what, or how much, Meg did there.

"Only by reputation, the Hotsy," he finally said. "Terrific Street and all."

"Yeah, terrific all right. *Cui bono?*"

"Ah, so you did your Latin."

"Well, I went to the nuns for school. Which means, one, I learned nearly nothing worth keeping, and two, they sort of taught me Latin."

They took a few steps before Blue ventured into deeper water.

"So. Always some of these things to haul around." Blue indicated the clutch of leaflets Meg was still carrying. "And your other... work... or whatever... at the printshop. And the café mural. And the Palace, too. Seems a mighty full plate."

She took a deep breath and exhaled slowly. "It is, at that."

"And are substitutions allowed?"

She stopped short and faced him. "You mean, like something on the side."

"No, no," he held up his hands. "It's just, you know... a full plate doesn't mean you might not still be hungry."

"Well in that case," she flapped the papers, almost in his face, "I could always eat my words... Say listen," she continued in nearly the same breath, shaking her head, "this is tiring. How about we try talking like normal people?"

He considered for a moment. "Yah, you're right, so. But... tell the truth... I don't think I know any normal people... Do you?"

She started walking; after a few moments she spoke. "Come to think of it, not since I've been in this town." They were silent for a bit before she spoke again, her voice now tamped down, sober. "There is one person. Though not around here. My mother. She always tries so hard for normal."

"And does it do right by her?"

"Mm... Not much. Though maybe now it's a bit easier, with me not around."

"Well I got to say, my mum tried it too. Normal. Never managed it."

"Is she here, in the city?"

"She was. Now she's nowhere. She passed."

"Oh. I'm sorry for your troubles."

Blue was surprised by the old world Irishness of this phrase from someone who otherwise seemed to have materialized, rootless, out of thin air, and he managed to say only, "So am I."

They had skirted the western edge of the Barbary Coast, then climbed the first block of Telegraph Hill's southern slope to Broadway—a wide, bustling street of shops, cafés, restaurants, bars, and meeting halls—where they turned east toward the bay.

"Glad you didn't hand me the usual shite about her being in a better place now."

"No." Meg paused, drifting away, before speaking again. "They used to say that about my father. But I never took to it, the 'better place' thing." She stopped in front of a large, barn-like building with bright bare light bulbs outlining the windows and a gaudy electric sign that read Barbary Palace. Meg looked up at the building and said, as if with a bad taste in her mouth, "Though this place here makes me hope there is one."

They faced each other awkwardly.

"Well…"

"Yes, well… Well, you want to come in, have a look at the joint? Quite a show they put on. And they've got a slummers' balcony, you know. So you'd be plenty safe."

"Ahh, no," he smiled, "I think I'll give it a miss. I've had enough folks for one evening… Not meaning yourself, of course. I think… well I think I'll be taking a stroll, so I will."

Meg looked up at the shimmering night sky. It was one of those soft, warm spring evenings following a sun-drenched day when the chill summer sea winds hadn't yet arrived, the notorious fog had remained offshore, and the entire hilled city seemed to sit on a magical perch, raised ever so slightly above the surface allotted to the rest of earth's mortals. "Yes," she said, "it is a delicious evening."

"Aye, it's all of that… So," he indicated the glittering edge of the bay peeking over the eastern slope of Broadway, "…you want to chance it?"

She seemed to consider for a moment but shook her head, then looked up: "Maybe another time. You know, when we're going the same way."

"Grand." He smiled at her mild mockery of his corny line from when he'd first joined her. But he couldn't read her face, couldn't tell whether she really was opening the door for another time or whether it was just a pro forma remark. Quickly his smile felt a bit obvious, foolish, and he took a step back. "Well then…"

"By the way, where are you keeping these days?"

"Myself?" He leaned towards her but resisted the impulse to close the distance again. "For digs, you mean? Well, I'm stopping at the Genova at the moment. Little hotel over on Mason, by the water. Dead cheap, it is. And they serve up grand Genovese grub, down the café at the bottom. Do you know it?"

"The Genova? No, I…"

"Ah, no, you might not so, like that, it's not the official name, which'd be New Pacific. But the folks 'round there are after calling it the Genova, on account of what's coming from the kitchen, and all the photos of the old hometown the cooks have put up around the place. But anyway," he asked, almost shyly, "why is it you'd want to know?"

"Oh, just trying to get the lay of the land," she bounced more of his words back at him.

Blue struggled to keep from smiling. "Good a reason as any. So I've heard… Well then…"

"Yes, well…" After a brief pause she turned, went down the building's adjoining narrow alley and into the Palace's side door, giving him a slight wave over her shoulder.

Blue didn't know what to make of their meandering conversation, and particularly of their parting terms. But he felt light on his feet. He hadn't actually thought of taking a stroll when he'd said it—they'd already had quite a hike from the Barleycorn—but now it seemed a fine idea. So he carried on walking down Broadway until it ended at the bay, then he turned and curled back through the Barbary Coast. He hadn't been in the notorious little district since he'd returned to the city, and not often in the years immediately prior to his departure. It was not yet the deep night hours when the Coast used to be at its wildest, but still it seemed obvious to Blue that the recent restrictive laws had done their work: the streets were quiet and tame, with numerous dark or boarded-up places interspersed with bars and music halls that were open but mostly empty. Blue passed through the few blocks quickly, and as he turned back toward North Beach, there it was: Purcell's So Different Club. Lights were on behind the painted front windows, and as Blue passed he could hear faint scratchy music, though from a gramophone not a band. The door was shut, there was no doorman as there always used to be to help handle the crowds, and no one going in or out. He thought he might stick his head in to see if Sid LeProtti was there, exchange greetings with his old *compagno*. But immediately he recognized that he didn't want to sit and listen to Sid talk about what had happened in recent years to Purcell's and Terrific Street; garrulous Sid would no doubt go on at length, and Blue wasn't interested in the grim details. Nor did he feel like giving even a truncated version of his own wanderings. And he wasn't ready to ask, or be asked, about Elijah DuPree. He kept walking.

8

Real-tor. When Mullally first said it, I heard "real tour." Which turned out not far from what the man, this other man, did for me this afternoon, showing me the houses. Except for the "real" part. Which always puzzled me in law school too. "Real property" they called it. Their idea of what was real and what was, what? More real? I suppose if you own land and buildings, you might feel that way. Or perhaps not feel. Just insist. "More real." I wouldn't know.

For me, though, this afternoon, it was definitely feeling. Foolish, the feeling. Looking through those two grand empty houses, pretending to be a buyer. Pretending to be a Jameson, a real Jameson. But going through the motions of house searching at least gave a respectable excuse to contact Mullally. Newspapers say he's to be grand marshal of the big Preparedness Day parade. So an even better connection than I first realized.

When Mullally used the word real-tor on the telephone and I said, "A what?" he told me that some property agents have just invented this name for themselves. Makes it sound as if it's some kind of profession, I suppose.

I wonder, was it curious to Mullally that I didn't know this?

Meant to add to my charade about relocating to SF, this looking at houses. But also used the time to chat with this realtor person about the war and all the Preparedness chatter around the city. Which after all is what I'm meant to be doing. As I understand it.

Wouldn't America joining the war likely hurt your business? I asked him. After all, people don't make big changes like buying houses when there's a war on, do they?

Oh, but they do, he told me. During the Spanish War, and "all that" in the Philippines afterwards, those years it went on and on, there was so much money pouring in around here, they were building big houses fist over fist.

That's how he said it. He had a way with words.

"All that" in the Philippines. Should have asked him. But asked him what?

Anyway, I knew he was right, about all the building. I'd seen it myself, when Jamey and Maggie and I were here in '99, the mansions going up, every hilltop.

So what do you think, I asked him, would we enter the Europe war?

Of course, he said, we need to be there.

I didn't understand "need," so I said but it's not our fight, is it? No one's attacking us.

Looked at me like I was daft. Well, but the Brits, he said. They're sort of us, aren't they?

Are they? I said.

Seemed he had to think on that for a bit, looking at me again as if I was odd.

Well, being white and all, he finally said.

But the Germans and Austrians, aren't they white?

Oh, he said, I suppose. But they're Huns, aren't they. Which is like Wogs. Isn't it?

You mean, like Italians? But they're fighting alongside the British.

They are? he puzzled. Well, I mean, the Brits, not just white, but they speak English.

But then what about the French? I said. They don't speak English. Or the Belgians either.

Yeah, well, them too, I guess you have to let them tag along, he said. Sort of like the Irish.

My people are Irish, I told him.

Ah, sorry. No disrespect, he said. Then after a moment he added, Oh, I see, Irish and English, a lot of trouble there. Just the other month wasn't it? The Easter thing? So, right. Now I think of it, he said, I suppose there are sides to choose from. But I wouldn't be bothered, one way or another. As long as we're in it. Too big a pie, he said, not to have a piece of it.

A way with words.

Drove me back to the hotel in his fine new motor car. Asked him to go along Clay Street. And going down the east side of the hill, just before Chinatown, I asked would he go slow.

Oh, you wouldn't want to look at any houses round here, he said. I didn't bother to explain, just asked him to stop. He already thought I was strange, so he didn't protest but once, for form's sake. I thanked him for his house tours and for the motor car ride, and got out.

Only a few yards away, it must have been, our rooms there, on Clay. You probably wouldn't remember, Maggie, too little you were. And too short a time there. Anyway it's gone now, the building, all the buildings of the block, done away in the quake. But never mind, I walked up and down the steep hill anyway, recalling, squinting to pretend the scene was still the same. And that's when I got to a spot. A particular spot I suddenly remembered. There'd been a metal grate or plate or something just there in the sidewalk back then. We were coming home one day, you and I, and you'd become tired on the steep hills, just age five you were, so finally I picked you up and carried you. It had been raining that day. The streets wet. And when I got to the metal thing, heading down the steep hill, I slipped. Feet flew out from under me. And holding you, falling, I wrapped both arms around you tight. Covering you. Which left me no way to protect myself from the hard collision and pain and damage to come. But here's the thing I want to tell you, Maggie. The thing I remembered on that spot this afternoon, something I had not thought of perhaps since that day itself all those years ago. And the thing was that, in the split of a second I was in the air, on my way to the ground, I did not decide to wrap you in my arms. No, what I realized and was amazed by right after the fall, and which I recalled again today, was that I did not have to decide. Because it was already a part of me. As I flew, my arms were already wrapping around you. And that was the moment, back then, when I understood. Perhaps in part because I knew, I already knew somehow, that your father was lost to me. To us. That we were alone. So I understood, in that moment, that in those few years you'd been in the world I had not merely changed, which was obvious, of course, any parent. But that I had become a different person. And now, missing you so, being reminded of it is a comfort to me.

I don't expect that you'd understand, Maggie. If I had the chance to tell you. Being the child, you're not meant to understand. You're meant to leave.

The beaux arts excess of the Palace Hotel's vast Garden Court was even further beyond Kate's experience than the Spreckels mansion where she'd attended the costume gala: massive marble columns supporting a high mezzanine topped by stained glass arches; glittering crystal chandeliers hanging from a vaulted glass and silver-leafed iron roof three stories above; two-story-high satin draperies alternating with full-mirrored walls; a highly polished marble floor most of which was covered by plush carpeting that softened the footfalls of the already low-voiced, round-gestured, white-liveried—black in the evening—serving staff; and dark mahogany tables with thickly upholstered chairs arrayed within fringes of impeccably trimmed, hand-shined dwarf palms. Passing by the Court each day in her comings and goings along the hotel's main corridor, Kate had seen businessmen lunching there, well-dressed ladies gathered over afternoon tea, and formally attired couples and foursomes at dinner. But fascinated as she was with this extraordinary gilded playground for the city's elite, she'd felt too self-conscious to venture into the Court alone, which is to say unaccompanied by a male, a status which already more than once had occasioned glances from other hotel guests that ranged from mildly quizzical to downright doubting. Even her one lunch foray to the hotel's regular dining room—not as large and opulent as the Garden Court but baroquely splendid nonetheless—had been preceded by an embarrassing false step into the men-only grillroom, and for the ten days she'd now been staying there Kate had taken all her other hotel meals up in her room.

So merely having a chance to experience the Garden Court first-hand was reason enough for looking forward to the Preparedness event to be held there that afternoon, an invitation to which she'd received several days earlier. More importantly, though, it would be an opportunity to assess the timbre of the Preparedness movement's call for US entry into the European war, as made by a certain portion of San Francisco's elite, and to see some of that portion firsthand.

It was also just a chance for some kind, any kind, of pointed activity to break up the tedium of her so far mostly aimless days. The introductions she'd made and bits of information she'd gathered at the Spreckels mansion gala had seemed a promising beginning, but she'd seen and done little else in the week since. Contrary to Lansing's foundational premise for this venture—that having once lived for a short time in San Francisco, plus the social status she'd reached through her marriage into the Jameson family, and her familiarity with the world of big business from her work at the upper-crust Boston law firm, made Kate the right person to insinuate herself within the city's upper crust—in truth she didn't know how to approach these people and in their presence felt a sense of anomie, a weightlessness. She'd felt it again when she'd forced herself to phone Mullally about her pretense of looking at a possible future residence, and again in the houses themselves, which were so unlike anything she knew, except for the Jameson manse in Boston, to which she was occasionally invited to highly fraught, for her, family gatherings. So the side trip on her return from the house tours—to Clay Street where she and Jamey and Maggie had stayed back in '99—was not so much an exercise in nostalgia as an attempt to reconnect with the city, to regain some sense of the place she had known, albeit slightly, those years before. And in the same vein, on her way back to the hotel after her wander on Clay Street, she had sought out the Municipal Clinic.

When she and Maggie had first arrived in San Francisco, shortly after Jamey had been returned there to recuperate from the Philippines war, she had known no one in the city and was dazed by the sudden dislocation of crossing the country with her small child to this very different place, this so different coast. Added to this disorientation was the extreme distress of seeing Jamey, during her visits to the army quarantine barracks on Angel Island, whom she found benumbed, in a near catatonia that was impossible to reconcile with the man who had left them in Boston little more than a year before. So for the two months she waited for Jamey's release she'd been consumed by the urge to maintain a sense of normalcy for herself and little Maggie. Routine became her sole ally, and her solace. She and Maggie filled the days with the most basic of tasks, in a calming repeated rhythm: breakfast together; a walk to the shops; return to lunch in the little two-room apartment; work with Maggie on her learning of numbers and letters; a walk to the bay to look at the boats; return to the rooms to cook and eat dinner together; picture-making with colored pencils or crayons or water colors; then reading stories and falling asleep together in the saggy bed. Kate sought out no company. Shied away from the friendly gestures of neighbors. And waited.

Things remained much the same when Jamey was released from Angel Island and joined them on Clay Street: he was too lethargic, too frail in spirit, to initiate anything, and Kate was too uncertain of what he was capable of—too unsure of who he'd become—to ask anything of him. The three of them went about their days as if on a pendulum, stiffly back and forth between their routine stops and their two little rooms, willfully ignoring everything around them. They put a little pad on the floor next to the bed, for Maggie to sleep on, but after a few days Jamey began leaving the table directly they'd finished eating in the evening and wordlessly going into the bedroom and falling asleep, still in his clothes, on the pad. He and Kate rarely talked. From time to time she would try to broach the subject of when they would return to Boston, to their life, but Jamey would not engage about it. Nor say a word about his time in the Philippines.

Slowly, Jamey became not exactly outward-looking but restless. On Angel Island he had come to know a doctor from the city who once a week made a boat trip out to the barracks to help tend to the many wounded, ill, and otherwise shattered soldiers pausing there upon their repatriation from the Philippines. Jamey and this doctor, the much older Benjamin Rothstein, had made a connection as fellow physicians. So when Jamey's pent-up distress finally pushed him out of the family's rented rooms for a few hours on his own—more to spare his wife and child from the toxins of his misery, it seemed to Kate, than in search of comfort for himself—he went to see Ben Rothstein.

Doctor Rothstein was high up on the staff of one of the city's main hospitals but, despite Jamey's medical credentials, he could not accommodate the younger man there: Jamey was too strange, too distracted, too unpredictable in his moods and expressions. So instead, Rothstein invited Jamey to join him at the more informal Municipal Clinic on Commercial Street, between Chinatown and the Barbary Coast, which the doctor had for years lobbied the city to open. At this clinic Rothstein and a few other volunteer doctors and nurses tended, without charge, to the many women in the city who regularly worked as prostitutes, and to numerous other women from the city's legions of poor who secretly supplemented their families' subsistence with occasional work behind the scenes in the Barbary Coast and other cribs around town, and who could afford neither the expense of private medical care nor the attention that might be occasioned by a visit to a regular doctor for treatment of an occupational disease. Part of the arrangement with the city was that the clinic would issue certificates of good health to the professionals who, if they practiced their trade within the confines of the Barbary Coast or Chinatown and kept their certificate current, were thereby rendered safe from arrest.

Despite the program's tremendous efficacy—in its first two years it had reduced by three-fourths the incidence of venereal disease among its patients—the social taint associated with the clinic meant that Doctor Rothstein had trouble attracting volunteer medical workers. So he was glad that he could not only bring Jamey out of his shell a bit during his visits to the clinic but also to make use there of Jamey's medical skills. Jamey took to his tasks with an energy he could not summon for anything else and even, Kate thought when on one occasion she'd seen him at work there among the motley patients, showed flashes of the man she had known before his time in the Philippines war.

The few times Kate and Maggie fetched Jamey from the clinic—though it was just a few blocks down the hill from their rooms, Kate gave Jamey a wide berth there—old-world gentleman Doctor Rothstein would remove his work smock and come to the clinic's front door to greet them with a ready warm smile under his big white moustache, twinkly eyes behind rimless spectacles, and a pale bald head that stuck out from his starched collar like a turtle's from its shell. On one occasion Rothstein took Kate and Maggie to the zoo; at the last minute, Jamey begged off joining them. And on another memorable evening, when Jamey did manage to come out with Kate and Maggie, they joined the portly doctor, a man who obviously loved his food, for supper at his favorite restaurant, a dark wood-paneled Dalmation place where the four of them shared a steaming tureen heaped to overflowing—little Maggie giggled at the sight of the grownups wearing large paper bibs—with a local stew called *cioppino*, the secrets of which, the doctor told them, the restaurant had stolen and brilliantly recreated from local Genovese fishermen's wharfside kettles: several kinds of fish—whatever had been brought in that day—plus oysters, mussels, clams, squid, and the region's famous Dungeness crab whose toothy claws delighted and terrified Maggie.

Kate understood that the clinic was a separate space for Jamey, a place apart from both his little family and the wider world and thereby from thoughts of how, so direly weighted from his time in the war, he might manage a future. Doctor Rothstein, too, seemed to understand Jamey's need for separation, so other than the two occasions of the zoo and the restaurant, the doctor made no attempt to socialize with the three of them. Over the several months Kate and Jamey spent together in the city before Kate was finally able to persuade him—by harping on the need for Maggie to begin school—that they must return to Boston, Jamey spent more and more time at the clinic and less and less with the two beloved strangers, his wife and young daughter.

Ben Rothstein. The closest there was in this city to someone Kate actually knew. Hardly someone Lansing was imagining when he sent her out to test the West Coast waters: a man with no business interests; a doctor to prostitutes; a Jew. It wasn't Lansing's project she was considering, though, when she thought now of Rothstein, but of its obverse: how isolated she felt here; how false. Ben Rothstein was someone in whose company she might feel, might be, a bit closer to who she really was. And not least, he was someone who'd known Jamey. Since arriving in the city, Kate had thought more than once of the old doctor. Recalled his kindness. So on her walk back to the hotel following the realtor's house tours and the stop by her old block on Clay Street, she decided to make a short detour to the Municipal Clinic. Of course, as with everything else in the central city after the great quake and fire, Kate knew it was unlikely the building would still be standing. But turning a corner, there it was.

Or not. Because while the pale stone exterior was close to how she remembered it, nothing else was familiar. There were no cheaply dressed women moving quickly in the front door or out the side—as Kate stood and watched for a bit before approaching, only two well-tailored business-suited men entered the building—and the wooden door with the painted sign announcing the clinic and its hours was gone, replaced by a new heavy glass and brass door and a brass plaque that read Pacific Maritime Assurance Ltd.

Inside too was utterly transformed: what had been a crowded anxious pasteboard waiting room with rickety benches was now a quiet, almost empty oak-paneled antechamber, with four dark leather chairs and a sober wooden table behind which sat a sober wooden woman with a notepad and a telephone. The woman's reaction to Kate's entry showed a mix of skeptical curiosity and discretion:

whoever this unknown and unexpected visitor was, she was at least tastefully and expensively dressed.

"May I help you?"

"Well, yes. Or I don't know. I was looking for Doctor Rothstein."

"I'm sorry?"

"Doctor Rothstein. Benjamin Rothstein." Kate looked at a heavy, polished-wood door that led into the rear of the building, what had once been the examining rooms.

"I'm afraid..."

"The clinic. Municipal Clinic. It was here. And I thought..."

The woman now looked more dubiously at Kate. "Oh that... place. Yes, I was told. But there's been none such here for two years now."

"Ah. Well... perhaps you could direct me to its new location."

"I'm afraid not. I would have no idea. About such a thing."

Outside, Kate noticed a man selling flowers at a stand directly across the road. She went over to him.

"Excuse me. Were you around here before, I mean when that was still the clinic?"

"Sure," he said, not looking up from his work cutting stems. "The shame of it."

Kate couldn't tell whether the man meant that the clinic itself had been a shame, or its closing.

"Well, do you happen to know where it's located these days?"

The man looked up at Kate, looked her over. "Nowhere. You're on your own."

"No, that's not... I mean..."

"Coupla' years ago," the man continued, "when they was cleanin' things up around here, for the big Expo and all. People comin' from all over to see the shiny new city. If it *looks* clean, must *be* clean, right?" The man spat on the ground behind him.

"And...?"

"Well, when they closed it down here, they told the old doc they'd find him a new place soon's the Expo was finished. Never happened, though, far's I heard. But what do I know?"

"But I mean... The women, where do they go now?"

"Yep, that's the question, ain't it."

When she got back to the hotel, Kate telephoned the hospital where Rothstein had been on staff all those years ago and asked whether they could tell her where the clinic now was.

"No such place," the woman on the phone told her. "City stopped funding it."

"Ah. All right. Well. But Doctor Rothstein then?" Kate asked. "How can I get in touch with him?"

There was a silence. "I'm sorry," the woman finally said, "but when they closed his clinic, he just..." her voice trailed off. "He passed six month ago."

$\sim$

Other than the realtor's house tours, Kate's only organized outing since the Spreckels mansion gala had been a somewhat puzzling visit to Alma Spreckels's "studio." Early in the Europe war, with the help of Alma's friend the dancer Loie Fuller, who was also a friend of Auguste Rodin, and with the added assistance of a significant tranche of husband Adolph's money, Alma had managed to whisk out of France and all the way to San Francisco a large passel of Rodin sculptures and related pieces. She had then arranged for many of them to be exhibited—in conjunction with some rather scandalous modernist performances by Fuller's dance troupe—at San Francisco's Panama-Pacific Exposition in 1915. All of which had added to Alma's growing reputation as a philanthropist, socialite and Europe-imbued avant-garde sophisticate. And to further plump the image, in all official pronouncements Alma referred to herself as Mme de Breteville Spreckels, making good use, she seemed to believe, of her "noble" French maiden name. Alma cherished all the notoriety. Particularly, as Kate would begin to understand on her visit to the studio, because certain segments of the city's fine families thought somewhat differently of the statuesque Mrs. Spreckels, whom they referred to simply as Big Alma.

She was donating many of the largest and finest pieces of her collection to the city. They were to be displayed in a new museum on a promontory overlooking the Golden Gate, which was to be purpose-built to house them and which, not coincidentally, her husband was paying for. But as part of her rather vaguely defined campaign to raise funds for European war victims—sometimes described as civilian casualties, other times just as victims, but always without references to "sides"—she was also auctioning off a number of Rodin drawings and maquettes, as well as numerous random *objets d'art*, some of it donated, some of it from Alma's own fast-growing personal collection. The auction pieces ranged from fine paintings and sculpture and rare books to cheap photo postcards and posters, plus an array of bizarre gimcrackery, including the silk bed sheets used as a backdrop for one of Loie Fuller's suggestive dance performances and, it was rumored, actually slept upon by the Queen of Belgium. And Loie. Together.

To help create an audience for the auction, and to hold informal social functions in which she would take center stage, Alma was putting on a series of invitation-only showings at a huge Victorian pile of a house that Adolph had bought for them to live in while the major mansion, where Kate had attended the costume party, was being constructed. After moving into the mansion, Alma had held on to the Victorian as a personal fiefdom and sanctuary physically, socially and aesthetically separate from her husband, with his blessing and—according to knowledgeable sources, Kate eventually heard—much to his relief, to be used as a storage facility and showroom for her art collection and for the particular objects to be sold for the cause of war relief.

The brochure that came along with Kate's invitation variously described the Vallejo Street Victorian house as a museum, a Temple of Fine Art, and the studio of Mme de Bretteville Spreckels. In addition to pictures of some of the pieces to be sold, the brochure featured a photograph of a bejeweled Alma reading to her angelic children; a picture of the Pope, though there was no mention anywhere of his having given the fund his benediction; and a full-page photo of a painting of the Franco-Danish General Louis de Bretteville being embraced by Louis-Napoleon, an item that was not included in the brochure's list of art for sale but the prominent caption of which served to burnish the de Bretteville name. Finally, the brochure's text trumpeted a curiously anonymous list of the fund's many purported patrons: "Kings, Queens, Presidents, Ambassadors, Ministers of State, Army and Navy, Diplomats, Notables, Consuls, Authors, Composers, Painters, Sculptors, Clubs, Colleges, Society, the People and the Clergy of the World." As they said, Big Alma.

The particular auction preview to which Kate had been invited was being put on specially by Alma for something called the Indoor Yacht Club, to which Thornwell Mullally belonged and by whom Kate's inclusion had been arranged. Kate hoped to get a sense from being there— something more than what was offered by the brochure's anodyne language—about what was implied by "war relief" and thereby about the attitude of Alma and her hugely influential Germanic husband Adolph toward the Europe war and the possibility of US entry: something, anything, she might be able to report back to Lansing.

A car sent by Mullally picked up Kate at her hotel and took her along to the Indoor Yacht Club's meeting rooms—dedicated, as the large nautical-themed sign on the wall proclaimed, to "encouraging yachting but without the terrors of the sea and avoiding all water except for purposes of bathing"—where Mullally greeted her and introduced her to a dozen cohorts, all men, as they gathered before heading together to Alma's studio. Though most appeared to be in their forties and fifties, and with their finely turned clothing and handsomely appointed meeting rooms clearly announcing that they were well-to-do businessmen, the group's forcibly clever chatter and loose physicality gave the impression of smug prep school boys on their way to mandatory chapel.

The yacht club men were only slightly less bumptious once they reached Alma's Victorian. Dressed in what seemed to Kate more of a ball gown, complete with long strings of pearls, than in something for a casual afternoon gathering, Alma was there to greet them. She was friendly and welcoming to Kate, whom she recalled from Kate's visit with Mullally to the mansion's library on the night of the costume ball, but the attention was fleeting: Alma immediately turned to the men, exuding a restrained but nonetheless obvious coquettishness and leading Mullally and two others into a room that held several large and a number of smaller bronzes. Kate and the other men were left to themselves, or almost, as a half-dozen well-dressed women flitted about the rooms making gushing remarks to the men about various pieces of art and related fundraising ephemera, though without, it soon occurred to Kate, actually having anything to say about them. For the men's part, they seemed comfortable if self-restrained, not particularly interested, and somewhat amused by it all.

Kate wandered through several rooms, each of which was filled with paintings, small bronzes, plaster and stone statuary—one room was devoted entirely to sculptures of big jungle cats and other wild animals, another to Japanese and Chinese fine art—and tables displaying presumably valuable books, either very old, beautifully illuminated, or signed by their famous authors. In one room, otherwise empty except for paintings of horses and dogs around the walls, stood a full size, remarkably well executed papier-mâché model of a racehorse, complete with racing silks and tack, and a placard with a photo of the horse, its name, genealogy, and racing accomplishments. Kate couldn't tell from the display whether the horse itself was actually to be auctioned, or simply the model of it. Or neither.

She didn't know what to make of it all. She found nothing in the rooms that described the auction's larger purpose or hinted at sentiments about the war; in fact, as far as she overheard, no one even mentioned the war. After an hour of slightly dazed art viewing, she found herself in a room where refreshments were being offered and discovered that most of the men she'd arrived with were already there, drinking and jabbering. They didn't particularly react to her entrance but pleasantly enough made way for her at the drinks table, one of them asking—without any apparent interest in her response—whether she'd enjoyed "Alma's little show." Since the many rooms chock full of material, much of which was impressive and some of which no doubt very valuable, certainly couldn't be fairly described as "little," Kate took the remark instead as something of a judgment about Alma herself.

After a few minutes the group was called into a large salon where Alma and several of her lady helpers were collected on sofas; Mullally and his club men arrayed themselves around the women, standing in a semicircle. When everyone had settled, one of the men stepped forward—Kate expected that it would be Mullally, but he remained to the side—with a plaque in hand and spoke to Alma, bestowing on her an honorary membership in the Indoor Yacht Club for her work "alleviating the suffering of mankind" in the course of which she "gave all her time and energy, even at the cost of her personal duties"—Kate thought she saw smirks flit across a couple of faces—and for which, "at a time that cannot be far off, she will finally receive the unadulterated appreciation she deserves."

Alma rose to her impressive height and accepted the plaque and applause graciously, with a small smile, murmuring pro forma words of thanks, but she seemed to Kate tentative in her reception of the "honor," or perhaps of the particular words of commendation. In any case it was all over quickly, with the men bustling toward departure and Alma and the ladies turning immediately to preparations for the next set of guests.

Outside, somewhat to Kate's surprise, Mullally hastily excused himself without making or seeking even perfunctory comment about the exhibition. He just said that he had an appointment but that the car was at Kate's disposal. He was already turning away as Kate thanked him, then he seemed to reconsider, stopped, and turned back to her.

"So nice having had you," he said with his Southern vowels appearing more prominently than they had earlier in the afternoon. The inflection he gave to the seemingly simple phrase was hard for Kate to read, but he smiled at her, and it seemed a more genuine expression than those she'd seen from anyone else that day. His parting words were, "I expect I will see you again quite soon."

On the short car ride back to the hotel, Kate found herself wondering about the syntax of "So nice having had you." And about the word "expect."

9

The Bull Cow... Frau Kaiser... Queen P... Genghis Khunt...

And that was from other women. Who were on the same side. Though not, as Blue came to learn, exactly the same.

Emmeline Pankhurst. *Mrs.* Pankhurst, as she insisted on being called by those in the struggle who toiled under her. Under her guidance, she would say. A woman in the movement explained to Blue that Emmeline Pankhurst insisted on the designation Mrs. simply to differentiate her from her three daughters with the same surname who were also involved in the suffrage cause, so that people wouldn't always have to be sorting through the four given names. Another woman nearby overheard this assertion. And snorted.

Following his months in Dublin, Blue had wound up treading time in London at the edges of two conflict zones: one between the suffragists and the British government, the other among different segments of the suffrage women themselves. And at the edges he mostly remained: he was an outsider, a Yank; and he was male, which severely limited, and with some suffragette cadres entirely precluded, his participation. On the other hand, the particulars of his otherness provided him with something of a benign mantle. As a Yank he was untainted and unhindered by the British Left's political baggage, especially the deep streak of misogyny that stained most of Britain's organized labor. Plus, Blue discovered to his unspoken amusement, being a San Franciscan afforded him a certain standing in the suffragists' eyes: California had granted women the vote four years earlier.

He'd been living in something of a shadowy, liminal space since fleeing across the Irish Sea from Dublin to Liverpool, then down to— though the Brits said "up to," one of many sources of disorientation for him—London. Women, and a few satellite men, in the suffragist network he'd first connected with in Ireland were lodging and feeding him; they passed him around, a few nights and meals at one place, then on to the next, a not unpleasant rhythm of acclimatizing similar to what he'd experienced in Paterson and Dublin. And they gave him small tasks, which made him feel, if not greatly useful, at least welcome. This hospitality and inclusion were in response to a commendation sent across the Atlantic by a Wobbly women's rights militant whom Blue had come to know during the Paterson strike. It was also in recognition of the mettle Blue had shown in Dublin amid the great citywide lockout struggle there, in particular during what was known as the Kiddies Scheme: what turned out to be a short-lived attempt to send near-starving children of locked out Dublin workers to temporary sanctuary with trade union families in England, an effort violently scuttled by the Catholic Church.

An English suffragette odd couple—East End London scrapper Grace Neal and manor-born, married-well Dora Montefiore—had come over to Ireland to manage the shakily organized Kiddies effort. Blue had shared with them his recent experience of a similar scheme for the children of Paterson strikers, then worked alongside the two women and their Irish cohorts in the chaotic Dublin version. He'd also shared a willingness to face down a screeching coven of priests and their hooligan enforcers from the Ancient Order of Hibernians—who arrived to quash the scheme with a combination of fists and threats of prosecution, not to mention damnation—even though he'd just arrived in Ireland and knew nothing much about the lockout, other than one side from the other. Which was enough. And now Grace Neal was continuing the comradeship by nestling him into her network of radical women in London.

Living in close quarters with these suffragette militants—as a reasonably well-trusted if mostly ignored member of a different species, something like a recently adopted stray dog—Blue overheard endless arguments about the two complex issues over which the suffrage movement was becoming increasingly fractured. Strategically, the question was what sort of suffrage to work for. At the time, no women at all had the vote in national elections in Britain but, because of property own-ership requirements, neither did a vast swathe of working-class men. For decades, some in the trade union movement, particularly its left wing, had been pushing for abolition of all property requirements for voting, and the women's suffrage campaign that had grown out of this milieu likewise sought universal suffrage, for both men and women.

This was the political trajectory out of which Mrs. Pankhurst had emerged. But over the previous decade, as her passion for the battle had intensified, her focus had narrowed. By the time Blue arrived in London in 1914, Mrs. P and her increasingly powerful Women's Social and Political Union had become single-mindedly devoted to obtaining women's suffrage "on the same terms as men," which meant leaving intact the extant property requirements that disenfranchised poorer men and women alike. Mrs. P initially justified the distinction as a kind of gradualism, a first-things-first realpolitik. But it soon became clear to many women in the movement that Mrs. P's politics had devolved into a nearly religious crusade focused solely on gender parity—meaning the vote for women of her own sort, without any abiding parallel concern for the women, or men, of a class beneath her—with herself as the crusade's mythic heroine and unassailable leader, a sort of rather better-dressed Joan of Arc. And about her abso-lute rule she would not be gainsaid: "We are a fighting body," Mrs. P had publicly declared when pressed on the matter, "which must have autocratic control to wage war. When going into battle, a general does not take a vote of his soldiers to see whether they approve." The irony of demanding autocratic power in a struggle for the vote was appar-ently lost on her.

Not that anyone doubted Mrs. P's righteousness and commit-ment: she'd been arrested many times, suffered serious damage to her health through repeated hunger strikes, and undergone the brutal assaults and indignities of prison force-feedings. But along with her increasingly dictatorial control over the movement, the line between righteousness and self-righteousness had begun to blur, and the com-bination of Mrs. P's tunnel vision and her regal decision-making even-tually led some women—including one of her own daughters—to leave the WSPU and form their own organizations, dedicated not to "equal terms" but to universal suffrage. These included the Women's Suffrage Federation, a working-class group based in London's East End, one of whose organizers was Grace Neal, Blue's initial London connection.

The other realm in which the suffragist movement developed serious fissures was that of tactics. Somewhat surprising to Blue, it was the substantively more conservative, narrower politics of Mrs. Pankhurst that tended to pair itself with the most militant actions. Increasingly over the past few years, Mrs. P and her followers had moved from rather tame street demonstrations to incendiaries and even explosives, albeit relatively small and often fumblingly unconsummated. Most of the universal suffrage groups, on the other hand, were less violent, tethered as they were to larger trade union movements whose national electoral aspirations and lumbering organizational structures, run by men without Mrs. P's singular passion, meant a more measured tactical approach.

But there was also a third rail: women who rejected Mrs. P's dictates, were independent of the large trade unions, and were willing to engage in extreme militant acts in pursuit of universal suffrage. This included a clandestine subset of the East End federation, a dozen or so women who moved within Grace Neal's orbit though not, as Grace and the others all made quite clear to Blue, under her direction. Grace was also a founder of the Domestic Workers' Union, which sought to be—unimaginably, to traditional trade unions—a labor syndicate for Britain's hundreds of thousands of household servants. Several of the women in the militant suffrage subgroup had formerly been "in service," a phrase—along with "downstairs"—which Blue came to learn meant one kind or another of live-in domestic servants; several others were relatively well-educated lower-middle-class women who'd labored as governesses or tutors to children of wealth and had suffered at the hands, often literally, of the heads of those households. It was this small network of militants, a cross-fertilization of socialists for universal suffrage and organizers for one of the lowest rungs of working women, among whom Blue found himself housed and fed and politically expanded in the spring of 1914.

Politically expanded. The more used to him they became, the more willing the women were to discuss in his presence their contested ideas and plans for action. For his part, Blue felt increasingly comfortable parrying with the women about their tactical choices; these conversations were initially one-on-one, usually late at night, often with Grace Neal, and after a while even more often with Nell Courtland. Nell was a well-traveled Irish actor in her thirties who, despite her classical theatrical training and range of experience, had to perform bawdy song and dance in music halls to supplement her infrequent roles—"No dogs or Irish" was a sign still common all across England—in serious London theater. Nell and Blue had become particularly close.

Though he didn't use the specific term to describe himself—he was too unclear about its varied, shifting tenets, and too uncertain of the extent of his own beliefs—Blue's own political flavor was broadly anarchist. That is, he viewed the modern nation-state as little more than capital's great cloaked enabler, its beard, and believed that abolition of the state apparatus—though Blue never applied himself to anarchism's great long-standing roil, "To be replaced by what, exactly?"— was the ultimate if admittedly very long-range political goal. His animosity toward the intersection of capital and the state, incipient during his youth in San Francisco's heavily immigrant working-class North Beach district, had burrowed deep into his marrow when his brother Declan had been killed in the Philippines, victim—as well as blinkered perpetrator—of a war waged in naked pursuit of American imperial expansion in the Pacific, with barely a fig leaf of patriotic pap to justify it: "Upholding the honor of the American flag" was the best Teddy Roosevelt could do by way of rationale. Teddy the Rough Rider: Blue wanted to fucking throttle him, with the fucking stripes torn from his honored fucking flag. And when little more than a year after Declan's death Roosevelt had come to San Francisco to dedicate a monument to American "heroes" of the Philippines war, if the young Blue had been able to get close enough… Well, no, he wouldn't have tried to kill him. True, there had been more than one young anarchist he knew around North Beach who would have welcomed the chance to help him if he'd wanted to give it a go. But by then Blue had marked the words of one of anarchism's venerables, in response to a string of assassinations by anarchists—including the one that put Roosevelt in the White House—who described such *attentats* as not only futile but counterproductive, declaring "I'd sooner kill a chicken than a king; at least you can eat a chicken." And marked as well the words of his own mother about the endless cycle of killing, the first words she'd spoken, some three days later, after receiving the news of Declan's death: "There is no reason good enough."

Blue was also attracted to the particular flavor of anarcho-syndicalism espoused by the IWW, the Wobblies. His coming of age in North Beach among often excluded Italian workers, plus the education he got from his friend Elijah DuPree about Black workers stonewalled by traditional unions, made him partial to the IWW's credo of breaking down the identity labels that separated different trades and crafts, and creating instead a single giant unitary union across all sectors of labor, all ethnicities, all national boundaries. Blue's practical experience of politics, too, had been along these lines, though in the context of narrower local industrial strife. These were prosaic labor actions geared toward making a particular company or industry suffer immediate financial pain in pursuit of immediate gain for a particular slice of laborers: quarry workers, gas and electric workers, and other industrial laborers in and around San Francisco; the silk workers during the Paterson strike; the tram drivers in Dublin. That was what he knew.

Now in London, though, he was confronted with another type of struggle, not against specific employers but against the state itself: how to pressure the government to grant universal suffrage. Initially, the goal was not of much interest to Blue. As with his anarchist and Wobbly acquaintances back in San Francisco, he'd never paid much heed to elections and voting: Why take part in choosing people to be your masters? Over time, though, he became more sympathetic to the women's project. In part, because he became more sympathetic to Nell Courtland. And she to him. But also in large part because Grace Neal and Nell and some of the others forced him to acknowledge that the labor struggles he'd fought in were no more politically sublime than these women's fight for suffrage. "Listen, Yank," Nell put it to him, "getting the vote might not rotate the world, but neither does winning tuppence more an hour for grinding coal out the ground." Moreover, Grace and Nell contended, forcing the state to grant suffrage could have enormous symbolic value for women, a foundational equality on the top of which other battles could be fought. Blue finally conceded, even if not fully convinced. Because emotionally, by then, he was already in: the sides were clear, and the women's political passion was itself a near revolutionary force, his own hesitations pale in comparison.

Once Blue had been swayed to their purpose, the women began to allow him deeper into their most contentious, and compromising, debates. Such discussions often spilled over to his pillow talk with Nell. Militant strategic planning and tactical decision-making might not be the type of late-night endearments whispered between most new intimates, but Blue and Nell were certainly not most: their attraction to each other was in large measure sourced from, and entirely wrapped up in, their shared passion for struggle in the streets.

Nell's growing trust in Blue was based in part on his experiences in California labor battles, which Blue had been slowly, partially revealing to her. Only slowly and partially because Nell was volatile, and sometimes hard for Blue to read. And what he'd seen within the provocateur-infested labor wars of the American West had made him extremely cautious, even with people he'd known much longer and better than he had Nell. But more than just political self-protection, his reluctance also stemmed from a deeply ingrained habit of personal restraint, a wall he'd erected around himself when his brother had been killed—the foundations laid even earlier, when his father had left—and he'd begun to horde every drop of his emotional energy to care for and protect his mother. A wall so tightly cloistering that when his mother died the year before, he'd had to leave the city in order to escape the clotted, oxygen-starved air within it.

So he was surprised—and not a little confused—to find an unfamiliar feeling welling up about Nell: wanting to tell her more, to open up for her inspection and response the closely held details that were an essential part of his life, of who he was. Nell was well-educated, at least for a young woman of her class, and more so from her experience in the theater, while Blue had little formal education but had long been an omnivore of the literary word, and on this they found another common ground. They read to each other almost every late night, Nell providing an exegesis of the otherwise impenetrable, to Blue, language of Shakespeare, and Blue laughingly offering a cultural lexicon for the abstruse, to Nell, American peculiarities of *Huckleberry Finn*, and producing local embellishments for her to Frank Norris's set-in-San Francisco *McTeague*. They also marveled together at the clarities of Emily Dickinson and the soaring sensibilities of *Leaves of Grass*.

But still… Despite the ways in which they meshed, there remained for Blue a certain distance between them that their common purpose, their affection, and their intimacy could not bridge. Their attraction for each other notwithstanding, they remained in some fundamental way, Blue felt, alien beings to each other.

Militant acts by various suffragette groups during the previous decade had been all over the map: geographically widespread across England, Scotland, Ireland and Wales, and tactically ranging through mass street protests, breaking high street shop windows, attempting to horsewhip Home Secretary Winston Churchill, burning post boxes and later an entire mail train, and trying to blow up the coronation chair in Westminster Abbey, among other actions. In recent years, they had increased in frequency and intensity.

The East End women of Grace Neal's underground group were disdainful of minimalist actions. Burning a postbox or breaking a shop window, they contended, might let someone briefly feel the hero but had no practical effect and, moreover, symbolically blighted the movement with a mark of pettiness. No, these East Enders were only interested in larger, more audacious acts. But they were in conflict about what and how. Various suffrage groups across Britain had engaged in arson and even a few explosions, though "bombings" was too grand a word for the minor charges they'd been able to generate. These attacks had focused mostly on churches—both Anglican and Catholic ecclesiarchs had been conspicuous in their derision toward and condemnation of the suffrage movement—and on the playgrounds and supernumerary abodes of men in power: cricket grounds, racecourses, golf clubs, and unoccupied country mansions and summer homes. Some of these efforts had been fairly spectacular and had garnered headlines, but had also led to arrests and imprisonments without seeming to move the government any closer to the women's goal. Grace and several others from the East End group were also deeply concerned that some attacks, in particular coming from Mrs. Pankhurst's direction, had risked—whether uncaringly or merely incautiously, the East End women disagreed among themselves—the lives of men and women who labored at these locales.

So the small cohort of women to whom Blue was appended was searching now for new and different sorts of targets, and also for more proficient means: many of the crude incendiary and explosive devices the various groups had cobbled together either did not work at all or were so haphazard in timing or execution that they risked serious harm both to the women involved and to unintended victims at the scenes. On top of that, the London chemist who had been providing certain suffragette groups with flammable materials and a modicum of knowhow about their handling had recently been arrested and imprisoned, so their ability to create devices of any sort had been severely curtailed.

Within the East End group there was no agreement on how best to proceed. Blue's intimate comrade Nell was a fount of bristling anger, impatient to do something to keep the group's momentum going. In particular, the vicarious satisfaction she'd gotten from another suffragette's horsewhipping of that little aristo-blowhard Churchill, as Nell called him, had set her to imagine kidnapping some government minister or other and subjecting him to the type of grotesque force-feedings that many jailed suffragettes had endured. Grace Neal, on the other hand, no longer had use for ad hoc attacks on symbolic targets and, given her wider political perspective developed in labor battles, now argued that the best, perhaps only, way to influence the government was to blow holes in industrial and other large commercial financial ledgers: racecourse grandstands and country houses can be easily rebuilt, she said, but interrupting major flows of capital into the coffers of men in power tends to rapidly focus their attention. From his sideline position, Blue gingerly added a few words of support for Grace on this point, and eventually she was able to convince the others. Except Nell, who didn't want to waste time on cumbersome grand plans; what she wanted was to get her hands around someone's throat, and soon. But the group made decisions collectively, which in this instance meant that Nell had either to tamp down her impatience or leave. She bit her tongue and stayed.

For the next several weeks the women pawed at the edges of various ideas for a foray but came up empty until late one night in early June when Blue and Grace were sitting at the end of a rickety old pier on the Isle of Dogs, gazing out over the Thames, waiting to greet Nell when she finished her last show at a nearby music hall. After yet another day of intense exchanges among various constellations of the East End women, Grace and Blue had been having a desultory conversation about nothing much, mostly just enjoying the rare balmy night air and long stretches of silence, when Grace suddenly sat up straight.

"Cor, now that would hurt," she said.

"What?"

"That. The electrics." Directly across the river from them loomed the colossal smokestacked edifice of the Deptford Power Station.

"Meaning?" Blue also straightened up.

"Meaning... well, I was just thinking on what you'd said about California."

Recently, suffragettes around Britain had been turning their attention to communications circuits and had managed to cut a number of telephone and telegraph lines. But these had all been easily accessible local targets that were quickly repaired. When similar actions were discussed and dismissed as trivial by the women in the East End group, Blue had decided to report to them about the analogous but far more successful union tactics during the California power company strikes of the year before, when crucial electrical transfer towers were identified and toppled with dynamite, causing serious disruption not only to the power company's profits but also to those of its big commercial customers.

"And I'm also remembering," Grace continued, "that a few years back there was a fire at the old Grosvenor power station in Bond Street. Knocked out the transformers, or turbines, or whatever they are… and the place was months out of commission. Which means they must have lost a bleedin' fortune in custom, all that time putting out no power."

She had Blue's full attention now. "And?"

"And? And… well, that one cross the river's much the bigger, innit? I don't know what, but I'd wager it's got all kind of important things sucking the electrics from it."

"And those important things… are they something maybe you could find out?"

"Something… maybe I could." She was quiet for a few moments, staring across the water at the smokestacks belching smoke into the night sky. "But… look at the bleedin' thing. Solid stone and concrete and all. Fucking massive. Can't just light a match and send it up, know what I mean?"

Blue had felt an immediate connection with Grace when they'd met in Dublin during the great lockout, and their bond had strengthened during Blue's time in London. Although he didn't spend nearly as much time with Grace as he did with Nell, it was time of a different sort. Blue was at ease with Grace in a way he wasn't with Nell. He felt he knew Grace. Trusted her. And so, sitting on the pier that night, he began to tell her things he'd not told Nell, the full extent of which barely anyone knew, even in San Francisco: that his father was Michael Cavanaugh, a fuse, timer, detonator, blasting cap legend in California quarries and oil fields and construction sites; that his father had passed down to Blue the better part of his special talents; and that Blue had not simply been part of a strike where electrical towers had been felled but had been—as he phrased it to Grace—tactically integral to it.

The possibilities suggested to Grace by Blue's revelations, when combined with her musings about the power plant, enlivened both of them: Grace could finally envision the group taking action that would not only be dramatic but also have real consequence, while Blue could finally see himself emerging from the group's fringes, where his status as little more than a mascot had begun to rankle.

Now the two couldn't sit still. Dropping their plan to meet Nell, they scurried back to Grace's room where they talked until dawn, alternating between excitement and grave doubts at the enormity and complexity of the task. They were still in high color when together they went to Nell's room the following morning. It was clear to Nell that the two had been up all night, and Blue could see that this bothered her. Of course Nell knew that Grace romantically engaged only with women, yet Nell's tone with and glances at Blue smacked of what he could only read as garden-variety jealousy. He was aware that Nell quietly chafed at the companionability which he and Grace shared but which Nell had with neither of them. And Nell now seemed to sense that, in this particular crackling moment, the two were not revealing to her all they knew. She was right: at Blue's request, but with Grace's immediate understanding and agreement, they decided not to disclose yet to Nell, or to the other women in the group, that Blue would be their source of technical expertise for potential action against the power station.

The notion was extreme, audacious, spectacular, and Nell and the rest of the group were quickly converted to it, utterly vague though it was. Over the next several weeks they set out to gather information, each of the women with specific tasks, according to her connections. Reports quickly confirmed what Grace had supposed that first night on the pier with Blue, that the London Electric Supply Corporation's Deptford plant provided power to an impressive assortment of commercial and public operations, including heavy manufacturing plants on both sides of the river, street lighting throughout south London, and several local tram companies. Most significantly, Deptford also provided all the power for the London, Brighton and South Coast Railway, a massive conglomerate that included not only a crisscross of train lines in the south of the city and throughout Sussex but also the main line from London to Brighton, where it connected freight trains to cargo ships for Europe. Knocking the power plant offline, in other words, would create large-scale commercial chaos—exactly the kind of top-level pain in the purse that the East End group was hoping to inflict.

Almost immediately after this inspiriting news, however, came a douse of cold water. Word from the plant revealed the near impossibility of actually getting at the works themselves: there were always security men inside and out; and even if somehow they could get in, and miraculously set explosives undetected, the plant operated round the clock, so they wouldn't be able to use charges large enough to cause serious damage to the massive machinery without risking the lives of workers, a matter about which the women were adamant. For the moment they were stumped.

Nell was immediately ready to give up on the plan and return to her more flamboyant idea of kidnapping a government official and subjecting him to what she called *foie gras*-ing: force-feeding in the brutal manner by which suffragette hunger strikers had been abused in jail. But Blue and Grace were both dismissive of it, Blue calling it theatrical, a "one-act melodrama," a choice of words that actor Nell very much did not appreciate. Grace, on the other hand, remained committed to the power station as a target. She and Blue holed up in her room for a day to consider other angles of attack. From Blue's experience in the California strikes he knew that power grids were vulnerable in many places, not just at main generating points. So he and Grace and a couple of the other women, minus Nell, set out to find spots outside the great Deptford station itself where the electric company might have weaknesses. They weren't long in learning that power from Deptford was sent into the world through high-voltage mains cables. And by following the cables out in various directions from the plant, the women discovered that they crossed the Thames on special railway bridges at Charing Cross and Blackfriars and through certain railway tunnels, none of which had pedestrian traffic to worry about harming, and each of which would conveniently provide cover for surreptitious activities. It was on.

Now it was Blue's time. He calculated a series of a dozen simultaneous detonations of the mains cables at different spots along the circuits, which would satisfy a combination of the group's goals and conditions. Ruining cables and switchboxes at many different sites increased the likelihood that power would be off to more of the company's customers, and for a longer time. Blue also figured that if there were a number of simultaneous blasts—which depended almost entirely on his skill with timers—the electric company wouldn't have the chance to respond, as they would following a single blast, by heightening security along the cable routes. Also, the relatively small detonations required would be easier to control, reducing the likelihood of collateral damage. And by using smallish devices at different spots, it would be easier and safer for each woman in the group to set one, making detection less likely; the women could also remain nearby to serve as lookouts to distract anyone who might accidentally stray near the site at the set time.

The first order of business was to procure dynamite—the kinds of fizzy concoctions the now jailed London chemist had previously provided being insufficient for the job—and Grace thought she might be able to prevail on a connection she had in the South Yorkshire coalfields. The miners' union itself tightly controlled its position on suffrage and certainly would have no truck with the East End group's plan, but Grace knew a couple of men among the more radical miners who might be willing to help. As it happened, the South Yorkshire mine owners were at that moment sinking numerous new shafts, deeper than ever before, which gravely increased the risk to the miners who worked them but which incidentally also meant that there were massive amounts of dynamite around the worksites. Widespread anger among radical mine workers—not only against the mine owners but also against the government for the totally free hand it allowed the coal companies—might well be enough for them to share with Grace some explosives they might liberate from one of the mine sites. So Grace headed north. She was well-known and likely to be watched, though, so she wouldn't be able to bring anything back with her and would have to send someone else later if she were successful in persuading the miners to take such a risk.

Blue's task was to assemble the equipment he'd need to construct the devices. Since he had no local knowledge, and Grace was heading north, he turned to Nell. Or as Nell saw it, turned back to Nell. Blue explained to her that he'd never turned away in the first place; that it was as much Grace's decision as his to tell no one about his experiences and skills, and the intention to make use of them, until they were certain they had a viable plan and were ready to begin putting it in motion; and that in fact he'd wanted to tell Nell but Grace had argued that, in the spirit of the group, an exception should not be made. Nell immediately countered that, in the spirit of the group, *none* of the women should have been excluded. But she soon relented, at least somewhat, recognizing the point of keeping such information under wraps, and she believed so fervently in the cause that she quickly moved past her personal hurt and got on with the job of helping Blue. Moved past it—but was never able to shed it entirely. She and Blue worked side by side daily over the following high-tension weeks, and she never again mentioned her grievance. They were an effective team, and some shade of their affection for each other resurfaced. Blue even took to spending some nights again with Nell. But that was mostly just a matter of exhaustion and convenience. They no longer read to each other in bed.

Blue and Nell visited electrical supply and hardware shops to locate components Blue might need, but it was difficult for him to prepare fully because he didn't know what form or intensity the actual blasting material would be. Moreover, the British versions of much of the equipment itself looked different, often with different names, from what Blue was used to. After several frustrating days of scouting various shops, Blue proposed trying to cut through the uncertainties by consulting at the North London electrical equipment and repair shop of Errico Malatesta, the great Italian anarchist theoretician and organizer who for many years had made London his exile home. When he'd first arrived in London, Blue had wanted to make a pilgrimage to the shop to see the great man in person. But Malatesta had recently left London and slipped into Italy again, as Blue learned from press reports, helping to incite a bloody insurrection in Ancona the month before. So Blue figured that now, since everyone knew Malatesta himself wasn't in London, Blue might unobtrusively consult about his needed materials with whomever Malatesta had left to run the shop. But Grace returned to London the day before Blue was to head to the shop, and she quickly shut down the idea: several years before, a notorious jewel thief had bought acetylene torch equipment from the shop, which the thief had used in a spectacular robbery, and the radical milieu in London knew that, ever since, the police had been keeping the shop under close watch, whether or not Malatesta himself was there. The clandestine East End suffragette group had so far managed to remain below the state's line of sight, but Blue going to Malatesta's shop, Grace argued, might bring them right to the women's front door. And at this point in the struggle, the police would not bother with the need for evidence of specific acts in order to roust the women and lock them up: just the week before, a small-time London printshop owner had been hauled away and sentenced to a long stretch in prison, his presses confiscated and his workshop barricaded, for "contravening a breach of the peace," which consisted of nothing more than having printed a suffragette newsletter that memorialized public speeches in which movement leaders, including Mrs. P, had sanctified attacks on property of privilege.

As it turned out, none of it mattered.

Grace believed she had convinced two of her miner comrades in Yorkshire to lift some dynamite for her. She now awaited word that the deed had been done, upon which she'd send one of the other women, someone without a public profile, to fetch the goods back to London. Meanwhile, Blue had managed to put together the material he'd need for fuses and timers, with only the matter of detonators on hold: he could not know what to construct until he saw the actual explosives. So they waited. Impatiently. Anxiously. July turned to August. And with August came the war.

The British state declared war on Germany immediately following the Kaiser's first bellicose moves on the Continent, even though Britain itself was in no direct jeopardy. Huge numbers of Britons in general, and suffragettes in particular, were outraged by this precipitous leap into the continental slaughter. Among the most virulent objectors was Grace Neal. But despite her rage, she also soon recognized that

Britain's entry into the war might present an opportunity to press the case for universal suffrage. The government would be consumed by the war effort, would do whatever it could to win cooperation from the populace—especially the laboring men being sent to the front lines, called on to kill and to die but not to vote—and would desperately seek to avoid any disruption of the state's massive military mobilization. All of which meant that acts of economic sabotage might have even greater political impact than in peacetime. So Grace thought the group should not only go forward with the attacks on the Deptford power circuits but also follow with other acts of disruption as soon as possible thereafter.

Except the Deptford attacks never happened. Thanks to Mrs. P.

In the first week of August, from the safe haven in France where she often went to recuperate when things got too difficult for her in England, Mrs. Pankhurst sent out a directive to all branches of the WSPU. Now that the nation was at war, she wrote, the women of Britain must rally to the cause and all militant suffrage actions must immediately cease. And since Mrs. P was not just leader of the WSPU but its embodiment and conscience, every local branch obeyed, albeit grudgingly in many cases and with the loss of numerous members. Of course, neither the Women's Suffrage Federation in East London nor Grace and Nell's smaller East End group took orders from Mrs. P. But Pankhurst's force as an almost mythic figure was so great that her manifesto created cracks of doubt even among organizations outside her control, including with several women in Grace and Nell's cadre. Which threatened the Deptford plan, since it required coordinated participation by the entire group.

In the end, the group's will was never tested. Because the dynamite never arrived. Grace's Yorkshire miners had also been buffeted by Mrs. P's declaration and refused to go through with their end of the plan.

Blue was deflated by the discord sowed by Pankhurst's declaration and by the resulting suspension of the Deptford scheme: it was not only frustrating that all the planning and work would go for naught but also disheartening to witness the leaching out of energy and spirit from the East End group. Still, it was only the latest in a string of political defeats Blue had recently experienced—following Paterson and Dublin—and as with those others this was not really his fight: he could leave it behind without a great sense of personal loss. But what Emmeline Pankhurst did next was of a different order. And Blue was enraged.

Within a few weeks of calling off militant suffrage action, Mrs. P returned to England and in one flag-draped rally after another, up and down the length of the country, exhorted women to support the war; chastised "ungrateful" war-opposed laboring men, calling on them to end all industrial unrest; and browbeat workers to join the military, with her followers patrolling the streets outside the rallies pushing white feathers—symbol of cowardice—onto young men not in uniform. To die in the name of king and flag, she declared, is a splendid way to go.

Declan. Blue's big brother Declan. Dead in the Philippines war. A splendid way to go.

And now she was here. San Francisco. Blue saw it in the newspaper. She was to be the featured speaker at a women's Preparedness gathering at the Palace Hotel. To drum up US entry into the war. Her visit sponsored, the advertisement said, by the Imperial Order of Daughters of the Empire, their motto emblazoned across the top: "One Flag, One Throne, One Empire."

Nearly two years later, and she's here. Emmeline Pankhurst.

"Genghis fucking Khunt," Blue said out loud.

10

Even before he got through the door, Blue could hear the delicious sounds of a full-bodied *disputa* in Italian.

"*Parmigian'!? On pasta alle vongole!? Minga! What are you, fucking French?*"

The meeting rooms of the *Gruppo Anarchico Volontá*—the Anarchist Will Group—were on the corner of Union and Stockton Streets facing Washington Square, the North Beach neighborhood's central *piazza*. When Blue entered the large ground floor front room, about a dozen men and a couple of women, most in their twenties to forties, were rustling about, some of them looking through newspapers and pamphlets and broadsheets held by clothespins to a wire strung the length of one wall, others moving in and out of a rear room where Blue could see there was another hive of activity.

The loud argument, though, was coming from one side of the front room where eight or so men were hovering over a laden table; it was difficult to tell how many were actually involved in the work at hand and how many were just volunteering opinions. Across its breadth were laid out various ingredients for the hot meal the group prepared each Saturday evening—in addition to the clothes and food they regularly donated to Lily Bratz's free clinic just up the street—and served to neighborhood denizens who might not see as good or filling a plate the rest of the week. On this occasion, the provisions cadged from local fishermen and foodstuff purveyors included a huge mound of clams in shells dumped onto layers of newspaper, an impressive pile of garlic, several bouquets of flat-leaf parsley, a two-foot high stack covered with grease paper out of which peeked the curled ends of fresh linguini, and a couple of clear bottles full of deep green olive oil.

A score of long crusty loaves of bread were piled atop and alongside a well-worn wine barrel next to one end of the table, while on the floor at the other end were two large iron cauldrons settled on gas-fired cooking rings.

The man who was loudly objecting to putting Parmesan on clam pasta held a block of the offending cheese in one hand, waving it over his head.

"*French!?*" another man shot back in Italian. "*Ehhh, you mule sniffer, what the hell does a farmer know about clams?!*"

Recognizing the two antagonists, Blue understood the "farmer" slur. Genio, recipient of the taunt, was in fact anything but a farmer: he was originally from Palermo and had spent an entirely urban childhood and young manhood there before moving across the ocean and then continent to live another entirely urban life in the center of San Francisco. But Genio's family name was Forcone, which means "pitchfork" and thus offered a convenient trajectory for barbed remarks during the frequent disputes that erupted among habitués of the *Volontá* rooms.

"*No, no, you're right,*" Genio replied, suddenly calm, "*not French, no. It's what...*" his voice pitched up again with each following word "*... a stinking... barbarian would do!*"

"*You... ignorant terrone!*" the first man sputtered a northern Italian pejorative used against southerners, meaning peasant, which in this case also conveniently fit the theme of the previous farmer jibe.

"*That's right... barbarian!*" Genio now noticed Blue and spoke directly to him, switching from Italian to Sicilian: "*Ehhhh-heh, Baldino, am I right? Only a barbarian would put cheese on clams. Or... an Englishman.*"

The other man in the argument, Mario Fraschetti, was from Torino in the north of Italy and didn't speak Sicilian but certainly could make out the final proper noun, and in reply howled "*Whaaat!?*" and lunged for Genio's arm to wrest the cheese from him but was restrained by one of the others, his reach flailing just short.

"*Hah! See, it's true!*" Genio continued to Blue, switching back from Sicilian to Italian so that his antagonist and all the others would understand. *"They do have short arms!"* The reference was to the Ligurian and Piedmontese reputation, among southerners, of being cheapskates: arms too short to reach into their own pockets.

Mario now turned to one of the other men and raged through an obviously impressive range of curses, but in Piedmontese, a dialect utterly unintelligible to either Blue or Genio.

Blue struggled to hold an expression that the two men would read as commensurate with what he knew was the seriousness of their emotions, despite the triviality of the subject matter. The men's vituperations were couched in *campanilismo*: the strong sense of identity with a local home region of Italy rather than with any broader sense of Italianness. It was only outsiders—particularly the Northern Europe–rooted San Francisco business elite and mainstream unions—who lumped all these men together as Italians, usually in order to denigrate and ostracize them, a categorization that, ironically, brought these otherwise fiercely anti-nationalist men together, from time to time, for collective self-preservation. But Blue had grown up around these men—was happiest, or nearest to happy, in their company—and understood that behind the *campanilismo* there simmered other, politically meaningful divisions about which the question of cheese on clams provided just one more in an endless stream of reasons, or excuses, for venting at one another.

In fact, because of their political differences, it was somewhat unusual to see Mario here among Genio and the other men of the *Volontá* group, despite the fact that almost all of them lived in the neighborhood and ran into each other daily on its streets and in its shops and cafés. Mario was one of the originators of the Latin branch of Local 173, a hodgepodge IWW-inspired multi-craft labor union organized among mostly Italian but also French, Spanish, Portuguese and Mexican workers who were excluded from traditional unions; their own, larger meeting hall was just a few blocks away. Mario self-identified as an anarcho-syndicalist. Some people of this tendency instead called themselves anarcho-socialists or anarcho-communists, and at times the terminology became so confounding that even the men themselves weren't sure what label to use, or what exactly they intended by it when they did choose one. For Mario, the term meant roughly that he believed—as did Blue—in the organization of all workers, skilled and not, into unions, but ideally into One Big Union, as the IWW coined it, without the trade or craft distinctions or racial or ethnic barriers that were typical of most labor groups. Many anarchist *organizzatori*, as Italians of this tendency were called, came from the north of Italy where there was a history of strong, militant labor unions. But there was no overall geographic consistency in these matters, and even members of the same family were known to fall on different sides of these organizational questions and consequently to become bitterly estranged from each other.

Contra the Wobblies and Mario, the *Volontá* men—and they were all men; although they made space in their rooms for meetings of kindred women's groups, and women were always welcome at any gathering, the *Volontá* itself was exclusively, if unspokenly, male— were *antiorganizzatori*. They disdained all formal associations as fatally bound to harden into hierarchy and bureaucratic inertia and believed that only fluid, free associations of working men—such as the *Volontá* group itself—had the capacity to adapt to circumstances and thus to ignite political fire wherever insurrectionary tinder might be found. They supported all kinds of militant labor actions, including by traditional trade unions—from the membership of which their Latin-ness mostly excluded them—but chose the what and when of their involvement without regard to the dictates of union bosses or IWW theoreticians. They also engaged in political actions completely outside the realm of labor struggles, particularly over matters of free speech and police repression, frequently arising from their deep hostility to nationalism and militarism. And to the Church: to a man they were *mangiapreti*—priest-eaters.

But these *antiorganizzatori* were themselves riven by splits, some of fine gradations, some of epic proportions. One subject that caused multiple, complex fissures was political violence. Most anti's were approving of some degree of violence, but many limited such support to actions conjoined with organized political or labor protest: doing battle against labor scabs or their security men; fighting police who roust an "unlawful" assembly; or attacking the machinery and property of big capital, as in the region's recent power company strike when electrical towers were toppled with dynamite. Others, however, were strident freelancers who operated entirely apart from labor struggles. Of these, there were the "illegalists," committed to lives of urban brigandage, arguing—though they rarely bothered trying to convince anyone—that since property is theft, as the old anarchist maxim had it, requisitioning it for themselves was a political act of reclamation, and that any incidental violence against the ownership class or the state was a form of self-defense. And most extreme among the *antiorganizzatori* were "propaganda of the deed" proponents who believed that spectacular acts of violence, including assassinations, against leaders of capital and the state would at some point spark popular revolutionary insurrection.

Then there was Blue. As for *campanalismo*, he was able to skirt its labeling strictures because he was *misto*, a mongrel: he was born in the US rather than in the shadow of any homeland campanile; and he was the issue of a Sicilian-Irish coupling that shunted him outside the bounds of all recognizable identities—though because of his maternal lineage, some local Sicilians included him as one of their own when it suited them, as with Genio in the *Volontá* rooms trying to recruit Blue to his side of the clam pasta dispute.

Politically, Blue never chose among the competing positions, not least because the militant milieu's ideological sands themselves, and their adherents, were constantly shifting. There was a bountiful if shuddering flow of local, national and international radical newspapers and journals presenting various shades of syndicalist, *antiorganizzatori*, illegalist and propaganda-of-the-deed arguments. A few journals in English or Italian had substantial lifespans, some of them produced in San Francisco itself, including a monthly publication by Alexander Berkman—infamous for his 1892 propaganda-of-the-deed attempt to assassinate Henry Clay Frick of Carnegie Steel—who had recently relocated to San Francisco and was publishing the paper out of his flat near Belle Lavin's boardinghouse in the Mission District, and who had given the paper the provocative or foolhardy, probably both, name *The Blast*. But there were also many other journals and pamphlet series that appeared, then quickly disappeared in sectarian chaos, seemingly every month. The joke went: lock two anarchists in a room; come back in an hour and you'll find either two dead bodies or a new newspaper.

Whenever the latest doctrinal pronouncement arrived in one of these publications, especially if it came from one or another anarchist or syndicalist venerable, the militant left-wing denizens of North Beach would argue fiercely among themselves about what exactly was meant—translations to and from various languages often clouding the issues further—and which argument, or riposte to it, was most convincing. And when the dust settled after any particular ideological scuffle, there was always a sorting-out process: which former comrades now had to be considered "reactionaries" (or "liberals," essentially the same thing), on one hand, or "premature vanguards," on the other, and which formerly shunned cadres could now be heartily embraced. That is, until the next *pronunciamento* appeared.

Blue's refusal to identify himself with any specific sectarian align-ment—part of his broader instinct to always leave himself an exit route—marked him somewhat among other militants, but opinion was split between those who were wary of it and those who admired it. Also, since Blue had never become personally dependent for paid labor on the enterprises of any particular group—his subsistence provided first by minor criminality, then by boxing and work for Flaherty's gym, and later by carrying on his father's legacy as a *pro tem* demoli-tion expert for explosives-dependent legitimate enterprises—he was never obliged by economic necessity to adopt any specific political position to the exclusion of, or in opposition to, any others. Also, the more extreme political groupings, who might otherwise have shunned Blue for his chronic nonsectarianism, gave him a free pass because of the value they placed on his combination of instrumental talents and discretion: the skills Cavanaugh-*père* had passed on to him had come in handy to some of these groups during several intense labor battles in recent years; and a small gang of Genovese illegalist *brigantes*, one of whom, Paolo, was an old friend and warehouse burglary partner of

Blue's older brother Declan—though Blue was never sure whether an illegalist political philosophy had led Paolo to criminality or the other way around—had turned to Blue for occasional technical assistance after Declan had gone off to the Philippines and got himself killed.

It was Paolo whom Blue was looking for at the *Volontá* rooms that morning. To borrow a suit of clothes.

About the last thing Blue would spend his dwindling money supply on would be a proper suit, collared shirt, and necktie. But to get into the posh Palace Hotel, and in particular into the room where Emmeline Pankhurst would be speaking at the Preparedness rally later that day, he'd have to look the part. He and Paolo were the same height and size, and he knew that Paolo would have a spare outfit that fit the bill: Paolo was a clothes horse, mimicking his illegalist hero, the foppish French anarchist bandit Jules Bonnot. Since returning to San Francisco Blue hadn't seen Paolo, but he knew his old friend would be happy to oblige. If Blue could find him.

When Blue had left the city three years before, Paolo and three of his illegalist comrades had been living in a ramshackle pre-quake building, perched perilously above the quarry on the east side of Telegraph Hill. Upon making inquiries now, Blue was pleased to learn that Paolo's building was still standing, and that Paolo was still there, rather than in some jail or other, which had seemed to Blue just as likely, or even dead in a shootout with police, like Paolo's idol Bonnot. When Blue arrived at the house earlier that morning he'd been surprised to find that such a haunter of late-night streets as Paolo was already up and out, and that Paolo and two other flatmates—as reported to Blue by another of the gang who hadn't been able to rouse himself that early—had gone off to the *Volontá* rooms. This latter piece of information surprised Blue, not because Paolo and his illegalist pals were anathema to the *Volontá* group, which they weren't; they were looked at somewhat askance, as self-indulgent, but were nonetheless welcome. It was simply that the political arguments carried on in the *Volontá* rooms had more complexity than Paolo could usually manage, and Paolo dreaded the occasional challenge from a *Volontá* to defend the political nature of his banditry. So he usually made a point only to consort with his several *Volontá* friends away from the confines of their official meeting place.

After wading through the cheese-on-clams argument in the front room, Blue went looking for Paolo in the back. Fifteen or so men and women were crowded around a rickety wooden table, with one woman and one man behind the table taking portions from half a dozen piles of uniformly stacked papers and passing them across to the others, along with vociferous commentary—in English from the woman, Italian from the man—and extravagant gestures toward the world beyond the room. The recipients of the papers were just as jabbery in response, all of them waggling and speaking at the same time, in a combination of languages and dialects. The overall impression was of a high-speed auction in which no one was sure who the auctioneer was.

Blue was familiar with many of the characters in the room and immediately saw there a combustible admixture of militant tendencies. He realized that this must be one of those unscheduled but not uncommon occasions when the various antagonisms among sectarian groups were set aside for the sake of a cause around which nearly all of the Latin left came together. This time, Blue learned from one of the broadsheets being distributed, the cause was birth control.

The broadsheet's headline, in Italian, shouted "Workers! Procreate Only When You Want!" and announced a demonstration for Washington Square on the following morning, Sunday, to protest the jailing in New York of anarchist firebrand and contraception agitator Emma Goldman for having publicly distributed birth control information to garment workers in Manhattan. The sheet's Italian text, which Blue briefly scanned, not only spoke of the injustice of arresting Goldman and of withholding birth control information from poor women, but also went on to excoriate the Catholic Church and to describe, in fairly explicit detail, various methods of birth control. No accident the demonstration was called for a Sunday morning in the square, where most of North Beach's observant Catholics would be passing on their way to and from Saints Peter and Paul Church, the center of Italian Catholic life in the district. The demonstration would thus also be taking place directly across from the enormous under-construction twin-spire edifice that was to become the new Peter and Paul cathedral, being built to lord it over the square and neighborhood.

In anticipation of the event, and to direct an extra frisson toward the passing Catholic sheep, as the *Volontá* referred to them, the group had moved two pictures from their interior walls to the twin Washington Square-facing windows on either side of their front door. One was a large photograph of the monument to the sixteenth century martyr for science and freedom of thought Giordano Bruno, erected in *Campo de' Fiori* in Rome, with the hooded figure of Bruno staring defiantly across the river at the Vatican, on the spot where the Church burned at the stake this heretical priest who'd dared publicly to doubt—on empirical grounds—the Virgin Birth, transubstantiation, and by implication the divinity of Christ. The statue's unveiling twenty years before had caused almost as much furor within the Italian Catholic world as had Bruno's teachings three hundred years earlier, so there was no doubt that the *Volontá* group's flaunting of the Bruno photograph would be read by many passing churchgoers in the confrontational spirit in which it was intended.

The other picture was more obscure but also—to those, including Blue, who registered its double meaning—more ominous. It showed the fortress on top of Montjuïc hill in Barcelona, with the caption *"Ricorda I Processi di Montjuïc!"* ("Remember the Montjuïc Trials!"). In part, this reference to the trials was preaching to the choir: the arrest twenty years before by the Spanish state of hundreds of Spanish anarchists, their torture and long imprisonment or exile to the Sahara, the execution of five, and the subsequent suppression of worker organizations across Spain, had been deeply imprinted on the anarchist world. On the other hand, local Catholics, mostly Italian, on their way to church, were unlikely to attach any meaning to the Barcelona fortress. Unless. Unless they happened to know of the event used by the Spanish state to justify the mass arrests and suppression: a crude bomb lobbed from a building roof onto a large group of Catholics leaving a church to begin a procession through city streets.

A procession of Catholics on city streets. Like the next day's North Beach churchgoers. And a bomb.

The woman handing out broadsheets and calling out instructions in English was Reb Rainey, indefatigable campaigner for labor rights, women's rights, free speech rights, and the overarching right to not have anyone, as she described it, tell her what the fuck she could or couldn't do. The man at her side, simultaneously giving parallel directions in Italian, was a buddy of Genio's and one of the founders of the *Volontá* group, a fierce Pugliese carpenter named Franco Caltrone. His heavy Barese accent and frequent relapse into Barese dialect was causing consternation and complaint from the men and women who were being handed the broadsheets to deliver around the district, resulting in an increasingly high-volume babel; several of the would-be distributors who were normally more comfortable in Italian were turning in frustration to Reb for English versions of what they couldn't parse from Franco's Barese.

Reb spotted Blue and called to him over the heads of the people around the table.

"Jayzus, Cavanaugh, if I'd known you were back in town, I wouldn't be wrassling with this boyo," indicating Franco, who was too busy arguing to react to the slight, if by some chance he understood it. Blue did. There had been a few other occasions over the years when Blue—usually the one called on first among local militants to translate texts between English and Italian—had been unavailable and Franco had stepped in. Franco was smart, literate, politically sophisticated, and fluent in street English. Unfortunately, however, Franco's less confident grasp of written English plus the heavy Barese slant to his Italian made his translation process difficult, and stressful to a wordsmith like Reb Rainey—who'd written this broadsheet, the English version of which was being distributed across the city, while Franco's Italian version was special for North Beach and the fishermen's haunts along the docks—and rendered the ultimate printed product somewhat problematic.

Blue laughed at Reb's remark but just then spotted Paolo and so simply gave Reb a wave and moved over to pull Paolo out of the crowd. Blue was hoping to make it in time to see and perhaps respond—though he had no idea what that response might be—to the appearance in a few hours by Emmeline Pankhurst at the Palace Hotel Preparedness event, and this rounding up of proper clothes was taking longer than he'd hoped. Paolo was delighted to see his old friend Baldino again and after a brief exchange immediately agreed to provide him with a suit—*"Ahah, two piece or three?"* Paolo beamed, pleased that someone was showing respect for, rather than the usual mocking of, his clothes collection—but was distracted by the parceling out of flyers and instructions about the section of the neighborhood where he was meant to distribute them. As he stepped aside to let Paolo finish receiving his directions from Franco and Reb, Blue was called to from behind by Genio Forcone, who had managed to extract himself from the *parmigiano* argument in the front room. Blue turned to see Genio standing in a corner alongside Treat, the printshop man. Next to Treat were two slatted boxes filled with more broadsheets; Treat must have been the printer. Blue found his eyes flicking around the room to see if Meg might be there but he didn't see her.

Genio left Treat's side and steered Blue away from the group at the table. After they shared a few banal remarks in Italian about how well each of them was looking and how long Blue had been back in the city, Genio switched to Sicilian, asking, *"And what are you doing with yourself?"* Blue paused, not sure whether this was just another generic remark or whether Genio was hunting for something in particular. Just then Paolo broke away from the table and approached, and though Paolo was Genovese and didn't speak Sicilian, Genio lowered his voice to rephrase his question: *"Are you getting back in the old games?"*

Blue still hesitated, not knowing which of his "old games" Genio meant, and didn't answer before Paolo joined them and Genio switched back to Italian, saying in normal voice, *"Well, I'll come see you soon. You're stopping at the Genova, huh?"* Blue's face showed his mild surprise that Genio already knew where Blue was staying. *"Ehhh-heh,"* Genio said in response to Blue's expression, *"I asked around."* With a satisfied purse of his lips, Genio nodded to both Paolo and Blue and returned to Treat in the corner.

~

The flag. And bunting. Red, white and blue bunting. And more bunting. And more flags. Enormous flags hanging over and nearly covering the Garden Court's two-story high draperies. Flags on poles at the back of the temporary raised dais on one side of the enormous room, swirls of bunting scalloping the wall behind. Flag bouquets in vases at the center of each four-, six- and eight-person table, the special linens a rotation of red, white and blue. Plus red, white and blue streamers twined from chandelier to chandelier, then over to encircle the Court's massive marble columns. And all of it reflected back in on itself by the room's floor-to-ceiling mirrored double side doors that alternated with the Stars and Stripes–covered draperies, a dizzying multiplication, a carnival fun house of American glory.

Kate waited in the Court's large open entryway from the hotel's main corridor until the room was almost full—pairs and small klatches of well-dressed women streaming in and milling about, talking in high spirits, maybe two hundred in all—before entering herself. Then she lingered at the back of the room, a vantage point from which she could watch the whole without feeling that she was being watched herself. There were name cards on the tables; Kate expected there was one for her since she'd received a formal invitation to the event, but she made no move to find it. Instead, she scanned the room, hoping she'd recognize at least one or two among the throng, to whom she could attach herself. True, at the Spreckels mansion masquerade ball almost all the women she'd been introduced to had their faces painted or masked and so by sight she wouldn't know them now. But that night there had also been the five unmasked women in evening gowns who'd been with Alma Spreckels as part of the small, more exclusive gathering in the downstairs library into which Mullally had introduced her. And there were the women who'd helped Alma at her charity fundraiser art preview a few days ago, with whom Kate had exchanged pleasantries and small talk about some of the pieces on display. Since this Preparedness gathering was also a by-invitation fundraising event, a gathering of the city's women of means, Kate assumed she'd see at least some of these women she'd met before. But she spotted none of them.

Near her at the rear of the room Kate saw a table without name cards, only two elderly ladies seated there, and slid into a chair on the opposite side from them. She wasn't entirely conscious of why she did this, except for a vague anxiety about what she would manage to say if anyone with whom she'd been assigned to sit at her name card table— And who would have decided that assignment? Who, come to think of it, had sent her the invitation?—should ask her opinions about the war and Preparedness. Of course she understood that, for Lansing's purposes, *she* was the one who should be asking *them* such questions, whoever they'd turn out to be. But she felt overwhelmed by the mass of unfamiliar, upper-echelon women: over her years working at the Boston law firm she'd learned how to cope with the crustiness and pretentions of men of elevated social standing, but in the rare instances when she found herself in close quarters with upper-class women— she cringed whenever she thought of the *grandes dames* of Jamey's family—she still felt herself thoroughly, uncomfortably, a Carey from Southie. Well, anyway, she now excused herself, she'd still be able to report to Lansing on the tenor of this gathering, and to describe its main actors, without having to put herself directly in the line of fire.

The room was now packed, women sitting or standing at their tables and talking animatedly, the bruit of voices echoing off the Court's mirrored walls. Suddenly, the noise dropped: at one end of the dais, a dozen soldiers appeared and moved ceremoniously into the room in an almost slow-motion single-file lockstep. The soldiers spread themselves evenly across the front of the dais, and when the first of them reached the far edge, all twelve turned in unison and faced the assembled audience of women, doing some sort of simultaneous formal foot stomp and coming to military attention. The people above them on the dais began to clap and the entire room followed. The soldiers remained still and impassive, except for what Kate thought was a slight jutting of jaws.

A woman on the dais approached the rostrum and motioned to the room; the applause receded and the audience, as well as those on the dais, took their seats. Kate could now make out more clearly behind the dais a white banner with what she now noticed, looking around, were the only words displayed anywhere amid the great room's forest of flags and bunting and streamers: in huge block blue letters edged in red, LOYALTY AND HONOR—PATRIOTS PREPARE.

When the crowd had settled, the woman at the rostrum announced herself as chair of the women's auxiliary, or something like that, of the city's Chamber of Commerce, sponsor of the day's event. Kate didn't retain the woman's name or exact title—she had brought her notebook but worried at the attention it might draw if she took it out of her bag and began writing—but silently remarked her surprise that it was the Chamber of Commerce sponsoring a Preparedness meeting.

The mistress of ceremonies now called forth a color guard of three more soldiers, the middle of whom carried yet another enormous Stars and Stripes; they marched in from the wings, just in front of the row of other soldiers, stopping at the middle of the dais and turning toward the audience. The rostrum woman now gestured over to the corner where a squawk of unseen bagpipes began; it took Kate a moment to realize that these were the opening bars of the Star-Spangled Banner. The mistress of ceremonies gestured to the audience, who pulled back their chairs, rose, and began full-throatedly singing. The weirdness, to Kate, of the anthem played on bagpipes was only heightened when, the singing finished, the bags continued for several seconds to wheeze out a discordant final breath. The color guard pirouetted and returned to the sidelines and out the door.

When the audience had reseated, the speaker began by calling out her personal pride, then proclaiming what she knew to be the pride of every woman in the room, for "our heroes in uniform." As she did so, she gestured toward the soldiers arrayed in front of her, which called forth from the room another round of applause.

"Of one thing there can be no doubt. . . no contradiction," the woman continued. "Our military is the best that is America. In fact. . . I can put it no other way. . . and every *true* American surely knows this in his heart and soul. . . America *is* its military." Again, applause from the crowd.

The woman went on in the same vein for two or three minutes, extolling with various platitudes the virtues of American men in uniform, in every sentence of which, Kate noticed, she managed to work in the word "heroes." Kate expected the woman to offer some commentary about the European war and why the US should join it—something Kate might report back to Lansing—but there was none. The speaker then announced that before she'd introduce the day's distinguished featured guest, the gathering would hear a few words from the grand marshal of the upcoming Preparedness Day parade, "our own" Thornwell Mullaly.

For a few moments Mullaly didn't appear. Kate was puzzled that the seemingly punctilious gentleman wasn't already on the dais when he was expected to speak. But quickly she understood: Mullaly appeared in a doorway near one end of the dais and, in what appeared to Kate the same uniform he'd worn at the Spreckels mansion ball, slowly entered the room, doffed his plumed hat and briefly glanced at the audience, then went along the row of soldiers in front of the dais, shaking each man's hand as if he were their commanding officer bestowing honors after a battle, finally turning again to the room and giving an ever so slight bow. The crowd gave him an ovation.

As she watched, Kate found herself bothered about the soldiers. There was something off-center about them, something slightly—she couldn't put her finger on it—wrong. At the same time, though, they were also somehow familiar. The combination was disquieting and she puzzled over it until her attention was drawn again to Mullaly who had gained the rostrum and started to speak, with what Kate noticed was once again his more formal diction and thicker Southern tones.

"I need not tell you," he began, "what brings us all here today."

Actually, Kate thought, I was hoping *someone* would tell me.

"We are patriots, all of us here," Mullally continued. "Americans through and through. And we share, all of us, the great certainty... that through our heroic men in uniform... we do... God's... work." He paused; if for applause, he wasn't disappointed. "Now, I have no doubt that every good person here today, every *true* American wife, mother, sister, daughter, will be standing shoulder to shoulder along Market Street come the 22nd of next month, on that *glorious* day when thousands of us... nay, tens of thousands," his voice began to rise "...will celebrate American ideals," and continued rising "...American strength... and American honor." The gathering responded to his vocal cue and applauded.

Mullally held up his hand. "But let me be clear. There are forces afoot... *alien* forces... *dark* forces... that seek to sabotage our great movement. And more than that, to stain and disrupt our fair city. Our state. Our nation. Indeed, to shatter the very foundations... of... our... world. Foremost the Huns, of course, upon whose horrors our guest"—he turned toward a woman on the dais, a rather ghoulish figure in black with a veil covering her face—"will no doubt expound. But also the Mexicans, Villa and his rabble, swarming on our border and *daring* to cross... with larceny and *sordid* menace... into our very farms and towns. And still closer to home, as to our disgust and horror we have all witnessed lately, the radical rabble in the heart of our very city... with their pestilence... their foreign notions... their foreign bodies... penetrating and poisoning our working men and women... on our docks, in our factories, on our streets and thoroughfares. And have no doubt, my good ladies, that these forces of darkness will try to interfere with our coming celebration. To interfere... with you. Indeed, some of the crudest of the labor gangs, the ones most deeply infected by alien ideas and alien flesh, have already called for workers to boycott our grand parade. So to you, the *cream* of our city, I should like to make a request. That you to turn your attention to the decent folk who labor for you, who cook and clean and sew for you, who mind your children, who garden and drive and fix and fetch for you. Allow me to ask that you spare them all a few hours that special Saturday next month, so that they might show the colors for *true* American workers. Spare them the hours. But be sure to remind them *clearly* where their duty lies in that time away from their chores. So that I may see every one of them on Market Street that day as I pass by in the great parade. So that *you* may be sure to see them there, standing next to you." The crowd burbled its assent. "Because no outsiders... no swarthy vermin from old world sewers... no, no one... and nothing... can be allowed... to stop us!" The women erupted, with an almost lusty quality to their ovation, different, it seemed to Kate, from their earlier polite applause and at odds with their previous seemly comportment and with the usual hushed opulence of the Garden Court.

Mullaly didn't so much acknowledge the crowd's response as momentarily bask in it, then offered a brief wave, turned, said something to the mistress of ceremonies, left the dais with another wave and went out the side door through which he'd entered.

The woman took the rostrum again and passed along Mullaly's regrets that he could not remain with them because he was off to engage in exercises with his cavalry troops that afternoon.

After a moment the words sank in. Cavalry? Kate puzzled. Troops? The man runs a railroad, doesn't he?

Kate's attention was brought back to the woman at the rostrum who was beginning her introduction of Mrs. Emmeline Pankhurst, the featured guest. It was a name Kate knew vaguely from years before when news from Britain had involved matters other than the war, but she did not recall having heard it in quite a while. The woman giving the introduction launched into gushing encomia about Mrs. Pankhurst's dedication to the British war effort and to the acclaim she had won on both sides of "our ocean" as a beacon and exemplar—here the introducer became almost reverential—of Western womanhood.

Kate missed most of the Pankhurst woman's opening remarks. From her spot at the back of the room it was hard for Kate to make out what Pankhurst said because the Englishwoman's accent was a bit difficult for Kate, and Pankhurst spoke quietly at first, as if demanding that the audience be absolutely still and pay the closest attention. But more, Kate was distracted by Pankhurst's self-presentation: amid polite applause she'd risen from her seat and moved toward the rostrum with excruciatingly slow movements, managing to remain absolutely erect while doing so, wearing a long formal dress, almost a gown, with a lace shawl, a choker at her neck, a lorgnette on a chain, and a round sequined hat from which a veil covered her face until she'd ever so slowly raised it at the rostrum, as if opening the lid of a treasure box. And all of it black. Kate imagined the grieving widow at a graveside service for some vaguely middling member of the British aristocracy.

When, after a minute or so, Kate was able to focus on Pankhurst's remarks, the Englishwoman was saying something about how wonderful it was to hear the "natural pairing" of bagpipes and the American national anthem, which led her into a complaint about "sulky" workmen in Britain who refuse to join in singing "God Save the King." Then, with a subtly deepening and strengthening voice, Pankhurst explained to the room that while they might know of her from her long struggle for women's suffrage, the moment her nation had been attacked and forced into war, she had become... as every woman in this room *must*, she added with a hint of prospective chastisement... first and foremost, "a patriot."

Now Kate was distracted again. Her nation attacked? After agreeing to Lansing's proposal and before coming west, Kate had spent many evenings—with Maggie gone, evenings that otherwise would have been empty hours alone at home—at the public library in Boston going through newspapers covering the war's first year and a half, to get herself up to speed for her San Francisco assignment. And she now tried but failed to dredge up from that reading any such attack on Britain that the Pankhurst woman might be referring to.

Meanwhile, Pankhurst had begun to declaim on what she called "patriotic motherhood." The best way for women to be patriotic, she declared in a voice that continued to swell, was to fulfill their duty to both nature and nation, which was to put all other considerations aside, to be mothers first and foremost, to bear and raise sons to perpetuate and build up the race physically, mentally and morally. The race that we share, she told the assembled women, Britain and America... the race that holds together the civilized world... against the barbarity and depredations of East and South, which in Europe for the past two years has come in the shape of the horrid Hun, overrunning the hallowed ground of France.

"And let me be clear"—Pankhurst was now gesturing toward some space above the heads of the gathering—"that these hordes will not be stopped unless we join together, all of us, to do the stopping, wherever they may appear... Which I must remind you, warn you, includes not only the battlefields of Europe but also the streets and shops and schools, the very homes where... we... live. Yes, you must be on guard, my good women of America, against the Huns in our midst, the Germanics amongst us, who intermingle and intermarry to subvert the house of our race from within."

"The intermarried Germanics among us." Well, Kate thought, no wonder Alma Spreckels didn't show up for this.

"So..." Pankhurst paused a moment, then tamped down the pitch of her peroration, which was threatening to become undignified "...the word of the day, my good ladies, is 'prepare.' As your sons prepare to take on the great challenge; as they prepare to cover themselves with glory; as they prepare to defend our sacred soil against the violators of our bodies and spirit. Whatever shadows might pass over your hearts at the sacrifices that await, you must be and remain steadfastly, first and foremost... mothers to your sons, your heroes!"

Sons. As Kate listened, she wondered whether the Englishwoman herself had a son whose fate in the war might cast a shadow over her heart. Or a husband.

Husband. Jamey. And then she understood. What had been bothering her about the soldiers in front of the dais. The uniforms. Not from the army of today but from her day, Jamey's day. The uniform of the Philippines Expeditionary Force. Jamey's uniform. Though not exactly: as a surgeon, Jamey wore an officer's uniform, which perhaps was why she had not immediately recognized it, because these were foot soldiers who had been trotted out here for the occasion, in their enlisted man's gear. But she remembered now; she'd seen many of these uniforms when she'd visited Jamey in army quarantine on Angel Island. And none of the soldiers here was young, Kate registered, not current soldiers but men of middle age, who would have served fifteen or so years before. When Jamey had served. Men who'd been where Jamey had been.

And what would Jamey think, to see them here, these men? As props for Preparedness. If only she could talk to him now, her Jamey.

Well, or back then, when he'd come home. If only she'd been able to talk to him then. If only *he* had been able to talk to *her*. If only.

Kate felt a presence behind her and turned to see Mullaly standing just a few feet away, blocked from the room's view by a drapery at the edge of a rear exit, his telltale plumed hat tucked discreetly under his arm. Unobtrusively watching her; waiting, it seemed, for her to notice him.

When she turned, Mullaly remained where he was but gestured toward the open doorway. And smiled a charming smile. Mrs. Pankhurst rattled on.

∾

After prying Paolo out of the *Volontá* rooms, it took Blue longer than he'd hoped to put together his outfit for the Palace Hotel. First, their progress back to Paolo's flat was slowed by Paolo's assignment to put broadsheets under the doors of all the homes they passed on the way—up flights of stairs, down flights of stairs, around to rear shacks, back to the street; Reb Rainey and Franco Caltrone had harped on getting the broadsheets into people's hands as soon as possible, since they'd held off until the last day before the rally in order not to give the police too much time to prepare. Then, because Paolo had only flamboyant colorful bow ties in his personal haberdashery, he had to hunt up for Blue a proper long necktie—limp and floppy, Paolo laughed, just like the *borghesia* themselves—from a neighbor. And, Paolo pointed out at the last moment, Blue badly needed to get a shine on his scuffed and faded shoes. So by the time Blue hurried in Paolo's suit down to Market Street, he feared he was cutting it close to get into the hotel in time to hear Pankhurst.

As he emerged from the shadows of the big office buildings along Montgomery Street and onto Market, Blue ran into the back of a large crowd, several hundred strong, filling the street in front of the Palace and blocking traffic in both directions. From across the wide avenue he could see a banner strung between two utility poles on the far side of the street, directly in front of the hotel entrance. Two figures, each high up on a pole, held onto opposite ends of the banner. One of the

145

figures was calling out to the crowd, who were replying with cheering and lusty-voiced calls of their own. Blue couldn't make out what was being said, but he could read the banner:

WORKING MEN PREPARE TO DIE!
$O THE BARON$ CAN MAKE THEIR PROFIT$

As Blue edged his way into the street he could see more clearly the two banner-holding figures who were clinging to the wooden poles, each with the help of linemen's foot spurs and a waist harness. The one haranguing the crowd was a diminutive, white-haired woman; the other was a lanky young woman whose extremely long hair was blowing around madly in the ineluctable west wind that cooled the oceanside city every summer afternoon. Blue continued through the crowd until he could see their faces clearly: Dr. B and Meg.

At the bottom of Dr. B's pole was a knot of police, alternately yelling up at her and arguing the situation with several firefighters who seemed considerably less agitated than the cops. Blue knew that a number of firemen's wives were among the patients at Dr. B's North Beach free clinic. So, Blue guessed, the firemen here were in no hurry to interfere with Dr. B's pole protest which, judging from the women's special footgear and harnesses, must also have had some assistance from a lineman or two. Dr. B was now exchanging remarks with one of the cops, and after she directed some particular comment at him— Blue was too far away to hear—accompanied by a scolding gesture, the man brought his eyes back to ground level, moved his head slightly from side to side, said something privately to the cop next to him, and moved away from the pole. Perhaps, it occurred to Blue, some police wives were also patients of Dr. B.

Blue made his way toward Meg's pole. Holding onto both banner and pole while fighting the buffeting wind, Meg remained in a fixed position looking out over the heads of the crowd. Blue planted himself a ways out from the pole, in line with the direction she was facing. There was lots of jostling and arm waving and rowdy cheering and sloganeering from the crowd, such that calling out to her seemed futile. So Blue waited and watched, and when finally she glanced near to where he was standing, he waved his arm and managed to catch her attention. Her expression of anxious excitement softened, and she smiled at him. A big smile. Blue grinned back and started nudging his way through the crowd toward her pole, hoping to actually speak with her if he got close enough. But after a few steps he stopped. At the base of the pole, alternately craning up at Meg and looking nervously at three nearby cops haranguing her, was Treat.

Fuckin' hell, Blue said to himself, this guy's like dog shit in Dublin: everywhere I step.

Meg now turned her head to watch Dr. B, who was launching into another round of passionate anti-Preparedness speechifying. Blue looked up to see people leaning out of the hotel windows and was reminded of his reason for being there and of the fact that he was already running behind time. He decided to shake off the whole Meg and Treat bother and head inside the Palace to try to catch some of Pankhurst.

A cordon of police was guarding the hotel's front entrance. Notwithstanding his spiffy outfit, Blue wanted no close attention from them or from the hotel employees stationed just behind them, evidently to identify hotel guests and event invitees. So he went around the side of the huge hotel, passed by the other main entrance on New Montgomery Street, and circled to quiet little Jessie Street in the rear. There was a back entrance to the hotel there, which Blue knew of from his many years of trekking to and from Flaherty's boxing gym, which was also on Jessie, though further along, in a more plebeian part of town near the Civic Center.

As he turned the corner, Blue saw a large covered touring car parked outside the hotel's rear steps; a liveried driver stood next to it. Blue hesitated, then continued toward the rear entrance after realizing it was a good thing for his own chances that other people were going in and out here. As Blue neared, a man and a woman came out of the hotel; the driver opened the car's rear door. The man was lean, middle-aged, sporting long, swept-back dark hair and some kind of fancy military uniform; he held a large plumed cavalry-type hat at his side. The woman was long and lithe and well-dressed in a tailored suit and stylish hat; as she stopped to put on a coat, Blue saw her clearly: the woman from the ferry on the morning of Blue's return to the city. Probably because he was staring at her—trying to come up with her name—from just a few feet away, the woman returned Blue's look but evinced no recognition: this well-washed, clean-shaven, hair-combed man in a dandy suit and tie offered her no connection to the soiled, scruffy, bearded, swollen-faced character who had engaged her in banter on the ferry some two weeks before. As soon as she had her coat on, she ducked into the car with the military man and they rolled away.

Jameson. Blue was able to call up the name only after the car had driven off. He also recalled that at the Ferry Building she'd directed the baggage boys to Market and Second Street, which must have been here, to the Palace. And he considered for a moment the fact that two weeks later she seemed still to be staying in the hotel. From which he deduced two things: first, that she must have a lot of money, in order to spend so long at one of the city's most expensive hotels; and second, that she was likely an outsider in town, or at least something of a loner, because why else would a woman, who appeared to be of a certain class, still be staying on her own in a hotel? The having money part didn't interest Blue. But the outsider, loner part did. At least vaguely. He was still focused on getting into the hotel to see Pankhurst, and still slightly agitated by the sight of Meg and Treat. So he spent no more time chewing on these inferences about the Jameson woman. But he did stow them away.

Blue finally got into the hotel and made his way to the Garden Court. He loitered in the central passageway next to the main doors into the Court, waiting for a moment when he could slip inside unobtrusively. His chance came after only a few minutes, under the cover of loud applause and the bustle of chairs and attendees moving about. Unfortunately for Blue, this disruption signaled the end of the gathering, and the only glimpse he got of Emmeline Pankhurst was of her black-clad back as she was led out a door on the opposite side of the great room.

~

Appears I'm well connected. Mullaly. Though no thanks to me, I'd say. He seems to do all the work.

And through Mullaly to the Spreckels. Even if it seems that they're sometimes on different sides. Maybe something useful in that, for Lansing. The Spreckels, powerful people, but a different take on things. Can't sort out yet how different. Still, it's the sense I got from the doings today. The Preparedness thing at the hotel. All those society ladies but no Alma Spreckels. Then the Presidio, the cavalry goings-on. What was all that, exactly? Exercise? Just show? "My troops," Mullaly called them.

In his big auto on the way to the Presidio army grounds, I asked was it knowing what the Pankhurst woman would say about Germans that kept Alma Spreckels away from the Garden Court.

Oh, she wouldn't have come in any case, he told me. Preparedness is awkward for her. That was his word, awkward.

I asked how so.

Because of all her charity work for war victims. There are different ways of thinking about these things, he said. Different camps.

But you manage to be welcome in her camp too, I said.

Oh well, yes. Because, of course, in the end. . .

He didn't finish. Looking to the side, he told the driver to stop, then pointed to a tall pillar in the middle of Union Square, the big plaza.

Alma, he said. The statue.

On top of the pillar a large metal sculpture of a curvaceous young woman in a flowing gown, balancing on one foot atop a sphere. The globe, maybe? Holding a wreath in one hand, a trident in the other.

Victory, Mullaly said. Admiral Dewey. A monument to his victory over the Spanish. Manila Bay.

The Philippines. Again. Oh, Jamey, it seems to lie in wait for me here.

Alma was the model for the statue, Mullaly told me. As a girl she'd come from poor, he said, and made her way doing artist's modeling. Raised a brow when he said that, but the words came out not unkindly. And that's where Spreckels first spotted her, Alma auditioning to be the statue model. Spreckels chaired the committee to choose the monument's design. Alma got the job. Spreckels pursued her then on, Mullaly said. Married her a few years later.

Poor girl to artist's model to society queen. I'm quite liking her more.

Then we were on to the Presidio, the army post, up above the Gate. Rolling hills, thick with green, and big trees, pines and cypress and so many of those tall gums, perfectly straight, that they brought over from Australia and shot up so fast like weeds. Beautiful place. Hard to think of it as an army post. But then, Angel Island was the army's too. That gorgeous wooded isle in the middle of the bay. Where the army held you away, Jamey. Quarantine in paradise.

Quite a display there, at the Presidio. When we rolled up to the huge open marching grounds the cavalry men and their horses were already there, about 40 of them, all in perfect new uniforms. Cut quite a figure. One of the newspaper reporters there told me they weren't actually army but friends of Mullaly. His polo club. And their polo horses.

The reporter. From the Examiner, the Hearst paper. And a photographer. To cover the spectacle. Knew all about Mullally's horsemen. Seems Hearst loves it.

Stars and stripes flying all around the grounds, must have been a hundred of them, poles hammered in deep against the wind. And the bagpipers too, same as played the anthem at the Garden Court. I mentioned them to Mullaly, while he prepared his horse, joked was he trying to make me feel at home, Irish pipes?

Ah, they're not Irish, he said, more serious than my question. They're Scots.

I must have looked puzzled, so he explained. To some people we Irish are still a bit too dark. So to speak. Maybe not the Jamesons. But I suppose you know what I mean.

Was he saying I'd understand because I was a Carey? And how would he know that?

The Scots, on the other hand. Can't be any whiter than the Scots, he said. Can't be any more American. And what people see and hear in the background, without actually thinking on it, is as important as the foreground. Especially if it's the same thing over and over again, he said. So pipers, flags and soldiers, all together in public. As often as possible. Sets an image in the mind.

Heroes, I said to him, thinking back on the Garden Court speeches.

He smiled. Yes it's all of a picture, isn't it? he said, looking over the whole scene around us there.

25 or 30 big fancy autos parked at edges of the grounds. Drivers and other helpers set up chairs and blankets and picnic baskets for the people they'd brought there. Men, women, children. All dressed to the nines. I think I recognized a couple of men from Mullaly's "yacht" club. And some women from the Garden Court. Mullally rode off to join his polo men, limbering up their horses. More limousines arrived. I waited with the reporter.

Two large delivery vans pulled in, unloaded maybe 30 schoolboys, young teenagers. A scruffy bunch compared with the children who'd arrived with their families in the limousines. Some regular army officers milling about, and two of them went over to these boys and their minders, began speaking with them.

Still trying, the reporter said to me, watching the army men with the schoolboys, shaking his head.

Sorry? I said. I'm new to all this.

He explained that the Preparedness crowd had long been trying to get military training into the public schools.

Had a big war chest to pay for it, from something called the Pacific Coast Defense League. I looked blank, so he said, You know, the big banks' group. I let it go, but maybe something for Lansing? If he doesn't already know.

Mayor hasn't allowed it, though, the reporter went on. Most working folks don't like the idea, he said. And they vote.

In the auto going back to the hotel I asked Mullaly about it, the military training for school kids. Oh yes, he said, public schools. It's the workers' children who need it most. Moral development, he called it. Instills the habit of discipline. Produces higher-quality Americans.

I passed over that, chatted instead about the horsemen, praised their performance. Mullaly was modest, said they were only an auxiliary. But we're improving, he said. Train every week now, "as we get closer." Closer? I suppose I should have asked.

I did ask how his private horsemen were allowed to use the army's parade grounds, and with regular army men helping out. Oh, General Pershing, he said, left instructions. Told me Pershing had been in charge of Presidio a few years before, and they'd become friendly. Pershing even took Mullaly along to Mexico, chasing Villa, earlier this year.

I asked him when Pershing had been here. In '13 and '14, he said. Right after Pershing came back the second time from the Philippines.

General Pershing, I said, quite some friend to have.

Well, more like good acquaintances, he said. Who see eye to eye. And with a close mutual friend.

I thought that might be something worth knowing about, for Lansing, so I asked, Anyone I've met?

No, not from here, he said. General Wheeler. Old friend of the family. From down home.

I went silent. Couldn't catch my breath.

Joseph Wheeler? I managed to ask.

That's right, Fightin' Joe Wheeler. He and Pershing ran a show together in the Philippines war, back in the early days. They finally let old Confederate Joe loose again, he said. Then asked me did I know him.

I turned away, said that I didn't. It's just that my husband, I told him, served under Wheeler. In those same early days.

Ah, your late husband. He said it in a way that seemed to know more about Jamey than just that he was gone.

My husband, yes, I said. General Wheeler his commander. In the Philippines.

I said no more. There was such a throbbing in my chest.

11

Blue stationed himself in front of the bakery on the northern, uphill corner of Stockton and Filbert Streets at the edge of Washington Square, one block further along Stockton from the *Volontá* rooms. The spot offered several advantages: it gave Blue a view down and across all of the square, along the verges of which the observant Catholics were passing up to and back from Sunday mass at Saints Peter and Paul Church one block further up on Filbert; he could see and somewhat hear the haranguing birth control speakers who'd set up on the side of the square directly in front of where the new cathedral was being erected; he'd be able to catch early sight of any massed police charge, which, if it happened, would probably come along Stockton; that part of the corner would almost certainly remain unblocked, and safe from projectiles, if things came to that, since *focaccia* from the bakery's wood-fire ovens was as hallowed by nonbelievers as it was by churchgoers, the neighborhood's very heated culinary schism—between those who revered *cipollotti* baked into the top crust and those who disdained any such baroque adornment (the bakery produced both)—not falling along confessional fault lines; and heading further north along Stockton from that corner would most likely offer Blue a safe retreat if he stuck with his intention not to join what had the makings of a fracas-to-be.

His intention not to join. Blue certainly considered the struggle over birth control to be worthy of his serious attention. Not least because it involved a frontal attack on the authority of the Church, for which he harbored a special loathing. And he definitely had no aversion to a street battle, into which the rally had a fair chance to deteriorate. But over the years, his assessments about when to jump into such melees had become more nuanced, the urge to use his skilled fists more tempered. In part because he had other things to do: he'd come to understand that his other special talent could be much more useful, more consequential, than his forays into ad hoc punch-ups—his technical assistance during the power company strikes just before he'd left San Francisco three years before and his similar involvement in London with the aborted suffragette attack at Deptford being prime exemplars. And if he was to continue providing that more serious kind of support, he needed to avoid the sorts of attention from police—harassment, arrests with or without cause, and most of all surveillance—that could result from too much notoriety achieved in street-level political scrimmages. There was also, as he was reminded at the docks upon his arrival back in the city, the serious risk of disabling injury, notwithstanding his one-on-one prowess: reminded by the bloody wound to Warren Billings's head that day; reminded by reports of a half-dozen men hospitalized after that dockside clash, one of them having been shot by a strikebreaker; reminded by his glimpse of Elijah's brother Isaiah viciously beating the prone longshoreman next to the pier.

Still, despite his resolve not to join any fighting that might erupt that Sunday morning, he wanted to be there, curious to see what would happen, to take the pulse of his old neighborhood after having been so long away. In particular, he wanted to see what members of the *Volontá* group might get up to. For future reference. How far they were willing to go. There was the Montjuïc picture that they'd moved to their front window; and, as at Montjuïc, this morning there would be a procession of churchgoers; and... and what?

When Blue first got to the square that morning, interactions between protestors and parishioners were fairly tame. Some *Volontá* men and a number of other men and women—Blue recognized some men from the Latin workers' local and a couple of women who used to work in Barbary Coast dancehalls—were stationed alongside and within the square, handing the birth control leaflets to people who were gathering in the square, and proffering them to churchgoers who passed by on the sidewalks. Some of the churchgoers accepted a leaflet without comment; others refused and looked away or spat words of rejection. But to that point no one on either side had gotten physical.

Soon a huge gray-haired woman—whom Blue had known forever, long respected in the neighborhood as a widow who'd raised a brood of ten children, somehow keeping them all mostly out of trouble and harm's way, supporting them through her work as the waterfront's most efficient fish gutter—climbed the wood box platform that had been jury-rigged directly across from the massive church under construction and began speaking. Although Blue couldn't make out much of what she was saying in her crackled leathery voice, he could tell that she was not only speechifying but also directly addressing—probably by name—some of the passing churchgoers, which seemed to be raising the temperature of things. She got several rousing cheers from the crowd.

Blue could see a two-man police team just below him on the corner of the square; another pair was on the downhill side of the speakers' box. One of the pair near Blue was clutching a rolled-up copy of the leaflet and both cops were looking at the gathering, but neither showed any stress from, or even much interest in, the crowd and they paid no mind at all to the woman speaker. Blue immediately understood their lack of engagement: he recognized one of the cops in each pair, from their long tenure in the neighborhood, and knew that they were of Irish stock. Their partners, too, looked like they had no clue about the heretical contents of the leaflet or of the speaker's provocations, both of which were in Italian. It was a long-standing police department policy not to have cops patrolling the neighborhoods they came from, an arrangement that encouraged them to mete out peremptory justice with less restraint while reducing the risk of repercussions for their home lives. But a consequence, in neighborhoods where English was a secondary language, was that cops often did their jobs through a gauze of linguistic incomprehension. At Washington Square that morning, these non-Italian-speaking cops seemed not to have a clue what was on the agenda.

That soon changed. A red-faced priest came flapping down Filbert Street from the church and confronted the two closest cops. The priest held a copy of the leaflet and began excitedly reading out loud and translating it for the cops, alternately jabbing a finger at them and gesturing violently toward the woman on the platform. The cops looked more annoyed than impressed by the priest's fulminations but, nonetheless, after a couple of minutes started slowly moving down toward the speaker's platform. The woman speaker now stepped down and was replaced on the box by the *Volontá* group's Genio Forcone, of the previous day's cheese-on-clams argument. Genio immediately spotted the cops heading toward him and, rather than beginning a speech, directed the crowd's attention to the pair, loudly and sarcastically asking the assembly what these gentlemen might possibly be doing there, then switched to English and repeated the question, in a faux polite tone, to the policemen themselves. The cops stopped a few yards away from the platform, in part it seemed from surprise at being directly addressed, but also because a number of men and women from the crowd, by now an impressive couple of hundred strong, advanced to put themselves between the cops and Genio.

Seeing this, the priest scuttled a few steps across the road and banged on the door of a house on the corner opposite Blue. When a woman opened, the priest pushed his way past her inside.

Now the second pair of cops headed toward the platform. But they too were quickly cut off and nudged toward a midway point between the platform and the edge of the main crowd, where the first two cops had now also been herded. Blue no longer had a clear view of them, so could not tell whether the cops made a foolhardy move toward Genio or instead were preemptively jostled by people in the crowd, but in either event they were now being harried toward the rear of the platform. There was an empty space along the sidewalk there, a kind of buffer zone that allowed free passage for churchgoers, and the four cops took advantage of the opening to begin a slow retreat up Filbert toward the corner where Blue was standing.

At first, the cops remained facing the crowd, backing up the street, brandishing but not attempting to use their batons. About two dozen men and women followed them, catcalling and gesturing hostilely but keeping a distance of ten feet or so. Halfway up the block, though, one of the cops turned his back on the group and began walking faster, then the other three cops also turned and sped up.

It's said that the worst thing to do when confronted in the wild by a predatory animal is to run. But these cops were from the city: as they made their escape up Filbert, they began to scurry, and the chase was on.

Several people from the chasers quickly closed the gap on the fleeing cops. But no one touched them; it looked to Blue that the pack was enjoying the pleasure of the chase itself, the theater of it, without needing to inflict any physical damage. Especially since the cops themselves hadn't struck or arrested anyone or tried to shut down the speechifying on the square.

Their faces twisted with anxiety and exertion, the four cops now turned just in front of Blue and went north on Stockton, the hecklers close behind, bellowing abuse, most of it in a variety of Italian dialects the cops wouldn't understand but the flavor of which they could certainly taste. The cops rumbled past the Telegraph Hill neighborhood center, where Dr. B ran her free clinic, and reached a local firehouse just beyond. The double wide doors were open; the cops dove inside.

The chase pack stopped and seethed on the pavement outside the firehouse. Probably wary of how the firemen would respond if they entered, and undoubtedly respectful of firehouse sanctity—firefighters' efforts during the '06 earthquake and ensuing citywide conflagration were universally admired—none of them tried to follow the cops inside. There seemed to be no one in the group taking a lead, and Blue wondered how long the stalemate would hold, curious to see whether the pack's anger would overcome its restraint and force a nastier turn.

Nastiness arrived soon enough, but from another direction. Blue heard shouting behind him and turned to see a swarm of uniforms surging up Stockton from the other side of the square. Twenty-five or thirty truncheon-waving cops were coming from the direction of their headquarters at the Hall of Justice, a few blocks away at the edge of the Barbary Coast. The brigade stopped at the far corner of the square to assess the situation, apparently trying to locate their fellow cops. The priest, who likely had telephoned the police from the house he'd forced his way into, was back on the corner, screeching and frantically waving to them, pointing along Stockton in the direction the four neighborhood cops had fled. The head of the large police detachment spotted him, and the big group of cops then hurriedly followed along Stockton, shouldering people out of their way but otherwise not bothering with the crowd in the square or the speaker on the platform.

Blue sensed that as soon as this big gang of police reached the firehouse and the crowd outside it, all hell would break loose. He decided not to risk getting swept up in the chaos and hurried ahead of them on Stockton. As he neared the neighborhood center, down its stairs and onto the street bounded the wiry, trousers-sporting—amid everything going on, Blue was struck that he'd only ever seen her in trousers—figure of Meg. She looked startled at the commotion over by the firehouse, and doubly so when she heard her name called and turned to see Blue rushing up to her. Without trying to explain, he took her by the arm and led her across to the quieter side of the street. He looked back to see the police reinforcements arriving and the priest along with them, screeching and gesturing violently toward the firehouse.

"*Va' fa'n cul*, you fucking pope-wanker!" Blue yelled back at the priest, accompanying the curse with the appropriate forearm-grabbing, raised-fist gesture.

"What?" Meg followed Blue's line of sight.

Blue just shook his head and hurried her past the firehouse. When they were clear of it, she gently but resolutely disengaged her arm from his and stopped.

"What is all this?" she asked, looking back at the crowd. "From the square? The leaflet?"

"Yeah, they chased some cops in there. But now all these other cops... It's likely to get ugly."

"Huh. And you? I mean, I would've thought..."

"Yeah, well, I like to keep my options open, so I do."

Meg considered for a moment. "Oh, that's... interesting."

Blue bit the inside of his cheek. "Well, not always." He waited to see how badly he'd erred, and when she didn't turn away, he took heart. They were standing at the corner of Lombard Street. A few feet down the steep hill a bright red motorcycle was parked.

"So," he pointed at the bike. "I've got this machine for the day. What do you say?"

"That's Mooney's bike, isn't it?"

"Mm. We, ah, do each other favors. So... As I'm recollecting, you did say, 'Maybe another time.' Am I right, so?"

"I suppose I did."

"And two can ride it. You know, if they're going the same way.'"

❦

Sunday morning. I've been sitting here in this elegant room on this elegant brocaded chair brushing out my hair. Brushing. And brushing.

How we used to sit like this, Maggie, you and I, one of us on our so very different chair in our so very different room, the other standing behind and brushing hair. Is it something you think of too?

I miss it so.

We began those quiet times together, brushing each other's hair, when you were still so small, soon after your father left for the Philippines. And we carried on while we were here in San Francisco, in the little rooms on Clay Street, waiting for him to return to us from quarantine. And then, when he was here with us, bodily here, waiting for him to return from his sorrowful silence. Which he never did. And after, through all the years after. After he was gone for good. We would sit and brush and brush, you and I. And talk. We would talk. Not much, it's true. But the sound of your voice, speaking softly, only to me. And my simple happiness, at touching your hair, your head, without you wanting to wriggle away.

Most of all, though, your touch on me. I know you loved

me brushing your hair, and the pleasure I got from your pleasure was a gift. Ah but when you were the one doing the brushing, that was of a different order. The heat of it. The sweetness. Not just in my hair, my head, but slipping under my skin and sliding down my neck and through my shoulders and coursing into the very center of me. All of me, the whole world, collapsing down into a single ball of warmth. And when, finally, you'd stop, I'd continue sitting, unable to move, or speak.

I wanted it to go on forever.

Less and less often as you got older. Inevitable, I suppose. In the natural order of things. But for me, my wanting it, my hunger for it, never slackened. My desire to hold onto that connection, different from any other. With you, with my child. I can't properly express to you what I felt in those last years when you were still at home and when, oh so rarely, you would bless me with a simple touch. Your hand laid on my hand, to calm me when you saw me upset. Your arm taking mine as we walked. And every once in a great while a hug that came from you, a hug not merely received but given. Such pleasure I would feel. And gratitude. Yes. Overwhelming gratitude. When you'd physically touch me.

Perhaps all the more because your father's touch was no more. I don't know.

But oh, most of all, when you brushed my hair.

$\sim$

Meg didn't try to compete with the motorcycle's roar, except once shouting in Blue's ear, "Where are we going?" when he took the bike past the city limits. But there was no uneasiness in her voice, and she accepted with a good-spirited smile Blue's response of a wave toward the forested hills that rose up south of the city between the bay and the sea.

The noisy ride gave Blue time to ponder. What the hell was he thinking—or not thinking—bringing Meg along? He had something important to do. Which didn't include a dallying overture with this girl. Or whatever this was. Which he didn't know. But then, it didn't exclude whatever this was, either. Because, he realized, having a female companion along offered him a patina of innocent purpose, an easily digestible explanation for anyone who might get curious about what he was up to.

So he headed for Palmiro Testa's Seven Mile House in Visitation City, just past the San Francisco line. Unlike bars and shops back in the big city, Palmiro kept his combination tavern and sundry provisions store open on Sundays. In part, as a stick in the eye to the blue laws passed by San Francisco three years before when it cleansed itself in anticipation of the world rushing in for the Panama-Pacific Exposition. But also as good business, to serve food and drink to the many workers from San Francisco who used their one day off to come to the fields in Vis City and tend their communal vegetable gardens, as well as those who just came to enjoy the gambling-enlivened poolroom in the back, the four brothel cribs above it, or the main room's evening music and dancing.

Blue pulled up in front of the tavern, shut off the bike and turned to Meg: "Wash out the dust?"

It was more than a mere figure of speech. Once outside the city proper, the roads were dry powdery dirt, which meant that Blue and Meg had eaten a fair amount of it.

"Well, since you haven't told me where we're headed," Meg replied with good humor but also a shadow of reproach, "or how far we're going, I'd say that's probably a good idea."

Though Sunday was the Seven Mile House's busiest day, at this still-morning hour the big front barroom-cum-shop had only a handful of customers. Most people who came out to Vis City to work their gardens headed straight for the fields, only repairing to Palmiro's at lunchtime or when their work was done for the day, and most of the tavern's other regular patrons, particularly its ample supply of gamblers and carousers, were not out of bed yet. Blue led Meg up to the bar where Palmiro was serving a customer and spouting barkeep wisdom from behind his enormous droopy moustache.

"*Who's this?*" Palmiro asked in a mock gruff tone, in Italian. "*Don't I know you?*"

"Yes, Miro, you do," Blue answered in English, in deference to Meg. "It's Baldo."

"Ah, yes it is." He paused. "But, oh, Baldino, your mother. *Ripos' in pace.* She was a gift to us all."

"Thanks, Miro... It's good to see you again. Been a long time."

"And who's this?"

"Oh, yeah, this..."

Meg cut him off to speak for herself: "Meg Carey. Pleased, I'm sure."

"Really? You sure? Maybe ask around first." He laughed and held out a hand. Meg smiled and shook it.

"You from the city?" Palmiro asked her.

"Well, I don't know. I suppose. For a little while now, anyway."

"Yeah, she's... Well, she used to stay at Belle Lavin's place."

"Aahh." Palmiro took a closer look, especially at the trousers. "Say are you maybe that painter girl?"

Meg looked sideways at Blue, as if he were somehow responsible for this piece of information having made it all the way to the Seven Mile House. He held up his hands in denial.

"Small town sometimes," he said by way of defense.

They each had a glass of beer, then bought some of Palmiro's house made *coppa*, a sourdough loaf, and some soft farmer's cheese, and from a barrel behind the bar filled a bottle with *primitivo* that Palmiro made with grapes from his cousin up in Sonoma. Blue then drove Meg the short hop over to a jumble of raised vegetable beds crisscrossing a stretch of flatlands at the base of the hills. He parked the motorbike and led her over to a particular section of beds, along the way greeting a few people who were working their plots.

"These were ours," he told Meg, indicating the garden beds. "My mother, my brother and me. Well, not just ours, but the ones we always worked, with some other Sicilians." He said a cheerful hello to a couple working in the plot who seemed surprised and pleased to see him, but after the brief salutation he didn't respond to their eagerness, in Sicilian, to engage him further. He turned away and led Meg back toward the bike.

"It's hard, so it is. Coming back here. My mother. I didn't realize."

Meg said nothing and both were quiet for a bit, but as they neared the motorcycle the silence seemed long. "And your brother?" she asked. "Where's he?"

Blue did not stop or look at her as he said, "Gone."

Head still down, he swung onto the bike. After a moment, though, he looked up at Meg, managing a smile that took effort but felt right and good when it arrived.

"C'mon. I've got some crackin' spots to show you."

He was relieved to see her distress recede at the rapid return of his own good cheer. She climbed on behind him.

The motorbike had an easy time moving up a narrow dirt road a short way into the hills. But soon Blue turned onto a narrow path that became damp and rutted and they had to stop. They left the bike and walked along as the path wound its way amid thick brush and manzanita, then dipped into a dark canyon within dense stands of willow, madrone and bay laurel.

"Not bad, eh?" he said of the canyon hideaway with its shade and cool air and its deep, lush green. "My brother and I used to come here. When we were kids. Hunt rabbits. Wild pigs. Even a deer sometimes. Well, once. With no luck. We'd come out here in someone's truck from North Beach, usually one of the other Sicilians. We were supposed to work on the vegetables with our ma, but she didn't mind if we went off with our little pop gun after we helped out for a bit. And the others, they all knew how much work my ma put in, so they had no problem with us bunkin' off."

They settled themselves in a little sun-mottled glade by a rivulet they could hear but not see, laid out the bread, cheese and *coppa* on Blue's rough serge jacket and opened the wine. For a couple of minutes they didn't speak but just looked around them, chewed the food, passed the bottle.

"So, listen," Meg finally broke the silence. "Back in town. With that priest…"

"Ah, well, sure you know how it is. You told me you went to their schools, so."

"Mm, I did. Had my fill of the nuns. But... that back there. I mean... you... that was... something fierce."

"Yeah, well, that feckin' priest. We got us a history, me and him. Though he probably doesn't remember how it started."

Meg looked at him expectantly, moved her hand slightly, opening her palm.

"Well all right, I don't know how you're getting me talkin' so, but anyways... So I was maybe six or seven, and I was out with m' da on some skiparound or other in the neighborhood. And we were crossing the square, Washington Square, when that priest, he's an Irishman, Joseph by name, just fresh out from seminary back then, so he was, and the new number two collar at Peter and Paul, and what does he do but decides he's going to have for himself a big old dog, some kind of wolfdog it seems to me in memory, but I don't know, I was only small. Anyway, this huge nasty piece of dog that I suppose made the priest feel the grand man. And m' da and me were crossing the square, and here comes Joe the priest crossing the other way and he's got the great fucking huge dog... sorry, feckin' huge dog... on a lead in front of him with his big old fangs growling, and it's looking at me, the dog, and it strains out tight on the lead, and I wasn't at all sure that dog wasn't about to leap away from the priest, or that he'd let it leap away, and come straight for me, and so I jumped back and ran around m' da's legs and grabbed on to him, hiding myself away as best I could. And that priest, that feckin' weasel of a priest, he doesn't pull the dog back or anything, no, he just lets it keep lunging and snarling at me, and he actually starts laughing, the priest, and then he says, 'Ah, now, don't be a little scaredy girl now. Be a man, yourself. You've got to teach him to be a man, now,' he says to me da, 'not scared of no dogs and such.' And m' da, for about the only time I can remember in my whole life that he did something I was proud of, or at least happy for, because I didn't really know what he meant by it, m' da he says, 'Oh, no, you've got it wrong, mister'—he never called a priest 'father' or any of that guff—'He's not afraid of dogs,' he says, m' da. 'He's afraid of priests.'

"And the priest said nothing after that, I don't think, I just remember him having this sickly sorta smiley sneer on his red ugly face and walking away."

Blue reached for the wine bottle and took a swig. He looked at Meg but didn't register her expression, too deep he was in the memory.

"And then this same priesty boyo, it wasn't long after, I don't know, maybe a few months, and I was with my brother Declan. M' da had disappeared again, like he always did, and things were tough around our house, making ends meet, my ma had taken sick at her work, you see. . . Well, anyway, we were at Panelli's, my brother and me, the butcher shop on Columbus, we'd gone there to get some *prosciutto* bones. If you knew to ask for them they'd sell you just the bones, for almost nothing, doncha know, after they'd sliced off all the meat to sell, and my ma would scrape and scrape the leftover bits off the bone to make a few pastas with, and then when there was nothing at all left to scrape she'd boil them, the bones, make a broth, then dump whatever vegetables into it for a few meals more. . . Sorry, I kind got lost there. Where was I?"

He took another drink; Meg drank too.

"So Declan and I are looking to go into Panelli's, the butcher's. But there's that monster dog again, tied up outside, and growling and snarling at us who's trying to go in, and your man the priest, he's inside, we can see him through the big front window, and he hears the dog making all this noise, and he looks out at us, the priest, but he doesn't move, doesn't do a thing, and finally Declan leads me around to a back door and we go inside and into the front of the shop, and the priest, he just looks at us like we're nothing, so he does, and soon it's his turn and he's telling the butcher, he's saying, 'A pound of your sirloin there, Mr. Panelli. No, no, not the round, make it the top sirloin, the best of the top' or something like that, all puffed up and snooty like. And while the butcher is getting the meat, our Declan, who was always full of cheek and had learned at m' da's knee all about the Church and priests and all that, he says to the priest, Declan says, 'Pretty fine eating there for a priest, ain't it, padre?' And the priest looks down his nose at us and says, 'The sirloin, you mean? Oh,' he says. 'That's for the dog.'"

Meg stared for a moment, then shook her head and said: "Yeah, the nuns too, back in my school days… Well, maybe not *that* bad. But plenty of them sour and nasty. Mostly, I just learned to ignore them. They hate that, you know."

"Aye, if only…"

She looked at him quizzically.

"Look," he continued, "I mean, it's not just the one-off arsehole priest, you know? It's the whole feckin' shebeen, innit?"

He saw Meg move back slightly from the rising heat of his reply.

"Sorry," he said softly, "it's… Never the mind. What say we move?" He picked up the bottle and began squeezing the cork back in.

Meg didn't budge. "'Never the mind,'" she repeated his words. With the whisper of a challenge, Blue thought.

He stopped fiddling with the bottle and considered her. What to say? How much to say? Because his feelings about the Church went far deeper—both older and newer, more personal and more political— than just the scars from his childhood scaldings by the dog-wielding priest.

The personal had begun before he was born. His mother Maricchia had been a sort of mail-order bride, sent halfway around the world as a twenty-year-old to marry a young man from a neighboring Sicilian town who several years before had gone to America, to California, and after a time wrote home that he was about to strike it rich in the gold fields. Well, the letters actually said silver rather than gold, but both the boy's family and Maricchia's surely knew what he must have meant, since the California gold rush was famous. The young man had agreed to the proposed marriage arranged by the families but neglected to send money for Maricchia's fare. So over the course of a year her family scraped together—Maricchia was one of five sisters who had to be married off—the punishing amount for her trip halfway round the world, and finally sent her on her way. When Maricchia's nightmarish months-long journey—to Palermo, Naples, Genoa, across the Atlantic to New York, then all the way around Cape Horn—finally ended in San Francisco in the autumn of 1880, however, the young man was nowhere to be found. The address he'd given was indeed a large house of three stories with many rooms, as one of his letters had described it. But instead of a *borghese* mansion as Maricchia and her family had imagined, it turned out to be a raucous boardinghouse on the waterfront where, yes, the landlady told Maricchia, the young man had, in fact, stayed but he hadn't been heard from for months. The last anyone had seen of him was in Nevada, where he'd recently returned to the mountains to try again for the get-rich silver strike that had eluded him in the several years he'd already spent toiling there.

This desperately disappointing news about Maricchia's putative *fidanzato* came from another miner—translated by a Sicilian woman at the boardinghouse—who'd known the young man in the Nevada silver fields, but who'd had more success himself at the mining game and was now back in San Francisco to begin enjoying his good fortune. He spoke a little Italian, this man—having worked for several years alongside a variety of Italianate miners—and so was able to communicate a bit in person with Maricchia.

The truth was he had suspected, this miner from Nevada, that Maricchia might appear at the boardinghouse one day; the young Sicilian villager had told the man all about her. Or, as much about her as the young Sicilian knew, having last seen her when they were still little more than children. And he'd shown the man a recent photograph of the lovely young girl, which Maricchia's family had sent to cement the match. So it might be said that this other man, this at least modestly successful miner, was expecting her. His name was Michael Cavanaugh.

Upon arriving in San Francisco only to find her betrothed gone, Maricchia had been bereft: she had no money; knew no one; and couldn't bring herself to write to her family for the hefty fare home because she knew they had nothing to send her. Plus the shame of it all.

A couple of local Sicilians helped her find occasional work and a bed in a sort of dormitory for young single women. It wasn't much.

Growing up, Maricchia and her family had been no more than routinely devotional. But Maricchia now found moments of calm, if not solace, by attending mass—and even more so by ducking into its dark quiet confines at nonceremonial times—at Saints Peter and Paul in North Beach, the neighborhood where she'd landed. So at least there was the Church.

There was also Michael Cavanaugh. He was young but seasoned, passably attractive, and reasonably civilized—he spoke some Italian, after all—despite what seemed to Maricchia an overfamiliarity with alcohol. Moreover, from all appearances he was financially flush from his Nevada mining strike; he'd even bought his own flat in the neighborhood. And he was a Catholic, albeit an Irish one and never seen at the church.

The courting rituals Maricchia had observed back home were highly ritualized, glacially paced, and closely monitored by family. In San Francisco, by contrast, it was all wide open. And fast. So Cavanaugh's courting of her seemed to Maricchia florid, his attentions overweening. On the other hand, she could see that he made considerable effort to remain respectful. Most of all, he was persistent. She held out for a time, because she thought she had to. But the girls at the rooming house told her what a catch she'd made, that she'd better latch on to him for good before someone else slid underneath him and stole him away.

When Cavanaugh finally was able to coax Maricchia to see his top-floor flat—in the middle of the day, while he pretended to retrieve something, and with one of the rooming house boarders as chaperone—with its view of the bay and the Golden Gate, and its back-garden apple and lemon trees, she knew she might make it her home. And who was to say no?

Well, someone, as it turned out. The senior priest at Saints Peter and Paul was an elderly Genovese who had his ear close to the neighborhood ground. He heard tell of the courtship and knew of Michael Cavanaugh. Had an opinion about him, the lapsed-Catholic Irishman. And one day as Maricchia sat quietly by herself in the pews, the priest approached her and asked whether it was true that she was being wooed. When Maricchia hemmed and hawed but essentially confirmed the fact, the priest told her she needed to visit the confessional. Maricchia was surprised and taken aback; she had nothing to confess, she told the priest. "Oh, but Jesus knows different," he said.

Maricchia avoided Peter and Paul for a while after that, but the damage had been done: she'd been anointed with a drop of guilt.

Cavanaugh soon proposed, and Maricchia soon became pregnant. She was only a couple of months along, and no one yet knew, so a Church wedding was still in the picture. But Cavanaugh would have none of it. Maricchia had made the mistake of telling him what the priest had said to her, which only added to his existing deep hostility; he wanted nothing to do with "them bead-snappin' sin grubbers." Since her pregnancy would soon be showing, Maricchia quickly gave up her argument with Cavanaugh about a Church wedding and went with him to city hall to do civil marriage papers.

During the pregnancy Maricchia kept away from Peter and Paul. And the neighborhood's church-going women—at the priest's suggestion if not outright behest, Maricchia presumed—kept away from her. Still, when Blue's older brother Declan was born, Maricchia insisted that he be baptized. Cavanaugh refused to participate, but he didn't try to stop her. Which turned out not to matter, because the priest wouldn't allow it anyway. In the eyes of the Church, he told Maricchia, she and Cavanaugh were unmarried. And so the bastard child of their union could not be baptized.

Maricchia was stunned. And badly wounded. In part because she feared for the immortal soul of her infant son, the jeopardy of which—a large second dose of guilt—the priest had clearly laid at her feet. But more, the priest's declaration confirmed her exclusion from the Church and its penumbra, which in North Beach of the time meant being shunned by many of the Italian women who otherwise would have been her natural pool of companionship, experience and support. This walling off of Maricchia marked the beginning of her withdrawal into herself, a shutting down of any hope that the world might have something to offer her, a withdrawal that would last for the remainder of her life, and which Blue was forced to watch, and to suffer silently with her, for her, during her long slow decline. Years later, when Michael Cavanaugh walked out on the family for good, the wider church-going community softened toward her. But the relenting was only partial, consisting mostly of tepid neighborliness that stopped well short of friendship, and from the priest a grudging acceptance, usually with an expression bordering on pity, of Maricchia's once-yearly appearance at Peter and Paul for Easter mass.

All of this left its mark on young Blue. On top of the legacy of utter disdain for the Church bequeathed to him by his father. Plus the aftertaste of his childhood encounters with the dog priest. But none of it would have amounted to much more than a garden-variety aversion toward the Church—his political objections to the institution not yet having matured—had it not been for Declan.

Blue's older brother had gone off to the Philippines war and Maricchia had gone off to church to pray for his deliverance. When the army's official death letter arrived, she went to the church to pray for his soul and to arrange a requiem mass for him. Which the old priest refused. Yes, a requiem mass for the unbaptized was possible, the priest told her, but only if the parents had intended to have him baptized and were somehow prevented.

But that's exactly what happened, Maricchia reminded the priest: she'd asked to have Declan baptized but he, the very same priest, had not allowed it. Ah, yes, the priest replied, he remembered. So, he said, if Maricchia would just bring Declan's father to the church, so that he could attest that he'd had the same intention for baptism as the mother...

On top of Declan's death, this rejection was crushing to Maricchia. It was a combination from which she never recovered.

As a result, Blue's rancor toward the Church burrowed deeper, becoming a seething personal rage that burned inside him and superheated all the subsequent anti-clerical antipathies he developed as he came of age within San Francisco's radical milieu, and which reached a boiling point years later when he was chased out of Ireland by the Church's claim to the police that his help with the Kiddies Scheme—to house and feed, in England and in Ulster, the children of Dublin's locked out workers—amounted to kidnapping young Catholics.

Seething. Personal. And too much of both, he felt at the nape of his neck, to expose to this girl Meg, this emotionally provoking, unsettling girl, whom he barely knew but who seemed so effortlessly to get around his guard and under his skin. So he decided on misdirection.

"All right, so." He put down the bottle. "But tell us, then. You must have read the leaflet from the square today, since sure you helped to paper up the thing, along with himself, your... printer friend. So now, is that something you can just ignore, the Church sticking its grubby nose all up into working women's privates? Or maybe you can so, not being down at the square this morning, as I recall."

"No, I wasn't," Meg said quietly but looking him in the eye. "I was at Lily's clinic."

Blue blinked. Swallowed. Because he knew that one of the main reasons Dr. B ran the clinic was to educate and minister to women on the very subject of the leaflet, and to sort them out when they got into a fix. Fuck me! he said silently to himself, thinking he'd blundered indelicately into this highly sensitive matter. Out loud he said, apologetic, "Oh, aye, so you were. And... well, sorry. It's none of my mind."

"Working," she said. "I was working."

"Ah. Of course." He tried not to sound surprised. Or relieved.

"Lily wants a nurse there, like Reb, or at least an almost-nurse, like me... I had some training back home, you see... to do the first talking off to the side about dicey things if a woman comes in who Lily doesn't know. To shield Lily a bit. From the law. Because if they arrest Lily, the whole clinic shuts down. So far the police have left her alone. But you never know."

"Yeah, you never know. And what with the feckin' Church trying to do its worst."

"Well, yes, them too, I suppose... You do have a mighty thorn about them, don't you?"

"Listen," he cut her off, "there's something I want to show you. What say?"

Meg took a glance back in the direction of the city, which Blue didn't fail to notice, but after a slight hesitation she nodded and they gathered up the remains of their meal.

Blue walked the motorbike back out through the glade. When they reached the trail, he and Meg got on and headed up the hill. The bike made more bumps and noise than progress, though, so after a few minutes Blue gave up and left it on the side of the trail, and they started walking up through the gradually thinning trees and brush.

"Declan and I," he said as they walked. "My brother. We'd always come up here at the end of the day, after we'd done with our little hunting trips down below, which truth be told didn't usually amount to anything, except for the thrill of it, for me, being alongside my brother, my big brother." He paused for a moment, allowing the memory to slough off a bit. "This trail thing wasn't here back then. It was just deer and wild pig tracks and such."

After a few more minutes they emerged onto an open hillside that, like another hill now visible south along the ridge, was naked of trees but lush with brush, shrub and tall grass. They were still about two hundred feet below the crest of the hill; Blue led Meg further up along a barely discernible path.

They reached the ridge top at a spot between two slightly higher crests. Meg drew in her breath at the view: in front of them, to the west, the sudden revelation of the Pacific, the immensity of the sea stretching away some twenty or thirty miles out where it disappeared behind a dense white wall, a bank of impenetrable fog the shimmer of which seemed to announce its imminent intention to close the distance and overwhelm all that lay before it, and just in front of the wall, glistening in the midday sun, a little group of island dots like a family of unsuspecting prey about to be swallowed from behind; looking behind her, the flatlands reemerged, with the tavern, a scattered settlement, and the vegetable beds dotting the ground, then the vast blue-grey expanse of bay and, ten miles across, a mirror image of flatlands and low hills on the other side; to the south, a narrow ridge of windswept, woodland-skirted hills like the one on which they stood, with the bay and the Pacific held simultaneously in peripheral vision; and to the north, the agglomeration of San Francisco sprawling across its own set of domesticated hills, its rows of pale houses ranging out in three directions from the downtown, and further in the distance, across the Golden Gate, deep green Mount Tamalpais looming like the watchful grown-up in a roomful of fractious children.

"I... had no idea," is all Meg could say as she took it all in. "Since I got here," she finally managed to add, "I've only been down in the city."

But Blue wasn't admiring. He was scowling, looking along the ridge tops to the south, then turning toward the northernmost ridge just beyond where he and Meg stood.

"Feckin' blight altogether."

He was looking at a line of identical metal towers, pyramids of thin beams and rods each forty or fifty feet high, that topped a half-dozen hills stretching several miles south. Connecting the towers, then heading down the northernmost hill toward the city, were electric power lines.

"I heard tell of them. But I had to see for myself. Like a stick in the eye, so they are."

"Does sort of spoil the spot a bit," Meg sympathized.

"A bit?"

"Yes, okay, *quite* a bit... I suppose they weren't here before. I mean, when you and your brother..."

Blue shook his head. "Nor even when I left a few years back."

"Well, there are an awful lot of people down there need electricity." Meg nodded toward the city.

"Oh, no. No, you see, that's why it gets me raging. The lines for the city, the public electricals, they're down there," Blue indicated the flatlands between the hills and the bay. "These here are private. Paid off all the right folks and got themselves a right-of-way. I'm just going to have a closer look."

Blue headed over to the nearest tower. After a few moments, Meg trailed behind. At the base of the tower Blue examined a corner foundation, peered up the length of the structure, then back down again at the corner. He paused for a moment, considering, then looked again closely at the spot where the tower's corner went into the ground. Suddenly he turned to Meg, whom he seemed to have forgotten.

"Oh," he said, as if she'd asked what he was doing. "Just curious. Dead interested in construction, so I am."

"Man of many hats."

"I suppose you could say... Except also *no* hats." He passed his hand over his uncovered head.

"Mm, now that you mention it."

To save it from blowing away, Meg had been forced by the ride to stuff her own hat halfway into the pocket of her jacket; it looked crushed and forlorn there as they both glanced at it. She reached up toward her head in a sort of mirror reflex of Blue's motion but could only pull one stray lock out of her eyes; despite the pins that still managed to hold parts of it in place, the rest of her long, thick, wind-blown hair was now a storm of solar flares.

"Yeah, seems everyone wears a topper these days. But mild as it is all the time, hereabouts," he nodded toward the glorious sun-swept bay, "I never could see the sense in 'em. And they always made my head feel captured-like. Besides, a hat could be a nuisance if you was to take a motorbike ride, eh? Though I guess it's not much better without one. I mean, with all that..." He gestured at her wilding hair.

"Yes," she touched her head. "It's just... I mean, I've always..."

"Oh, it's stunnin' lovely. Which is... a comfort, I'm sure. Even with a hat, eh?"

Meg's face showed a mild discomfort. "Well, anyway, hats can be useful, can't they? I mean, it does rain sometimes. 'Hereabouts,'" she lightly mocked his phrase.

"Well, yeah, true enough. But I'm a city boy, and in cities there's always an indoors close to hand. Also, if you think about it, with everyone else wearing a hat, it makes me easy to spot in a crowd... If someone was a mind to." He smiled, but not too broadly. At least, so he hoped.

"True... if someone was." She glanced over his shoulder. "Speaking of the city..."

Blue followed her gaze, then his mouth turned down. "Ah, right you are, so. Don't want to be getting anyone agitated, do we?"

"What does that mean?"

"Nothing. Just, I suppose..."

"Well don't," she said sharply. "It's not like that. And anyway, he doesn't get agitated."

"Yeah, come to think, I didn't see him at the square this morning. Got to be careful 'bout that agitation."

"Excuse me. He does his part. He just doesn't… lose his head over things."

"Ah, right so. But tell me, wouldn't that be terrible altogether? Never losing your head over anything?"

Meg seemed to consider for a moment—whether about Treat or about him, Blue couldn't tell—then looked hard at Blue: "Why are we talking about this?" she said crossly. "I need to get back. Some people, you know, have things to do."

They didn't speak on the way down to the motorcycle, and Blue was glad for the machine's roar on the ride back to the city. She asked him to let her off at the Barleycorn.

"Thanks for the tour. See you around," is all she said.

12

Each time Kate thought about going again to see Breyer, the Bureau of Investigation man, she became aware of a dull ache behind her eyes. He'd been polite enough, if stiffly so, on the one occasion she'd been to his office, and had said he "stood ready" to assist her. But beneath his politesse she'd sensed something contentious, hostile even. And while she hadn't actively tried to dissect it—she knew too little about him—she found that whenever she considered visiting him again, her mind would roam across various possible explanations for the lack of goodwill she'd sensed: that she was a woman was the most obvious, a phenomenon she knew well from her years of important, top-quality, low-pay, never openly appreciated work at the Boston law firm; that she was an amateur, not an experienced police or political operative; that she'd been sent from the weighty but clueless East Coast into what Breyer felt was his professional bailiwick, even though officially his Bureau's brief only covered criminal matters, not the political reconnoitering Kate had been sent to do; that she had what might appear to him a bloated financial check from Lansing that shaded Breyer's own constrained office budget; or that Breyer believed that the question she'd been asked to look into—the likelihood and level of support from San Francisco's business elite if America entered the war—was already settled and needed no exploration. Or was there more? Other things that Breyer somehow knew, or thought he knew, and that made him contrary: Jamey's complicated history? The dark clouds that obscured his death?

Still, Kate felt she needed Breyer. Connections to the local elite made through the Jameson family introduction letters were continuing to prove fertile—she'd attended two mansion dinner parties the previous week—but had led only to one side of the story, Preparedness mania. At one of the evening gatherings there was talk about marshalling more resources against the striking longshoremen so that the docks would be ready for the war's "bonanza," and at the other event the women with whom she'd been shunted into a separate room after dinner spoke animatedly about where they would place themselves along the route of the city's big Preparedness Day parade in a couple of weeks' time, what they would wear, and how they'd manage their household help there, all of whom they would require to attend. But there had been no discussion at either gathering of the war itself or of the wisdom of direct US involvement: support among these people for American entry seemed to be a given.

Lansing, though, also wanted a sense of the other side among the business barons, of opposition to and potential abstention from US participation in the war. Alma and Adolph Spreckels seemed the best route. The costume ball evening had provided a good introduction to them and Kate intended to seek out more of their company. But to prepare herself, she wanted to learn about them from the outside. And Breyer was the only potentially knowledgeable source to whom she could make direct inquiry without appearing suspiciously indiscreet. Besides, she might also ask for his help on something else.

So she'd made an appointment to see him, telling him of her interest in the Spreckels. And was now climbing the stairs to Breyer's office on Market Street, down near the Ferry Building. The ache behind her eyes was back.

Breyer already knew a fair amount about the Spreckels; they were, after all, among the most celebrated couples in the city. But he told Kate that, prompted by her call, he'd done some extra digging about them. When she thanked him, he told her that the information might be as useful to him as to her. Her impulse to ask what he meant by this was halted by the expression on his face, simultaneously blank and dark.

Adolph Spreckels was enormously important on the West Coast, Breyer told Kate. Not only for the sheer bulk of his enormous fortune but also—as Lansing, of course, would already know, Breyer said in a way that seemed intended to diminish Kate's project—because of the strategic significance of his holdings. Beyond the Hawaii and California sugar empire for which he was famous, he owned a major shipping line that carried a large share of Pacific trade with the Far East and Latin America, a controlling interest in several shipbuilding enterprises, railroads, and steel and ironworks, and rapidly expanding holdings in the burgeoning California oil fields. Moreover, his family owned vast tracts of land along the entire length of the California coast, including much of the strategic port city of San Diego. So Spreckels's cooperation with a US war effort would be invaluable in securing American interests against Central Powers influence in Latin America, where Germany already had a strong foothold in restive Mexico, and in the Far East should Germany seek to expand there. On the other hand, a Spreckels refusal to become engaged—and the influence that might have on other West Coast titans—could make US diplomatic and military efforts in both Latin America and the Pacific much more difficult. Not to mention seriously restricting what would be a much-needed mobilization for the war effort of California's enormous ship-building capacity.

And there seemed to be grave doubts, Breyer said, about where Spreckels stood. His connections to Germany were substantial and long-standing: both parents were born and raised there, Adolph himself had gone to school in Hanover—a time he spoke of often and fondly—and he had extensive business interests in the *Heimat*. Of particular note, Breyer said, was the fact that Spreckels had pointedly rejected any contact with, let alone support of, the local Preparedness movement. And he made sure that his wife's fundraising efforts for war victims were—Breyer paused, barely an instant, his eyes flicking away to a spot above Kate's head—"scrupulously ecumenical."

You little shit, she thought. Are you testing me? Or do you think you already know where to put me? And just want to make sure I remember to stay there?

"Ecumenical," she repeated, standing up and moving over to a window, vaguely aware that by doing so she reminded Breyer that she was taller than he was. "Are you referring to a religious component to her efforts, Mr. Breyer? Or do you just mean it in the. . . literary sense?"

He didn't flinch. "Yes, without her taking sides. Regarding the war. And as for what Mrs. Spreckels herself. . . Aalmaa" he elongated the name, as if it were awkward to pronounce, "actually thinks about all this. . . Well, that's also difficult. Because of her. . . other sympathies."

Breyer let this comment sit there. Kate sensed that he was trying to draw her out, get her to say something that would reconfirm how little she knew. But she didn't see how a battle of wits with him, or whatever it was he was trying to induce, would be helpful to the job she'd been given. And doing her job well—moreover, being *seen* to do her job well—was important to her: she suffered under the burden of feeling a need to prove herself. A burden that, once strapped on, is almost impossible to shake off. A burden that she'd carried ever since marrying out of her depth into the Jameson family; which had become crushingly heavier after Jamey's death; and which had accreted daily, milligram by excruciating milligram, in that damnable law office. So, she didn't take Breyer's bait. If that's what it was. She simply cocked her head slightly as a call for him to continue and sat down again to emphasize that she was ready to listen.

"Mrs. Spreckels, you see, has. . . tendencies," Breyer said. "Against. . . the stream of things."

Kate wondered about Breyer's continuing reticence, his tiptoeing language. Perhaps he was slightly squeamish, feeling the need to maintain what he perceived as professional dignity. Or, it occurred to Kate, he might be uncertain of what he could safely say to Kate— what sorts of things, and with what degree of forthrightness—about members of a class to which the Spreckels and Lansing, and the Jamesons, belonged but to which Breyer didn't. It was an uncertainty she knew well herself.

"Tendencies," she repeated.

"Yes. Beginning. . . well, at the beginning."

With slowly increasing if muted relish, Breyer began to paint a portrait of Alma Spreckels as a tenacious social climber with artsy pretensions whose deepest loyalties, he suspected, lay not with Adolph, who had "rescued" her from poverty and inconsequence, and his caste but rather with the "troublesome sorts" she'd associated with before meeting Spreckels and with whom she continued to consort: artist types, bohemians, dancehall performers, women of easy virtue. Even socialists: "that writer" Jack London, Breyer reported somewhat sourly, was one of Alma's frequent guests.

"Of course, partly she clings to these sorts," Bryer said, "because of the way so many society people treat her. Something of a vicious circle, that."

"But I was at her society ball the other week," Kate interjected. "It was overflowing."

"Yes, I'm sure. But it's the people who *weren't* there who nettle Alma. Some of the 'best' families shun her, you see. Even mock her. Especially the women."

Bryer explained that, even by San Francisco's notoriously thin and porous standards, to these local society *grandes dames* Alma's personal history was shamelessly covetous, bordering on the sordid. Alma's parents had a decent enough name, de Bretteville, its French and Danish origins sufficiently northern and white. But that, according to these arbiters of class position, was the upper limit of Alma's claim to social standing. Alma's father had been a failure at various meager efforts to support the family, so her mother had turned to running a laundry in their flat near the city's north shore, later adding a makeshift bakery there. And while such homely enterprises alone may have been no worse than déclassé to the society ladies, Madame de Bretteville's other business, providing "European" massage services in the flat's back bedroom, reportedly with the participation of buxom teen Alma, pushed things well over the line.

And it only got worse. The teenage Alma enrolled herself in art school, and to pay for it began to do modeling. For a wide variety of, well, artists. Given her "striking physique," as Breyer put it, she was extremely sought-after. On one notorious occasion she even appeared as an olive, her naked body painted purple and embracing a long stick—perhaps representing a toothpick—in a giant martini glass ice sculpture displayed at a society bachelor party.

Then—all this when Alma was still a teenager—along came Klondike Charlie.

Charles Anderson was a rough-and-tumble miner who'd made a sizable pile in the Alaska gold rush and came to San Francisco to spread it around. After seeing Alma's attributes displayed on one of the cheap postcards that were sold in certain parts of town, he decided to spend some of his good fortune on her. Given her growing reputation around the city it wasn't difficult for Charlie to find her, after which he began squiring her to fine restaurants and nightspots of Alma's choosing—Charlie wouldn't have had any idea—and showering her with gifts, among which were numerous pieces of expensive jewelry, also selected by Alma, a piano complete with lessons and, again at Alma's suggestion, a box at the opera. He even tried to give her a horse. But she had nowhere to put it.

There was a question as to whether Alma and Charlie had become betrothed; Alma contended that they had. There was also a question as to whether Alma was pregnant; in the end, one way or another, she wasn't. But apparently the scare was enough for Charlie to back away, and when he did, Alma did the unthinkable: she sued him. For breach of promise. And "unlawful deflowerization." With the help of some eccentric blowhard lawyer, Breyer said, she actually took Charlie to trial. And won.

Though "won," Bryer explained, was a relative term. Because Charlie skipped town before paying her a dime. And while the trial served to thrust Alma into much-craved public attention as a free-thinking modern woman—the city's several newspapers had all covered the case with unmitigated glee—it also created a legacy she'd never be able to live down among the genteel society sorts by whom she'd later vainly hope—as wife of Adolph Spreckels, as patroness of the arts, as benefactress to the city—to be embraced.

As a result, Alma kept alive a parallel social world populated by various characters whom Breyer described as "dubious." And over the most recent few years, Breyer said, she'd given even freer rein to her more unorthodox tendencies, associating more and more brazenly with members of these other, well, sectors. Breyer was still choosing words gingerly, though at this point his sympathies and antipathies were clear.

"All that may be so," Kate finally said. "But what does it tell me about the Spreckels and the war? I mean, her charity for war victims. Couldn't that mesh with wanting the US to join the war and defeat the Germans?"

"Well yes. . . I suppose," Breyer replied with a bit of impatience. "But think about some of the types Alma consorts with. The arty ones. The 'new' women. The literary crowd. Not to mention her fondness for worker sorts. All of them against joining the war. Even though it would mean jobs for them, good pay. Which they're always on about. . . these endless strikes. You'd think. . ." Breyer's tone was suddenly aggressive, irritated.

"Because. . . it means. . . other things, too?" Kate said. Despite choosing an anodyne phrase to avoid ratcheting up Breyer any further, the close mention of men and war sent a shiver along her scalp: a sense memory of Jamey. She looked away, over Breyer's shoulder out the window onto Market Street.

The ache behind her eyes was becoming more insistent, and the idea of engaging Breyer in conversational fencing about the war made her slightly nauseous. To her immense relief Breyer said nothing more, and after a few moments it seemed to her that the meeting was over. She began gathering herself, which Breyer made a bit easier by looking at some papers on his desk.

"There is one more thing," Kate said, more timidly than she'd hoped, "which perhaps you can help me with."

She gave a very brief, affectless summary of Maggie's departure from Boston the year before, and told Breyer that she'd last heard from Maggie from San Francisco.

"Looking for wayward children is not exactly what the Bureau does, Mrs. Jameson."

"She's not a child. And she's not wayward."

Breyer's brows arched but he said nothing.

"She's. . . on a road." Kate added weakly.

"A road."

"Well... yes."

"And what, ah, sort of road would that be?"

Kate hesitated, never before having tried to describe what might have been in Maggie's mind's eye when she'd left Boston. "I... don't really know," she finally said, looking away. Then abruptly she turned back to Breyer. "Her own."

"Well, Mrs. Jameson, we follow criminals, not roads." Kate thought she detected the shadow of a smirk on his plaster of Paris face. "But let me refer you to someone who might be able to help. An investigation agency. The Public Utilities Protective Bureau. Private, you understand, despite its name. Quite private. And discreet. Run by someone called Swanson. A former Pinkerton man. We've had occasion to consult with him from time to time. He's extremely... resourceful. Just tell him that I've sent you."

Kate scowled. "That you sent me? Surely, Mr. Breyer..."

"Ah, yes, of course," Breyer immediately acknowledged Kate's concern that by using his name she might compromise the covert nature of her presence in the city. But he seemed utterly unbothered by his blunder. "Well, I'm sure that if you mention your friend Mullally," he went on quickly, "they'll be more than willing to help you. They and Mullally are... associated, you see."

Mullally. Again. And "your friend Mullaly"? How would Breyer know that? But the thought of spending another moment with Breyer in what suddenly seemed an airless little room was more than Kate could bear, so she remained silent while he scribbled the protective bureau's address, thanked him without actually looking at him, and tried not to seem in too much of a hurry as she turned and left the office.

Kate's notebook sat on the hotel room's polished wood writing desk, looking up at her in the reflected glow of the reading lamp. She had finished jotting down a summary of the things Breyer had told her about the Spreckels, details that ultimately might inform and lend credibility to her final report to Lansing about Adolph and Alma and the war.

But she didn't put the notebook away. Because her head was now brimming with thoughts—random, disorganized, pulsing—about Maggie. About what Kate would say to the detective Swanson when she asked him to try to find her.

She'd rung Mullally as soon as she got back to the hotel from Breyer's office, and he'd just now returned her call. She'd explained very little to him about Maggie, downplaying the significance of it all: "Oh, she'll be back in Boston after the summer, it won't be long. But until then I can't have her bumbling into some local misfortune. Not with the family seeking to establish itself here, you see. A young woman on her own. A town like this." And she'd asked if he could recommend someone who might locate Maggie, someone quite experienced and discreet, echoing the very words Breyer had used about Swanson. Perhaps someone Mullally knew personally, she added. As a favor to… the family. And as Breyer had suggested he would, Mullally had given her Swanson's name.

He doesn't take on private clients anymore, Mullally had told her. Because we keep him quite busy. But he was certain Swanson would agree to help Kate if she told him that Mullally was referring her. She thanked him—not too profusely, maintaining the semblance that this was a minor matter—and said she expected she would see him again soon, at one gathering or another. He took a cue she hadn't intended and apologized for his recent "inattention"; he'd become terribly busy, he told her, with all the bustle in advance of the big Preparedness Day parade. And he rang off without making any specific proposal for a rendezvous. Despite his value to her regarding the project for Lansing, she found that she was relieved.

Now she picked up the notebook again and began to make jottings. To "rehearse," as she thought of it. To grab hold of the twirling strands of her thoughts about Maggie and tame them into a description she could present to Swanson—carefully circumscribed to reveal as little as possible about the true nature of the two women's lives but nonetheless helpful to a search—whom she intended to call first thing the next morning.

Photograph.

Kate had brought with her a photograph of Maggie. To have her near. It was Kate's favorite. From six years earlier, Maggie in ballet costume, holding her toe shoes, immediately after her final dance recital, a high-quality image taken by the man who'd done the formal performance photos. In the picture, the teenage Maggie had just let down her long tresses and was beaming, exultant to be relieved of the constricting pins and clips and bands that had so tightly clamped her mass of hair for so many hours that day, and of the shoes, both symbol and locus of classical ballet's painful constrictions. And, Kate knew, exultant as well that the years of dance and its multiform bondage—which Kate had channeled her through, beginning when Maggie was four years old, first at the Jamesons' urging, then on Kate's own account, though she had struggled mightily to pay for it, the training, the costumes, in the years after Jamey's death—were now finally done: at age fifteen, Maggie had said, "Enough."

So the photo. Not recent, but it showed Maggie's face and her magnificent fall of hair. It would at least give Swanson the visual idea of her.

Nursing school.

Kate wasn't sure what she'd say to Swanson about Maggie having gone to nursing school. Because Maggie had left just before finishing, without taking a certificate. Turned her back on it. And on their plan—well, Kate's plan, Maggie had taken pains to point out at the time—for Maggie to follow it on to medical school. To become a doctor. Like her father. Though Kate had never invoked Jamey's name in that regard. Rather, it was always Kate's own trajectory toward becoming a lawyer, which she'd never had the chance to complete, that was the exemplar—of a modern, educated, and most of all independent woman—she repeatedly held up for Maggie.

When Maggie had decided to drop out, Kate had protested.

"But this idea, Kate,"—when most irritated with her mother, Maggie called her by name—"don't you see what it is? It's you. . .

wanting me... to be you. And you have to get it through your head: *I'm... not... you!*"

The charge had hit Kate hard. Because Kate knew the truth of it. And more, knew that Maggie didn't understand the whole truth, its added dimension: that Kate didn't exactly want Maggie to become her, but to become the her that Kate had wanted for herself but had not achieved, to be a "better" version of Kate, the fullest Kate that Kate had imagined of herself.

Imagined. The key, Kate had finally understood. A failure of imagination. A tunnel vision that had led her to encourage Maggie, consciously and not, toward a life Kate conceived for her. No, not just encouraged. Pushed. Because she'd been unable to grasp that Maggie might be just as complete, just as fulfilled, on some other path. Some road—that word, that notion, that had popped out of her head in her conversation with Breyer—entirely of Maggie's own making, regardless of her unwillingness or inability to map it out ahead of time. Pushed her not from an overabundance of love, as Kate had always excused herself when along the way she'd been put in doubt by Maggie's resistance. But from a failure of imagination.

Kate decided that she would tell Swanson that Maggie had finished nursing school and was taking a year "away" to travel before she'd start medical school. In the Jameson family, she would explain, this was an accepted, even expected, thing to do. Normal. Kate was not trying to rein in her daughter, she'd tell Swanson; she just wanted to make sure that Maggie was all right, she would say, in this bumptious, unpredictable and, so it seemed, violent town.

Painting?

Kate struggled to bring into focus other things that might help describe her daughter to Swanson. Since early childhood Maggie had spent countless hours drawing and painting. Always alone: she was never interested in taking art classes or instruction, and in her regular school when they did art projects Maggie refused direction and always made something different, something completely her own. At home she didn't exactly hide her work, and even allowed Kate to put a few things on the wall, but she was never keen to show anyone else what she'd done and never spoke of it. She immersed herself in the work not so much for interest or pleasure, it seemed to Kate, as for solace. Safety, even. On the rare occasion when someone would visit their apartment and Kate called attention to one of the drawings or paintings, Maggie would leave the room.

Maggie's attraction to the concentrated act of entering a purely visual world had begun when she and Kate had been in San Francisco, cooped up in the little rooms on Clay Street, waiting for Jamey to be released from army quarantine on Angel Island. At the time, Kate could see that little Maggie sensed the doubt-filled tension that gripped Kate during the many weeks of their purgatory, and the even greater tension after Jamey was discharged and stayed with them on Clay Street, rarely speaking, never physically touching his wife or daughter, unable even to look fully at either of them. It was during this time that Maggie began to cling to her pencils and crayons and water color brushes as if they were protective amulets.

When the three of them returned to Boston, Maggie entered school and took to it gladly, a relief from the world of her parents' silent pain at home: her father incapable of speaking about what haunted him, her mother not knowing how to draw him out. After school, she'd spend hours drawing and painting in the sanctum of her room. On a trip to the library she discovered art books, both technical manuals and picture books of the world's great works. Then Kate took her to the Museum of Fine Arts, at Copley Square; Maggie was entranced. And in one of his few moments of initiative in an otherwise nearly inert six months before his death, Jamey had called on a family connection to obtain a special pass for Kate and Maggie, for entry into the museum even when the galleries were closed to the public. Maggie made frequent use of it, first with Kate alongside, then on her own when she was a bit older and the museum was relocated closer to the small apartment Kate had moved them to in the South End. Maggie had continued frequenting the museum right up to the time she'd left Boston the year before.

But as Kate had chewed on it, worried it, during the past year, she'd come to realize that Maggie's insistence on a solitude of drawing and painting was not the only change that had been visited upon her daughter by the time they returned to Boston, especially after Jamey was gone for good six months later. Kate herself had had to cope with the unfathomable loss of Jamey and at the same time hide its full inexplicable reality from her daughter. But the hiding had not been enough, Kate eventually came to see: Maggie had been deeply marked by it all.

Of course, in part, Maggie had suffered from the simple fact of her father's disappearance, his absence. But in truth he'd already been gone for the previous two years: first, away in the army; then physically returned but at a distant remove from his wife and child, and from the world. So, since she was four years old her father had had little direct impact on her daily life; she was really only half aware of who he was. And therefore his loss, by itself, was only half a loss.

Thinking back on it now though, sitting with her notebook, Kate considered how the echoes Jamey had left behind, the reverberations not just of the suicide but also of Kate's struggle to keep it hidden, had inflicted a greater harm on Maggie than just his absence: Kate's slight wobble whenever someone mentioned Jamey in Maggie's presence; darting eyes and awkward posture by the person who'd spoken the name; Kate's inability, in all the years of Maggie's childhood and youth, to say more than a few words to Maggie about her father, in those few instances—having departed her life so early, he rarely surfaced in Maggie's thoughts—when Maggie directly asked something about him, or about Kate's life with him before Maggie was born; the tears that would invariably well up in Kate's eyes at those moments, and her turning away from Maggie's gaze.

In unconscious response to it all, Kate realized, Maggie had created a protective superstructure, a carapace, to ward off these echoes about her father. And thus also about her mother. And so, about herself. But underneath that shell, Maggie was silently storming.

She hated change. Desperately she resisted even the smallest adjustments to her routines and patterns, clung to things she knew, even if she did not particularly like or want them: clothes she'd out-grown but refused to stop wearing, most of which Kate managed to keep alive only through extreme, awkward alterations; the quartet of stuffed animals from her toddlerhood—each of which had been bought for her by her father, though Maggie never adverted to that fact, if even she knew it—not to be touched by Kate even though by age seven or eight Maggie had dumped them in a jumbled dust-gathering pile in a corner of her room, where they remained, undisturbed, throughout her teenage years; exactly the same brushes and paints as she had begun with as a small child, even though many varied and more sophisticated instruments and supplies were available; her hair—she had refused, for the entire fifteen years since they'd returned from San Francisco, to allow any cut of her thick, lustrous hair which, by the time she'd left Boston on her own a year ago, reached below her waist. Like a protective cloak. And companion.

She had no patience for the pedantry and peremptoriness of adults; she didn't trust them, neither their judgment nor the hidden realities of their intentions. As a result, she was a difficult child when forced outside the bounds of her carefully self-controlled private space. Not by active disruption but simply by quietly refusing the dictates of grownups. For several reasons, though, her intransigence was mostly indulged, or at least conveniently ignored. First, she was extraordinarily bright, talented, and articulate, which meant that the adults who suffered her resistance also basked in the reflected glory of her excellence. They also learned that, in many cases, it was simply prudent to avoid—especially as she grew older—the trenchant bite of her replies to unwanted prodding; if left alone, she tended to cause no problems. And more, she was tolerated because she was a Jameson. Even though she and Kate had been almost entirely cast out by the Jameson family after Jamey died, the name still carried weight: in the church and its school that Maggie attended; and among Kate's own family, who sensed from the great intelligence mother and daughter shared, enhanced by their exposure to the Jamesons, that Kate and Maggie were just different from the rest of the large Carey family, and from most everyone else in the Southie world.

Then there was her temper. Occasionally explosive but more often sulfurous: a dark seething that overtook her when she was confronted with anything she deemed illogical, uncalled for, ill-conceived or sloppily executed. It sometimes took the form of a rage against inanimate objects. Once, Kate came home from work on a cold, dark winter's eve to find ten-year-old Maggie banging a hammer, again and again, not so much angrily as punishingly, against the iron coils of the often balky steam radiator. Mrs. Doten, the elderly widow from the apartment across the hall, had stuck her head out to see about the commotion. Through the open door to Kate and Maggie's apartment she saw Maggie turn toward her mother, a nearly tearful frustrated fury contorting her face. Kate turned and apologized to the neighbor. Mrs. Doten said, "Anger's never about just one thing, is it dear."

When Maggie became a teenager, Kate several times pointed out the senselessness of these eruptions. "It's not *about* making sense!" Maggie would reply. "And anyway, why do you care? I'm not mad at *you*." Kate was unable to speak further, more deeply, about it to Maggie, unable to tell her that the outbursts themselves didn't bother Kate as much as the notion that Maggie needed them. That they might be a sign that the daughter carried within her the father's unbalance. Disturbance. Illness. Whatever it had been.

But there was also Maggie's vast capacity for tenderness. Which seemed to arise from the same well of buried emotion as did her rage. Kate thought now of Maggie's loveliness when she spent time with little Joey Carey, one of her myriad Southie cousins. Joey was "slow," and his raucous immediate family of twelve seemed to make no concessions for him, clattering noisily around their ramshackle old house in Dorchester without paying him much attention. But Maggie, when from time to time she and Kate visited this branch of the Carey family, would sit patiently for hours with Joey, reading to him and drawing with him and playing games, despite him being three years younger and having little to offer her except the gratefulness in his eyes.

Then there was old Mrs. Doten, the nearly housebound neighbor. Maggie fetched groceries and medicines for her. Helped her down the apartment building's four flights of stairs at the crack of dawn each Sunday morning so Mrs. D could go to mass, and an hour later returned to fetch her home. (Despite the church school's injunction that all its students attend mass, after Maggie reached the age of twelve Kate relented to the girl's insistence on the matter and Maggie never again went into the church outside of school hours; the school, in one of its many little concessions to "the Jamesons," let the matter slide.) Maggie would also frequently visit with Mrs. Doten of an evening, sit with her for an hour or more and listen to the old lady's stories, the same few repeated again and again. Upon returning from these visits, Maggie would sometimes speak to her mother of Mrs. Doten's loneliness, more than once with tears in her eyes.

And, between bouts of recalcitrance, such tenderness toward Kate herself. Kate thought back now on their three annual command appearances at the main Jameson manse, after Jamey was gone: Easter; New Year's Day; Grandmother Jameson's birthday. Thought of how Maggie would speak softly with her, like soothing a skittish animal, in the days leading up to each visit; how they'd spend an afternoon together planning what they'd wear, trying on their few dress-up outfits and giggling like school chums, Maggie's laugh a balm for Kate's anxiety; how Maggie would hold Kate's arm, softly stroking the skin of her wrist, on the long streetcar rides from the South End to the mansion in Brookline.

And their suppers together. How, as the years moved along, Maggie took on more and more of the meal chores. She'd shop for food after school and help prepare it for the two of them, to the point that by age fourteen or so Maggie would have a meal ready and waiting when, finally, Kate dragged herself home at 7:00 or later, after her nine-hour workday and her hour-long, two-trolley ride back from the law office. How they would sit together and share their meal, Maggie gently prodding Kate to talk about her workday, listening closely and asking precociously thoughtful questions about the various office characters she'd learned about. The roles of mother and daughter reversed.

And oh, Kate thought again with a surge of heat in her cheeks, how Maggie would patiently, lovingly, for far longer than needed for its care, brush Kate's hair.

Kate sat up straight in the brocaded chair. But how would any of this help Swanson to find Maggie? She clapped the notebook shut. The warmth from her reverie was suddenly gone and she found herself back in the same agitated mind as when she'd fled Breyer's office that morning. She looked around the luxurious hotel room. There was nothing of consolation. She got herself ready for bed. Though she didn't brush out her hair.

13

"In sum, your honor, I must remind the court... nay, I must *insist*... though, of course, with such respect as the court... may have... coming to it."

In the yard upon yard of white linen that made up his summer suit, the enormous cumulous cloud that was Cornelius V. Clay billowed from the lawyer's rostrum in the packed Hall of Justice courtroom.

"Yes insist... that the discomforts of mind purportedly suffered in North Beach on Sunday last, by certain... ovinities within the Catholic flock"—at this last choice of words the remarkably square, remarkably pink face of Judge Diarmud Philbert was moved from blank passivity to disturbed puzzlement; C.V. was gratified that the judge was at least awake now, but sensed that he might have nudged the torpid jurist a bit too far, and so quickly moved on—"which the prosecution mystifyingly contends amounted to 'outraging public decency,' arose from nothing more than the mere distribution of information... of *knowledge*, your honor—and how can knowledge possibly be an outrage!?—concerning the subject of women's control over their own procreatory inclinations, which is to say their own... human... destinies! Information, I might add, that is readily available to those in our fair city with the means to procure it." C.V. turned to the first row of spectators, expensively dressed middle-aged and older women, all of whom nodded in agreement, several staring defiantly at the judge.

"But in the end, your honor, whatever one makes of such ephemeral discomforts as might have glancingly grazed a few passersby, they must *perforce*," C.V.'s already impressive basso voice rose a notch, "be outweighed by the freedoms enshrined in our great Constitution. Most prominently, in the *glorious* First Amendment, which *sanctifies*...

and I do not use the word carelessly, your honor, or in this case with any... irony... the *fundamental* right of assembly to those who gathered on the public square that morning. So too sanctifies the *fundamental* right of freedom of speech, to all those who spoke there that day, and to all those who listened. And as pertains particularly to the matter before this court, to those who wrote, printed and distributed the paper in question," C.V. flourished a copy of the offending birth control leaflet, "the *fundamental* right of freedom of the press! Though I must admit," C.V. lowered his voice a notch, "that if the Founding Fathers had foreseen the redoubtable Mr. Hearst's newspaper..." he glanced at the claque of reporters clustered at one side of the room, "this latter right might have fallen considerably further down the Amendments list."

Blue was watching C.V.'s performance from the last row of the courtroom. Sitting next to him was Reb Rainey, author of the leaflet and collaborator, with *Volontá* translator Franco Caltrone, on the Italian version.

Blue hadn't planned on being at the courthouse. Didn't know that this morning was the conclusion of Joseph Macario's trial. Had only vaguely heard about the police raid on the *Volontá* rooms. Moving unimpeded through the always unlocked *Volontá* doors on the morning following the Washington Square birth control rally, angry about the harassment of their uniformed brethren on the square and looking for the "perpetrators" of the offending leaflet, the raiding cops had found only one person on the premises. Earlier that morning twenty-year-old Joseph Macario had come off a three-day shift on his cousin's fishing *felucca*. Instead of returning to his noisy boardinghouse where he knew he'd get no rest, and knowing that the *Volonta* rarely used their rooms until later in the day, he'd gone there to get a bit of sleep on one of the two cots the group kept in the back room for wayfaring radicals. Macario had been out at sea when the Sunday morning rally and subsequent police imbroglio had occurred, and knew nothing about it. But when the police raided the *Volontá* rooms and confronted him, demanding to know who was responsible for the leaflet they shook in his face, Macario took a look at its bold heading and first couple of lines of text and said, "We all are." They took him away.

At about 8:00 the morning of the court hearing, Blue had been staggering toward the Bohemian Cigar Store on a corner of Washington Square, a Basque café that he'd frequented since his early teen years—at the Genova, where he stayed, the eating room was far too busy in the morning; people would actually try to talk to Blue before he'd had coffee—when he ran into Reb coming across the square. She veered toward him, calling his name. When she reached him, she linked his arm as if to prevent an escape.

"Come with me," she said gruffly.

The two had known each other for years, Blue serving not only as a translator into Italian of the indefatigable Reb's various radical political tracts but more generally as a bridge for her into the deep reaches of Italian North Beach. They liked each other immensely.

"You might turn out to be useful," she added when he stopped and squinted at her but didn't respond. "For a change."

"Ah, thanks a lot."

"Oh, shut up and listen."

"But I need..." Blue gestured plaintively toward the café.

Reb looked him over and, knowing him well enough, understood that he'd be useless until he'd had one or two of the café's notoriously virulent coffees.

"Okay. But quick. And you don't have to talk yet, but you do need to listen."

As they stood at the café bar and then walked the few blocks to the courthouse, Reb gave Blue an account of the Macario arrest, of C.V. Clay's planned defense, and of the quickly patched together tactic of populating the courtroom as much as possible with women whom the judge would immediately recognize as coming from the city's upper strata—with Lily Bratz's help in contacting some of the many women she'd discreetly assisted over the years.

"Yah, okay, but what do you want from me?" Blue finally asked as they entered the courtroom and grabbed two of the last available seats. The morning's session was being called to order.

"I'm not sure yet," she whispered. "You have so many talents." She gave him a comradely grimace.

It was now an hour or so later. The prosecutor had spent the first part of the morning's session delivering his closing argument, recapitulating in high dudgeon the evidence presented in court the day before: testimony by two cops who'd been at the rally; the leaflet itself; and a reading into the record of statements of shock and horror by three church patrons who'd been "assaulted" by the pressing of the offending paper into their hands while on their way to church. This the prosecutor followed with the accusation of "desecration," by the leaflet's "carnal impiety," of the "hallowed ground" next to the cathedral under construction, and to the court's duty to maintain the city's good name, its hard-won honor as a beacon of decency and morality.

The utter absurdity of this latter claim—for a city that had come of age as a no-holds-barred playground for gold miners and whose raunchy Barbary Coast had reached worldwide notoriety—was so obvious that C.V. couldn't contain a short, sharp snort.

C.V. then began his own final argument, mounting his ringing Constitutional defense and concluding by returning the courtroom's attention to the young defendant.

"And so my client, your honor, the estimable young Joseph Macario"—Blue didn't know Macario but was impressed by the baby-faced fisherman's calm dignity, sitting straight-backed and silent next to the massive figure of his lawyer—"presents himself to you not only wrapped in the mantle of the First Amendment but also proudly asserting the *essential* righteousness of the cause for which not only he but also very many of the good women of our fair city..." C.V. half-turned his body to include the courtroom gallery, "...are being vilified!"

"Bravo, Joseph!" and "Well done, C.V." burbled out of the gallery. But since the women who filled most of the seats had been tasked with presenting a picture of high respectability, the remarks were muted and quickly died out.

The judge did not move or speak for an excruciating few moments, then leaned forward ever so slightly and with remarkable flatness said to C.V., "Anything else, counsel?"

From long experience at the bar, C.V. knew only too well what that meant. He quickly turned toward Reb at the back of the courtroom, pursed his lips and gave a short shake of his head. Reb nodded in reply.

C.V. turned back to the judge and said that indeed there was something else but that he'd need a short recess of the proceedings, until late in the day, when he would bring before the court certain other matters of "considerable import" to the resolution of the matter.

The judge looked sourly at C.V. "Considerable? Well, Mr. Clay, I suspect that you and I might differ, considerably, about what is considerable. However, since the delay you seek is a relatively brief one, your request is granted. We will reconvene at 4:00 p.m."

Blue heard Reb exhale, then felt her tug his sleeve and they were climbing over other spectators toward the exit. As they made their way, the judge continued: "However, since you haven't yet managed to gather up these mysterious 'matters,' Mr. Clay, I think that your client would benefit greatly by allowing you to carry on your efforts unhindered by concern for his well-being. Therefore I will provide him with a safe and quiet place in which to repose himself while we all await your… quest. Bail is hereby revoked." A burly bailiff stepped up to Macario, gripped his arm and pulled him away to the holding cell at the rear of the courtroom.

Outside, Reb spoke to Blue in a rush. That nod from C.V. had meant that he knew they were losing the case and that the judge was ready to sentence Macario to a stretch in jail which, under the charges against him, might be for as much as two years. Reb and C.V. had discussed the night before that if it looked dire for Macario in the morning's closing trial session, C.V. would stall for time while Reb and others rounded up people to appear at the courthouse that afternoon in a show of strength, and implicit threat of further action, if Macario were to be convicted and sentenced to jail. Reb told Blue that she was heading to a couple of dancehalls where women, aware of the court case, had been gathering, and that Blue was to head for Lily Bratz who'd be at the North Beach free clinic—it had no telephone—to tell her what had happened. "She'll know what to do," Reb said.

Blue could tell there was no time to question Reb about exactly what was going on, so immediately he agreed and headed up the hill toward the clinic while Reb hurried off toward the nearby Barbary Coast.

~

"Fuckers be going to send him down, I bet."

"Ay, that's what it looks like altogether."

On his way to the clinic, Blue was intercepted by an agitated Genio Forcone, who came hustling onto the square from the *Volontá* rooms. Blue kept moving; Genio strode alongside.

"But maybe I have an idea." Genio switched from his rocky English to Sicilian. *"And maybe you're a part of it."*

Blue looked quizzically at Genio but didn't slow down.

"Okay, so you have important," Genio switched back to English. "But you come to see me. Soon's you finish your important. I also have. Very."

Blue wondered for a moment whether Genio thought that speaking English somehow made his appeal more compelling. He slowed briefly and searched Genio's face. The combination of energy and barely contained anger he saw there led him to say, "Okay. As soon as I can."

Genio nodded, stopped, and let Blue carry on alone across the square.

A minute later Blue was climbing the stairs to Lily's clinic. Two women sat on rickety chairs just outside the dispensary door. Blue didn't know the protocol for going into the dispensary itself, but feeling the urgency imparted by Reb, he nodded at the women and carried right on past them to the door. One of the women said, "Ehhh!" but Blue kept going.

Inside the dispensary a woman lay on her back on an examining table; Lily was hovering over her. The doctor's head shot up at the intrusion and she barked "Out!" Blue froze. But then she saw who it was and understood from his expression that it was something serious. Her face softened and she nodded, but the command stood and she watched until he backed out the door.

The two women waiting in the hall glared at Blue and one of them stood to confront him. Blue lifted his hands in a gesture of surrender. "It's all right," he said. "There's no trouble. I'm after knowing Dr. B for ages." The woman hesitated but sat back down. "Good woman yourself," Blue said to her and moved away from the door to lean against the opposite wall.

As he waited, two things occurred to him. First, he remembered the unspoken neighborhood understanding that men on their own didn't go into Dr. B's dispensary unless they were invited; Blue had been to the clinic several times with *Volontá* friends when they'd brought donated food or collections of second-hand clothing, for the free box Dr. B maintained there, but only into the clinic's little office next door to the dispensary. And he admitted to himself that although his assignment from Reb gave him a free pass to find Lily as soon as possible, part of the reason he'd barged into the dispensary was that he'd hoped to find Meg there, helping Dr. B.

After a minute Lily came out.

"From Reb," Blue said. "A message."

"All right. In one moment. I will just finish." She went back inside.

Kate's meeting with Swanson earlier that morning had left her disquieted. And adrift. Why had she agreed to this strange venture, for which she felt so ill-equipped? Yes, the money from Lansing, surely. And the relief to be, for a while at least, out of the narrow, lidded box that was her life in Boston.

But perhaps just as much, she admitted to herself now, it was about Maggie. Even though she'd known that the odds of finding her were extremely slim. If she was even still here. And more sobering, now that she had spoken about Maggie—which had given her daughter shape and substance again—she recognized that if by some blind chance she were to find her, Maggie would be mortified. Furious. And most likely fiercely reinforced in her will to put distance between herself and the life, her life with Kate, that she had known.

Because how could Kate hope to convey to Maggie what had driven Kate to undertake this mad search? Convey anything of what Kate felt? A mother. The fear, the haunting, that terrible things happen to a child only when she's out of the parent's sight. And worse, when the parent, for even a moment, lets the child slip from mind. Maggie had left Boston a year ago. And each morning since, when Kate went out the front door onto the landing, she found herself looking down to the bottom of the stairwell four floors below. Expecting to see a body that had plummeted there in the night.

Nor would Kate know how to speak to Maggie of an opposite truth that Kate had come to understand during her past year of furrowed late-night agonizing. That it was not, after all, the unforeseen hazards of the world that were most likely to cause Maggie grief but, rather, the things that Maggie had already experienced: from Jamey and his disappearance; from the Jamesons; from school and church; and—a terrible accretion of burdens—from Kate herself.

Seeing Swanson hadn't helped.

Whether the detective had actually spoken with Mullally— Kate saw as she entered the building that the headquarters office of Mullally's United Railroads was there as well, one floor above Swanson's—she didn't know. But in any case the reference from Mullally had done the trick, since Swanson had agreed to meet with her that very morning, immediately following her phone call to him.

Like Breyer, Swanson presented himself without affect. But Breyer gave the impression of having to work at such a presentation, a function of wanting to appear professional, and was not always successful at it, as Kate had seen during her second visit with him when a slight flush about Alma Spreckels and the antiwar cohort with whom she consorted had peeked through his mask. Swanson, on the other hand, seemed to have no blood whatsoever. Part of this was his otherworldly paleness: translucent skin, white-blond hair and eyebrows, colorless narrow lips, and eyes that Kate couldn't decide between grey and blue, mostly because there was so little of either. But also his manner. He was an extremely large man—tall, very broad, big shoulders, thick neck—yet he seemed not to take up much space in his office, perhaps because during the entire time Kate was with him he hadn't moved a muscle except once, barely, to glance down at the photo of Maggie that Kate slid across his desk. He hadn't reached for the photo; his massive hands had lain flat on the top of his desk and stayed there the entire time. His voice too was motionless: Kate couldn't recall ever speaking with someone whose tone, throughout a half hour or so conversation, remained so thoroughly, immovably neutral.

Swanson told Kate that he'd have a photo made of Maggie's picture and would distribute copies to his men. Then he listened without interruption to Kate's description of her daughter—Margaret, we call her Maggie, five-foot-six, very slim, long-legged, masses of chestnut hair—and a brief history of Maggie's passion for drawing and painting, and of her nursing school background.

"Does she have money?"

Kate was caught off guard. It wasn't something she'd thought about, either in regard to how Maggie might have fared the past year or as to what she'd say to Swanson on the subject. Fortunately, she remembered that in answering him she was meant to be describing a Jameson, and that for the sake of her mission for Lansing she needed to conceal that Maggie wouldn't have taken any money with her because at the time Maggie left Boston, and for all the years before that, she and Kate had had no money.

"Uh, not really," she stumbled. "That is, not much. She made it a point of honor, you see. Wanted to make her own way. To show us that she could. You know how young people can be."

The likely inaptness of this last remark, to Swanson, left a metallic taste in Kate's mouth.

She waited to see if he showed any distrust of her answer. But there was nothing. Absolute nothing.

"Well, that gives us a little something to go on. Looking for her where she might be working. Unless," Swanson continued without hesitation or change in tone, "someone is keeping her."

Kate was momentarily stunned. She'd never suffered any thoughts along those lines. Of course, the predations of men were one of the wider world's dangers about which Kate feared for her daughter. But it wasn't a vivid fear. Maggie had never given Kate any cause for concern in that way. She'd shown no typical young woman's interest in boys or men during her high school and nursing school years. Between school, ballet, a dedication to helping Kate with domestic chores, and her obsession with art, she'd had little in the way of a social life. And Kate knew her to be both wary and savvy: she'd been out and about on her own in the city, managing to take care of herself, since she'd been little, when Kate had gone back to work after Jamey's death. But now Swanson's remark brought her up short. Because of the notions it conjured. She swallowed hard and barely registered that Swanson had gone right on speaking.

"...nothing much to be earned with drawing and painting. So I'd say the nursing is most likely. I'll have my men check the hospitals. Also, in case they have a record of her... for any other reason."

A surge of images: Maggie ill; Maggie injured; Maggie abused and abandoned; Maggie... under a sheet.

"Then there's the dancing," Swanson continued, his eyes flicking down at the photo of costumed Maggie holding her toe shoes. "That could be a way for her, in this city."

"Ballet? Oh, no," Kate replied, "she's definitely done with that. I know my daughter, and when she says..."

Swanson let the subject drop. It was only after Kate left him a few minutes later that she realized he probably wasn't referring to ballet.

Kate wandered aimlessly for a bit among the crowds around Market Street. Swanson had triggered something in her, and it took a few minutes for her to figure it out. It was the mention of calling the hospitals. As Kate had done a couple of weeks ago, looking for Dr. Rothstein, who'd befriended Jamey at the women's clinic fifteen years before. And then she understood: she'd come to San Francisco not only hoping to find Maggie but something of Jamey as well. Some taste of him. Some piece he might have left behind. And she knew what she'd do next. Because it came back to her now that there'd been someone else at the old clinic besides Dr. Rothstein. Someone with whom Jamey had spent some time, though Kate had only met her once, briefly. Kate didn't remember the woman's name. She was another doctor, quite a bit older than Jamey; Slavic or Baltic or something like that. It was enough, she hoped. She hurried back to the hotel.

She again phoned the hospital where Dr. Rothstein had worked. After speaking with several people, Kate was finally given the name of a doctor who had assisted Dr. Rothstein at the women's clinic and who fit the description: Lily Bratz. Kate had immediately phoned Dr. Bratz's Union Square medical office and was told that the doctor was not in that day but could be found at the free clinic in North Beach. Kate got the address and rushed out the door. As she waited impatiently for the hotel elevator, she paused to take stock. Calm down, she told herself. What's the hurry? Jamey's been gone fifteen years. And Dr. Bratz, if she remembers anything about him, won't suddenly forget in the next few minutes. Anyway, what's the likelihood anything will come of this? Except to find someone—away from the judgments in Boston—with whom she can speak Jamey's name.

She took a few deep breaths. Composed herself. But the lift took a while to arrive and first went up several floors, then stopped at several on the way down. By the time it reached the ground floor, Kate was nearly in tears.

∾

Dr. B's patient came out of the dispensary and gave Blue a dirty look as she passed him in the hallway. Lily emerged a moment later and stood aside for Blue to enter, after which she acknowledged the two women waiting outside the door and told them she'd only be a minute.

"And that's what you have, Baldino," Lily said when she had closed the door behind them. "One minute. What can be so important that you come gallooting in here like this?"

Blue told her: C.V.'s message to Reb in the courtroom about the imminent conviction of Joseph Macario, and Reb's instructions to Blue to get the message immediately to Lily.

Lily was quiet for a moment, sighed, and said resignedly, "Yes, I said I would."

"Would what?"

"Thank you, Baldino," she said, ushering him to the door. "Do not wait so long to visit me again. Though maybe not here, eh?" She spoke kindly but was too preoccupied to smile. "You must catch me up on yourself."

She opened the door and stepped into the hall.

"Madams, I am sorry," she addressed the women waiting to see her. "I must rush away. But I will be here again in three days, and I will be happy to see you then. If something cannot wait, please come to see me in my other office tomorrow. And you will have no fees there."

The two women got up. Lily took each of their hands, one after the other, in both her own, and pressed them warmly. Though the two women were obviously disappointed, Lily managed to get a small smile from each of them before they turned and left.

It was only when the two women had moved off that Lily, and Blue standing behind her, noticed a third woman in the hall, who now stepped forward. She was more formally and expensively dressed than the usual clinic patient.

"Dr. Bratz?" Anyone who knew her called her either Lily or Dr. B. "I was hoping to have a word with you."

"Ah, I am so sorry, but as perhaps you heard, I must be leaving just now. Can it wait until I am back, in three days' time?"

"Can it wait? Yes, well…"

"Jameson, isn't it?" Blue asked from over Lily's shoulder.

"Um, yes," Kate said, startled to hear her name, "that's right."

"First name, 'Mrs.'… As I recall."

Kate regained her composure: "Yes, that's also right."

"You two know…?" Lily puzzled.

"Ah, sort of…" Blue began to answer.

"No, I think not," Kate cut him off.

"Well, I must be going, right away." Lily turned and locked the door to the dispensary. She looked again at Kate, glancing at her tailored outfit. "Perhaps it is best you come to see me in my regular office. You can telephone to make an appointment. On Post Street…"

"Yes, thank you. I will."

Lily looked quizzically for a moment back and forth between Kate and Blue, then moved past Kate, speaking over her shoulder. "Then I will see you again, Mrs... Jameson." If the name meant anything to Lily, she didn't show it. "And you Baldino, soon, yes?" She didn't wait for a reply and hurried down the stairs.

Kate looked at Blue, trying to place him.

"I'm sorry. Baldino? Is that...?"

"Just call me Blue. But you wouldn't know that either, I'm afraid, since the last time we met I failed to introduce myself. Unforgiveable."

Kate looked at him, befuddled.

"The ferry. A few weeks ago. Coming into the city. I was a bit... scruffier then. 'Undercover'?"

"Ahh," Kate recalled now. But she didn't know what to say to him, her head too full of the things she wanted to speak of with Lily Bratz, and her wits jangled by actually having found her. Kate had no capacity at the moment to cope with the forward-pressing energy that Blue presented, so she turned and moved toward the stairs. "Fancy that," was all she could manage. "I... have to be going."

He followed her toward the stairs. She went down without looking back.

"You're settled?" he said when they reached the courtyard.

"Settled?"

"Or are you still at the Palace?"

"What?" Kate was taken aback, looked at him with some dismay, but kept moving along the street.

"The barrow boys, remember?" Blue walked along beside her, though maintaining an unthreatening distance between them. "They carried your bags? You told them where you were staying. I was standing next to you." From her expression it dawned on Blue that the one-sided information he had about her might seem a bit much, so he didn't mention that he'd also seen her some weeks later, leaving the Palace in the fancy car when he'd been heading in toward Emmeline Pankhurst. "I'm sorry, I didn't mean to distress you." And after a few more steps: "But anyway, I mean, if you're someone who knows Dr. B..."

Kate slowed. Lily's name acted like a winter muff in which they both found their hands being warmed.

"Know her. Not really." For the first time she looked at him directly. "Maybe, long ago." Her voice became almost wistful. "I... hope so."

Her sudden earnestness disarmed him. "Well, whatever it is," he said quietly, "she's the one for you. She's the best."

Kate didn't exactly smile but looked on him softly, as if they'd shared something. Her abrupt thaw prompted Blue to back away from their newfound connection, to allow her room for whatever was preoccupying her. As they reached the top corner of Washington Square he slowed and let her move ahead. Which was a good thing in any case because Genio Forcone had spotted him, and was moving toward him across the square.

"But your name, your given name. I still don't..."

She stopped.

"Katherine." She took a few more steps before stopping again, turning, and giving him a small smile. "Kate."

❧

Blue and Genio huddled at the back of the Bohemian Cigar Store, the dark and smoky Basque bar and *pintxos* café on a lower corner of Washington Square, where Blue had taken his morning coffee with Reb. The place was neither Bohemian—the original owner had sold it thirty years before to a Basque named Iriarte—nor a cigar store—it had only a few cheap cigars behind the bar to sell to inquiring strangers; the locals knew better. Blue had been coming to the café since he was a youngster, when Iriarte had hired him to sweep up at the pre-quake version of the place and to make deliveries to the several cheap Basque hotels in the neighborhood that catered to the many homesick shepherds—almost all young single men—who worked the ranches of the Sierra Nevada foothills but made San Francisco their home when they were seasonally or temperamentally off work. As Blue got older, the café remained simpatico to him in large part because its patrons were almost exclusively Basques, which meant that since he neither spoke nor understood the language, he could spend time there in relative peace, or carry on private conversation in English or Italian, neither of which most café patrons spoke very well.

And especially not Sicilian, which Genio and Blue now spoke with each other and which thus provided a protective wall of relative privacy. Also, the place was empty except for a few old guys playing cards at a table near the front; the young Basque shepherds who filled the café during the idle winter months were now in the Sierra mountains tending the flocks.

"So almost for sure they'll move him down to the Ranch, right?"

Blue had confirmed to Genio what the neighborhood already assumed, that Joseph Macario was likely to be convicted and sentenced to a sizeable stretch in jail. And Blue now agreed with Genio that since the offense was nonviolent, the authorities likely would move Macario from the cells at the Hall of Justice to serve his sentence at the "Sheriff's Ranch," as it was known, a larger but lower security jail in the nearly rural Ingleside district at the southern edge of the city.

"And so...?"

"And so, we break him out."

"Break him out? You mean, we get our guns and storm the place? Madunnuzza santa, are you Jesse James or something now?"

"'Madunnuzza santa,'? Ehh, what, you found religion all of a sudden? You sound like my mother!"

"No, I sound like my own mother." Blue's face was stern.

"Ah, okay, okay. But anyway, not break him out exactly... Blow him out."

In reply to Blue's more than dubious *"What?"* Genio raced on to explain that the high double fencing at the Ranch was made of wood, and that two relatively small charges of dynamite, in the right spots, could blow holes in the walls when Macario was outside in the exercise yard.

"But the charges would have to be just right," Genio continued, *"and the fuses or detonates or whatever they are, to get through both walls at the same time but not wipe out a bunch of the guys in the yard. That's where you come in."*

The proposal was utterly outlandish, which was no surprise since it came from Genio, whose eternal rage at authority often substantially outstripped his capacity to think straight. Fortunately for Blue, there was a truth that spared him from having to say so.

"*Genio, I don't have any work in the quarries. Or anyplace else where I could get my hands on blasting stuff.*"

"*Ah. Well anyway I think I could get what we need. Might take a little time, but...*"

Blue looked at him doubtfully. As far as Blue was aware, Genio had never before had any access to blasting material. And of the various people Blue knew who sometimes lifted jobsite dynamite for use in labor struggles, he was pretty certain that none of them would hand over any of it to an unpredictable hair trigger like Genio.

"*I been talking to a guy. No one you know,*" Genio continued, seeing the look on Blue's face. "*But I think maybe. Even so, we'd still need you to set it up. The caps and timers or whatever.*"

Blue was at a loss. He didn't want to reject Genio out of hand, in part because Genio was an old friend and dedicated comrade, and in part because while the idea seemed wildly impractical, it occurred to him that it wasn't entirely out of the question. Mostly. But not entirely. So he stalled for time.

"*But Genio. You know, doing time at the Ranch, it's pretty easy. My brother, he did time there, said it wasn't bad. And we don't even know how long Macario will go down for. Maybe only a few months, eh? Besides, things happen when you blast. Things you can't control. No matter how well you plan it. And I mean, if it's wood, the walls, why not get some carpentry guys, drill or saw right through the damn things. Nobody gets hurt. But anyway, even if you get Macario out, then what? They just track him down and haul him back in.*"

Genio was never any good at the "then what" part of plans, but had at least a vague answer ready for Blue.

"*Nah, nah, he's a young guy, got no family or nothing, we just slip him out of town, easy as can be, and set him down in Monterey and he'll keep right on fishing, or up to our comrades in Seattle, no problem. And the carpenter thing? Takes too long. They'd be spotted, unless you do it middle*" *of the night, but the prisoners aren't out on the yard at night. And anyway, that way's too sneaky. A blast, you see, that's the point."* He held up a finger, poked the air. *"How a blast feels. And the idea of it. Putting the picture of it in people's heads. Remind folks what we can do when we need to. It's not just against the jail, you see. It's against* jailing."

Genio was positively bubbling. And while Blue was no less skeptical now of the plan's viability, something in his gut responded to Genio's enthusiasm.

"Well, let me think about it. It'll be at least a few days before they even send him down to the Ranch. Then we'll see what word we get from inside. See if it could work. But I don't know, Genio. I'm not... Well, anyway, let's see. We'll talk again soon. But right now I want to get down to the courthouse. Reb Rainey's brewing up something, and I want to see what it is, see how it plays."

Genio didn't seem to register Blue's doubts and gave him a big hug when he stood up to go, as if they'd actually struck a bargain. Blue decided there was no point in restating his misgivings and left the café.

Walking back toward the Hall of Justice, Blue found himself trying to identify what it was about Genio's jail plan that had struck a chord with him. But he couldn't sort it out; now that he was out of the penumbra of Genio's effusiveness, no matter how he looked at it, it was a crackpot scheme.

Only when he neared the courthouse and saw the huge crowd of women gathered outside there did he realize that it was neither the jailbreak plan itself, nor any of Genio's rambling rationales for it, that had stirred him. Rather, it was just the possibility of being engaged. In something. Anything. There, outside the courthouse, he was struck that once again he was little more than a spectator: as he'd been at the Washington Square event itself; and again this morning, watching the trial, then acting as messenger boy for Reb; and now returning to watch the women surround the Hall of Justice. It took him back to all those months he'd spent in London, feeling costive and dull while the East End suffragettes raged around him. Which all finally changed when he and Grace Neal had come up with the plan to knock out the

Deptford power station, and he himself had joined in making the plan operational.

Yes, true, as soon as he'd returned to San Francisco after his years away he'd made contact with old comrades, talked with Billings about joining Villa in Mexico, and showed up to support Tom Mooney at the United Railroads strike meeting. His sympathies hadn't changed. Nor his intentions. But he knew that the distance between intention and action was a measure of character. Knew it. And now felt it.

Outside the courthouse, hundreds of women—and a few men, hanging back around the edges—were gathered in front of the building's entrance, filling the entire block of Kearney Street all the way across to the edge of Portsmouth Square. Blue had envisioned going back to the courtroom, finding Reb and sitting with her for the judge's final decision. But the dense, pulsing crowd meant that just getting to the building, let alone into the courtroom, now seemed out of reach. Instead, Blue climbed halfway up the slope of Portsmouth Square on the other side of the road, from where he could scan the scene below.

Police were lined up in two phalanxes at the courthouse doorway, struggling to keep open a path to the entryway. The crowd of women kept pressing forward and clogging the makeshift lane. To Blue's surprise, the police seemed restrained, even though they were defending their own territory: the central police station and jail were located on the courthouse building's top floors. They held their nightsticks across their chests, adding to the sense of a barrier, but did not swing or jab with them, even when surges from the crowd bumped some women up against them. Something held the cops at bay. The crowd was all women, yes, but that alone wasn't it; at other times Blue had seen cops wade into groups of striking women factory workers, wielding their clubs with no such reluctance.

The women, too, Blue noticed, were... what? He groped to sort out what it was about them that differed from a strike crowd, or from the birth control crowd at Washington Square, or any other crowd in a standoff with the cops. They were certainly loud: yells, catcalls, raised fists, gesturing arms. Aggressive: they continually pressed forward, threatening to overwhelm the cops and storm the building. And they had the numbers, hundreds of them, far more than the cops would be able to hold back unless they split enough heads among the closest swathe of them that the ones behind would recoil in self-defense.

The closest swathe of them. That was it. The rank of women closest to the cops was definitely not the cohort he'd expect to see here: they were well-dressed, well-coiffed—the floridly embellished hats of leisure class women were a tip-off—and well-behaved; all of them middle aged and more. Behind them in the crowd many of the women were young and boisterous, and while these younger women all wore Sunday dresses and hats, most of them had a ragtag, bottom of the hill look. Among them Blue spotted several women he knew who'd worked the Barbary Coast dance joints, including a cluster of four from Lew Purcell's So Different Café who stood out because of their brown skin.

Blue's attention was drawn away by movement in the alley at one side of the courthouse. The crowd there, a bit thinner than out front, parted a bit to make space at a doorway directly opposite a large touring car automobile parked there. Two people emerged from the doorway: one, a very tall, broad-shouldered woman elegantly dressed, including a long-feathered hat and a fur neckpiece; the other a tiny, plainly dressed woman with very short white hair. Blue thought he recognized the big woman from the newspapers, some kind of high-society dame, but he couldn't come up with her name. The small woman he had no trouble naming; it was Dr. B—Lily Bratz. The two women climbed into the big auto; the crowd made room for it as it slowly pulled away.

As Blue turned back to the main crowd in front of the building his eye was caught by the sight of a particular head in the midst of a group of rowdy young women; unlike all the women around her, she wore no hat. When she turned, Blue saw her face. It took him a few moments to be sure who it was. Because all of Meg's massive, lustrous hair was gone.

He hadn't seen her since the decidedly poor ending to the day of their motorcycle ride. He'd wanted to speak to her ever since but hadn't known quite how to approach her, or even where he could find her where she'd be on her own. Now, the sight of her with the radically short haircut so startled him that he immediately headed down the hill. But he hadn't made it more than a few yards when the crowd seemed to convulse as one, then after another moment issued a huge roar. Blue stopped. Emerging from the courthouse front doorway was the enormous white-clad figure of C.V. Clay. And at his side, his diminutive client, Joseph Macario. Just behind them were Reb Rainey and a clutch of well-dressed older women.

A policeman in the uniform of a ranking officer came out and announced something to the cops who formed the protective barrier; they immediately melted back into the building. C.V. grasped Macario's hand, turned to the small group of women behind him and gestured for them to join him. The group of women stepped forward with C.V. while maintaining a dignified, chin-raised stillness. C.V. and Macario, though, raised their arms to the sky in triumph. The crowd roared again and surged forward. Some women in the crowd started singing and many began to swing each other around in joyful dance.

Blue looked for Meg again, but he couldn't see her. He headed for the part of the crowd where he'd spotted her. When he got to the general area he looked all around, but she was nowhere to be found.

14

Blue needed work. Though he wouldn't have said it quite that way. Work was something that mattered. Or at least something you cared about. No, he would've said that he needed paid labor. But however he'd describe the eventuality, the impetus was straightforward: the fast-approaching end of the modest roll of cash he'd put together from the odd jobs and itinerant boxing he'd done on his way back across the country to San Francisco.

Over the previous couple of weeks he'd made the rounds of the region's quarries and big construction firms for which he'd regularly done blasting tasks before he'd left California. Back then, his skills had been highly prized and ad hoc jobs—always just for a few days or weeks, then he'd collect his specialist's relatively high pay and be on his way—had been easy to come by. But now, nothing. Blue couldn't tell whether each of these places really did have a full roster as they told him—after all, there were a number of others who had skills roughly comparable to his, if not quite with the same precision, and he'd been gone three years—or instead that rumors of his explosive involvement in violent labor struggles during the several years before he'd left San Francisco had seeped into the industrial grapevine despite the caution he'd always taken to remain behind the scenes. In either case, none of them offered him anything, and none was particularly promising. So he turned to the only other paid labor he knew well. He headed to Flaherty's gym to see if he could get back into the local boxing game.

Flaherty was delighted to see him. The crusty old Irishman, known as "Flat" to people at the gym, had grown very fond of Blue during the years he'd overseen Blue's training, beginning when Blue was a young teenager, taking over for Blue's brother and boxing mentor Declan after he'd left for, and never returned from, the Philippines. Flaherty had proudly presided over the rapid growth of Blue's fighting prowess and reputation, until Blue had reached the top of the area's light and middleweight divisions, then shepherded him, in Blue's twenties, into the often higher-paying heavyweight class—though these were only informal categories, with the lines between them vague, shifting and frequently ignored—despite the fact that Blue never topped more than about 180 pounds. Blue's success had brought not only a cut of Blue's purses to Flaherty but also notoriety to his gym, and with it lots of paying amateur customers as well as other box-for-pay fighters whom Flaherty then trained and managed.

At first during their reunion, the two old friends just made small talk, Blue glossing over his three-year absence with vague references to time on the East Coast and in London, and to a few of the fights he'd had on the way back across the states. When Blue mentioned his short stint in Dublin, though, Flaherty's eyes widened—Flaherty was originally from Cork, but he'd spent much of his twenties as a boxer in Dublin—and so Blue gave him a descriptive tour of the city Flaherty hadn't see in nearly forty years. He didn't risk mentioning his involvement in the lockout battles, though, and especially not the Kiddies Scheme: Blue needed Flaherty again, and since Flaherty was a somewhat practicing Catholic, Blue worried that news of the Church's rabid demonization of the Scheme in Ireland might have reached all the way to San Francisco.

Despite Flaherty's obvious pleasure at seeing Blue again and listening to his travelogue, Blue could sense a shadow. And he knew what it was: his abrupt departure from San Francisco three years before. He'd given no warning, said no goodbye. He had stopped by the gym to tell Flaherty that he was leaving, but Flaherty wasn't there and Blue had simply left a message with one of Flaherty's helpers to the effect that he was going away "for a while." He hadn't tried again to see Flaherty and had left a couple of days later. He'd made no contact in the three years since.

Of course, Flaherty knew that things had been tough for Blue before he'd left. Knew that Blue's mother had been very ill, that Blue was spending most of his time caring for her, rarely leaving their flat; that he'd had no time for the gym, for training, for bouts that would have made money for them both; and that his mother's death, a few weeks before he'd left town, had hit him terribly hard. Flaherty also knew, though, that Blue's final fight, three months earlier, had been by far his biggest, with the correspondingly fattest payday. And that if only Blue had followed up that knockout win with more bouts, he could have done extremely well for both of them, likely stretching his reputation and thereby gaining a chance to make even bigger fights and paydays not only locally but across the West and beyond.

But Flaherty also understood that final fight had left a mark on Blue. Had pained him beyond the tough beating he'd taken on the way to his victory. Knew that caring for his mother was not the only reason Blue had stopped coming to the gym in those last months. Though Flaherty did not know, Blue hoped, the full why of it all.

The shadow receded a bit as Blue told Flaherty that he wanted to start fighting again and Flaherty explained how the landscape had changed while Blue had been gone. A new state law now banned professional boxing altogether and limited all amateur matches to four rounds each, as opposed to the grueling twenty-rounders or more that previously had been common for most higher-end prize fights. The game still went on, though, Flaherty assured Blue: prize money had simply moved under the table. And ironically, the purses had grown larger, since many more quality fighters from around the country were eager to come to California and fight the much easier, and usually much less damaging, four-rounders. The fight crowd responded to the bigger names and higher-quality boxing by packing arenas and paying higher ticket prices: the promoters gave the audiences the same amount of entertainment by stacking several bouts back to back, and the action in the much shorter bouts was fast and furious every round, as opposed to the necessarily plodding pace of most of the old marathon fights. The result was steadily rising unofficial prize money, such that a good boxer now could make two or three times more per bout than before the ban. And because the fights were short, that boxer could generally recover and return to the ring much sooner for the next good-paying match.

All this was good news to Blue, who might have taken months to get into proper shape for a twenty-rounder: although he'd been boxing his way across the country, those had mostly been small-town five- to ten-rounders against unschooled fighters, and he'd usually made out without exerting too much energy and rarely having to go the distance. He figured he could get ready for a four-rounder in a matter of a few weeks, and he and Flaherty made plans for Blue to start working out at the gym.

Although it was the first thing Blue had wanted to ask Flaherty, it was only when he got up to leave that he finally managed to speak the unspoken question between them: "Arrah, you, ah, you been seeing anything of Elijah?"

Flaherty looked down at the floor, then back up to a place somewhere around Blue's cheek. "Well, he disappeared for a while. But lately he's been fightin' around again, so I heard. Sacramento. Central Valley. Gold Country too, I think. You know, small places where they don't pay much attention to the four-round limit thing." He finally looked Blue in the eye: "But not with me. I don't know, we was close, him and me. You remember?... Least, so I thought. But after the fight, your big fight, he never came back to me."

～

From the very first hint of it, Blue had been against the big fight three years earlier.

Yes, he and Elijah had fought before. Three times as teenagers: one no-decision and two draws, any of which arguably could have gone to either fighter. Then two fights when they'd grown to be young men and had made local names for themselves as the region's best young middleweights. The first, a brutal twenty-round no-decision—a common phenomenon at the time, which served to whet the fight crowd's appetite for a rematch—when they'd both just turned twenty-one. Then another bout two years later, at a time when Elijah had no one helping him prepare: his older brother Isaiah, his trainer, had a new wife and baby to support, and finding enough decent paying work was a constant struggle that left him no time for Elijah and boxing. Blue, on the other hand, was by then training full-bore under Flaherty's tutelage, the generous time for which was afforded by the little side jobs that Flaherty fed him, in addition to the increasingly frequent, well-paying blasting jobs he was getting as heir to his departed father's explosives skills. Flaherty's honing of Blue's boxing, and in particular of tactics to use against Elijah, was enough to make the difference from the previous fight, and Blue had won a hard-fought decision in front a big crowd at Dreamland, San Francisco's premier boxing venue.

That history, well-known in regional boxing circles, would have made for great interest in yet another fight between them. The rubber match. Or, from the perspective of those who'd favor Elijah, the revenge match. And for quite a while after the Dreamland bout, the idea of a rematch was frequently mooted. Both fighters had gone on to embellish their reputations by winning more bouts, including against several common opponents; if promoted well, a rematch between Blue and Elijah could generate a really large purse. But other things had changed since their last bout. Things that seemed to put another match between them out of the question.

Since Elijah no longer had anyone training him, Flaherty had invited him to come under his wing. This meant that Blue and Elijah became regular sparring partners, giving each other the best, toughest possible workouts; they kept a long-running unofficial personal scorecard which they'd banteringly tally after each session. Their training against each other improved both of them, and for a couple of years helped each continue to get and win better-quality fights and higher purses. But since they now boxed under the same Flaherty gym colors, boxing rules didn't permit them to stage an official fight against each other. Which suited them both just fine. Because in the meantime they'd become friends. The best of friends.

They rotated between their two homes. Blue enjoyed spending Sunday afternoons amid the warmth and noise and big Louisiana-spiced family meals of Elijah's multigeneration household—mother, grandmother, younger sister, older brother Isaiah, Isaiah's wife and their baby daughter—all crammed into a little bungalow in Butchertown. Elijah, meanwhile, regularly found a peaceful retreat from the chaos of his own house by spending nights at Blue's mother Marrichia's little North Beach apartment, on a pallet that Marrichia made up on the floor next to Blue's bed. By then, Blue had taken a boardinghouse room of his own further north along the shore, but Marrichia continued to sleep in a little alcove in the front room and to keep Blue's bed made up for him in the back room. Blue often joined his mother for an evening meal and sometimes spent the night there, and Maricchia always delighted in making a big breakfast for both boys on the occasions when they'd tumbled there in the early morning hours—saving Elijah the long trek home to Butchertown—following a night of carousing at the So Different Café, Sid Purcell's "Black and Tan" music club in the nearby Barbary Coast.

But everything changed in early '13, when the two friends were in their late twenties. Everything.

Blue had sensed that lately things were getting more difficult for Elijah. E, as Blue called him, had always been moody: easily joyous and exuberant but just as often quietly pensive. Now, though, he was uniformly sullen, silent. Sparring with Blue, Elijah's punches seemed angry. He snapped at Flaherty's correctives during training, something he'd never done before. And he rarely came by Marrichia's, after a night at Purcell's club or any other time, to see how she was doing, even though Blue knew that Elijah cared about her enormously.

One late night Elijah showed up at Blue's room at the boardinghouse. He was skittish, edgy. He'd been approached by a promoter, he told Blue. Someone who was ready to put up a purse if Elijah and Blue would fight again. A big purse, Elijah told him, a lot more than they usually got. And, he added uncomfortably, he could really use the money.

Recently Blue hadn't taken any bouts and had slacked off from his training, to spend more time with Marrichia, who had been slowly fading for years—since Blue's brother Declan had died in the Philippines—but whose health was now markedly poorer. The specialist doctor that Lily Bratz had sent her to said that Marrichia's lungs, damaged from her years working in the cigar factory, in turn had damaged her heart. Blue thought otherwise: that her heart had gone for its own reasons.

But lack of boxing fitness aside, Blue had no interest in fighting Elijah again. And wondered how his friend could consider it. But Blue didn't want to embarrass him, so he didn't press him on what it might mean about their friendship that Elijah was willing. Or how their friendship would stand up after such a fight. Instead, Blue stuck to tangibles. He reminded Elijah that Blue was in no shape to fight him, particularly because lately Elijah had been fighting, and winning, every bout he could find. And Blue didn't want to go back to heavy training just now, what with his mother...

Elijah knew well how much Marrichia was declining. For years, whenever Elijah showed up, she would scrabble together some morning—or, given what time the boys usually dragged themselves in to bed, midday—food for them and stand over them, grinning, teaching Sicilian idioms to Elijah while they ate; on Elijah's most recent visit a couple of months before, though, she'd barely been able to make them a coffee before she went to lay down again. At Blue's mention of Marrichia, Elijah lowered his gaze.

"Besides," Blue said, "we're both Flat's..."

Blue was uncomfortable even bringing this up, that two fighters from the same trainer didn't fight one another. Uncomfortable, because of course Elijah knew it, too.

Elijah just said, "Well..." and trailed off. He quietly asked how Marrichia was doing, then abruptly left.

One evening a month or so later Elijah showed up at Marrichia's, where Blue was now spending most of his time caring for his mother. When the two friends had repaired to the back room, leaving Marrichia to her bed, a mix of Elijah's woes and plans came spilling out.

"I gotta do something, man. And you gotta help."

Elijah began slowly, telling Blue that his brother Isaiah had lost his decent-paying job as a scudder and limer at a tannery, after a race-shadowed ruckus with a foreman. "And that cracker piece of shit put out the word to the other tanneries. Now Isaiah can't get nothin'. He finally got himself a trade, you know? A good payin' trade. And now they won't let him work it. All's he got now is just sloughing waste over at Moffat, the slaughterhouse. Don't pay him but punk money. And the new baby and all..."

Blue hooded his eyes; he'd been so preoccupied with Marrichia recently that he hadn't been to Elijah's house in months, hadn't even seen Isaiah's new child.

"And Victoria"—Isaiah's wife—"can't work 'cause there's no one to take care of the babies." Elijah waited a beat, to see if Blue reacted.

"But Gloria?" Blue said. "And Gran...?"

Since Isaiah and Victoria's first child several years earlier, Elijah's mother Gloria had babysat during the days so that Victoria could work. Elijah's grandmother too had pitched in to the extent she was able, but she was badly hobbled by arthritis and various other untreated ailments and needed almost as much care as she was able to give.

"Yeah..." Elijah's eyes flicked toward the other room, where Marrichia lay. "Gran's gone all over sickly, ya see. Can't help with the babies anymore."

Blue blew out a long breath but didn't say anything.

"And Mama's gone back working uptown again. So, you know..."

For years, Elijah's mother had cleaned houses in the rich neighborhoods in the north of the city, even though the time and cost it took her to travel all that way and back home again had made it barely worthwhile. In recent years, Elijah's boxing purses had finally allowed her to stay home and help with Gran and the grandchild. But with Elijah's purses now shrinking, and Isaiah's formerly good pay now gone, she'd needed to go back to work.

"And Alicia?" Blue asked, tentatively, about Elijah's younger sister. Tentatively, because she'd always been the family's wild child and for several years now—she was in her late teens—was hardly ever at the house, day or night.

"I'd see her more if I was still going to Purcell's. Which I'm not."

Although Blue's nights caring for Marrichia meant that he hadn't been going to Purcell's for a while either, he'd somehow imagined that

Elijah's life, including nights at the music club, had carried on the same without him. He realized now that for Elijah nothing was the same.

"Sure and all the fights, though? I mean, you're after winning all these purses, eh?"

Elijah slowly shook his head. "The more I fight, the less I make. I already whupped most of the top guys, and the rest of them don't want to get gloves on with me. So I just been beatin' up a line of stiffs. And people ain't much interested in seein' that. Crowds are small and the tickets cheap. Meanin' the purses been low and gettin' lower."

He looked hard at Blue: "And then there's this." Elijah pinched the dark skin of his cheek. "Remember? Flat says he don't hear nothing 'bout it when he's trying to book me fights. But just 'cause he don't hear it don't mean it ain't there. And anyway, who's to say what he hears for real? Look, I been in this skin my whole life. I know what I know. And fact is, they ain't gonna pay me shit to watch me beat up another no-name white boy punchin' bag that ain't got no chance. But *you...* If it was you and me, Blue. That'd be different."

Blue lowered his head and shook it.

"And I'm not with Flat anymore," Elijah said. "So there's nothin' stoppin' us."

Blue jerked his head up. Elijah's jaw was set, grim.

"Yeah, already left him. Signed with Braxton."

"Braxton? That bum? He couldn't train..."

"Don't matter. I don't need him to train me. I'm the best shape of my life. Anyway, he's just a name, him and his gym. He ain't even gonna get a regular cut. It's all taken care of. Maloney's the one. He'll be promotin'. And payin' big."

Blue had never met Maloney. Flaherty didn't like to book fights where Maloney was promoting because Maloney wanted to run the whole show and take a bigger than usual share of the gate. Still, on a couple of occasions over the years Flaherty had relented and booked Blue into bouts arranged by Maloney, and they'd all drawn good crowds. And since then, Maloney's reputation as a slick promoter had soared because of the huge Jack Johnson world title bout against James Jeffries, the "Fight of the Century," a couple of years before.

Maloney had squirreled his way into a piece of the promotion action of that fight, and was thought to have been behind the bout's move from San Francisco to Reno just two weeks before fight time. Maloney had seen Reno as a better place to drum up support for the former world champion Jeffries, coming out of retirement as the "Great White Hope," whereas the Black champion Johnson had spent a lot of time over the years training—and partying—in San Francisco and was very popular there, at least among the city's ranks of boxing fans.

Turned out Maloney scored big. Twenty-five thousand people showed up to see the fight at the purpose-built outdoor arena in Reno, paying premium ticket prices. And the betting action back in San Francisco had been frenzied, the move to Reno having turned Jeffries from less than even money to a three-to-two favorite by the day of the bout. The move hadn't helped Jeffries in the ring, however: Johnson knocked him out in the fifteenth round. Whether the late change in venue, and thus in betting odds, engineered by Maloney the promoter had proved highly profitable to Maloney the gambler was a subject of some considerable discussion in boxing circles. But, in any case, it was clear that Maloney had become the hottest boxing matchmaker in San Francisco.

"He can make it big, Blue. He's got all the ideas. He'll play it that I'm lookin' for revenge, see, from the last fight. And since I been with Flat but now I left him, Maloney's gonna put it around that you and me had a big blowup and we got scores to settle. And then, since you ain't fought for a while, he'll be making it out that you'd be sort of coming out of retirement."

"Out of retirement. Like Jeffries."

"Yeah. Sort of. That's just the way he'd flog it."

"So, you'll be Johnson…"

Elijah looked down.

"…and I'll be the Great White Hope."

"Well…"

They looked at each other without speaking.

"It don't matter what I think about it, Blue. I can't afford to think. I can't get fights that pay anymore. I got no other work. Isaiah got nothing but shitwork. Victoria got to stay home with Gran and the babies, and Mama's scrubbin' white folks floors again. We all got to eat. Eight of us got to eat. And it wouldn't be just this one payday, see. 'Cause if we put on a top fight, it'll mean more good bouts'll come my way... Blue, I *need* this."

Blue just stared, unable to get a hold of his thoughts.

"I mean, sure, Flat'll always take care of *you*," Elijah went on in the face of Blue's silence, a combination of sadness and anger now in his voice. "Well, I ain't got that, do I? And there's always those dynamite jobs for you too, ain't there? Good money jobs. But I ain't got that either. And Isaiah ain't got that. Victoria ain't got that. Mama ain't got that... Listen Blue, understand me: it don't mean I *like* this. Hell, I *hate* it... But I *need* it."

∾

Maloney, the promoter, did his job. Better than Blue had imagined. And probably better than Elijah had, too. Though Blue didn't know what Elijah thought of it all once Blue had agreed to the fight: Elijah steered clear of him after that evening at Marrichia's, and Blue respected the distance. He told himself that Elijah was just making sure they weren't seen together, in order to maintain the promotional illusion that they'd had a falling-out, the better to pump up the rivalry and revenge aspects of the fight. Told himself. But didn't believe it.

San Francisco had built a big new baseball park after the '06 earthquake, to house the Seals, the city's longtime Coast League professional team. Recreation Park—Big Rec—was in the Mission District, close to the center of the city, and for a boxing match could hold well over twenty thousand people. There had been occasional prize fights in the Emeryville baseball park across the bay, and now Maloney convinced Big Rec management to let him put on the Cavanaugh/DuPree bout in the ballpark. Maloney had a temporary ring built in the outfield, up against the fence, with tiers of benches placed on two sides of it on the grass, with the overlooking left field grandstand and bleachers creating an amphitheater effect. Blue went with Flaherty a few days before the fight, to take a look. He was amazed; he'd never fought in front of a crowd anywhere near the size they were setting up for. And then there were the posters Maloney had plastered all over town, showing photos of "Gentleman" Blue Cavanaugh and "Black Jack" Elijah Dupree superimposed against a background of enormous crowds that they had never actually fought in front of. All of which added to Blue's sense that the whole thing was happening to someone else, that he was simply standing in until this other person, this other Blue Cavanaugh, showed up.

Despite his disorientation, Blue trained hard. Throwing himself into training offered a physical counterpoint to, and a respite from, the emotional drain of long hours sitting with his mother, unable to slow her precipitous decline. He also knew that to serve his own best interests, however unclear they might be, he ought to perform well in the ring.

His best interests. Maybe he'd begin to take more bouts again, and a good fight against Elijah would put him back in the spotlight; Flaherty certainly hoped so and was working Blue hard. His best interests also included helping his friend Elijah, and in order to propel Elijah into better bouts, they'd both have to put on a great show in this one, whatever the outcome. Blue could also use the money he'd make with a win—he hadn't been fighting at all in recent months, and had turned down several blasting jobs that would have meant leaving the city and, therefore, his daily care of Marrichia—though to protect the interests of both fighters, the winner's share of the purse was to be only slightly bigger than the loser's. The problem was that despite the good ticket sales for the ballpark, the expected purse was turning out to be a lot less than Elijah had at first been told and had reported to Blue. "Ah, me expenses, ya know," Maloney had quickly skimmed across his excuse, "Big Rec and all. But it's going to be huge. Fierce enormous. You'll be the talk of the streets, and reapin' rewards years to come."

There was also pride. Blue simply couldn't imagine fighting poorly, at least not in his hometown, in front of thousands of people. And though he didn't admit it to himself, the old boxing rivalry with his friend had resurfaced, abetted by a persistent, low-level resentment that Elijah had pushed him into the whole damn thing.

So, all in all, he trained to win.

The day of the fight dawned classically summer San Francisco: a deep thick fog blanketed the city in the morning hours—Blue had been up since well before dawn, had hardly slept, had walked ragged along the piers soothed a bit by the sonorous foghorns—only slowly burning off as the afternoon arrived. It was replaced by glistening cloudless sunshine but also by the first ripples of the west wind that by late afternoon, fight time, would be charging in off the ocean. "Wind at your back, keep it at your back," were the only words Blue retained from Flaherty's slew of last-minute advice as they rode together to the park and entered the dressing room immediately behind one of the baseball dugouts.

As Flaherty rubbed him down, Blue could hear roaring out in the park as the preliminary bouts whipped up the big crowd's enthusiasm, its blood lust. Blue, though, was now calm. Part of his success over the years—in early petty thefts and later burglaries with big brother Declan; in boxing against older and bigger fighters; in stealing dynamite from worksites and carefully controlling its clandestine use—stemmed from an ability to slow himself down in situations where others would become rattled. Still, a corner of his brain was raging: What would this be like, the two friends—grown men now—going out to fight not in a friendly sparring session but trying to take each other down?

When the call came for Blue to head out to the ring, Flaherty stopped him. "Not yet. Make him wait." So for two or three more minutes Blue sat on a stool, head bowed, listening to the shuddering crowd noise that suddenly pitched up at what Blue assumed was Elijah coming out of the other dugout. Finally, Flaherty said, "Right so. Let's fucking do this," and the two of them marched out into the bright daylight and the belaboring wind.

The crowd, on its feet, was too dense for Blue to catch sight of Elijah until Blue climbed through the ropes, and suddenly there he was, pacing back and forth across the other corner, as if he weren't in a ring but a cage. He didn't, wouldn't, look across at Blue. In the chill wind Blue would have expected Elijah to be wearing a robe to keep warm until the bell, as Blue was. But Elijah stood bare-chested, rippling, pacing. Blue was struck by how big Elijah had become since Blue had last seen his torso, all of it hardened muscle. He looked to be in the best shape of his life. Given this impressive form and his recent string of lopsided ring victories, measured against Blue's long inactivity—he'd last fought almost a year before—he understood how money bet on the fight had driven the odds to Elijah as three-to-one favorite. Betters weren't going to make the same mistake, fantasy over probability, as they had with Jeffries against Johnson. Maybe the newspapers were buying the Great White Hope stuff, but not the punters.

Elijah still avoided Blue's eyes as they met in the center of the ring for the referee's instructions. Only when they were about to return to their corners did Elijah finally glance at Blue, his face betraying the same mix of sadness and anger that Blue had seen and heard at Marrichia's the night Elijah had talked him into the fight.

The bout started slowly, as these twenty-rounders usually did: fighters had to pace themselves. But even with their cautious, tentative early jabs and short, follow-up rights, Blue knew right away that he was in trouble: Elijah was a hair quicker, several of his jabs getting through to Blue's head while Elijah's own gloves and forearms effectively parried Blue's slightly less crisp attempts; Elijah's footwork was more nimble, bouncing in on his toes to hit, then backing just out of Blue's reach; and he was stronger, already in the first round Elijah's jabs were beginning to sting, Blue's face was becoming hot, and he knew that swelling would soon follow. Blue was certain that Elijah knew it, too, although unlike in their scores of sparring sessions and in their fights from earlier years, Elijah didn't look Blue in the eye but focused instead on a spot in the middle of Blue's forehead.

Through the second, third, and fourth rounds, Blue was just about able to hold his own, not really inflicting any damage on Elijah but getting through the occasional partially deflected punch and avoiding any big hits in return. Nonetheless, the cumulative weight of Elijah's jabs and body punches was already taking a serious toll on Blue. He had to find a way to slow Elijah down.

Elijah's left jab was doing the most damage; his right hand—straight short rights following the jab, and the occasional right cross—was curiously less accurate, almost careless, most of those punches glancing off Blue rather than landing solidly. Between rounds Flaherty, who could already see that Blue was marginally but steadily losing, told Blue to move in close to Elijah, not to let him just pop away at Blue from distance, then to tie him up in clinches, to frustrate him and tire him out that way. But Blue knew that repeated grabbing and clinching would look bad to the crowd, not to mention the judges, and decided instead to focus on Elijah's left arm. He would move in closer, to pound Elijah's left shoulder with his own right, short punches that wouldn't leave himself open to a big counter blow. Any one of these shoulder punches by itself would not be particularly effective, and certainly wouldn't impress the judges, but Blue hoped that the mounting effect of them over a couple of rounds would numb and tire Elijah's left arm enough that his jabs would get a bit slower, a bit weaker, and would come from a lower angle, which would mean they'd have a tougher time getting through Blue's defense and might—now Blue's only hope to actually win the fight—drop far enough that Blue could land a big right over the top. If Blue could last that long.

And it seemed to work. Over the course of the next two rounds, Elijah's left jabs dropped fractionally but steadily lower. And then something odd happened. Near the end of the seventh round, Elijah for the first time in the fight pushed himself into Blue and grabbed him in a clinch. Hooking his chin over Blue's shoulder, Elijah hissed in his ear: "I could fucking clock your ass." Then he pushed Blue away and the bell sounded.

"What was that?" Flaherty demanded as he iced Blue's swelling face between rounds. Blue shook his head. "I don't know." And he didn't. Although Elijah was certainly winning the fight, his reliance on his jab, and the relative ineffectiveness of his right-hand punches, meant that in fact Blue wasn't likely to get clocked. So Blue went out for the eighth round with the same idea of pounding Elijah's left shoulder to weaken his jab and to continue getting him to lower his left arm.

Halfway through the round, Blue could see that the tactic was now paying off more rapidly: Elijah's left arm was sinking noticeably lower, his jab coming from a level at the top of his ribs, not straight out from his shoulder. Blue sensed that this was the moment to try the second part of his improvised plan, to launch a long, looping right hand that might at least partially pass over the top of Elijah's now-lowered left. Not that Blue expected to knock out Elijah with one punch: Elijah was too quick, he'd certainly get his left arm up at least part way to take some of the power out of Blue's punch and would in any case see it coming soon enough to turn his head away, mitigating the effect. But Blue hoped at least to land a solid enough punch to slow Elijah down, to make him more defensive with his left hand, to stop the incessant jackhammer of his jabs. And then hope for the best.

Blue began slowly to position his feet—much of the power of a long punch coming from the legs—to sharpen the angle from which he'd throw the punch. Elijah's eyes locked onto his, then quickly darted away. Blue threw two more short rights to Elijah's left shoulder, then saw Elijah's left arm drop several inches. Torquing his lower body, Blue dipped his right shoulder and began the long arc of his right arm to rise above Elijah's left and toward his head. But instead of bringing up his left arm to try parrying the punch, which he could surely see coming, Elijah instead kept his left arm down. And instead of turning or ducking his head so the blow would catch him, if at all, above the ear or higher on the side of his head, almost imperceptibly Elijah turned toward Blue's oncoming fist.

Even as his punch toward Elijah's head was still in the air, Blue understood. Understood why, on Elijah's last visit to Marrichia's apartment, he'd bid her such a wistful, valedictory goodbye. Understood—as the blow came crashing down squarely into Elijah's left eye, its full force unimpeded by any defensive move—why Elijah remained so committed to the fight, so passionate about it, even when they were told that the purse would not be nearly as much as had first been suggested to Elijah. Understood—as Elijah crumpled to the canvas, blood already spurting out of his left eye, his right eye looking up at Blue with something akin to sorrow—that given the heavy odds in Elijah's favor, big money bets on Blue to win would pay off enormously. Understood, that Elijah had taken a dive.

Throughout his childhood, Blue had been plagued by nightmares that someone was moving in on him, was about to hurt him, and that Blue could not stop it. The dreams finally began to fade in the years after his father disappeared. Beginning shortly after that final bout with Elijah, though, and during the three years since, the nightmare had returned. Only now it was not some looming menace closing in to strike or throttle Blue, but the opposite: it was Blue moving toward someone else, closer and closer, readying to strike. Unable to stop himself.

15

Lily Bratz and Kate reintroduced themselves—following their brief first meeting outside the North Beach free clinic the week before—in the examining room of Dr. B's Union Square medical office.

"My colleague says that on the telephone you did not tell your condition." Lily indicated with her head the woman who sat at the reception desk on the other side of the door.

"Condition?"

"But it's all right. Your privacy, I mean. Many people prefer to not speak about such things until they are here with me, in the person."

Privacy. True enough, that was part of it. But the main reason Kate hadn't said on the telephone why she wanted to see Dr. Bratz was that she couldn't have articulated why she wanted to see Dr. Bratz. At least, not in any specific way. Except that she wanted to talk. About Jamey.

~

In the first years after Kate and Jamey met and soon after wed, they'd had each other to talk to. About anything. And everything. It was part of their special admixture, an intense companionship that helped sustain them against the incomprehension and exclusion they faced from their two sides of Boston, from both Jamesons and Careys. And what the two of them had together was so full and unconstrained that they barely noticed their isolation.

Until Jamey came back from the Philippines. And soon was gone for good. Leaving Kate—never a Jameson but no longer a Carey—with no one. Except her six-year-old daughter.

He'd always been an odd man out, Jamey. An only child. Sort of. His parents had given his four older brothers the same traditional

Scots-Irish names that had been repeated through all the previous generations: John, James, William, Robert. But as if sensing the new, and likely final, child's difference even at birth, they had named him Wistan, after the ninth-century Anglo-Saxon warrior saint. His brothers could find no suitable diminutive for Wistan, so they just called him Jamey, taking their cue from the little boy's early attempts to pronounce his family name. The brothers looked on their quiet, thoughtful youngest sibling with distant bemusement; they didn't bully or tease him much, and only mildly, but neither did they include him in their childhood roughhousing or later in their young men's carousing. He remained an outsider to them, a curiosity, as he was to his shipping magnate father and to his mother, a doyenne of Boston society. Not that he was utterly unloved: the eldest Jameson child was his sister Margaret—after whom Jamey and Kate named their daughter—who favored Jamey with some of the attention and affection that was unforthcoming from the rest of the family.

Jamey spent most of his growing-up years inside the quiet but fertile gardens of his own head. And preferred it that way. His sister Margaret's occasional company and love, as later with Kate's, was enough; he could do without the rest. Which meant that while he was often solitary, he was rarely lonely. Though not visibly cheery or rambunctious in the usual ways, for the most part he was a happy child.

And happiest when in Cuba. Several generations of Jameson family wealth had been made in shipping, first in Ireland and England, then in Boston as a New World hub. Jamey's grandfather had developed a large portfolio of interests in Cuba, triangulating shipping routes among Havana, Liverpool, Dublin and Boston, moving vast quantities of Cuban sugar, tobacco and rum. So deeply did the Jamesons engage in the island that the grandfather bought a Spanish colonial mansion on the Bay of Matanzas, the old Afro-Cuban stronghold east of Havana, along the rum and sugar route to the port. During Jamey's childhood, the family would escape frigid Boston winters to their island home for a time each year, as well as for stretches each July and August when the Caribbean breezes of Matanzas were surprisingly more tolerable than the heavy, mosquito-bearing, grime-suffused air of summertime Boston.

As at home, Jamey's family mostly left him to his own devices in Matanzas, though under the eyes of minders and maids and other retainers, all of whom were Afro-Cuban, many of them former slaves. Over years of sitting in the kitchen with the cooks and helping in the gardens with the groundskeepers and roaming in the fields with the workers' children, Jamey came to absorb a passable fluency in both Spanish and local Creole. His informal local education also included exposure to the workers' public humiliation by and private disdain for "the Spanish," as the Black, mulatto and mestizo *Cubanos* referred to both segments of the paler ruling class: the top-of-the-heap Europe-born *Peninsulares* and the somewhat lesser-caste island-born *Criollos*. And though he usually ventured off the family property only on swimming expeditions to the sea or shopping trips to Matanzas town, or occasionally on visits to other gringo family enclaves, he couldn't help but witness, often enough to make a deep impression, ugly scenes of slave labor maltreatment in the surrounding cane and tobacco fields.

Of his own family's place in island hierarchy, and that of the several other US big business families whose local residences were scattered throughout the district and with whom his own family socialized, Jamey never formed a clear notion: as a child he was not privy to commercial arrangements among the various elites; his family's interactions with the Afro-Cuban workers on the estate were superficially benign, with *Criollo* overseers handling the actual daily management; and the estate's workers and their children themselves were too discreet to express their feelings about his family, whatever they might have been, in Jamey's presence.

Jamey spoke often and lovingly to Kate about his childhood experiences in Cuba but she never got to see the place for herself. By the time he and Kate met, Jamey had become distanced from his family—more distanced, that is, than by his natural inclination to solitude—and was no longer accompanying them on their trips to the island. His desire to attend medical school rather than to join his father and brothers in the family's vast shipping enterprise had been opposed by his father, then poorly received by the family when he went ahead anyway. In their view, to practice medicine was to become merely a slightly elevated tradesman, a role back in Ireland where you'd find a middle-class Englishman. Or in Boston, a German. Or a Jew, for goodness sake.

Medical school, followed by dedication to his downtown Boston practice, plus one day per week volunteer work in a Quaker clinic in South Boston, kept Jamey fully occupied, but he still felt acutely the loss of his Cuban world. Then his whirlwind romance and marriage to Kate entirely sealed off the island to him: Jamey's decision to become a doctor may have been somewhat puzzling and distressing to his family but his marriage to this Carey girl from Southie was utterly unfathomable. And unforgiveable. Estrangement from his family was now complete.

When she met Jamey, Kate was in her first year at "normal school" teacher-training college, one of the only routes—nursing being the most prominent other one—by which brighter, or simply more tenacious, Boston Irish working-class girls could avoid a life of domestic service, factory labor or seemingly endless childbearing. Jamey, the young doctor, had appeared one day at the normal school, on behalf of the nearby Quaker-run clinic, to give a tutorial on hygiene pedagogy for the teacher-training students. He was immediately smitten by the striking, exceedingly verbal young Carey girl, and naively crossed multiple unspoken rules and boundaries by singling her out with an invitation to visit the clinic. Kate happily crossed the boundaries in the other direction; she was already waiting for him at the clinic when he showed up there on his appointed day the following week. And that was that. The two of them fell instantly and hard, finding in each other not only a lover and soon a spouse but also a best friend and confidante. In one magical stroke, Jamey was rescued from his deepening isolation while Kate was freed from the social and economic manacles of Southie, to a degree that becoming a teacher, by itself, never could have matched.

Their first couple of years together were blissful and overflowing. Jamey continued in his small medical practice and once a week at the Quaker clinic in South Boston. Kate busied herself setting up their new flat in the Brighton district and commuting from there to South Boston to finish her first year of normal school. The journey they took home together from Southie—she from the college, he from the clinic—one day each week, sitting on the hard wooden trolley bench with arms linked, facing the world as a unified pair, were the happiest moments Kate had ever known.

The next summer, Kate considered switching to a normal school closer to where they lived. The trip to and from Southie was long, and occasional visits there with the large Carey clan, after her classes, had become rare: her single-parent father, and her aunts, uncles and cousins, had long viewed her as a somewhat alien creature because of her restless, questing, book-inflamed intelligence, but her linking with Jamey and her move up to Brighton had strained things even further. In response to Kate considering a different normal school, Jamey wondered whether perhaps she might want to aim higher. Was there anything else she could imagine herself doing, he asked, rather than teaching school? And for the first time in her life she allowed herself the notion.

An elderly couple, the Kaminskys, lived in the flat below. Kate had gotten into the habit of sitting with them for cup of tea and a chat on the evenings when Jamey was late coming home from hospital rounds. The old man was a jack-of-all-trades lawyer, or had been when still able, and as they sat in the parlor he'd tell Kate stories of his cases. He enjoyed stopping in mid-tale to ask the bright young Southie woman what she thought of some strand of a case's tangled web, and he was often delighted by how perspicacious she was, how she not only cottoned on to the legal issues but also had a feel for the human lives behind the litigant "parties." So while it came as a surprise to both Jamey and Kate when she immediately responded to Jamey's query with, "You know, I think I'd like to be a lawyer," in fact, the idea may have been simmering in her for quite some time.

They set to it. Many would-be lawyers got their training through apprenticeship in a law office rather than by attending a law school, but finding an office that would welcome a woman apprentice was a task too tall. Of course, Jamey's family had connections with a number of big law firms, but none of them was likely to accept a woman, and certainly not one with Kate's Southie genes. Not that Jamey would have wanted to ask for his family's help in any case. But Kate and Jamey learned that there was a local law school that had recently begun to admit the occasional female student, and she applied. Jamey accompanied Kate to the admissions interview, as some male personage was required to. And whether it was his patrician carriage, medical profession and Jameson name, or Kate's well-spoken, whip-smart responses, the two of them never knew and did not care, because Kate was admitted to the school's night classes, if not its full-time curriculum, to begin the next matriculation period. On top of that, the neighbor Mr. Kaminsky prevailed on his former law partners, a two-man operation, to let Kate spend mornings at their office as an unpaid assistant, observer, and—when they recognized her talent with the English language—amanuensis-cum-editor.

Then came Maggie. Kate and Jamey were ecstatic with the pregnancy in the second year of their marriage. At first, Kate carried on with her law studies and unpaid work at the law office. But the latter months of the pregnancy became difficult, so Kate stopped her night classes and her law office work until the baby was born. She would return, she and Jamey agreed, as soon as they were able to settle into a new rhythm as parents.

Maggie was born several weeks premature, so Kate and Jamey paid the tiny little girl especially close attention and Kate postponed her return to work and school. By the time of Maggie's first birthday, however, it was clear that she was a healthy, hearty child, and Kate decided she would return to the night law school classes, when Jamey would be at home to look after Maggie. The law school, though, made it difficult: Are you planning on having another child and stopping again? What's the point of training to become a lawyer, taking up someone else's place in the school, if you'll be minding children instead of practicing? You've been away for almost two years, so you'd have to start again from the beginning...

Eventually the school relented, and Kate reentered the following semester. It was a logistical struggle, with Jamey rushing home from work in time to take over Maggie's care while Kate headed off to class, but they made it work. Until the war.

The Spanish-American War. Or as Jamey thought of it, the war for Cuban liberation. Through his sister Margaret he'd kept up on doings at the family property in Matanzas, in particular the marriages and births and growing-ups and deaths of the workers there, with whom he'd become so close during his childhood and youth. As the Cuban rebellion against the Spanish grew in strength in the mid-nineties, Jamey followed it avidly, wondering at times whether there was some way for him to help.

His chance came when the United States declared war on Spain and sent ships and troops to the island. Newspaper editorials trumpeted the glorious virtues of American armed intervention, while the government proclaimed that the United States had no territorial aims and merely sought to help the Cuban people throw off the Spanish yoke, which aligned with Jamey's own dreams for the island's locals, that is, the Afro-Cubans of Matanzas. The fact that Cuba's liberation would likely mean little more than replacement of Spanish and *Peninsulare* overlords by the more rough-hewn and compliant—from the point of view of their international, mostly American, business partners—*Criollo* mid-bourgeoisie was lost on Jamey. Anything deeper than surface political assessments was beyond him. He was a romantic.

And, romantically, he decided to join in the war. Though he first discussed the matter with Kate.

So where should she stand on this? His enlistment surely meant another postponement of law school, Kate knew. Meant raising Maggie without him for as long as the war lasted. Meant being alone—acutely so, given their insular life—while he was gone. But she had lived with him for four years now and had witnessed the depth of his passion for Cuba, his sorrow at its disappearance from his life. And he'd given her so much. He had rescued her—though he would never have thought in such terms—from Southie. He had supported her entrance into law school and her struggle to reenter after Maggie was born, taking on Maggie's care when Kate went to class in the evenings and when she had to study on the weekends, things that would have been inconceivable to most men. But by marrying her he'd given up the last vestiges of connection to his family and, thereby, to Cuba.

Besides, the war would surely be over quickly; the newspapers all said so. And the hastily arranged terms of enlistment for doctors would allow him to return to civilian life "immediately upon the cessation of hostilities." Also, since he would be going as a doctor rather than as a fighter, the chances were he'd be out of harm's way.

Even the Jameson patriarch was approving, having heard of Jamey's intentions from Jamey's sister Margaret. He sent Jamey a note of congratulations for carrying on the family's proud military tradition—Jamey's uncle, great-uncle and two earlier forebears had been high-ranking officers in the Royal Navy—though his enthusiasm was muted by disappointment that Jamey would be going as a healer not a hero.

It didn't take Kate much time to decide. She'd waited this long to return to law school; a bit longer didn't seem so much to concede. And she and Maggie could manage on their own for what promised to be the short time he'd be gone. She gave Jamey her blessing.

Jamey enlisted. By the time his brief training had finished, however, the war in Cuba was already over. But the army didn't muster him out. Because, they told him, there'd been no "cessation of hostilities"—they continued in the Pacific. They sent him to the Philippines.

～

"Widow."

"Excuse me?"

"My 'condition.' Widow."

Lily looked puzzled.

"You asked about my condition," Kate continued. "The reason I'm here. You see, I think I might have known you. Well, not exactly. But my husband. Perhaps. We were here, years ago. And, well..."

Kate stopped, shook her head, looked down.

"Come," Lily said and gestured to a chair in front of a small desk, away from the examining table. And instead of going around to the chair behind the desk, Lily moved a stool next to Kate's chair and sat at her side. Kate was silent for a few more moments.

"He was in the war, my husband." Kate resumed, speaking toward the air just over Lily's shoulder. "The Philippines. And when they sent him home, the army, they first put him here. On Angel Island. To... recover."

"Yes," Lily said quietly. "I knew the island in those days."

"We came out here to be with him. In '99. Across country. My daughter and I. She was five. To visit with him. To wait for him. And after he was released from the island, and from the army, we stayed here six months more, together, the three of us. While he... Well... Then we went home."

Kate finally looked directly at Lily. Lily said nothing; her expression didn't urge Kate to go on but gave her room to.

"I'm a widow. There are things I don't understand. Large things. And perhaps you... I don't know." She shook her head.

"But..." Lily struggled. "How is it I could help?"

Kate took a deep breath, closed her eyes, and after a few moments opened them again.

"When we were here, you see. Those years ago. My husband, he was a doctor, and he spent some time working at a clinic. A clinic for women. Down at the edge of the Barbary. With Doctor Rothstein. And there was another doctor there. A woman. I never met her. But from the few things he said, my husband, it seemed that he liked her very much. And perhaps... A Russian woman, I think. Or like that. I couldn't recall. But I asked, at Dr. Rothstein's hospital. They gave me your name. And I thought..."

"What was his name, your doctor husband?"

"Wistan. Wistan Jameson."

Lily paused for a moment: "Jamey."

"Yes, Jamey. You... remember."

"Of course. He was a... rememberable man."

Kate was suddenly overcome. For fifteen years she'd kept her emotions tightly packed away, the self she showed to others armored against any intrusions. But now here she was, cracking the vault herself, asking to speak about Jamey. She immediately recognized that she could not stop herself from weeping but also knew that somehow with this woman, this Dr. Bratz, she need not try. She kept her head up, made no sound. But the tears welled up and flowed. Lily reached out and took Kate's hands, and the two of them sat there in silence.

"He was always so calm," Lily finally said, lifting her eyes as if searching through the past for her words. "So much patience with the women at the clinic. Not something I often see in doctors, especially with their women patients. And some of the women who came there, the night-working women, they could be plenty difficult." She paused, looked directly at Kate, then looked away slightly. "I always thought he must be a wonderful husband. And father."

"He was," Kate managed.

"I think you are correct, that we never met, you and I. It seemed in those days that Jamey wanted to keep his work and his family apart, is that right? Maybe because of the kind of work at the clinic, with the women? Or maybe not that, because he always had complete respect for everyone he saw. But whatever his reason, it was his choosing, and I did not push against it. Bernard, though... Dr. Rothstein... I think he saw you outside, time to time?"

"Yes, my daughter and I. He was lovely to us, Dr. Rothstein. But not often. Jamey didn't want it. Things were... difficult for him."

"Difficult. Yes, I saw that. But it never got in the way of his work at the clinic. This I can tell you."

"Well, maybe not his work."

"Or in the way of his kindness."

"Yes, there was always that. Until he was gone. Then, you see, his kindness was... nothing."

For a few moments Lily remained silent in the face of Kate's swell of memory. When Kate didn't continue, Lily spoke in a tone that eased the moment.

"Back those years ago he told us that he was returning east. New York was it?"

Kate was glad for the respite Lily tendered; she hadn't intended to reach so deep inside herself so quickly.

"Boston. Yes, we did."

"So then, if I may ask, what is it brings you back to San Francisco? Surely not just to see small me." Lily offered a kindly smile.

Although it was an obvious question, Kate had been so consumed by her own thoughts that it took her by surprise.

"Ah. Well. Some business matters... Family business... Jameson business..." She couldn't come up with anything more clarifying and shifted uncomfortably in her chair, which opened a sightline out the window behind Lily. They were on the fourth floor overlooking Union Square, and the view was straight to the statue atop the square's Dewey Memorial pillar, the voluptuous figure in the long flowing gown whose model, Thornwell Mullally had told Kate, was Alma Spreckels—Big Alma.

"Yes, some people to see here. About possible. . . dealings. Connections." Kate was reluctant to let go of the momentum she'd achieved in speaking about Jamey but at the same time she was distressed by it. She wanted Lily to share recollections of Jamey—because why else had she come to see her?—but she was still so deeply constrained by her years-long habit of silence, misdirection and avoidance when it came to any mention of him that she didn't know what she herself was willing to say. "I have legal training, you see."

Lily tilted her head appreciatively: "And these connectings. They are going well for you?"

"Ah, some." Kate couldn't tell whether Lily was interested or just polite. "That statue up there." With a slight move of her head Kate indicated the pillar. "Did you know that the model is now Mrs. Adolph Spreckels?"

Lily didn't turn to look. "So I understand."

"She is one of... Well, her husband. One of the people... Out of the ones I've met, she's... an interesting sort."

"This I also understand."

Kate realized that they'd now moved a great distance from talk of Jamey. She didn't know whether she'd made that happen or Lily had.

In the outer office the hallway door opened. Someone came in and was greeted by the woman at the reception desk. The sounds of this new arrival made it seem as if Kate and Lily had suddenly been redeposited in the office from somewhere else. Kate felt that her odd visit with Lily was over.

"Mrs. Jameson, I..."

"Yes, of course, you have patients. I've taken up your time. I'm sorry."

"No, please."

"But... perhaps. Well, perhaps another time?"

"Yes. Yes certainly. I... I don't presume, Mrs. Jameson, but I have the feeling that there is more to say. I would like to hear more about Jamey. Your Jamey."

"My Jamey. Yes. Well, and yours."

16

The original Woodmen's Hall had been destroyed in the '06 quake but its constituent lumber, sawmill and carpentry workers had quickly rebuilt an almost exact replica. Groups booking the hall for meetings and events mostly came from the further left side of the city's political divide, in part because of the hall's location in the thoroughly working-class Mission District but also because the Wobbly-saturated lumber and wood workers' unions that made the hall their home were among the most radical in the local labor landscape.

So the hall was an obvious choice for Tom Mooney when he called a meeting to test the strength of his push to unionize United Railroads: URR workers, under threat of firing if seen attending such a meeting, might be more willing to show up if they thought the gathering was at a relatively safe site. To further encourage and protect these train and trolley workers, Mooney recruited Warren Billings and several others whose experience in the power company strikes of the past few years meant they'd crossed paths with and, therefore, would recognize some of the operatives from Martin Swanson's detective bureau, on which URR relied in its anti-union efforts. Mooney also brought in a dozen longshoremen whose part in the current dock strike had similarly brought them into close contact with Swanson's men who'd been escorting scabs on behalf of the shipowners and skirmishing with striking dockworkers. Mooney's recruits, joined by a handful of disgruntled former URR employees, were screening people as they entered the hall, trying to keep Swanson's men and URR foremen from slipping in, and were patrolling the surrounding streets to keep URR spies from identifying and intimidating carmen on their way to the meeting.

As a youngster, Blue had fought a couple of bouts at the old hall; he had fond memories of the place. But the density of his anticipation about what might lay ahead for him that night left no space for nostalgia. Before going to the hall, he went to Belle Lavin's boarding-house, a couple of blocks deeper into the Mission District, to make sure Tom Mooney's motorcycle was there. Blue had enjoyed dropping in at Belle's a couple of times over the past several weeks, to catch up on local doings from the years he'd been gone and just generally to have a jaw with the great proprietress herself and whatever other voluble characters might be there. But this night he kept his distance; once he'd spotted the motorbike stashed in dark shadows between two small sheds set back from the house, he carried on to the Woodmen's Hall without showing himself inside Belle's.

At the Woodmen's Hall entrance he said hello to Billings, and once inside he nodded to a couple of men he knew, but he didn't stop to chat as he made his way toward a small stage. The hall was moderately loud with talk—maybe two hundred people were spread out through rows of benches, most of them standing in small groups—but only by dint of accumulation: individual voices were low, gestures restrained, with little of the boisterousness of many strike meetings. The room seemed to sense how long the odds were against Mooney's campaign.

Blue looked over the crowd. There were numerous men wearing the telltale flat white caps of the longshoremen, and he recognized several men from the electrical workers' union, whom he'd met during the strikes back in '13. He also saw a claque of quarry workers, whom he knew from his paid blasting jobs over the years. Over on a far side he spotted Mario Fraschetti and a dozen or so other members of the North Beach–based Local 173, the catchall Latin union group, many of whom would show up for almost any contentious labor event. And close to Blue was a contingent of women who, judging from their odiferous penumbra, must have come straight from work at a fish cannery. What he didn't see, however, was anyone wearing a URR uniform, though he realized that for security's sake these workers might well have shed their identifying clothing before appearing there. And for good reason: with so many people milling about, chances were high that, despite Mooney's precautions, a URR management spy or two or a Swanson operative would have made it inside.

A man standing near him at the edge of the stage turned around. It was young Franco Costantini, who worked the graveyard shift in the reception cubbyhole at the Genova boarding hotel where Blue had his room. He didn't know anything about Franco: Blue liked to hold onto some privacy wherever he was staying, and so didn't engage in too much chitchat with other hotel regulars. And he'd particularly held Franco at a distance because the young man always seemed to have a slight grin lurking, which gave Blue the impression that if he so much as cracked open the door of conversation, he'd have a hell of a time shutting it again.

"*Good evening, brother Cavanaugh,*" Franco said in Italian, in a tone that seemed to reach for far more gravitas than the youngster had under his belt.

This wasn't the time for even brief chumminess with Franco, so Blue simply nodded and turned the other way.

Which was when he saw Meg standing at the other end of the stage front. Her sudden presence disarranged him: he hadn't seen her up close since she'd cut off all her hair; hadn't spoken to her since their motorcycle ride into the hills; had given her little thought over the past several preoccupied days. Considering now their uncomfortable last parting, he didn't know where they stood, and trying to find the right tone, the right posture, was more than he could manage at the moment. She didn't seem to have seen him yet, and though he couldn't help staring at her, he made no greeting.

"*Madonna santa!*" Franco said from just behind Blue, who turned to see the young guy staring at Meg. "*What a beauty. I got to talk to her.*"

"*Stay right there,*" Blue said quietly but with enough authority that Franco retreated from his forward lean and looked quizzically at Blue. "*You know her?*"

Blue didn't answer.

Meg now noticed Blue. And smiled. Though perhaps more wryly than forthrightly. After a moment's hesitation, she slowly made her way over.

"Herself, is it?" Blue said when she neared. "And how are we at all?"

"All right yourself?"

Blue gave a shake of his head that could just as well have meant okay or not so. For another moment they didn't speak.

"I'm Franco, pleased to meet you," Franco said to Meg from over Blue's shoulder.

Meg smiled lightly, said "Meg," and shook the proffered hand.

"I stay with Baldo," Franco offered. Blue turned slightly and glared at the young man.

"I mean, I work where he stays," Franco corrected. "I'm a security."

"Well," Meg replied, "I'm sure I'd feel secure."

Blue now turned again to Franco and said firmly, in Italian, "*I need to speak with her.*"

Franco was a taken aback but got the message.

"I'm pleased to be knowing you, Miss Meg. I hope again." He smiled at her, made a little bow, then shuffled off.

Meg was holding a stack of leaflets, which Blue assumed were the announcements for this meeting; they'd begun to appear the day before on poles and walls around town. He glanced quickly at them, then back up.

"Don't say it," she said sharply.

"Truth be, I wasn't. It's... well, at the minute, it's yer man the haircut there that's gettin' all my attention."

Meg ran her free hand back through what remained—maybe two inches—of her thick hair.

"Yeah, I'm not used to it yet, either."

"So... and what's it all about then?"

"About? I don't know... Or, maybe... It... frees me, I suppose. Of something. I don't know what."

"Free? It's that easy?" Blue ran his hand back over his own hair, longer now than Meg's.

She looked hard at him. "No. No, it isn't. Nothing is, is it."

Blue was on the verge of asking more but held back: he couldn't take a turn down some serious road with her, not just then. So instead, he mollified: "Ah, sure and you're right there." Then sought a return to tamer ground: "And... are people takin' to it, the cut?"

"Oh, well, some people are a little... agitated."

Blue involuntarily glanced behind her to see whether Treat was lurking. Meg didn't seem to notice and went right on.

"But I really don't care. Mostly it's just Ledesma. He's stage director at the Palace. You know, where I work? He's steamed at me, says the long hair was part of my dance show. It's this stupid jungle act, you see. I'm in these leopard skins. And they've got these big cats. Anyway, Ledesma tells me I have to get a long hairpiece now. As if it's actually my hair our fine clientele are gawping at."

"Well, maybe I'll see for myself sometime."

Meg appraised him for a moment.

"Maybe you should. You know... I have a midnight show tonight. And this Mooney thing ought to be over by then."

Blue looked around, uncomfortable.

"Ah, sure I'd love to, so I would. But, well, I've got to be... elsewhere."

"At midnight? Oh... I see."

"No, no it's not what you think."

"You don't know what I think."

He looked at her closely for the first time since she'd approached. "No, I don't, do I."

So soon upon seeing her, here again was the irritation of having to claw back something he'd said. But without what had been, on previous occasions, a parallel sense of getting closer to her.

Tom Mooney stuck out his head from behind a curtain and peered around. He spotted Blue and nodded.

"Well, for what it's worth," Blue said to Meg, considering her hair, "I think you're lookin' fierce."

Meg moved her head from side to side in tepid thanks.

"But I, ah..." Blue's eyes went up to the rear of the stage.

"But..." Meg repeated, then paused. "Well then..." Her words were flat, toneless.

Blue wanted to make another a start. But he had to see Mooney. And it couldn't wait. He gave Meg a last brief, rueful look, then hopped onto the stage.

Mooney was standing with two men whom Blue didn't know. Mooney excused himself from the men and steered Blue to a corner a few feet away from the nearest of several knots of conversation. He was the center of attention, Mooney; people all around kept their eyes and ears on him. So, speaking to Blue, he kept his voice as low as possible without giving the appearance of whispering.

"Fucking labor council still won't back us. And those two?" Mooney nodded toward the men he'd just been talking with. "They're inside at United, working for us on the quiet. But they've been checking the crowd out there, and they've only spotted a couple of dozen carmen."

"And so?"

Mooney shook his head. "A couple dozen out of two thousand? So we decided not to call the strike for tomorrow. It'd look bad if we called it and hardly anyone came out. So we'll wait." Mooney looked Blue in the eye. "At least... for the strike."

Blue gave a slight nod.

"I'll make a speech, and some of the others will, too, to keep spirits up. Then we'll listen to any of the carmen who want to speak."

"And where will you be... later?"

"Right here. After we're done out front I'll call a meeting backstage here. Plenty of the lads will stick around, I'm sure. Keep me company 'til the wee hours."

"Well, the later the better. Things... take time, so they do."

"Yeah," Mooney said. "Story of my life."

~

Bombs Topple Electric Towers
Power for United Railroads:
Union Radical Suspected
San Francisco—Three high-volt-
age electrical towers on San Bruno

Mountain, owned by Sierra Light and Power Company, were toppled by bombs late last night. The towers serve United Railroads, providing electricity to its trains and trolleys. A spokesman for United said that service would barely be affected. Power from a reserve source would come on shortly after the first morning trains were scheduled to run. "We were well-prepared," said the spokesman.

Suspicion for the attack has fallen on Thomas Mooney, a labor radical who was arrested for bombings of electrical towers in 1913 during strikes against power companies, and who is currently engaged in a campaign against United Railroads.

Martin Swanson of the Public Utilities Protective Bureau, speaking on behalf of Sierra Light and Power, asserted that timing devices and fuses used in the attack were the same type as those previously found in Mooney's possession, and that Mooney spoke out violently against the railroad at a meeting earlier last night before leaving the gathering at 10:00 p.m., well before the bombings. Also, witnesses reported seeing a man at about midnight, toting two valises on a motorcycle similar to one owned by Mooney, on a road near the towers. Swanson will provide this

evidence to District Attorney Fickert
and will press for Mooney's immediate arrest.

Kate saw the article in the early edition newspaper that was
delivered to her room each morning. Her eye was drawn to the headline that mentioned Mullally's United Railroads. She was further
engaged—and not a little disturbed, though she didn't know exactly
why—to see the name Martin Swanson, the man Breyer had sent her
to about searching for Maggie.

Her discomfort about Swanson was heightened when she read
two later edition papers. They repeated the information from the
earlier story but added that, in fact, Mooney had not left the meeting
at Woodmen's Hall at 10:00 p.m., as claimed by Swanson, but had
merely left the stage and had remained at the hall in various caucuses
until 1:00 a.m., in the company of dozens of people. If, after this revelation, Swanson made any further public statement about Mooney,
it wasn't included in these newspaper reports.

For days now Kate had been waffling about revisiting Swanson
for some kind of progress report about Maggie. Kate knew he'd get in
touch with her if there was any significant news. But she felt remiss—
not toward Swanson but toward herself—about remaining entirely
absent and silent while she waited. Now, with Swanson in the news,
and somewhat compromised at that, she was even more reticent about
getting in touch with him.

Later that morning, though, it was she who had something to
report to him. The hotel's front desk sent up a messenger with an
envelope for her. The return address was Breyer's office. Inside was
a postcard. From Maggie. Sent to Boston. Dated two weeks earlier.
Lansing had promised that he'd have her personal mail at home monitored and would forward to her anything that arrived from Maggie.

On the front of the card was a photograph of a dance troupe:
a dozen barefoot women in outlandishly long flowing white silken
robes, caught in midair performing a leaping flourish in front of a
large outdoor crowd at a water's edge. At the bottom was printed

"Panama-Pacific Exhibition, San Francisco." As with all of Maggie's cards, the message on the other side said very little: "Dear Mother, Still San Francisco. Maybe for a while. Don't really know. Don't really know much. Dancing again. Sort of. Makes me think of you. Much love, Maggie."

"Still in San Francisco." "Maybe for a while."

And "Makes me think of you." None of her previous cards had said that. Or anything like it.

Kate's face was hot. She read the card again, read "think of you" again, got up and circled the room, held the card tight. She would go see Swanson. Show him the card. "Still in San Francisco." And the dance troupe on the front. "Dancing again." Kate would see him and hope to transfer to him some of the electrical charge that was now juddering up and down her spine.

She immediately went to the telephone, rang Swanson's office. He wasn't in, said the gruff-voiced man who answered. Kate asked when he was expected. There was a slight pause before the man said that being expected was not something Mr. Swanson made a habit of doing. Kate pressed, asking for an appointment. The man suggested calling back the following week, when things might be quieter. Kate told the man that she was already a client, that she had some new information, and that it was important.

"Jameson, did you say?"

"That's right."

"Important... You mean, about your relative."

"Relative? Well, yes, my daughter."

"All right, tell *me* then."

"But... No, I'm sorry, I want to speak with Mr. Swanson. As I said, it's important."

"Yes, you did say that. But it so happens we got us a dock strike, with hundreds of ships choked up, millions of dollars, and fifty people beat up all the way to the hospital just the last couple weeks. And then we got people setting off bombs to knock out the trains. But you want me to tell Swanson to stop all what he's doing, to come sit here at a desk so's to listen to you talk about how you want to see your daughter, who happens to be a grown-up, who left home on her own dime and, oh, by the way, who don't necessarily want to see you... because it's *important*? Is that about it, Mrs. Jameson?"

Kate was mortified. Said nothing.

"I'll leave him a message you called," the man said.

~

Blue knew there was no chance he'd be able to sleep, so he stayed abroad all night, wandering in and out of several dives in the Mission District, until Flaherty's gym opened at 6:00 and he could put on some training gear and go for a run. He didn't really need to run in order to get in good enough shape for the short four-round fights that were now all the law allowed. But it would be a way to show Flaherty that he was taking his training seriously. Which in truth he wasn't, having put in almost none of the sparring Flaherty wanted from him before he'd book Blue a fight. Mostly, though, he just hoped that a run out by the ocean would help him clear his head.

He allowed himself a moment's pleasure when, hoofing it up to Geary Street, he saw that no URR trains were running along either Mission or Market, the two big thoroughfares. At Geary he picked up a municipal trolley and rode it out to Ocean Beach. As usual on summer mornings, the wide expanse of rolling dunes was socked in by fog. But the anonymity it created suited him at the moment, offering him the sense that he was alone, in one place, while the world was someplace else. He ran up and down the punishing dunes. Ran. And ran.

He was both exhausted and exhilarated—from the previous night's adrenaline spike, from lack of sleep, from seeing the empty URR tracks, from the run—as he rode the trolley back into the central city. But the exhilaration was short-lived: back in town he saw that URR trains were already running again along Market Street. He picked up a couple of newspapers and read the conflicting stories: Swanson's charge against Mooney and the later reports of Mooney's ironclad alibi. There was a bit of consolation in Swanson's comeuppance. But not much.

Flaherty was there when Blue got back to the gym, and pleased to see him. Pleased that Blue had been on a training run. But more, pleased just that Blue was there at all. Flaherty hadn't seen anything of him for the past week and wondered whether he was still keen—or at least intent—on returning to the ring under Flaherty's colors. But pleased or not, the old trainer didn't mince words, telling Blue that he was lining up something, maybe something good, and that if Blue didn't get his ass ready to fight he could go look for another gym right now.

"Whoa, Flat. I wasn't to know you're so shook."

"Shook I'm not. I just want to make sure you ain't more mouth than trousers."

"No, no. Don't be wearing out your patience, now. I'm in."

"Right then. And… well, what about now? Where are you for just now?"

"Now? Ah, I don't know exactly. You got something a mind? I do have a bit of a throat." Blue grinned. "Your shout?"

"No, I'm not talking a drink. Jaysus, it's 10:00 of the morning. Anyways, you're in training, remember?"

"Oh, yeah, right so. Then…?"

"Well, I been talking around about making you a match. A 'comeback match' we'd bill it, since you still got some kind of name here-abouts. Could work out to a good dollar or two."

"And?"

"And, well, the most interest I got so far is down to the Railroad Club. You know, by the carbarn, in the Fillmore."

"You mean United Rail's place?"

"Yeah, that's your man."

"No, no way."

"Now listen up. Maloney's promoting for 'em nowadays, so they've been booking the best fights in town."

Blue shook his head. He knew that the good fighters the Railroad Club gym produced, most of them faux workers on the United Railroads payroll, were popularity feathers in URR's cap. So, given the ratcheting up of the struggle against URR, making a fight arrangement with them felt out of the question. Not only that, but Maloney had been the promoter of his final fight with Elijah. And while Blue wasn't certain that the promoter had played a role in Elijah throwing the fight, the strong possibility made him want no part of him.

"Now hear me out," Flaherty continued. "Maloney was telling me they've got three good middleweights training there right now, and we can have a look-see for ourselves, decide if there's one we think looks tasty. We'd get to choose, doncha know. Three mornings a week they're working out there, he says. And one of them mornings is right now. So what do you say? Let's us chase down there and see for ourselves. I mean, ain't no harm in taking a look."

Blue was still extremely doubtful and his expression showed it.

"As I recall, Blue, you fightin' again wasn't my idea in the first place."

Blue was sleep-deprived and frazzled. Too much so to argue with Flaherty. And, as Flaherty's final gibe reminded him, he was almost broke and needed a fight.

"All right so. Let me get a wash and my proper clothes back on, and we'll shift down there. No promises, though."

Flaherty held up his hands, showing his palms in concession.

～

The United Railroad Club boxing gym was on Fillmore Street, directly across from one of the URR carbarns that housed its city trolleys. Hopping a URR trolley down by Flaherty's gym would have taken Blue and Flaherty directly to their destination. But Blue refused, insisting instead that they look for a jitney, the nickel-a-ride autos that darted around the central parts of the city in competition with URR. Flaherty looked puzzled at Blue's vehemence but didn't press him.

The URR gym was large and amply embellished, with four elevated boxing rings—Flaherty's had only one, and a small floor ring—plus an abundance of training equipment: the usual medicine balls and climbing ropes and varied punching bags but also weightlifting benches, a couple of pulley machines that Blue had never seen before, and even a gadget on a tripod, flanked by two huge electric lights, that

Flaherty explained was a moving pictures camera the gym used to record some of their top fighters, to help them and the trainers study their movements in the ring. There were a dozen or so people on the gym floor, including fighters working out, a couple of trainers moving around from fighter to fighter, and some helpers fetching and cleaning up. It was impressively busy.

Two of the four raised rings had sparring sessions going on, with a trainer at each ringside. Soon after Flaherty and Blue entered the gym they were greeted by Walter Braxton who, though technically a fight trainer, was more of a glad-handing front man for the gym. His walrus mustache and the waistcoat over his prominent belly managed to give off an emanation of beer despite the gym's otherwise overpowering odors of sweat and liniment.

Braxton had obviously been told that Flaherty might come around and greeted him with a cordiality that was undisguisedly disingenuous: their respective gyms were competitors, and Braxton clearly wasn't happy that Maloney—the promoter who was higher on the gym's ladder than Braxton was—had invited Flaherty to get a preview of URR fighters. As Braxton shook Flaherty's hand, he eyed Blue warily.

"And who's this, then?" Braxton asked. "Could it be?"

Despite Blue's three-year absence from the local fight game, Braxton recognized him immediately.

Blue nodded but said nothing, and after a glance at Blue, Flaherty decided to make no small talk either.

"All right, then," Braxton said, "I'll give you thirty minutes."

Flaherty nodded.

"So this one here's Billy Flamm," Braxton lifted his head toward the fighter working out in the ring just above them. "I don't think you know him. He just come out from Denver. Hell of a record out there. Long reach. Well, you'll see. Take a good look. And over there's Tomlinson," Braxton indicated the next ring over. "Him I suppose you know, Flaherty. Young and a little raw, but he's been scarin' the hell out of everybody this last year. You probably never seen him, Cavanaugh, bein' gone and all."

Flaherty looked up attentively at the two fighters in the adjoining rings, back and forth from one to another, deciding which one to study more closely. Blue only glanced. Stepping into this gym with its sights and sounds and smells, stepping tangibly closer to another fight, brought to the surface the real reason he hadn't been training as he'd promised Flaherty he would: he had no stomach for it anymore. Part of it was that his young man's satisfaction from the sense of dominance brought by a boxing victory had dissipated, a process that had accelerated during his deep company with the East London suffragettes. But it wasn't the physical act of boxing itself he was done with: fighting was still sufficiently routine for him, uncomplicated by qualms, that he'd had no trouble climbing into rings all across the country the past year to earn his keep on his way back to San Francisco. No, it wasn't so much boxing he was deeply tired of but the world of boxing: the publicity and promotions and posturing and reputations and purses and odds-making and payoffs that created so much smoke and noise, and that diminished nearly to silence and invisibility the exaltations and humblings of the fighters themselves. All culminating in the sickness of heart he'd suffered following his last San Francisco fight three years before. The fight with Elijah. Which, on top of his mother's death, had driven him to leave the city.

"Ah, but no doubt," Braxton continued after a moment, "you both know who that is."

Braxton indicated the raised ring at the back of the gym, near a double door to a changing room. Coming out of that door and climbing into the ring were two more fighters. One of them was Elijah DuPree.

Blue shot Flaherty a look of dismay, of betrayal discovered.

"Hey, I didn't know," Flaherty replied. His expression convinced Blue that he was telling the truth. And the calmness in his voice and the innocence of his shoulder shrug were enough for Blue to understand that Flaherty had no idea how complex Blue's emotions were at seeing Elijah; that is, to understand that Flaherty didn't know Elijah had thrown the fight. And since Flaherty was as savvy and well-connected a fight man as there was in the city, it also meant that the truth about Elijah's loss had not been put abroad in the boxing world.

Blue and Elijah hadn't spoken since the moment Elijah had been led out of the ring at Rec Park, blood-soaked towel pressed against his eye, Blue in shock at what Elijah had done, a celebrating crowd swarming the ring to carry Blue away in triumph. Shortly after the fight Blue had tried to get news about him from Elijah's family, but they had no telephone, and he got no reply to the brief inquiring note he sent to the DuPree house in Butchertown. Of course, he might have gone there in person. But he hadn't known what to think. Let alone what to say. So he'd said nothing. And a few weeks later, shortly after his mother's death, left the city without another word.

Elijah was all business over in the training ring, preparing for and beginning his sparring session, and didn't look in the direction of the two outsiders across the gym. Blue's first instinct was to turn and leave before Elijah spotted him. But his head refused to turn away, his body made no move. After a few moments he slowly began to cross the floor. Flaherty started to say something but Blue put up a hand to stop him and held it there to keep Flaherty from following him over toward Elijah.

Blue took up a vantage point behind a hanging workout bag, still fifteen feet from the edge of Elijah's ring, and watched. Elijah looked much the same as when Blue had last seen him, except that he'd cut his hair down to the scalp. Like Jack Johnson, Blue thought. Blue watched Elijah begin to spar. He looked to be in great shape. A bit bigger and more muscular than when he and Blue had last fought but, despite the added bulk, just as quick on his feet, always one of his great boxing attributes.

As Blue watched for a couple of minutes, though, it seemed to him that Elijah's fighting style was slightly different from when Blue had last seen him. Curious, even. Instead of using his quickness to move side to side, right and left, in and out, as he'd always done, with no pattern an opponent could home in on, Elijah now moved almost exclusively to his right. Still with quick feet, at unpredictable intervals, but only in the one direction. The result, Blue noticed, was some power lost from what had always been a punishing left jab. Also, Elijah held his left hand higher than he used to, and closer to his head, which meant that it took a fraction of a second longer for the jab to reach its target. The jab's accuracy, too, was off, frequently just missing. The almost constant movement to the right also meant, Blue could see, that in order to throw the combination right cross that had so often devastatingly followed his left jab, Elijah needed to come to a stop, ever so briefly but enough for Blue—who had sparred with Elijah for hundreds of hours over the years—to notice, and to realize that in that instant of stopping but of not yet regaining the balance necessary to throw an effective punch, Elijah was momentarily but crucially vulnerable.

After a few minutes the trainer called for the fighters to take a break. Elijah came over to pick up a towel from the corner. He still hadn't spotted Blue.

Blue didn't know what he'd say, what he wanted to say, but he stepped forward.

"Hello, E." Blue stopped, leaving a space between them he would not cross unless invited.

Though that space was only a few feet, Elijah leaned over the top rope and squinted at Blue as if he didn't quite recognize him.

"Long time," Blue added.

Elijah wiped his face with the towel, then leaned over further, peering.

"You," he finally said.

"Yeah, me."

"Come to say hello, have you?... You never said goodbye."

Blue looked down, shook his head. "No excuse, E. It was just... all that was going on, I suppose."

"Yeah? Well guess what. Most of what was going on... kept going on."

Blue hesitated. His encounter at the docks with Elijah's brother Isaiah popped into his head but he knew he had no standing to mention it.

"I got no doubt about that," Blue said quietly. "But still... I mean, what are you doing... here?"

"Why? Where you think I oughta be?"

Blue shook his head again.

"That's right, you don't know," Elijah continued. "You been gone what... three years? And you come in here thinking you know something? Well, you don't, Cavanaugh. You don't know shit. So whatever you think you got to say, keep it to yourself."

Cavanaugh. Calling him Cavanaugh hurt almost more than the rub of what Elijah said.

"C'mon DuPree," the trainer barked from the other side of the ring. "We got work to do."

Elijah leaned a bit further over the top rope, squinting hard at Blue, then turned and went to join the trainer. Halfway across the ring he stopped, turned and took a couple of steps back.

"So I'll be the one to say it: Goodbye, Blue."

Elijah turned on his heel. Blue went back to where Flaherty was watching the two other URR fighters but walked right past him toward the door.

"I know, I know," Flaherty said, catching up to him as they stepped onto the street. "But what about the other two? Which one do you want?"

Blue took a few more steps before answering: "I don't care. Either one. You pick. I'll see you after a time." Blue turned the corner and, without looking back at Flaherty, headed away.

Only when he'd gone a few blocks did he begin to piece it together.

Elijah squinting at Blue only a few feet away. Not to recognize him after Blue's years away but merely to see him clearly.

In the ring, Elijah moving always to the right, his left hand held inordinately high. To protect the left side of his face. From punches he couldn't see coming.

And Elijah after their final fight, three years before. Blood pouring not just from the ridge over Elijah's left eye but also seemingly from the eye itself, a towel unable to stanch it. Elijah's left eye. That he'd left unprotected. And that Blue had hit flush on.

Elijah's left eye. That no longer saw enough of what it needed to see.

A while before, when Blue had asked him if he'd seen anything of Elijah, Flaherty had said that for quite some time Elijah hadn't been fighting in San Francisco but up and down the Central Valley instead, small towns, small fights, always moving. Not staying in one place long enough, Blue now thought, for people to figure out about the eye. But Flaherty certainly would have spotted it soon, if Elijah had come back to box for him. No wonder Elijah hadn't.

And what about the URR gym? Did the trainers there see what Blue saw? Blue couldn't tell: he didn't know the trainers, didn't know how well they knew Elijah's style, didn't know how long Elijah had been working out there. Maybe Elijah was able to keep it from them. And they'd put Elijah out there in harm's way, with much tougher fights in the city than Elijah had been facing in the boondocks, without realizing the risk.

Or they knew about his eye. And put him out there anyway.

17

Transubstantiation. Like the Host, bread and Christ's body at the same time. Something like that. Or do I mean syllogism? Should have looked it up.

Kate had just returned from a long day in the city's main public library. She'd gone to read back issue newspapers, Chamber of Commerce reports, and the social register, in order to pick up more information on the coven of men she'd joined for dinner the night before at the secluded Crocker estate in the wooded hills south of the city. She now brought out her notebook and tried to take what she'd heard at the meeting and piece it together with what she'd found at the library.

However to describe it, this doubling, this circle. At the center of their conversation. One half, desperate to put all the striking workers back in the bottle, so if US enters war they won't miss any big gov't contracts. Especially now with new canal open down in the Panama. Apparently US desperate for ships. And lumber and iron to build them. And fuel. These men own it all.

And the other half, wanting war to control the workers for them. War will shut them up, old Captain Dollar said. Once we're in it, the gov't will break up anything that slows the effort. "Discipline," Dollar called it.

So a clear report for Lansing re this group—all champing for the war. And Preparedness, to make it seem there's no choice.

Different group than at Spreckels. Different set. Got the sense they don't get along, the two sets. Except about the unions.

Forming Law and Order Committee. Big push against the dockers. And all other strikers. Called meeting of businessmen, tomorrow at Merchants Exchange building. Open war on unions. The "other war" they called it. Expect hundreds at meeting. Raise millions. War chest. Will use some to hire 500 more enforcers, to break the dockers. Someone said arm them, the others agreed, but vague. Didn't mention that docker shot dead by strikebreaker over in Oakland the other day.

They went again to see Rolph, the mayor. To deputize their private army. Crocker himself, and a couple of other bigwigs. Rolph wouldn't budge. Crocker furious. Said nasty things. Even though Rolph's brother was there at dinner. Coarsest language. Even with wives present. And me. Means they really are including me, I suppose.

Surprised me, that they included me, since I never say exactly my business here. But after their talk of the canal last night, understood why. Shipping. Many of them big, big in shipping. Vast money. Especially with war. And with new canal, they're raring to connect with East Coast. And Europe. So, seems that's why, through me to Jameson shipping. Atlantic connection. Been worrying about convincing them I'm for real, and they had own ideas all along.

—William Crocker. Railroads. Banks. Hosted dinner. Seemed to run things. Open talk about war means money. Someone joked peace and money were good for him too. All laughed. Stories in old papers explained. In '14, he started Belgian War Relief fund. Rivalry with Spreckels fund. But then exposed, his fund money meant to buy flour for Belgians, but all to come from Crocker's own mills. Gave him bad name with public, had to withdraw from fund. Also wanted to build

new opera house, but with donors to get free boxes forever. Rolph the mayor vetoed and told the public why. Another reason they hate him. Though Rolph himself seems all for Preparedness. Turns out Rolph also owns ships. Crocker's bad image probably why he didn't put himself on Law & Order Com.

–Robert Dollar. Big shipping. Lansing will know. Introduced to me as "Captain" Dollar. Made a blunder, asking him about his sailing days. Frozen look, no answer, turned away. Mullally explained later that Dollar never sailed, just took the title when he bought ships. Mullally matter of fact, no embarrassment for Dollar. Also ranted about strikers, Dollar, says send them all to hospital, best way to get results. Will bring in all the new enforcers, even without mayor deputizing. Said Fickert, the district attorney, agreed to cover for whatever they do. Knows where his bread is buttered, Dollar said.

–Frederick Koster. Prez of Chamber of Commerce. Biggest barrel and crate mfct'r. Gets his lumber from his lumber friends. Makes containers for his shipping friends. Newspapers showed he already has army contracts. To head the L & O Com.

–C.R. Johnson. Lumber, steamships, railroad—seems a common trio with this bunch. Owns huge forests north state. L & O Com. Was almost as vicious as Dollar about unions. Kept barking Wobblies, Wobblies.

–George Rolph. Mayor's brother. Sugar—rival of Spreckels. Didn't say much. Got sense the others included him just to poke eye of mayor. And maybe Spreckels too?

–Mullally. Not on L & O Com. But everywhere else. Getting awkward with him. Called me Dear Katherine. Took my hand as car delivered me to hotel. Lucky for me, he's too busy now with Prepare Parade to pester me. But then what?

∾

Kate sat down to begin a note to Alma Spreckels.

She'd brought Maggie's photo postcard to the library when she'd gone to inform herself about the industry barons she'd met at the Crocker estate. She'd hoped to track down the dance troupe pictured on the card. Did choosing that card mean that Maggie—who'd written "Dancing again. Sort of."—was connected to this troupe? This was what she wanted to report to Swanson when she'd called his office, the lead she wanted him to follow. But her phone encounter with Swanson's man made it clear that she'd have to wait to get Swanson's further attention, and since she didn't know how much longer she'd be in San Francisco, waiting was not something she was willing to do too much of.

With the help of the legend at the bottom of the card—Panama-Pacific Exposition, San Francisco—and a little digging, a librarian had been able to identify the location of the performance in the photo as the city's northern shore on the bay, site of the Expo throughout the previous year. And by sorting through newspaper coverage, plus the Expo's extensive catalogue of promotional materials, the librarian was able to name the dancers: the Loie Fuller troupe. A bit more digging found an Expo handbill that described the troupe as being based in Paris. Kate's hopes sank. But then she wondered if there might be a dance school or troupe in San Francisco affiliated with Fuller that Maggie might have joined, a connection that might have prompted her to choose this card. The librarian could find no likely candidates, though, and Kate feared she'd reached a dead end. But at the very bottom of the handbill was a line giving credit and thanks for the troupe having been brought from Paris to San Francisco through the "good offices and generosity of Mrs. A. de Bretteville Spreckels." Big Alma.

So Kate now had two points of reference for a visit with Alma Spreckels that might prove to be more personal to Alma, and thus divulge more than Kate's previous encounters with her: the competing war victims' funds—Alma's and the one started by Crocker—and Loie Fuller's dance troupe.

By now Kate had an unambiguous report to give Lansing about the vehemently pro-war cast of characters at the Crocker estate, as well as about Mullally and the other sponsors of the Preparedness Day parade. But she still had only vague notions of whether and to what extent different views might be held by what she now knew was a separate—at least socially—and perhaps rival set of industry barons centered around Adolph Spreckels. Contacting Alma now, she could mention Alma's war victims' fund and, when they saw each other again, inquire delicately about the competing Belgian Relief fund. If she could interest Alma in conversation about her fund—and according to all reports, Alma loved to self-promote her role—Kate hoped it would reveal more about the degree to which the Spreckels might be opposed to American entry into the war, and potentially even refuse to join a war effort.

"Hoped" it would reveal: without fully recognizing it, Kate was beginning not merely to look for opposition to entry in the war but to wish for it. In part, so that she could provide the U-1 bureau with a more complete, more nuanced report than any of Lansing's disdainful Washington crew expected from her. But also because of something buried within her about Jamey and his war, something that, being once again in San Francisco and speaking Jamey's name to Lily Bratz, was moving to the surface.

Then there was Loie Fuller. A mention of the famous dancer and her connection to Alma Spreckels might also offer the vain and seemingly insecure socialite a different, lighter subject for self-congratulatory conversation. Which might offer Kate a thread—extremely unlikely, she knew, but she had nothing else—to Maggie.

As the highly prized drafter of correspondence for the law firm where she worked, Kate had learned that the first step toward an effective missive was to conjure the mind of the person for whom it was intended. She closed her eyes, brought forth images of begowned and bejeweled Alma in the library of her mansion, and began to compose.

18

At the first ragged edge of waking, Blue found himself on top of his bed covers. And still in his clothes. His narrow third floor room at the Genova boarding hotel had a single small window; it only offered a view through a metal fire escape to the featureless wall across the alleyway, but the slant of the sun was enough to tell him that it was no longer the afternoon he'd returned from the URR gym but instead sometime the next morning. And not early.

He slowly swung his feet over the edge of the bed. Rotating his body hurt his head. His feet hitting the floor hurt his head. After a moment's pause, turning to look at the little bedside clock hurt his head; it read 10:30, but he didn't know whether the clock was running, and trying to recall when he'd last wound it hurt his head. Shifting himself brought a foot into contact with a bottle on the floor; it clanked into a twin standing next to it. One bottle held an inch or two of red wine; the other was empty.

Blue now vaguely recalled his return to the Genova the day before. He'd wandered the streets for a bit after the shock of his encounter with Elijah, and by force of habit more than purpose had come back to North Beach. He hadn't wanted to see anyone. Hadn't wanted to articulate thoughts about Elijah that hadn't yet congealed but neither had he been willing to talk about anything else. So he'd gone straight to his room, stopping only at the ground floor bar to pick up a bottle of wine. Two bottles, apparently. And that was it. How long he'd drunk before he passed out, and whether he'd managed any consolation regarding Elijah, he didn't know.

After downing half the ewer of water sitting next to the bed, he did manage to recall one thing: he was meant to meet Tom Mooney at noon. He grabbed the clock, heard that it was running, and understood that he had to stir himself. He took off his wine-stinking shirt, poured the rest of the ewer's water over his head, toweled himself off, put on another shirt, and briefly smoothed himself out a bit in front of a little cracked shaving mirror.

He staggered downstairs but as he made for the front door the man in the reception cubbyhole called to him. There was a note for him from Genio Forcone. The man told Blue that Genio had been there earlier that morning and had gone up to Blue's room but had gotten no response to his knocking. Blue dimly recalled noise at his door, hadn't known or cared what it was, and in any case had been incapable of responding. The note said that Genio needed to see Blue right away, and that Blue could find him at the *Volontá* rooms.

Blue couldn't cope yet with the idea of seeing the always intense Genio, and so headed to the Bohemian Café where he downed two sugar-loaded espressos. He still felt shaky and had to get to his meeting with Mooney but knew that Genio wouldn't have left such a note unless it was something serious—at least, serious to Genio—so he made his way up along the edge of Washington Square toward the *Volontá* rooms.

Genio came out and intercepted Blue at the doorway, as if he'd been keeping watch out the *Volontá* front window, waiting for him. He steered Blue away from the *Volontá* rooms and over to an unoccupied bench in a quiet corner of the square.

"*I need you, complice,*" Genio said quietly but urgently in Sicilian, without any greetings or small talk. "*We need you.*"

"*What are you talking about?*" Blue hadn't seen Genio since the day Genio had proposed blasting Joseph Maccario out of jail, and he had no idea what Genio might be up to now. He also wondered about Genio's odd use of *complice*, which meant more partner in crime than pal or comrade.

Two old men settled themselves onto the other end of the bench. Genio looked around; the square served as an informal neighborhood community center and on this mild summer morning there was no spot without either clusters of people nearby or passersby, many of whom knew Genio or Blue or both, and so were likely to stop for a chat.

"*Ah, maybe not here.*"

Blue glanced toward the *Volontá* rooms.

"*No, no,*" Genio said quickly. "*Too many. . .*" he wiggled a hand. Blue wondered too many what? But Genio added, "*Maybe my room, eh?*"

"*Listen, I can't. I got to be somewhere. What's going on, anyway?*"

"*Baldino, this is. . . something. Trust me.*"

Blue shook his head. "*Okay, if you say so. . . but I can't right now.*"

"*What you got that's so important?*" Genio challenged, a combination of irritation and disdain creeping into his voice.

"*Mooney. I gotta see Tom Mooney.*"

"*Oh, madunnuzza, that mick and his little union shit. C'mon. . .*"

"*Mick?*"

"*Ah, sorry, sorry. I didn't mean anything. You know how it is.*"

"*Yeah, yeah.*"

Blue wasn't really bothered by Genio's slur or by his dismissal of Mooney. He knew well that the more extreme of the *Volontá* anarchists—and Genio was certainly one—had little sympathy for many local unions, particularly the several Irish-dominated locals that had never made room for Italian workers. But in any case Blue wasn't about to debate just now the relative importance of Genio's business, whatever it was, versus Mooney's.

"*But I still gotta go,*" Blue repeated, a bit stronger, and in English so as to gain an upper hand.

Genio looked as if he didn't understand how Blue could possibly be making this choice.

"*Okay. Okay. But we need you. Soon. Got to be soon. See me tonight, okay? Okay.*"

"*I'll try,*" Blue returned to Sicilian as a small sop to Genio. He turned and left without waiting for Genio to say anything else, and without trying to read anything more in Genio's expression.

∾

Rena Mooney gave piano and violin lessons at her fifth-floor studio in the Eilers Music Company building on Market Street at Sixth. She was well-regarded as a music teacher and had a steady stream of students, which was particularly important lately because husband Tom had been proving even more than usually indifferent to contributing to the family budget. So much so that since he'd thrown himself into the United Railroads organizing effort he and Rena had been forced to give up their flat in the Mission District and take up residence behind a folding screen at the rear of Rena's studio.

Tom had sought to balance out the domestic financial scales somewhat by starting a planter box vegetable garden on the Eilers building's flat roof, its seven stories height opening it to considerable sunshine. In San Francisco, however, an open roof was also prey during the summer months to the relentless ocean winds, and by June Tom had needed to jury-rig cage-like supports to hold up his tomatoes, peppers and beans. As the plants and their vegetables grew heavier in July while the winds grew stronger, Tom was having to rerig and reinforce the makeshift cages almost daily; after a while, the planter boxes and their scrap wood and metal supports looked like nothing so much as miniature beached shipwrecks. Or dynamite-toppled electrical towers. Nonetheless, Tom continued to assure Rena that they'd have homegrown food by August. She wasn't holding her breath.

Rena was as committed to radical union work as Tom was, and she never suggested that Tom should slacken his organizing pace in order to take on paid labors. Nor was she averse to frequent meetings at the studio, though sometimes the presence of music students forced Tom and compadres to climb several flights and meet on the roof. For larger gatherings they sometimes met at the Barleycorn Vegetarian Café a few blocks down Market Street, but the café was open to the public, so if the discussion would involve *sub rosa* activities, Tom usually preferred a less public space.

Blue went first to the studio, then at Rena's indication climbed to the roof. Tom was already up there with Israel Weinberg of the jitney drivers' association, Mario Fraschetti from the Wobblies' Latin laborers group, and Warren Billings. Since the subject of the urgent meeting was what to do next in regard to the URR organizing effort, Blue was a bit surprised and disappointed not to see any URR workers there. Unless, it occurred to Blue, Mooney was considering some kind of sabotage, in which case the circle of people in the know had to remain very small. But knocking out the power transmission towers had done little to disrupt URR's business and, more importantly, had failed to embolden URR's workers to walk off the job. So Blue had hoped Mooney would have something else in mind. On the other hand, if Mooney's next step was a more traditional organizing effort, why did he need Blue there? These thoughts knocked rapidly one against the next as Blue crossed the roof toward the trio of men sitting precariously on the edges of Mooney's planter boxes.

An agitated Billings was in the midst of a rapid-fire delivery as Blue approached.

"H'lo Blue," Mooney interrupted Billings. "Warren here's just telling us of a little business deal he's got going."

"Don't fun me, Tom," Billings said.

"I'm not, I'm not. Just... Anyway," he turned to Blue, "it's Swanson, and he's hard at it."

"Swanson the goon?"

"Yup. Hit up Warren and made him an offer. Give Swanson something to tie me to the tower bombs, he says, and he'd fix up a soft job for Warren at the power company. And... give him five grand cash."

Blue let out a whoosh of breath at the staggering amount.

Billings nodded and simultaneously shook his head. "Said he was gonna nail Tom for one thing or another, and I might as well get in on it."

"And Izzie, too," Mooney said, indicating Weinberg.

"Yeah," Weinberg explained, "first he names a bunch of places I've driven Tom in my jitney. How'd he know that? Then he offers me five grand to say I drove Tom out near the towers on the bomb night. And when I told him I couldn't because it wasn't true, he turned all ugly and threatened to get my jitney license pulled. Said he'd get the DA to see to it... And let me tell ya, I believed him."

"I don't guess he's gonna let up," Mooney continued, "so we got to get something moving fast with the trolley men, before Swanson and them find some way to shut all this down."

"And?" Blue asked, still wondering why he'd been included in this meeting.

"And? And I thought maybe you'd have an idea. Someplace to hit a jugular, you know?"

"Tom, we've been over all of this."

"Yeah, yeah, I know. Just hoping. Anyway, why I really asked you is just, well, we got us a plan… but not many bodies."

Rena came clattering onto the roof. She was obviously distressed and stood for a moment looking at the little group of men before she approached.

"Just got a message," she said. "Guns on the docks. A scab shot another striker. Dead."

She let the information sink in for a moment before adding, "I thought you ought to know." She turned and went back down the stairs without waiting for any response.

The men were visibly sobered. They all knew the history of the previous long, violent and ultimately disastrous strike against URR—which had resulted in the collapse of the previous carmen's union—ten years earlier, on a particularly gruesome day of which two strikers had been shot dead and twenty others wounded by gunfire from strikebreaker security men firing from one of URR's carbarns. At the very spot where Blue had visited the URR boxing gym the day before.

"It doesn't change a thing," Tom finally said. "Except maybe now's the time more than ever," he added with his irrepressible energy. But without, Blue thought, much conviction.

∽

Blue's mood hadn't been improved by the meeting, though at least time on the rooftop had helped clear his head. Mooney obviously had made little progress organizing the URR workers but remained dogged, despite the new pressure from Swanson and the escalating gun violence from the big employers in the city's several other strikes.

The plan Mooney revealed on the roof was to engineer a wildcat strike of URR trolley cars that would tie up all traffic on the busiest street at the busiest time—Market Street during the evening rush hour—the dramatic effect of which he hoped would snowball into a walkout by the operators and conductors of the other URR cars on the streets at the time. The major flaw in the plan, Mooney had been forced to admit when pressed by Mario Fraschetti, a man with long labor-organizing experience, was that he hadn't "yet" been able to secure commitments to join the wildcat move from more than a handful of URR carmen.

"But don't worry," Mooney had told the rooftop gathering. "Once they see it happening, lots of them will join in. That's how it works."

Mooney said that he and his URR inside men were still trying to figure out the best day to call the strike, and that he'd get word to the rooftop group as soon as it was on. They'd probably only get a day's notice, though, because Swanson and Mullally always seemed to get wind of things somehow and Mooney didn't want to give them time to prepare.

All the others had looked skeptical except Billings, whose excitement at going into action completely shaded any thoughts he might have about its likely outcome. Nonetheless, Mooney got a pledge from each of them to show up and take a role. Fraschetti also promised to bring along some people from his Latin local. Weinberg said he'd try to get some other jitney drives to join—they were in direct competition with URR trolleys—but he was doubtful because rush hour was when they made most of their fares.

Blue had agreed to show up whenever the call came, but to Mooney's request that he bring along "some of the *Volontá* boys" he'd been noncommittal. Blue hadn't spent much time around the *Volontá* since he'd been back in the city and didn't know the tenor of thinking and feeling there about the URR organizing push; he was well aware that many in the group thought and felt as Genio Forcone did, with disdain not only for this type of traditional single-employer organizing but also for Mooney in particular.

Genio. Who wanted to see Blue soon. "Got to be soon." Another reason, Blue thought, for avoiding the *Volontá* rooms just now.

As he came out of the Eilers building onto Market Street, Blue thought he might head up to Flaherty's gym, to make peace with old Flat, straighten out the mess from the day before at the URR gym. But after going only a block up Market he realized that he didn't have the heart for it and stopped. And stood there. And tried to figure out what the hell he *did* have the heart for. Then he saw that he was just around the corner from Barleycorn Ike's printshop. Or rather, the printshop which Ike used to run but had sold to that guy Treat. The printshop where Meg lived... with that guy Treat. Through the tumultuous two nights and days since he'd seen her at the Woodmen's Hall, a trace of her remained on his mind, just below a surface teeming with so much else, so much Mooney and electrical towers and strikes. And Elijah. But now an image of her breeched. Without thinking about what he'd say to her, let alone how he'd deal with Treat if he was there, he headed toward the printshop on Stevenson Alley, just behind Market.

He made his way over to the warren of sheds that had grown around and behind the little brick shop whose walls had survived the '06 quake and fire. Blue had only been there a couple of times over the years—leaflet and pamphlet and journal production never having been much in his line—but knew that the original brick front space was used for commercial transactions and that the actual designing and typesetting and printing workshops, as well as the living quarters, were in the little outbuildings. He turned down a side alley in hopes of spotting a way to get to the rear buildings without going through the shop. But he couldn't find an entrance or break in the wooden fences, so he returned to the street side just as someone went in through the front door. He glanced through the front window and there was Treat, coming out from a back room to greet the person who'd just entered; Treat immediately gestured for the man to come with him into the rear. It was Genio Forcone, from whom Blue had parted just a couple of hours before. Probably there, Blue thought, to get something printed regarding whatever doings Genio had been so anxious to rope Blue into. And just about the last person Blue wanted to see at the moment. Except for maybe Treat. With a gauntlet of those two, he decided to give up his idea of seeing Meg there.

He started walking back down Market Street and had just crossed over to the north side, about to angle away from the chaos on the waterfront and back up toward North Beach, when he remembered that on the next block of Market was the Barleycorn. He hadn't been back there since the night of the earlier Mooney strike meeting and in the meantime had completely forgotten something about that night: Meg and the mural, her painting project on the café's rear wall. He found himself recrossing Market and heading down the block. When he got to the Barleycorn he could see through the big front windows that the mural had progressed in the previous weeks. But there was no sign of Meg; the paints and brushes and tarps were all neatly stored on the scaffold. He considered going in, to ask Maysie or Ike when Meg might be around. But that would mean a conversation with one or both of them. And more, would likely make them wonder—and unless he could come up with a different, misleading but plausible reason, would lead them to figure out—why he was looking for her. He knew that Maysie was discreet about such things, but Ike was known to be a bit of a barber, a ready source of local gossip, especially when he was in his cups. So, Blue decided not to go in. And determined to shake off the itch to see Meg. There was too much else going on. Too much he didn't know what to do about.

19

Kate saw the Cavanaugh fellow coming the other way down Market Street. He appeared preoccupied, didn't seem to notice her among the throngs on the sidewalk. She thought he looked rough and unkempt, almost as much as when she'd first bumped into him on the ferry and unlike the more recent version she'd seen in their brief encounter outside Lily Bratz's North Beach clinic. Still, she found herself pleased to see him. He was someone she knew. Sort of. She was feeling increasingly isolated. Lost. Almost foolish, at least to herself.

She was coming back to the hotel from Swanson's office. First thing that morning she'd handed the hotel concierge, for delivery, the note she'd composed to Alma Spreckels the night before, then had returned to her room for what had become her usual slow morning ritual. But after so much agitation the previous two days—the disturbingly revelatory dinner at the Crocker estate; Maggie's postcard and the library search for the dance troupe; the writings in her notebook and to Alma—just sitting in her room over breakfast, doing nothing but reading the local newspapers, had quickly become insufferable. So she'd gone to see if by chance she'd find Swanson in his office, to show him the postcard. She knew it was unlikely, but at least it was something, it was movement.

She hadn't actually made it to his office. As she reached Swanson's building she got cold feet, didn't want a repeat of the humiliating conversation she'd had on the phone with Swanson's underling or colleague or whoever he was. So she stopped in a bank next door to his office and used the public phone there to call ahead. Thankfully, someone other than the man from the previous call answered the phone. Without identifying herself, she asked if Swanson was in. He wasn't. She asked if he was expected anytime soon. He wasn't. She hung up without leaving a message.

Kate waited until Blue almost bumped right into her.

"Are you following me?"

Blue looked startled, took a moment to recognize her. Then scowled.

"How could I be following you if I'm coming from the other direction?" He turned his faux scowl into a weak but, it seemed to Kate, genuine enough smile.

"Maybe you circled around behind me. To make it *look* like you weren't following me."

"Arrah, or maybe you're following me, Mrs. Jameson... given name Kate."

"Ah, you remembered."

"Well, I had help."

Kate was momentarily distressed. Help? From whom?

"Sure what do they call it, for helping to recall? A demonic device? Jameson the whiskey, you see. I'm dangerous fond of it. When I can afford it."

"And here I thought it was just the force of my personality."

"Ah well, it might yet be so... You know, you remind me of someone."

"Oh, and who would that be?"

"Someone else I don't know very well."

"And are you getting to know her better?"

"How do you know it's a her?"

"Well, some guesses are easier than others."

～

Blue liked this woman. It helped that she seemed to have some connection to the great Lily Bratz. And at this moment he was distracted by her. From the storms of his previous couple of days. And from what had become a gnawing agitation about Meg.

Though part of what attracted him to Kate was how she reminded him of Meg. The same pale skin and traces of Boston Irish rhythms and tones of speech. The same long-limbed frame and loose yet gracefully balanced carriage. And the same sort of sparky, intelligent banter. Seeing her was like getting a small taste of Meg without the weight of hope. Because despite the fact that Kate was smart and gingery and more than a little good-looking—in what Blue thought of as a stylish if buttoned-up sort of way—he felt no stirring of his innards about her. Which was a relief.

His innards were definitely stirring in another way, though: he hadn't eaten for almost two days. And the alcohol that had filled the void during the course of two nights had left him queasy as well as empty. So, a meal. And why not—more distraction—with this Jameson woman? The problem, he quickly recognized, was where. Given her air of respectability, he didn't feel he could pull her into one of the many workers' saloons thereabouts, which offered dirt-cheap bar food along with their steam beer and rough whiskey. But his money supply was now down to crumbs, so inviting her into a more substantial restaurant might prove financially painful. Especially because there were two of them, and he didn't know if he could count on her—this expensively dressed, staying-at-the-Palace woman—to divvy up the bill with him, as any woman within his ambit of friends would do. Of course, he could steer her up to North Beach where several of the low-cost family-style Italian places were already feeding him on credit. But they wouldn't look on that very kindly, his bringing in a stranger, and a *borghese* to boot, and asking for credit for two, especially because he'd feel obliged to order a decent meal. In fact, it occurred to him, among his North Beach circle it would be a little awkward just being seen with her. He'd surely be pressed later to explain. And how would he do that?

But then where? He thought of the Barleycorn, which he'd just passed on Market, and where Maysie and Ike would certainly front him a meal if he took one of them aside and asked. But, oh, the food there: he could barely face it himself, and how would it reflect as nearly this Jameson woman's first impression of him? Besides, he'd have the same problem there as in North Beach, being chivvied later to explain who this uptown woman was. And wait, what was he even thinking? The Barleycorn? Meg might walk in there at any moment to work on her mural.

All this flashed through Blue's head in the time it took him to slowly drawl, "You know, Mrs... Kate... I was just thinking..." and, when he paused, for Kate to answer, "Well, that's probably a good thing, isn't it? From time to time."

Over her shoulder Blue noticed a flyer tacked to a pole. It advertised the week's Seals baseball games being played at Recreation Park in the Mission District, with a special inducement for the week of two-for-the-price-of-one hot dogs. There was a game that afternoon. Rec Park hot dogs, Blue thought: the Molinari family sausage makers had the concession, so the dogs were great, sourdough buns, and dead cheap, plus two-for-one today, and hey, nobody could think you're a piker for making a meal of hot dogs if you're at a ballgame.

∽

Kate immediately took to his suggestion that they go to the game. It seemed a relaxed, uncomplicated way to spend a bit of time with and get to know someone who was, whatever else, at least outside the oppressive orbit of fakery that was her Lansing project. She knew nothing about him, except that he seemed to be a friend of Lily Bratz, for whom Kate had felt a great affinity during their conversation at Lily's office and whom Kate very much wanted—needed—to see again.

"Sure we'll just hop the trolley," Blue said. "It'll take us straight there. Ten, fifteen minutes."

Kate nodded and started crossing the street toward a streetcar that was stopped in front of them, headed west up Market Street.

"No, no," Blue said, "not that one."

"But... it's headed for the Mission District, isn't it?"

"It is. Right route, wrong tram."

Kate thought she knew what she was doing but recognized that she was the stranger, Blue the local, so she came back to the sidewalk.

"There'll be another one soon, on the farther tracks." Blue indicated a separate set of rails, closer to the opposite sidewalk, parallel to the rails that the standing tram was on. Altogether there were four separate sets of rails along the length of Market.

Kate moved her head in a way that asked a question without having to speak it.

"Tracks on the outside are the city's line. Inside ones are United Rail." He shook his head. "We don't do United Rail."

"But they go to the same place?"

"Yup. But that's the least of it."

Kate knew well enough from the newspapers that Mullally's railroads were in a deep struggle, including the bombed towers, with radical union people. It just hadn't occurred to her that she'd have any part in it, even as small as this.

"Sure there's only two sides, you know," Blue said

"I think I've heard that from someone before."

"Oh aye? And who was that?"

"If I recall correctly, it was a man on a ferry boat."

He smiled: "Ah, might have been so."

They crossed to the other side of the street to wait. A city streetcar soon came along but Blue shook his head.

"Nah, that one keeps going all the way up Market. We need one that bends into The Mission."

The tram left; there was no other in sight on the municipal line.

"Could we walk?"

Blue shook his head: "Game's already on, be mostly over by the time we got there."

"How about a taxi?"

Blue grimaced slightly, moving his head a bit side to side, and Kate realized that a taxi ride might be expensive for this scruffy fellow. She'd be happy to pay but didn't know the etiquette of it and didn't want to offend or embarrass him.

They looked east, down toward the Ferry Building. There were several trams going in both directions on the two inside rows of URR tracks, and several on the outside tracks on the other side of Market heading toward the Ferry Building. But none in sight coming along the city tracks in their direction. Kate turned to Blue and opened her hands in defeat.

"Life lesson," Blue said. "You gotta believe."

She looked at him quizzically.

"That there'll always be another trolley," he said.

~

The clanging clacketing streetcar was so loud that Blue had a chance to think without having to talk—smiling, nodding, laughing easily with Kate at the sight of a bicyclist running into the back of a low horse-drawn cart and tumbling forward into the cart's load of tomatoes—as they rode toward the ballpark. Recreation Park. Big Rec. It hadn't jumped to mind when he'd first suggested the ballgame, but the last time he'd been at the stadium was for his disastrously momentous boxing match with Elijah. Now it weighed on him. Especially after having just seen Elijah the day before, for the first time since the fight.

But would I never go to Big Rec again? he asked himself. Never again to a ballgame? And with this woman here, unconnected to that time, that world, what better way to return? He shook off jagged images from the fight and concentrated on the sunny afternoon and the intriguing Mrs. Jameson, given name Kate, standing next to him.

"A delirious day, wouldn't ya say?" The tram had made a stop next to an empty lot that framed the city's green hills to the west and a shimmering bright blue sky made more vivid by the massive dense white ridge of fog that hung, like a vaudeville theater curtain, high over the ocean lurking behind. Kate smiled broadly and nodded; it seemed to Blue that she was enjoying herself.

The trolley dropped them off right next to the high wall of the grandstand side of the stadium. The game had been going for more than an hour already, which Blue was actually counting on: if you didn't get to the game until the later innings, they tended not to bother checking tickets and you might just walk right in without one. If so today, Blue could save the ticket price as well as the cost of a regular meal that he was avoiding by coming to the game.

Sure enough the front gate was only casually manned, and the lone ticket taker was busy hassling a bunch of kids who were trying to get in. Blue and Kate strolled on through; Kate hesitated for just a moment and darted a mildly concerned look at Blue but kept going at his side and said nothing. After a moment, Blue was pleased to see that her expression had changed to something he thought was pleasant surprise.

The next matter was where in the stadium to go. Blue always sat in the cheap outfield bleachers. But a big section of the bleachers was a wild and wooly zone known as "the cage," closed in with chicken wire so that the unruly, booze-soaked fans there wouldn't be able to terrorize opposing players or rival fans with a rain of pennies, random debris and even an occasional bottle. The cage was a consequence of the fact that a ticket to the bleachers also entitled a patron to a beer or a shot of rough whiskey. This highly questionable piece of marketing enticement dated from when the stadium first opened, a year after the big quake, and later couldn't be withdrawn because so many fans now considered it not merely a tradition but a fundamental right. One which they often abetted with additional cheap whiskey that entered in hip pockets. So, rather than subject Kate to the cage and its spillover into neighboring sections of the bleachers, Blue turned toward the grandstand.

∼

Kate was momentarily nonplussed that Blue led them through the entrance to the park without stopping to buy tickets but found a frisson of guilty enjoyment from the little transgression and from Blue's confident stride as they sailed along. She was also surprised when Blue lightly linked his arm in hers to direct her toward the grandstand, gliding past the separate ticket checker there without so much as a glance. And was pleased to recognize that her presence likely played a part in their minor masquerade as grandstand ticket holders.

She was also pleased, even more so after he withdrew it once they were within the grandstand, to realize how warm and absorbing his arm had been. It was her first real touch by another human since Maggie had left home a year before. And the first touch by a man—at least one that was neither avuncular nor patronizing—since Jamey had been gone. Fifteen years. The heat of it remained.

Almost half the grandstand seats were empty, so they made their way all the way down to the first row of the open deck, which hung over the narrow section of box seats immediately below and nearly over the edge of the field.

"Very posh," Kate said as they settled into their prime spot.

"Well, I'm usually out there," Blue gestured to the left field bleachers, which were packed to overflowing. "But makes a nice change to see it from this side."

"Ah, right, two sides. So you said."

Blue smiled but didn't reply. Kate wasn't sure how he'd taken what had been an innocent remark. At least, she thought it had been innocent.

She looked around at the relatively sparse crowd in the grandstand, then back out to the bleachers. "They don't seem to have any trouble filling those seats out there."

"Aye, well there's a lot of folks not going to their jobs these days. You might have heard. And if you take a break from the picket lines, the bleachers is a cheap place to spend an afternoon. And to stretch out your stresses."

The cage denizens' banging on the chicken wire enclosure and hollering at the opposing players in the field was impressive even from where Kate and Blue sat all the way across the park. They watched the ranting and railing for a few moments.

"And here I was thinking of a baseball grounds as a peaceful meadow."

"Well, sometimes what people rage at is just a stand-in for all the other things they want to rage at."

"Oh, something of a... what do they call it, psychologer, are you?"

"No, no. Just lots of experience... being angry. But also hungry. So, may I obtain for you, madam, one of the city's finest examples of popular cuisine, the humble but glorious Recreation Park *salsiccia panino*?"

Kate puzzled at him.

"Hotdog."

"Ah, well, I'd be much obliged."

Blue smiled, then scuttled up the aisle. Kate was left alone, her attention drawn back to the antics of the men and women in the cage bleachers directly across the field from her. They were all of them rowdy, these bleacher fans, more out of their seats than in, many of them yelling at the opposing players in front of them but just as much calling and responding—a sort of performance—with the several thousand others surrounding them in the bleachers. And despite their vituperations at the other team, the overarching mood they projected, it seemed to Kate, was good-natured, a pleasure in their own unrestrained exuberance, a sense of freedom springing from their collective situation, not just together there in the bleachers but also together in the wider world.

Kate felt a welling of affection for them. Even kinship. She thought back on her own childhood trips with her Carey cousins and uncles to the old Walpole Street baseball grounds in the South End, once each summer, to sit in the outfield bleachers and watch the Beaneaters team, Boston's own local heroes. She remembered the shared feelings among the cheap-seats crowd there, and of her own mini-crowd, the chaotic Careys—usually eight or ten of them, a slightly different family mix each time—and their trolley rides together to the park, and the scrambling and tumbling of the cousins once let loose on the street and in the stands, beyond the control of whatever couple of uncles had undertaken the outing that year, and the greasy bangers with beans, and the soda pop, and most especially the warmth of the slow ride home, all of them sweaty and dirty and exhausted and crammed together on the trolley benches among the jam of others, the other loud, beer-soaked characters and Carey-like families also heading home. Home to Southie.

Suddenly she missed them, the Careys. And more, she realized, had been missing them all along: not just for the years since Jamey had been gone but also before that, through all the years since she'd left Southie. Not missing Southie itself, with its small-minded, cosseting Irish Catholic strictures, its grinding sameness, its unspoken acceptance of multigenerational hopelessness. But the people: her life-confounded but good-hearted father, and her big clamorous family. Who had never forsaken her. Despite the fact that she seemed to have forsaken them.

But she hadn't, not entirely. Not in her heart.

Kate's precocious intelligence and the oddity of her being an only child of an only parent—and a father at that—in a world of many-child families had set her apart early in life. Her mother had died when she was a toddler. Her father, who never remarried, was clueless as to the ways of raising a daughter and so had become dependent for Kate's upbringing, through all her growing years, on her aunts and uncles and cousins with whom they lived in a large but still crowded ramshackle old house.

The lack of any clear place for her in the household, plus her father's indulgence toward his beloved but to him unfathomable only child, had both led her and given her the freedom to seek a world outside of Southie. Teacher-training college had a been a first small step; meeting Jamey had been the second enormous one.

When she'd married Jamey and moved up to Brighton, Kate's physical distance from Southie had lengthened her emotional distance from it. Then, with Jamey in medical practice and Kate beginning her legal training, there was little time to see her family and little left in common about which to "visit" with them when she did. Still, she could have managed to keep the connection stronger if she'd made a greater effort. But she hadn't. And neither her sweet but feckless father nor her aunts and uncles and cousins had known how.

After Maggie was born, Kate was determined to give her an avenue of life that was not the lot of all the Careys. Something more. And so she maintained a distance from her family, almost fearing that too much contact with the Careys might somehow infect little Maggie with the virus of Southie. And that once the virus was in her bloodstream—the pull, on an only and sometimes lonesome child, of a raucous world of cousins hard at play—it might be more than Kate could overcome.

When Jamey died, Kate's rejection by and isolation from the Jamesons was immediate, and almost total. The Careys, though, were there for her. Kate hadn't known how to ask for help, but they helped anyway: aunts or cousins stayed with her and Maggie in the weeks immediately after; brought her meals and filled her cool box with food; slipped her a few dollars, of which they had but few themselves; and once Maggie returned to school and Kate found work at the law firm, regularly invited her and Maggie down to Southie for weekends.

In the following years, though, there remained a strain, a distance, between Kate and her family; the differences between the Careys' lives and the life Kate had created with Jamey, and the differences between how she viewed her family and how she viewed herself and Maggie, were never bridged. Nonetheless, through all the years, her family remained loyal to her. And despite her own lack of reciprocal loyalty, she continued to love them dearly. Though she was never able adequately to let them know it.

And now here she was, spending the afternoon with this rough-edged, Irish-inflected man who could easily have come straight out of Southie. Enjoying herself. Enjoying him. Such a relieving change from the miseries of her treatment by the men at the law firm; from Lansing's men in Washington; from the horrid pretense of her time with the likes of Spreckels and Crocker and Dollar; and from Mullally, the insufferable Southern gentleman.

"Hot dogs!" Blue broke into Kate's musings. "Cold beer! Hot dogs! Well, sort of hot. And the beer's... sort of cold..." He hesitated. "I got us beer too. I hope..."

"Yes, yes," Kate said. "Beer is a good thing."

Blue smiled, handed Kate her hot dog and beer, and sat down.

"So, what happened?"

"Happened?"

"In the game. The board says the Seals scored another run."

"Ah... sorry."

"Hey, did we just come for the hot dogs?"

"I don't know," Kate said. "Did we? You said they were awfully good."

"Well..." Blue gestured toward her dog. She elaborately freed it from its newspaper wrap and took a careful bite.

"And...?" he asked.

Kate chewed for a few seconds, slowly and overlong for effect, then swallowed dramatically and sat back, closed her eyes, exhaled through her nose and sat perfectly still. After a few moments she opened them again and turned slowly toward Blue: "Without doubt the best hot dog I've had... since I've been in San Francisco."

Blue smiled and raised his beer: "*Cento di questi giorni!*"

They each took a sip.

"*Cento...?*" Kate wondered.

"Ah. 'A hundred more days like this!'"

"That's... something of a grand wish, isn't it?" she said smiling. "I mean, since we've only spent a total of about two hours together."

"Yeah, well, I'm Sicilian, you see."

Kate hesitated, not knowing whether the remark was meant to be serious.

Blue turned back to look at the game and without looking at her said: "Stereotypes can be useful sometimes. Depending on the source." And still looking away, broke into a grin.

They settled in to work on their hot dogs and beers, and even to watch a bit of the game, most of which they'd missed. The next half inning was over quickly. And the crowd slowly began to rise for the seventh inning stretch. Kate and Blue had only been there a short time, so they remained in their seats.

Almost immediately Kate heard a muffled but nonetheless familiar squawking from somewhere below her. The sound soon burst forth from the players' dugout as three bagpipers marched out onto the field immediately beneath where Blue and Kate sat.

"*Madunnuzza,*" Blue complained, "didn't I hear this guff enough when I was over there? And what the hell's 'God Save the King' doing here anyways?"

But while the melody was indeed Britain's "God Save the King," they soon made out the words of "My Country 'Tis of Thee," sung by a chorus of schoolboys who came onto the field through the other dugout, though their reedy voices could barely be understood against the overpowering screech of the pipes. Kate couldn't be sure—their backs were to her, and she didn't have a very clear recollection of them anyway—but the bagpipers wore outfits similar to those of the Scots pipers who'd appeared at the Preparedness occasion in the hotel's Garden Court and later at Mullally's cavalry exercise at the Presidio.

In a moment, though, she was certain. Because following them onto the field were a dozen men wearing army uniforms from the Philippines war: the same soldiers, or some version of them, who'd appeared with Mullally at the Garden Court. This time, one of them was carrying what appeared, from its faded colors, shredded ends, and several holes, to be a large battle flag.

"Jayzus fuck!" Blue spat out when he saw them. He turned briefly toward Kate on the occasion of his cursing but there was no apology in his expression.

These former soldiers in their old uniforms were immediately followed onto the field by a unit of spit-polished current soldiers, all of them carrying field rifles and one of them an enormous American flag. Boos and catcalls from the bleachers could be heard over the noise of the pipes and the singing.

"What the hell is this?" Blue complained loudly, not to Kate but to whoever was nearby in the stands. Several people turned toward him, some with disapproving looks.

When the soldiers had formed up on the field and the bagpipes and children had finished the song, a man with a large megaphone stepped to the third base line.

"Today," the man hollered through the megaphone, "we ask you to join your San Francisco Seals in honoring our men in uniform. From wars past," he looked toward the veterans, "and in current wars," he gestured toward the present-day soldiers, "our heroes keep us safe in our homes... safe in our beds!" Catcalls from the bleachers grew louder. "So, let's hear a hearty thanks from the people of San Francisco to the men of Company K, of the California Volunteers, heroes of Manila!" he swept his free arm toward the veterans; their flag bearer waved it feebly back and forth. People in the grandstand cheered and applauded; Kate could see a few people in the bleachers also applauding, but they were well outnumbered there by those who were not.

"What does he mean, 'people of San Francisco'?" Blue said very loudly, now rising from his seat. Several people around him turned and scowled. Kate slowly got to her feet, too, so as not to be conspicuously seated.

"And to the men of the Presidio's finest," the megaphone man continued, "Pershing's own crack regiment, fresh off driving Villa and his Mexican bandits away from our border, our families, our children..." He gestured toward the current soldiers.

"Wait, what the hell does the army have to do with a baseball game!?" Blue now called out loudly. More people now turned toward him, grumbling.

"...and they are... prepared..." the man on the field called out, "for that moment surely coming, to defend us... against the Hun!" The soldiers snapped their rifles to shoulder arms. Most in the grandstand crowd cheered and applauded, as did a few in the bleachers. Kate could see, though, that there was considerable agitation out there in the cage section, many people shouting and rattling the wire fence.

The bagpipes now struck up the "Star-Spangled Banner," and when after a few moments people in the grandstand were able to recognize the tune and the words sung by the boys' chorus, quite a few joined in the singing. Blue made a conspicuous point of sitting back down. Kate noticed that most out in the bleachers sat down too. Surrounded in the grandstand by people standing, however, she remained on her feet.

"What the hell does *killing* have to do with a baseball game!!?" Blue yelled now from his seat. Several people nearby now hollered abuse at him.

Kate was getting increasingly uncomfortable with the hostility being directed at Blue and by extension at her, and by Blue's increasing vehemence itself, the extent of which—and limits, if there were any—she had no idea about.

The song droned on with Blue steaming in his seat. As it concluded, he shot to his feet.

"What the hell does *getting* killed have to do with a baseball game!!?" he screamed at the top of his voice. The last gasps of the pipes finished just as Blue pronounced "hell," and his final words reached a wide swathe of the grandstand seats. Many people now turned and yelled at Blue to shut up, sit down, go home.

"That's right! That's right!" Blue swung around from side to side, addressing the entire grandstand in a fierce, crackling voice with what seemed to Kate as much pain as anger. "Killing. And getting killed. That's what the army is! So, what the fuck does the army... have to do with a baseball game!!?"

Insults now came at Blue more thickly, more roughly, and Kate saw a couple of men starting to move menacingly toward them. She was now genuinely frightened and touched Blue's elbow.

"Yeah, you're right, let's get out of here," he said to her. "The place is making me sick. A baseball game... making me sick! What the hell's happened to this place?"

He took her arm and they walked up the aisle toward the exit, Blue going slower than Kate would have liked, seeming almost to invite, to relish, the insults aimed at his back. She, on the other hand, walked with her neck tight, her head jammed down into her shoulders, expecting at any moment to be hit by something thrown at them, but they made it to the exit without anything more damaging than a ringing in her ears.

Kate didn't know how she felt about Blue's outbursts. Her project for Lansing had tasked her with uncovering what others, certain others at least, thought about the nation joining the Europe war. But it never required her, or prompted her, to examine her own feelings on the matter. She certainly had no love for the army and its wars. Jamey had returned physically in one piece from his time in the military but an utterly changed man; though he never spoke to her about the Philippines during the brief remainder of his life, his suicide just a year after his return left no doubt in her that somehow he'd been massively damaged there. At the same time, though, she recalled how proud Jamey had been to join the army, to go off to fight for a cause, with an unalloyed integrity of purpose, such that an all-encompassing enmity for the military, which is what she seemed to have heard from Blue, felt like an affront to that memory.

When she and Blue got down to the walkway behind the grandstand, she stopped.

"I had a husband who was in the army."

He looked at her for a moment before replying.

"Well, I'm sorry to hear that. For both of you. And where was that, so?"

"The Philippines."

"Ah. Well, me too. My brother... *Had* a husband?"

"Yes. He died."

"In the Philippines?"

"No, Boston. That's where I'm from, Boston."

"Well, you're luckier than me, then. My brother never came back... So what do you think: Was he a hero, your husband?"

Kate took a few moments. "I... don't know."

Blue's face softened. He gently took her arm and led her out to the street without saying anything more. She was grateful for it.

$$\sim$$

Blue knew that he'd distressed this woman by his outbursts at the game. And by his blunt talk about the war in which her husband had fought. But he'd been impressed by her willingness to confront him with her history. Impressed too by her composure in presenting it. She was formidable. And it seemed there might be more about her to learn, more of interest. So maybe he'd make a plan with her, to meet again. And why not?

Boston. She'd said she was from Boston, as he'd guessed from her speech. No wonder she reminded him of Meg. But the intrusion of thoughts about Meg now clouded his idea of seeing this woman Kate again. Jesus, he admitted to himself, I really don't know what the hell I'm doing.

As they reached the street outside the park, Blue's attention was caught by a newsboy hawking the afternoon papers.

"Negro arrested for dock killing! Get the latest!"

The shooting death of a striking longshoreman the day before, the second on bay docks within a week, had sent shocks through Mooney's rooftop gathering, and no doubt the city's entire labor movement. What none of them knew, though, was whether the killings would galvanize the dockers and, by extension, other embattled workers to redouble their strike efforts. Or instead would terrorize them toward submission.

Blue wanted to see what the first press reports had to say. Which certainly could wait until the evening, after he'd returned Kate to her hotel. But the newsboy's words "Negro arrested" gave him a chill. He excused himself to Kate and went to buy a paper.

There, under the front-page headline, was a picture of the waterfront scab arrested for shooting to death a striking docker. Blue didn't need to read the story to know the man's name: Isaiah Dupree. Brother of Elijah Dupree.

20

Kate was stunned by Blue's abrupt departure; suddenly tightlipped after looking at the afternoon newspaper, he'd showed her the right trolley to ride back to her hotel from the ballpark, then had slumped away with barely a nod and a mumble. Which only added to Kate's discomfort from his outbursts during the game, so at odds with the free-flowing geniality that had attracted her during her initial encounter with him on the ferry and their brief exchange outside Lily Bratz's clinic, and which he'd displayed again in their chance meeting and first couple of hours together that afternoon. His parting words to her outside the ballpark were all but unintelligible. Whether he might call on her again she couldn't tell. And didn't know whether she wanted him to.

Her consternation took a back seat, though, soon after she entered the hotel. Because a note from Alma Spreckels was waiting for her with the concierge. The heretofore snooty functionary seemed impressed: in one of those perverse class reversals by which minions of the rich take on the values and airs of their employers, this particular concierge seemed to have decided early in Kate's hotel residence that there was something unseemly in a woman staying there alone for so long. And by tone and expression had made his judgment known to her, including early that same morning when she'd entrusted him with her note to Alma, insisting on immediate delivery. The fact that Mrs. A. de Bretteville Spreckels, as the gold embossed envelope read, had replied within a matter of hours apparently changed this man's view. Kate allowed herself a moment's satisfaction.

Alma wrote that she was delighted to have heard of Mrs. Jameson's interest in her war victims' fund. And, apologizing for the short notice, invited Kate to lunch the following day—at the house where Alma had put on the fundraiser rather than at the mansion where the costume ball had been—when "a select few friends" would be discussing the "dreadful" situation in Europe. The only shadow on Kate's pleasure at receiving the note and its invitation was the lack of any mention of the Loie Fuller dance troupe. But Kate quickly brightened herself: the visit, which sounded distinctly smaller and more personal than either of the other two Spreckels events Kate had attended, might very well give Kate a chance to ask in person.

～

Blue found himself on a trolley heading to Butchertown, where several generations of the Duprees had lived for years in a cottage behind a slaughterhouse at the edge of a slough on the bay. But as the trolley entered the pungent neighborhood, he woke from his stupefaction at the news about Isaiah. Woke into the pained recognition that, despite his many warm, embracing visits with the Duprees over the years, he would no longer be welcome there. At least, not by Elijah. And, he now admitted to himself, what did he think he had to say to them anyway?

So he climbed down from the streetcar, wandered around aim-lessly for a few minutes, then, not knowing what else to do, climbed onto a trolley heading back into the central city. He rode all the way to the Ferry Building. The streets there were eerily quiet, and after a moment he realized why: the longshoremen who'd been daily picket-ing the nearby piers were nowhere to be seen, and the corresponding gangs of strikebreakers and their security men were either on the docked ships working or were staying away in light of the fatal shoot-ing the day before.

He trudged along the waterfront toward his room at the Genova, only stopping at the Anchor Caffe on Columbus, which also served locals as a sort of after-hours grocery, to pick up a loaf of bread, some smoked *porchetta* and a bottle of wine produced by one of the neigh-borhood's basement presses. At the Genova he avoided the evening crowd gathering in the ground floor bar-cum-eating space and headed for his room. He was stopped by a hail from the reception desk man.

"Ehhh, Baldino," he said in Italian, shaking his head, *"that guy Genio has been busting my balls about you. As if I got a string tied to you or something, to know where you are all the time! He's been here two more times looking for you. And his eyes, when he talks, madonna, this is one crazy mook, eh?"*

Genio. Damn! He'd forgotten all about Genio. That morning Blue had said he'd see Genio tonight. Which meant now. But after the long, tumultuous day had piled itself on top of his already jumbled and frayed emotions, he couldn't imagine now taking on Genio's intensity. He just shook his head.

"So, anyway, wait, he left something for you."

The man went into the reception cubbyhole and came out with a folded piece of paper. Blue took it without looking at it and went up to his room.

He took off his clothes and lay on his bed before finally reading the note. The text was simple, merely repeating the uninformative plea of earlier in the day, and again using the same vaguely portentous term of address: *"Complice, we need you NOW. See me at Volontá. G."*

Normally, Blue would have responded; he and Genio were long-time neighborhood chums. And from the sound of Genio's entreaties, it seemed the matter was serious. But Blue knew that Genio's agitation could mean that he was preparing to embark on something egregiously reckless, or melodramatic, or both, and at the moment Blue couldn't face whatever it was. He broke off a hunk of break, wrapped it around some *porchetta*, and mechanically chewed. He took a sip of wine, but after his two previous nights of drinking he was almost nauseated by it. He put the bottle on the floor and lay down again.

His brain didn't know where to go. He tried to shake off the image from that morning of Genio's bristling moustache and piercing black eyes. But that sent his mind bouncing jaggedly to the strange pairing of Genio and Treat at Treat's printshop earlier that afternoon. And Treat's shop led to images of Meg. Which led to the Jameson woman. Then Isaiah Dupree on the front page of the newspaper. And, finally, Elijah. Then round and round again until he could no longer bring any of them into focus and he fell into a restless sleep.

An insistent knocking on his door woke him. The light at the window told him it was early morning.

"*Baldo. Baldo.*" Franco, the annoying young night reception man was calling through the door. "*Telephone. He says important. Telephone. Baldo!*"

"Shit, Genio again," Blue thought through his waking fog but nonetheless asked who was calling.

"*Mister Tom Mooney,*" Franco told him through the door. Blue's mind switched gears.

"*What should I tell him?*" Franco continued, sounding all too eager to insert himself into the two men's business.

"*Nothing,*" Blue answered, "*except I'll be right there.*"

Blue hurriedly stepped into his trousers and went downstairs to the phone.

Mooney spoke without preliminaries: the wildcat action was on, that afternoon, rush hour, Market Street.

Blue spluttered: "Huh? So fast? What's happening?"

Mooney explained that the Chamber of Commerce had just formed a Law and Order Committee and had immediately raised over a million dollars to hire hundreds more scabs and armed security men, intending to break not only the dockers but every troublesome union in the city. And rumor had it that the killings of the two longshoremen, plus all the new security goons and their guns, meant that the longshore union—one of the largest and most powerful in the city—was about to cave in and settle their strike, which certainly wouldn't encourage the URR workers to embark on one of their own. There was no time to lose, Mooney said, they had to act now, before things got any bleaker.

Blue told Mooney that he hadn't had a chance to recruit any of the *Volontá* men, and Mooney snorted, "Huh, how many of them would've shown up anyway?" Blue didn't argue. What he really needed, Mooney said, was just a few guys to help him and Billings stop the crucial cars on Market and create a blockade. Fraschetti had promised to be there with at least a few Wobbly comrades. So was Blue in or not? "I am," Blue told him. "You know I am." "Great," Mooney said, and told Blue to meet at the Barleycorn at four that afternoon.

21

*So odd, this Alma. Different each time. And at lunch today,
different within different minutes. Even with all her Spreckels
fortune, still always trying to impress. One minute so formal,
with gown and jewels and necklace pearls and gold serving
dishes. The next, as soon as she turned to Lily, like a street
girl, with slangy rough talk.*

*Strange pair, Lily Bratz and Alma. Didn't expect Lily
there. Seems they go back a long way. When Alma was young,
Lily the doctor "helped her out."*

*Then another Alma, trying to be intellectual, artsy, to
Cora Older. Who's written some books or something. Married
to Older the newspaper chief.*

*And still another different Alma, fluffy charming flirty,
when Rudolph Spreckels came in to our "ladies' lunch."
Alma's brother-in-law. Much younger than his brother, her
husband Adolph. Handsome. Charmer himself. Flirted with
all of us. Except Lily.*

*Alma talking about "dreadful" Preparedness Day parade
and "dreadful" war—used the word over and over. Hard to
know what she meant. To herself. Or to us listening. What
does it tell Lansing?*

*Lily so glad to see me. Almost relieved. Strange. Took
me aside, very serious, said must get together again soon.
We made a date. She gladdens and frightens me at the same
time. I don't know why.*

*The lunch was to talk about next step for Alma's war
victims' fund. Some big fundraiser they want to put on soon*

after the Prep parade. Not just for funds, it seemed, but for appearance, to not let the Prep people get too much upper hand.

I could have mentioned the baseball game. Soldiers and Prep even there. Didn't want to explain how I got there.

Cora Older brought message from her husband that his paper would give front-page coverage to Alma's event, whatever it turned out to be.

Alma and the others are dedicated to her fund, and all of them put off by all the Prep noise. But then what about Mullally being Prep Day king and yet Alma so cozy with him? How do these things work with these people?

Rudolph S, a banker. Gave me his card, said happy to make bank available for Jameson plans in SF. Never met him before. How did he know about supposed Jameson plans, which would need a bank? Guess these things move around, in certain circles.

RS spoke harshly against Prep, against the parade. Doesn't want nation's wealth to go into war—too few "winners." War disrupts good relations, and good trade, he said. His family Germanness behind this? Sounded more like the bank. Maybe Lansing find out who his bank does business with, give leads to who might be against joining the war?

RS to be a main speaker at big anti-Prep rally two nights before the Prep parade next weekend. Dreamland arena. Cora Older's husband, the newsman, speaking too.

Maybe why Lily was there. RS and Older knew she's friends with the Goldman woman, Emma Goldman. The radical. EG scheduled to speak at a different anti-Prep meeting same night as RS and Older at Dreamland. They think she'll pull in big crowd, take away from theirs. Want her to cancel, so only one giant anti-Prep event, at Dreamland, with photos and big numbers in Older's paper the next day. Tactics, RS said, just tactics. EG can speak the following week, he said. Asked would Lily speak with EG. Lily said she would.

*A few moments alone with Alma. Invited me to supper
at the big house the night after Dreamland, night before the
Prep parade. Maybe learn something for Lansing about how
far Spreckels' anti-Prep feelings will take them.*

She put down her pen. Yes, maybe something more for Lansing.
But nothing more for Kate. As she was leaving, she'd asked Alma—
rather awkwardly, she felt, but didn't care—about Loie Fuller and her
dance troupe. Alma had replied with that word again: so dreadful
how the war has trapped Loie in Paris, and how Alma can't visit her
because of those dreadful U-boats. But Loie must have acolytes here,
Kate had continued, a local troupe that follows her lead? Oh, no, Alma
had replied, no one would presume—there's only one Loie.

But what about when she was here for the Expo, Kate had pressed,
had she worked with any local groups, to spread her style of dance? No,
no, Loie is a great artist, Alma had said a bit sniffily, not some huck-
ster of art fashion. Anyway, Alma had ended the conversation, Loie
wouldn't have worked with any of the local dance troupes—they're
all too dreadful.

~

Gathered at the Barleycorn—in addition to a smattering of patrons
at this post-lunch, pre-dinner hour—Blue found a group of only nine.
They were split between two adjacent tables at the rear of the restaurant, partaking of food and drink so as to appear to anyone passing
by the front windows—Mooney was sure that Swanson's men were
tailing him—as nothing more than friends having a meal together.
There were Rena and Tom Mooney; two former URR drivers who'd
been active in trying to help Mooney penetrate the railroad; Mario
Fraschetti and a couple of his fellow Wobblies from the Latin union
local; and two characters whom Blue recognized from Belle Lavin's
boardinghouse, friends of Warren Billings whose hearts were no
doubt in the right place but the remainder of whose bodies and
minds, Blue had noticed on occasion, seemed overly burdened by
beer.

And Meg. Off to the side, below the scaffold, wearing painter's overalls, holding a brush, and looking up at her mural. Blue studied the wall: it was considerably fuller than when he'd been there last but still too inchoate for him to get a clear sense of the final composition. Meg turned and noticed him. He would have hoped for something better, but at least her expression wasn't hostile. Just blank.

In what had become a reflex whenever he saw Meg, Blue glanced around to see whether Treat was there. Two stacks of leaflets sat on a table near the gathered conspirators but the printer himself was nowhere to be seen. Small mercy, Blue thought.

Mooney beckoned Blue over to the tables. When he'd pulled up a chair, Mooney said they'd get started.

"This is it?" Blue blurted, looking around at the small group.

"This is all we need," Mooney snapped.

Blue scanned the gathering: except for the two guys from Belle's, whose faces were too mushy to read, they all displayed grim determination clouded by anxiety—everyone knew the blood-soaked history of the previous URR strike—but nothing that could be described as confidence.

The central labor council was still refusing to sanction a strike, Mooney reported bitterly; it was now rumored that the council was even pushing the longshoremen to give up theirs. And without council support, Mooney had so far been unable to get many URR carmen to officially sign up with his incipient union. So the plan was simple—it had to be. At 5:15 that afternoon, two from this little gathering would ride URR trolleys heading in opposite directions along Market Street toward the central business district's busiest intersection, where Market, Kearney and Geary Streets converged. Another from the group would hop the Kearney Street trolley heading down to Market. Warren Billings, who had already left the meeting, would be riding a Geary Street tram back down to the same spot. At 5:30, when all these trolleys should be reaching the intersection, the plotters would pull the emergency brake on each car, then coax the drivers and conductors— quite a lot of whom, Mooney claimed, were anxious for the union to succeed and were ready to take action—to abandon the vehicles. If any of them didn't, the saboteur on that car was to hold onto the brake and keep the tram from moving. All of which would block this crucial intersection, creating a massive traffic jam—for maximum attention and publicity—in the center of town at the height of rush hour.

The rest of the group—Blue's eyes strayed toward Meg, wondering if it included her—would hop onto other URR cars that the logjam perforce will have backed up along each of the lines, handing strike leaflets to drivers and conductors, and to riders, and verbally urging the carmen to jump off and join a growing crowd of rebellious carmen celebrating their new freedom in front of the duly impressed throngs of citizens. At least, as Mooney imagined it.

"First chaos! Then victory!" Tom closed his description of the scene.

The trolley car assignments were quickly devised. The job of pulling a tram brake and making first contact with a driver and conductor was thought to have the greatest risk of physical confrontation: from a URR security man, if one happened to be riding that tram; from an irate passenger; or—they had to admit the possibility—from a carman who wanted no part of a wildcat strike. So that job had to be parceled to those who could handle themselves in a grapple.

Mario Fraschetti and two fellow Wobblies, both originally from Mexico, whom Mario had brought with him from the Latin local, were all tough labor men who had plenty of experience in picket line battles. But in this plan a certain amount of persuasive rhetoric might be required to get each tram's two carmen to join the protest, such that the three's lack of fully fluent English created a problem in giving them lead roles. Not to mention that, depending on the background and character of the drivers they would wind up encountering, having Latin "foreigners" make the crucial pitch might be met with extra resistance.

As for the two guys Billings had brought from Belle Lavin's, their unfamiliarity with the particulars of the strike meant that they too would only be backup leafleteers. There were also the two former URR carmen but, Mooney confided to Blue as they prepared to go, one of them was so full of rage against the company that Mooney didn't trust him not to get seriously ugly if a driver or conductor on the stopped tram proved recalcitrant. That left three: the other former carman, Tom, and Blue. They would handle the two Market Street cars and the one coming down Kearney, and Billings would be on the Geary Street tram.

The gathering shifted into two groups: Tom discussed with Blue and the former URR worker the details of stopping the trams and coaxing the carmen to leave; Rena took the stack of leaflets and coached the others about mounting the trolleys that would be stopped behind the central jam-up, and speaking with their drivers and conductors, as well as handing out the leaflets and explaining to tram riders what was going on.

When everyone had their instructions, the plotters grew quiet. Even Mooney. The two waterfront killings over the previous days plus the weight of the previous strike's bloodshed pressed on all of them. From time to time Blue touched the bulge made by the small revolver he'd tucked into his waistband under his jacket, at the small of his back.

There were still a few minutes before it was time to head out. During the hour or so that Blue had been there, he'd glanced repeatedly over at Meg. She'd been climbing back and forth on the scaffold, alternately working on the painting and coming down to view it. Paying no attention to the intense meeting going on behind her. At least, so it seemed to Blue. For the past several minutes she'd been cleaning her brushes and tidying up but paused when Rena came over to speak with her. Shortly after, Maysie—the Barleycorn proprietor who, with husband Ike, had been bustling around the restaurant during the meeting but had not taken part—noticed Rena speaking with Meg and came over to join them. Maysie looked to be interceding, speaking alternately with the other two, and after some back and forth, the three women appeared to come to an agreement and the two older women left Meg alone.

Blue sidled over. Meg picked up her brushes and continued to clean.

"Some mighty progress on your man the painting there," he said, looking up at the mural.

Meg turned to glance at it.

"Yeah, I suppose. Though I don't get the chance too often. Which must mean you haven't been here for a while. You know, to see how it's going."

"Ah, true enough. It's the food here, ya see. Gives me... a bit of a hard time."

"Really? Seems pretty mild stuff."

"Well, you know, vegetables and all."

This got a small smile from her, which Blue gladly reciprocated.

"So all this... business," he nodded toward the group. "Are you meant to be part of it?"

Meg shook her head. "Rena was asking me. To hand out leaflets on the trolleys. But I've got an early shift at the Palace. And I can't afford to miss it. Especially... these days."

She hesitated an instant. But Blue didn't understand the reference and still felt too awkward with her to ask what she meant.

"I thought I'd have time even so," she continued, "but Maysie reminded me that, well, things don't always go as planned out there."

"Sure and that's the truth. So... an early shift. And just so's I'm clear, what would early mean?"

She gave him an uncomfortable look, seeming to wonder what he was getting at.

"It's just I thought," he continued, "you know, when all the smoke clears out there on the streets, that... I might come over and take a look. See what you're up to at that place. I mean, you did invite me... once upon a time."

"Yeah? And do I believe you'd actually make it there?"

"Hey, now, there was never a time I said I'd be there and then didn't show up, was there?"

Meg took a moment. "I suppose that's right."

"So now I'm the one asking. What time will you be on later?"

"I go on at 6:00. Four shows. Til midnight."

"That's the early shift?"

"Pff. Another shift goes 'til 4:00 a.m."

"Well, all right, so. For sure I'll be making it... if you wouldn't mind."

Meg's expression didn't formally change but he noticed the muscles of her face loosen.

"Well, then, I'll see you... if I see you," she said and returned to fiddling with her brushes.

Blue smiled modestly, then turned to rejoin the group. He arched his back as he walked away, trying to make sure the bulge under his jacket didn't show.

"Be wide out there," Meg cautioned him, looking toward Market Street.

He turned back, nodded thanks and, appreciating her use of a shared Irish-ism, smiled a bit more broadly.

~

Because Mooney assumed that Swanson was having him watched, members of the strike party left the Barleycorn one or two at a time, at intervals of several minutes and by various routes: out the front door alongside and seemingly accompanying patrons who'd finished their meal, others out the rear kitchen door onto the alley, some then moving west, some moving east.

Blue went out the front and onto the crowded sidewalk while joking with a couple of café patrons to whom he attached himself on their way out, then headed along Market the short distance to the corner of Third Street. There he crossed, through a thick rush hour welter of trams and autos and delivery wagons and pedestrians, to Kearney Street where it ended at Market. He looked around to see if he was being followed but didn't spot anyone obvious, then walked up Kearney several blocks until he spotted a URR trolley coming his way. He checked the clock on an adjacent office building and saw that it was 5:20, right on time.

As the packed trolly stopped, he took a look at the driver but couldn't tell anything useful from his expression: the strain on the man's face could have just as well been from his rush hour tasks as from awareness of the impending wildcat action. Blue went to the rear door and hopped on. The conductor squeezed himself over to collect fares from Blue and the several other passengers who'd just got on.

Blue couldn't read the conductor's face either, but at least he was a small, older man whom Blue would have no trouble fending off if he made trouble when Blue pulled the emergency brake.

The emergency cord ran along the rear wall of the car, so Blue positioned himself there, with a view out the rear and side windows. Because the car was packed, though, he couldn't see out the front to know what was happening ahead, at the intersection with Market. It was only a couple of blocks to go, so when the trolley rumbled on, he braced himself and waited.

A hundred feet or so north of its regular stop at Market, in the middle of the last block of Kearny, the trolley slowed perceptibly. Blue couldn't tell whether it was because of the normal press of traffic backing up from Market or because the Market and Geary Street trams had been halted by the other saboteurs. But he decided it didn't matter; it was time. He reached up and pulled down hard on the emergency cord. The wheels screeched and the car jerked to a halt.

People lurched against one another; there were cries of surprise and protest. After a moment Blue called out.

"All right lads! All right you carmen! No more slaving for Mullally and the other thieves. Your time is now! We're taking these cars outa commission! So off with you now! Onto the streets, with the other train lads. All gathering up on Market. Go on with yas!"

He aimed this last remark directly at the conductor, a few feet away, who seemed more bewildered and uncomfortable than hostile. The man looked back and forth between Blue and the street, and when he saw out the side window that the driver had gotten down, he moved his head slightly from side to side in a helpless sort of gesture, then climbed out the rear door himself. It wasn't exactly a ringing endorsement of the strike, but Blue allowed himself a small moment's satisfaction.

Most of the passengers were craning at the doors and windows to see what was going on. One man called to the two trolley men to get back on the damn car, and several people were looking daggers at Blue, but no one made any threatening moves toward him as he clung to the emergency brake. After a minute Blue leaned out the rear door and took a look toward Market. It was pandemonium: three trams stopped in the middle of the intersection, their drivers gone, another stopped where Geary ran into Market; Blue couldn't see the rear of that tram but he was certain that Billings had been there and was probably now down in the streets enjoying the show. Passengers were abandoning the stopped trams and were jamming the streets around them. Blue could make out Tom Mooney leaning out the rear door of one of the Market Street trolleys, hanging on with one arm and pumping the other arm into the air.

Since nothing was moving, Blue felt he could let go of the emergency cord and step down to reconnoiter. He went out and up to the front of the trolley. As he got a better view, he could see that at each of the stopped trams a concerted group of five or six men was bulling its way through the crowds toward the cars; two of the men in each group were wearing the URR carman uniform. At the tram stopped on Market immediately in front of Blue, two men grabbed Mooney and, despite Tom's ironmonger's strength, ripped him off his perch at the rear of the car and threw him to the ground. The whole group then clambered onto the tram, which was mostly empty at this point; the uniformed driver and conductor went to the front and the rear while the other men took up positions at the doors. The same scene was taking place at the Geary Street car, though Blue couldn't see Billings, and at the tram stopped on the other side of the intersection, across Market.

Blue turned to see a similar group of men coming out of the crowd on Kearney, about to reach his tram. He rushed back toward the rear door as the first two men arrived; he grabbed one by the shoulder, pulling him back and spinning him around. He had a flash of recognition at the man's face, twisted in anger, but it was only after he had ducked under the man's punch and thrown one of his own, which landed in the man's midsection and dropped him to his knees, that Blue recognized him as one of the fighters he'd watched training at Mullally's gym a couple of days before. He had only a moment to think on it, though, before someone grabbed him and yanked him back. He tried to get his arm up in time but a blow from the big man who'd come from behind was already on its way; the brass-knuckled fist smashed Blue on the side of his head, and he blacked out.

The next thing he was aware of was someone holding him under the arms, roughly dragging him on his back, and a voice above him shouting something about "Got this one" and "This one's done." He was barely conscious and not making sense of what was happening but when his eyes cleared for a moment he could make out a face, a dark brown face, just above him, showing the strain of pulling Blue off the street and into an alley, away from the crowds and out of sightlines from the tram.

"Elijah?" Blue struggled to sit up straighter against the wall where Elijah Dupree was propping him.

"Well, at least you remember my name. That's a nasty piece of work upside your head." Elijah took out of his pocket a bright red patterned bandana, a vestigial vanity that Blue recognized from their younger days, a signature flourish that Elijah had used to accompany their jazzy dancing when the two of them had frequented the Barbary Coast's So Different Club. Elijah folded it, crouched, and pressed it hard against the copiously bleeding wound above Blue's ear.

"But what…? What are you doing here?" Blue looked around and out beyond the alley to Kearney Street, trying to focus on where he was and what had just happened.

"Working."

"What?"

"I'm working. That's what I'm doing here."

"Working?" Blue looked out toward the street.

"That's right. For United. Who gave me a job. And let me train in their gym. And get me fights. And *pay* me. Pay me good. Which nobody else was doin'."

"But… bustin' up workmen?"

"Oh yeah? Well guess what. I'm a workman too. Who needs to work."

"Yeah but… this?"

"Oh?" Elijah replaced his own hand with Blue's to keep pressing the bandana on the wound, then pulled from his jacket pocket the pistol that had been in Blue's waistband. "And what about *this*? What the fuck you were gonna do with *this*?"

"Hey, there's… a history." Blue's head was howling from the blow he'd taken; he struggled to find words. "There was… a lot of guns last time. And… you know… still a lot of guns."

They stared at each other without speaking. Though he hadn't intended it, Blue's remark instantly made Elijah's brother Isaiah their subject. Isaiah who, two days before, while scabbing on the docks, had shot and killed a striking longshoreman.

"I wasn't planning to use it," Blue finally said.

"Neither was Isaiah." Elijah's voice was scratched, stretched.

"I've *never* used it."

"Yeah? Neither had Isaiah."

Elijah tucked the pistol into the space between Blue's arm and ribs, then straightened up.

"You'll live," he said, and turned to look at Kearny Street.

"E, you can't do this."

Elijah turned back to Blue.

"Oh yeah? What the fuck do you know about it?"

Blue closed his eyes and opened them again. Sorrow and mortification were competing for his heart.

Elijah again moved close and leaned down; their faces were only two feet apart.

"What the fuck could you *possibly* know about it, Blue?"

"C'mon, E. I been…"

"No, no, no," Elijah cut him off. "You been nothin', Blue. You *know* nothin'. Maybe Marricchia, your blessed mother, maybe she would know, bein' as how she was marked Sicilian and all that, and paid for it her whole life hereabouts. But you? Mr. Cavanaugh? With all your sweet jobs from Flaherty—you never saw *me* gettin' any of those, now did you?—and your good payin' fights, being the golden boy and all, and all those easy-money blasting jobs, just 'cause you was a Cavanaugh…"

Blue struggled to say something but couldn't manage.

"And you. With nothin' to look out for 'cept yourself, 'cause you never wanted no people close, no connection, no one countin' on you. No love. You don't want no love, man. And that's harsh. That's a harsh way to live. But it ain't that way for most folk. And not for us Duprees, Blue. We got kids to look out for and old ones to look out for and each other to look out for, and nobody in this stinkin'-with-money city gives a good goddamn what happens in Butchertown. And I used to think different about you, but I was a fool, Blue, a fool, 'cause the only thing that matters to you is that you make sure nothin' matters, and you ain't never lookin' out for no one, Blue. No one but your own damn self!"

Elijah straightened up, turned, and headed back toward Kearny Street. After a couple of steps he stopped and looked back.

"You can keep the damn bandana."

22

Something nudged his leg. He opened his eyes. Looked up. A woman, standing over him, middle-aged, pale, heavy makeup, coiffed hair, low-cut red velvet dress.

"Oi, you alright?" she said in a tone that was part solicitous, part censorious.

Blue was still sitting against the alley wall where Elijah had left him. He realized that he must have passed out again; his head still rested against his hand, which held Elijah's bandana pressed against the wound behind his ear.

"Listen," the woman continued. "You been here a while, and you got to move along. Not good for business, you being sprawled out here. Customers coming to the house, they don't like to see it."

She indicated with her head the door just a few feet from where Blue sat. Although it was still daylight, a small red electric lantern glowed on each side of the door.

"Here," she said, "maybe this'll help." She tossed a nickel onto his lap.

His head was a mess, both inside and out, and he couldn't sort out what was happening. He began slowly to shift himself to a more upright sitting position.

"Jesus, Mary and Joseph!" the woman piped, then backed away, a frightened face, holding up her hands, until she disappeared through the door.

Blue looked down and saw that, with his slight movement, his small pistol had slipped from under his arm, where Elijah had tucked it, into his lap.

After a few deep breaths, he began to take stock. Very gingerly he removed his hand from his head and with it the bandana that had been covering the wound; the ferocious bleeding had stopped, but he felt a trickle begin again as soon as he pulled away the cloth, so he pressed it back into place. He looked around the alley: Morton Street, he now recognized, former home to a bevy of brothels, with only a couple of higher-price joints remaining after a post-quake clean-up. He turned his head slowly and looked out to Kearny Street. People seemed to be going about their normal pursuits, without any sign of the earlier ruckus. He noticed a few passersby looking at him queerly, and he decided he'd better get out of there before the velvet dress woman—the presiding madam of the adjacent house, he gathered— called her local cop-on-the-take, or a beat cop happened by.

He tucked the gun into his rear waistband and struggled to his feet. He was trembling, his head was roaring, but he managed to totter out to Kearny and to look down to the intersection with Market. It was as if the events of the while before had never happened; he had no sense of how long it'd been since Elijah had dragged him into the alley, but an office building clock read 6:30, so less than an hour. Trolleys and other traffic were rolling smoothly along Market and up and down Geary and Kearny, and the early evening pedestrian crowds were moving around without any evidence of stress or confusion. There was no sign of the Mooneys, Billings or any of the others from the wildcat action.

Dizzy. Nauseous. He needed to get off his feet. The Mooneys' studio was the closest place of refuge, just a few blocks along Market, so he made his way over there. But he spotted a cluster of four or five men loitering near the entrance, didn't like the look of them, and turned away. The Barleycorn was the next closest place he could think of, so he backtracked along Market and barely made it in the restaurant's front door before collapsing. Maysie ushered him into the kitchen and began tending to his head wound while he gave her a brief account of what had happened out there. He didn't mention Elijah.

She in turn told him what she knew, which had come in a staccato report from Mooney, who had ducked in there immediately after the skirmish. Somehow, Mooney had said, Mullally and his people must have known exactly what was going to happen and when; they'd had extra carmen on standby if any driver or conductor left his post, plus a group of enforcers for each tram, to handle the wildcatters. Mooney had been physically thrown off a trolley onto the street and badly bruised by it, but in the confusion had managed to slip away. He didn't know what had happened to Billings or most of the others but, from a hidden vantage point within the street crowd, had seen police take Rena away. He'd used the Barleycorn's telephone to try to reach C.V. Clay, the lawyer, to see about getting her out of jail, but hadn't been able to find him so he'd gone out looking to round up bail money, starting by touching up Maysie and Ike.

Blue was disheartened. Almost ashamed. Though not, when he considered the recent history of things, surprised. He was revived a bit by Maysie's ministrations and by the cup of hot tea she brought him, followed by a few spoonsful of Ike's signature barley soup, which he found surprisingly soothing considering he'd thought it tasted like boiled rope the one other time he'd tried it. And by the time he'd finished a second cup of tea, to which Ike had added a dose of patent medicine loaded with opium, the pain in his head had subsided enough that he felt up to heading back to his room at the Genova.

As he made to go, Maysie came back into the kitchen. She'd just had a call from Mooney, who asked her to tell any of the strike crew she saw that he would be at Belle Lavin's place at 11:00 that night, to try to sort out what happened and what might happen next. Maysie told Blue that he should give it a miss, though, to go rest up instead. Mooney could manage without him, she said; there were plenty of others who'd help out.

"Oh, yeah?" Blue said. "Like who?"

Ike accompanied Blue out to the street, walked him up to Kearney and hailed a jitney cab for him. The Kearney Street jitney route would take him up to Broadway at the edge of North Beach, from where it was only a short walk down to the Genova.

It was almost dark when Blue got out of the jitney. The lights were on at all the restaurants and bars and clubs in both directions along Broadway. Including, Blue saw just a block away, the Barbary Palace.

Where Meg worked. And where he'd told her he'd come see her dance. See her that night.

He was woozy. He wanted to go lie down. But he understood that if he went to ground now, he probably wouldn't be able to get up again. He leaned against a wall and considered. He wanted to show up at Belle's later, to see Mooney and whoever else managed to make it there, to find out what the hell had gone on, gone so wrong. And the bit of rest he'd had at the Barleycorn, and no doubt the opium, had at least reduced the pain in his head a little. So if he could just keep himself upright for a couple of hours, he could probably make it to see Mooney. Besides—he looked again over at the Palace dancehall lights—this time he'd promised.

～

It was an enormous cavern of a place. The main floor, which took up the front half of the building, was open to the ceiling three stories above; fifty or so tiny tables were spread around the floor, with several small straight-backed wooden chairs at each table. At the rear of the ground floor was a raised stage, with wings that suggested a large backstage area. Between the tables and the stage was an open wood-floor dancing area, and to one side a small bandstand. Along the other wall was a long bar.

Jutting out at an angle from the wings, about twelve feet above each corner of the stage, were two large platforms with low protective railings; the supports for each platform disappeared into the backstage area, connected there to a second backstage floor. Along the side walls of the main room, at about the same height as the platforms, were two spectator balconies, reached by open staircases.

Blue had come in the side door, where he'd seen Meg enter when he'd walked with her there from the Barleycorn a couple of weeks earlier. He was still acutely aware of his precarious finances, so although admission was only fifty cents—the clubs made their money on booze after they got patrons inside—he thought he might use Meg's name to slip in for free. The security guard at the side door was unmoved when Blue said he was a friend of Meg Carey and that she'd invited him. Blue tried to insist, but the parlous state of his head meant that he could summon neither his argumentative skills nor his normally formidable physical self-presentation. His wound, the clumsy bandage that Maysie had affixed to it, and his blood-soaked collar, all added to an overall unimpressive appearance. In response to Blue's pale attempt at assertiveness the bouncer took a menacing step closer. Blue's instincts kicked in and he retreated a step, positioning his feet, crouching and raising his arms in a highly evolved boxing stance.

"Say," the bouncer said, stopping his advance, "ain't you Cavanaugh? Blue Cavanaugh?"

Blue lowered his hands.

"Yeah, that's me."

"Well, why didn't you say? I sparred with you at Flaherty's a few years back. Mo Pidulski, you remember?"

"Oh, yourself is it? Sure you are, so," Blue said with a bit of false enthusiasm; he had no recollection of the guy.

"You taught me a thing or two back in the day, I gotta say. And I saw you win that big Dupree fight. That was somethin'. You was a helluva fighter. All the palookas was lookin' up to you. So, hey, glad to see you 'round again. And sure, come on in."

"That big Dupree fight." "Come on in." Blue winced at these echoes of Elijah's plaint from a few hours before, of how San Francisco always fell so easily into place for Blue.

"Meg just finished," the man added as he ushered Blue through to the main floor, "but she'll be on again in a few minutes, up there." He indicated one of the platforms sticking out above the main stage. "So you're a friend of hers, huh? What a crackerjack she is!"

It took Blue's eyes a few moments to adjust to the deep darkness of the Palace; the empty stage was only dimly lit, and the only other light in the large open room came from faint lamps in wall sconces. The place was about half full, maybe a hundred people, most of them men. Blue watched as lacily dressed waitresses sashayed among the tables serving drinks, here and there sitting with, which is to say on the lap of, a patron. Blue noticed two men leave the bar and carry their drinks up the stairs to the near side balcony; looking up, he saw only a few people up there, and no servers. Besides offering him a chance to watch without having to buy a drink, the balcony had an unobstructed, almost level view of the platform where the bouncer had said Meg would appear. So he hauled himself up the steps. Since it was still relatively early and there was no performance on for the moment, the audience up there was sparse and he was able to make his way along the benches to a spot close to the platform. He sat, rested his twice-sized head in his hands, and waited.

After a few minutes he heard a rustling below and leaned over the edge of the balcony to see some musicians listlessly taking their places on the bandstand. Shortly after, they began a slow dance tune. Several couples got up and began to dance. Blue also saw a couple of waitresses put down their serving trays and accompany patrons to the dance floor. After about fifteen minutes of alternatingly slow and fast tunes, the band played a fanfare, the lights over the stage flashed off and on and off again, and a stage curtain descended. Blue could hear shuffling behind the curtain, then silence, then the band struck up a lively number with some kind of exotic back strains played on a clarinet. The curtain slowly lifted to reveal a dozen women in ragged formation in front of large cutouts of thick-canopied trees, complete with hanging vines, interspersed with large brightly colored cutouts of gorillas, lions, tigers and hippos. The women were barefoot, dressed in grass-like skirts and one-shoulder leopard skin "jungle" tunics, with gapes along the ribcage sides revealing that, at least above the waist, they wore nothing underneath. As soon as the curtain was fully raised, they began their performance.

Artistic it wasn't. At least it was energetic. The music was loud and jazzy, each tune including a sort of tropical backstory with too-tling clarinet, hand cymbals and drums. The dancers mostly stretched, gyrated and jumped in a marginally organized choreography that seemed designed primarily to maximize the revealing flapping of their outfits. Many patrons watched, but others drank and talked without paying any attention, and a dozen or so couples continued their own dancing on the floor in front of the stage.

After four of these numbers, the music stopped, the dancers retreated to the rear of the stage and the stage lights dimmed. Blue could see and hear movement in the dark shadows of the raised platform near him. A few moments more and a deep-toned drum began to beat, its rhythm slowly increasing until it ended with a flourish and a bang of cymbals. As it did, a spotlight snapped onto the platform, and at the same moment there came an astonishing live roar from what sounded, however implausibly, like a big jungle cat.

And there she was: Meg. She was holding onto a long green sash that seemed anchored to a beam or something in the darkness above her. Her costume was similar to the one worn by the women on the stage below, except that the grass skirt was replaced by a short loin cloth that emphasized Meg's long, lean young legs; the tight brief garment underneath it was beige, giving the impression of no garment at all. To top it off, she wore a waist length blonde wig, held to her head with a leopard skin band, to replace her own long hair which she'd so recently lopped off.

The animal roar had come from a large wild cat—a mountain lion, Blue thought, though absurdly it had been dyed yellow and given black stripes—held in a wooden cage that had been rolled out onto the platform to a spot a few feet behind Meg, and through the bars of which the animal was able to stretch a clawed front paw. In the shadows behind the cage Blue could just make out a man with a long pole, who every so often poked it through the bars to provoke a roar from the big cat. The jungle motif was meant to be enhanced, it seemed, by more tree and gorilla cutouts alongside the cage.

Blue watched in amazement as Meg was able, in the midst of so much ridiculous tat—including frequent pole-prodded roars from the big cat—to put on a performance of grace and even a kind of dignity. Her movements were slow and sinuous but somehow avoided salaciousness, despite the costume and the lurid setting. She used the hanging sash as a prop, allowing it to wrap and caress her as she flowed around the platform in movements that drew on her years of training in classical and modern dance. These sources were lost on Blue, as no doubt on all the other gobsmacked men, but he was struck by the beauty and elegance of her movements. At the same time he was mesmerized, along with the rest of the male audience, by her shapely long bare legs, made to seem even longer and barer by the skimpy costume.

He was sitting at the stage end of the balcony, just a few feet from the edge of Meg's platform. As she danced, she stared out into space, looking neither down at the people on the main floor nor over to the near balcony where Blue sat. In any case it was quite dark in the balcony, especially in contrast to the spotlighted platform. Still, Blue thought he saw her eyes flicker in his direction.

She did four numbers, the first three of which the dancers below shadowed with their own performance; for the finale, however, the stage went dark and the spotlight on Meg went from gold to rose. When it was over, the platform went dark and the audience heartily applauded and cheered. With not a little lustiness. After a few moments some of the stage lights below came back up, and the place seemed to exhale. Blue found himself leaning forward, holding onto the rail. He slumped back on the bench, and only then remembered the pain. He held his head in his hands, not yet able to think about what to do next.

"Excuse me." There was a tap at his shoulder; he must have drifted off. "Are you Blue?"

He lifted his head to see a young teenage girl at his side.

"Hey, I'm blue, too," came from a man nearby. "What about me?"

The girl flinched, looking back and forth.

"Take no notice," Blue said to her kindly. "Yeah that's me."

"Well, Meg asked me if I'd show you back to where she's taking her break. If you..."

"Ah, yeah. Of course. Lead the way."

He was unsteady on his feet and his eyes had a hard time focusing, but the mention of Meg's name helped him keep moving as the girl made her way down the stairs to the main floor, then around to where Blue had entered the building and up a back stairway. They came out onto a second-floor backstage that appeared to wrap around the entire rear of the building. It was cluttered with props and broken furniture and had a strong rank smell coming from the big cat's cage, which stood between the top of the stairs and the entrance to the platform. Wearing a kind of kimono over her stage outfit, minus the wig, Meg came around from behind the cage.

"Thanks, Oonagh," Meg said to the girl, who beamed at Meg with adoration. "I owe you."

Meg stared at Blue, then looked at Oonagh and shook her head slightly. Oonagh hied off into the backstage nether reaches.

"I'm sorry I had to send the girl," Meg said, "but it's not exactly a good idea for me to show up in the bleachers there." She peered hard at him. "Jesus, are you alright?"

"Well, other days I'd have something smart to say to that... but not today."

He slumped against a stack of chairs. Meg came closer, looked at his bandaged head, the blood on his clothes, the daze in his eyes.

"Good lord. Come on."

She took his arm and led him around the cage. Against a wall was a cot with rumpled bedding, a table with some notebooks and a block of paper and a tin of colored pencils, and an open clothes trunk. She sat him on the cot and sat down next to him.

The big cat stirred in its cage and snarled.

"It's all right, lovely," she said softly to the animal; at the sound of Meg's voice, the cat lay down again. "She's just curious about you. She'll be all right. But I don't know about you. What happened?"

"Yeah, it was a bad doin' over there, with the trolleys. They were waitin' on us. We were well and truly fucked."

"What about the others?"

"Mostly okay, I think. Except Rena got pinched. Tom's trying to get up bail money."

She looked him over for a moment: "And what are you doing here, anyway? Like... this." She indicated his battered head.

"Well, I don't know if you recall and all, but I said I would."

Meg paused and looked at him.

"Yes, you did," she said softly. "Here, let me look at this," she said, suddenly brusque, and put her fingers to the edge of the bandage.

A pained grunt escaped from Blue, and in response the big cat leaped up at the cage bars and snarled.

"*Ma'don'!*" Blue said, jerking away from the cat despite the fact that he and Meg were safely ten feet away.

"Oh, she's okay. Good thing the other one isn't here. He'd be eatin' the bars." She went back to investigating the bandage and the wound. "So who did this patch-up for you?"

"Uh, Maysie. I went over there, after."

"Yeah, well," Meg said, "it's about the same as her cooking."

"Hey, I thought…"

"Don't get me wrong. I love Maysie. And the Barleycorn. I just don't go when I'm hungry."

"Hah. I knew you and I'd be snug about something or other."

"Hold still." She pried up the edge of the bandages.

"Inclined to this sort of thing, are you?" he said.

"Don't worry, I'm trained."

"Well, sure *that's* not a word I would've put on yourself."

She frowned at him briefly then returned to her examination of the wound.

"This needs to get cleaned. And a proper bandage." She looked around at the table and the trunk. "I don't have anything right to hand. And I've got to go back out there in a minute… Tell you what. You wait here. Lie down. Rest a bit. And I'll see what I can do when I finish work. A couple of hours."

Blue sighed. "Nothing I'd like better. But I've got to go. Things to… tend to."

The stage curtain was lowered and the musicians struck up below.

Meg's face turned sharp. "Suit yourself."

"Ah, now, don't be like that."

"Like what?"

"Arrah…" But he didn't have the energy to spar with her. And more, didn't want to. "I don't know."

"No, you don't, do you?"

The curtain lifted on the dancers' next performance below. The man with the animal prod appeared from backstage.

"Time, Meg," he said.

She stared at Blue for a moment, shook her head, and got up. Blue got to his feet.

"Your dancing. So... gorgeous... I... had no idea."

Meg picked up the long wig, looked at Blue: "You still don't."

23

Chained-Up Father
Won't Press Charges

San Francisco—An 81-year-old man told police his daughter chained him to a bathroom pipe for a week, forced him to eat cold gruel from a dog bowl, and beat him with his own hat.

When police arrested the daughter, she told them that she treated her father that way because she "didn't like him anymore."

The daughter was released, however, when the father refused to press charges. "With children, you have to overlook some things," he said.

In this afternoon's paper, Maggie.
I saved it to show you. When we see each other again.
For us to have a laugh together.
I'd hope.

24

It was about 2:00 in the morning and Franco the night clerk was asleep in his cubbyhole. For which Blue was thankful. The nosy youngster would certainly have noticed the large bandage on his hatless head when Blue moved past on his way to the stairs. And even though Blue would have ignored Franco's inevitable attempt to engage him in conversation, word of his injury would surely have made the rounds of the Genova by the time Blue next emerged from his room. The occasion for the wound would certainly be met with respect around the hotel, if Blue were to explain it. But that would give people there an opening into Blue's doings. Which was something he assiduously avoided.

By the time he got back to the Genova he was in a storming foul mind. He still had a lot of pain, though it had been transferred somewhat, from a physical sensation to an idea of pain, by the second dose of medicinal opium he'd been given at Belle Lavin's just before he'd left there, a little while before. More than the wound, though, he was miserable because of the multiple helpings of bad news he'd been served over the past several hours. It all seemed to be falling apart.

Tom Mooney had shown up at Belle's as he'd promised, along with Rena whom he'd managed to bail out of jail. Also around the big communal table there were Warren Billings; Izzy Weinberg, organizer of the jitney drivers; Mario Fraschetti from the IWW Latin local and the two Wobbly compadres who'd been with him at the Market Street action that afternoon; Belle's two boarders whom Billings had recruited to hand out leaflets on the backed-up trams; plus the two former URR carmen who'd been most involved in talking up the union with their erstwhile workmates.

Tom, normally irrepressible to the point of delusion, was despairing. Despite months of recruiting and the bravado of the wildcat action, in the end only six carmen had left their posts on the trams that afternoon. Six, Tom repeated. Yes, they'd managed to tie up rush hour. But none of the drivers or conductors of the following trams had joined, and Mullally had men standing by to replace the wayward six. The trains had begun rolling again in half an hour.

Somehow, Mooney said, Mullally's henchman Swanson had found out in advance about their move. Mooney wondered whether Swanson had gotten an early view of the strike leaflet. The day before, Mooney heard, Swanson had been spotted going into Treat's printshop. Mooney had assumed it was to make Treat the same offer as Swanson had made to Billings and to Weinberg: a big reward for tying Mooney to the electrical towers bombing. But maybe while Swanson was at the shop he'd gotten a peek at one of the leaflets that Treat was just then printing, announcing the wildcat strike. Mooney hadn't been able to find out anything more because Treat hadn't been heard from after he dropped off the leaflets at the Barleycorn. Anyway, what does it matter, Mooney finally said. It's over.

Belle then added her own depressing piece of news. The longshoremen, she'd been told, were going to end their strike the following day. The largest, longest-running, most effective and most contentious strike for years was collapsing. What's more, the dockers were going back to work without so much as a penny's wage raise or other concession except for a vague promise by the shipowners that the union would still be "recognized." The killings of the two dock workers over the previous week, on top of the many who'd been sent to the hospital at the hands of the shippers' security men, without District Attorney Fickert prosecuting a single one of them, plus the formation of the million dollar–supported Law and Order Committee which promised to bring in hundreds more strikebreakers and armed security men, with the aim of creating a nonunion waterfront, had finally pushed the dockers to capitulate.

When Belle finished talking, the room was quiet. Billings was the only one whose energy seemed unflagged; though as usual he'd said nothing during the discussions, he fidgeted in his seat as if he couldn't wait to get on to the next thing, whatever that might be.

Blue moved away from the table to have his wound tended by Lily Bratz, whom Belle had summoned. Billings came over and leaned close: "Mexico!" he half-whispered to Blue. "Villa! Because you know, freighters'll be sailing again soon." Blue was grimacing with pain as Lily cleaned and stitched the wound, and had to keep his head still while she worked, so he couldn't respond. Which was just as well since he didn't know what he'd say. Not because Billings's suggestion seemed outlandish. But because, at that moment, it didn't.

The gathering was about to break up in a fog of absolute defeat. Mario Fraschetti, though, wasn't ready to let them go.

"But what's about the Preparedness shit," he challenged the room in his forceful if ragged English. "Saturday this fucking parade, and we got nothing on plan. Nothing, 'cept everybody stay away. Don't nobody go near, people is saying, so we don't make it seem like a bigger crowd behind it. But this is weak, this way, a weak thing. I say we got to show ourselves... maybe march right into the middle, something like this. *Something* to show anyway. Something..."

The group around the table shifted uncomfortably but no one said anything.

"I mean, I was talkin' to the dockers, you know, so many of them on the streets down by the piers every day anyways, the Ferry Building, the 'xact place the parade gonna start. But now they say to me no, they're all tired out, and like that, and they going off the streets, like Belle says. So they not even gonna be down there on parade day. And so nothin'. We got nothin'. And this parade, it's gonna go on like all the rest of us isn't even livin'!"

For a few moments nothing came from the dejected group. Lily finally spoke up. She reminded everyone, in a moderately positive voice, that there was to be a big anti-Preparedness rally the next night at Dreamland. That they expected thousands of people. That maybe there they'd make some plan against the parade. And at any rate just having all those people show up at the rally, that was something.

By the shake of his head, it was clear that Fraschetti was unmoved.

So was Blue. He was too battered, and too thick with a new dose of opium, to say anything, but he and Fraschetti exchanged a look of shared anger and frustration.

Izzy Weinberg had his jitney car and offered Blue a lift back to North Beach. Fraschetti and his two Mexican Wobbly mates hitched a ride with them. Fraschetti took the opportunity to speak his mind to Blue in Italian without having to consider what any of the others would think.

"*Baldo. I got to say. The Volontá. I don't understand. They* hate *the war, what with Italy telling them they're traitors for not joining. Hate it more than just about anyone in this town. But when I went there, two times I went, to talk to them about doing something against the parade, all they said was just stay away. Not all of them—I was talking to Parenti and another Lucchese, and they were hungry to do something, but they said it'd been impossible to get anybody else there to agree on anything, all these fucking antiorganizzatori, you can't get two of them to agree the sun's gonna come up. So Parenti said maybe he'd do up a leaflet or something himself, saying people ought to jump into the parade and block it up, or anything else to foul it, you know. But the next time I went over there he wasn't around, so then I'm talking to that Pugliese Centrone… you know he doesn't talk to me much, since he hates Wobblies, or at least he says he does, but I think mostly he just can't stand Parenti, 'cause after all I'm a Wobbly through and through and he talks to me, at least sometimes. Anyway, he was agreeing with me that just stay away was no kind of stand to take, when that crazy Forcone came up to us…*"

Blue interrupted: "*Genio, you mean?*"

There were two Forcones, unrelated, within the extended *Volontá* galaxy.

"*Yeah, Genio, the really nutso one. Ahh, he's a friend of yours, eh, I'm sorry, but…*"

Blue raised his hand slightly to signal that he wasn't bothered and for Fraschetti to continue.

"*Anyway, he says to us, to me and Centrone both, he almost orders us—I don't know who the hell he thinks he is—but he says, 'You heard what everyone's doing, so don't be no hero. Just make sure you do what everyone else does.' This coming from mister individualismo himself, eh? And then he raises his voice like he's my father or something, no, worse, like he's a fucking priest, and gets right in my face and he says, 'So JUST... STAY... AWAY!'... Can you believe it?"*

Blue was dispirited by Fraschetti's description of the *Volontá* group's failure, or refusal, to galvanize against the parade: if the *Volontá* wasn't going to do something forceful, dramatic, to oppose the crude propaganda of Preparedness, who the hell would? But he had no ideas to offer Fraschetti, or even the energy to respond. He could do nothing but let Fraschetti's words hang there as Weinberg stopped the jitney to let Fraschetti and his Wobbly mates out on Broadway, where the IWW local's office was.

"I don't know, Baldino," Fraschetti said as he got out. *"Except I'll never stop."*

Not only was Fraschetti's report disheartening to Blue but the mention of Genio Forcone reminded Blue that he still hadn't responded to Genio's urgent request to come see him. Genio, whom Blue had last seen through the window of the printshop. The printshop run by Treat. Who Mooney said was suddenly nowhere around. The printshop where Meg stayed. With Treat.

Genio. Treat. Meg. In his ragged, pained, opium-addled state, it was all too much. The only thing he wanted, desperately, was to get to his room, lock the door and crawl under the bedcovers.

He hauled himself up the stairs to the Genova's third floor. The place was dark and still. But as he neared his room, something made him stop: a slight noise from inside, or a change in the moonlight that filtered under the door: in his fog he wasn't sure what it was that had stopped him. He stood very still and listened, watched the bottom of the door. Nothing. But his insides told him something different. He reached back and touched the pistol at the small of his back, then quietly made his way over to the hallway window. Slowly he raised the bottom pane, stopping with each slight creak, until there was enough room for him to crawl out onto the fire escape.

He picked his way silently over to the window of his room. When he reached the ledge, he pulled the gun from his waistband and slowly edged himself to a position where he could peer through the space at the bottom of the partially open window. He could see that a figure was sitting on his bed but the room was too dark for him to make out any features or whether there was more than the one person. He took a deep breath, then yanked up the window with his left hand and pointed the pistol with his right.

"Freeze!" he barked.

The figure turned, but relatively slowly, without alarm.

"Why don't you come in?" Meg said calmly, her voice a bit slurred. "No need for both of us to freeze."

Blue was simultaneously stunned and relieved to see that it was Meg. Then annoyed. Then also pleased. He climbed into the room and stood by the window, staring at her. A half-empty bottle of something sat at her feet.

"You know, that's exactly how I got in," she said cheerily if thickly. "Except for the 'freeze!' part... And the gun."

"Aye, I might wonder." He lowered the pistol.

"Well, the young guy downstairs, he took a shine to me and told me which room was yours. Then he sort of left me... to my own devices."

"Yeah, a piece of work, he is. So now I know *how* you got in."

"Next question's going to be tougher, right?"

"Right, so." He put the gun on a little table next to the bed and sat down next to her, but kept a couple of feet space between them.

"You want to take a guess?"

"Arrah... maybe you... got hungry for something."

She shook her head. "Nope, I wouldn't say that."

He looked down at the wine bottle. "Well, thirsty anyway."

She also looked at the bottle. "Yeah, I took the liberty."

"You take anything else?"

"Mm, no... Not yet."

He considered her a moment. She leaned down, picked up the bottle, took a swig.

"So, if it wasn't 'cause you're hungry...?"

She took a few moments to respond, and when she did her voice was huskier, suddenly serious. "Well, you... showed up. At the Palace.

You said you would. And you did. Even with all that…" She indicated his wound.

Blue moved his head slightly to acknowledge what she'd said, but its significance escaped him.

"I had an art teacher once," Meg continued, "and she always used to say that half of producing good art was just making sure to show up at the easel. When the world is always pulling you away."

Meg let the remark sit there, as if it were an explanation. Blue furrowed his brows.

"Sure is it art, now, we're gonna talk?"

"Things got bad for you out there." She reached out and put both hands gently on Blue's cheeks as if to hold his face still for her to see him better. "But the thing is… you didn't… disappear."

Blue didn't move or speak; he still didn't understand her but didn't want to do anything that would rend the intimate cloak she was weaving. She, and the opium.

"So…" he finally said as she slowly withdrew her hands, "showing up is the half of it. And what would be the other half?"

Blue could see her grin through the darkness: "Talent."

"Ahh, I'd be afeared to claim any of that. About my own self, I mean."

"Oh, I'm not asking you to. I'll judge that myself."

∼

"Come to Mexico."

"What?"

It was almost light out. The opium had worn off during the night, and the pain had returned fiercely to Blue's head, but so had a certain clarity. Or at least, so it seemed to him.

He hadn't really slept, had spent the last hours before dawn thinking over all that had happened in the weeks since his return to the city. Including the young woman next to him whom he now roused from her sleep.

"Mexico. Where it's still… I don't know… possible."

"Possible?" She looked at him closely, as if his face might explain what his words weren't managing. "Ooh. . ." She reached out to the bandage on his head, full of blood. "This's gotten to be a right mess."

"Yeah, and whose fault is that?"

Between the opium and his concussed head on his part, and the wine she wasn't used to on hers, their first attempts at requiting their mutual attraction hadn't been very satisfactory. After they'd dozed a bit, Meg had insisted that Blue lay on his back and keep his head still, and had then coaxed him to life. After which, he definitely hadn't kept his head still.

"Listen, I've got some gear," she said, looking at the wound. "Come back with me, and I can fix this up again."

"To Treat's place? No thank you."

"No, to the Palace. That's where my things are. The night watch, he's been letting me stay there for a while. Until I get sorted. I'm. . . I don't stay at Treat's anymore."

Blue stared at her, surprised and greatly pleased but not wanting to show too much of either.

"Ah, I wasn't to know."

"And why should you? At least. . . before now."

"So, if you're already out of there, it's even simpler to head for Mexico."

"What is this with you and Mexico?"

"This place. . . is finished."

"Place?"

"This city, so."

"But you just got back. I thought this was home."

"Yeah. Well, it was. But it's gotten. . . ugly. And it's going to get worse. Let me tell you. Much. . . worse."

"Not everybody sees it that way." She swung her legs over the side of the bed, edged a bit away from him. "There are people here who are still. . . alive."

"Sure I don't know who you been talking to, but all I've been hearing is the same old dead duff."

"Well, duff answers don't make the questions less important, do they?"

"Look. The docker strike is over, which means the ships are gonna start moving out again. I know some guys in the sailors' union, maybe help get us cheap passage out of here. Down past the border, we could hook up with Villa. Or maybe all the way down to Guerrero and over to join Zapata. Where real things are happening."

"'Real things.' But what do those things have to do with you? Or me? I mean, since I've been here, well, from what I've seen, you have to be truly dug in someplace... for things to matter."

"You saying things don't matter to me?" The phrase had painful echoes of Elijah's charge against him.

"Maybe some things do. But I don't know *what*. Or who."

"Hey, who was it kept running away?"

"Running away? What're you talking about? You knew where to find me... if you'd wanted to. And what the hell's Mexico if not running away?"

Blue stood up. Too abruptly, given his state, and he staggered against the little table. The gun clattered to the floor. They both stared at it as if it were alive.

After a few moments Meg exhaled slow and long, as if she'd been holding her breath. "I think," she said quietly, "I'll... take a walk."

Blue didn't want her to leave. But he could tell that what they'd only barely managed to put together had just exploded. And that the shards were too hot to touch. For now, at least, it was better for her to go. Because he didn't know what to think about what she'd said about him. Let alone what to say in return.

25

Kate was meant to go to that night's rally at Dreamland where the banker Rudolph Spreckels and the newspaper chief Fremont Older would be speaking against what they saw as the dangerous, fraudulent drumbeat of Preparedness. Others too were to speak. The full lineup hadn't been announced in advance, but if it included men of Spreckels's status in the business community, Kate knew it was a prime chance to learn who else might be of interest to Lansing and therefore to whom she should seek introduction in order to learn more.

Except that now she wasn't going. She'd made a plan with Lily Bratz, who not only was to accompany her to Dreamland but also to provide her with commentary on the various speakers. It was a perfect arrangement. Until it wasn't. Because Lily Bratz was also, now, the reason that Kate wasn't going.

She and Lily had arranged to have an early supper together beforehand. Kate went to Lily's flat in the cusp between Nob Hill and Russian Hill, halfway between Lily's Union Square office and the North Beach free clinic. And so close, Kate saw as the taxi drew up, to the tiny apartment where she and Jamey and Maggie had lived after his release from Angel Island. So close, too, to the women's clinic where Jamey had worked with Doctor Rothstein and Lily. A proximity that, as she crossed from the taxi to the entrance of Lily's building, began to break apart her flimsy focus on the Dreamland rally and send her into the raging waters beneath. The matter of Jamey. And what Lily might know.

It didn't take long for the floodgate to open all the way. Kate sat at the table waiting for Lily to serve up their supper. Lily was at the stove, chattering away about the upcoming evening's events. Kate heard little, said nothing, her chin sinking slowly to her chest.

"He... took his life," she finally whispered.

"Say again?"

Kate could only raise her head slightly, only manage a bit more breath for her words: "Jamey, he... Suicide."

Lily clattered a pot back onto the stove. Wiped her hands on her apron. And came to sit across from Kate.

"I had no idea."

"No. I realized that, when we spoke before, at your office." Kate still had not raised her head enough to look Lily in the eye.

"Until you came to see me," Lily said, "I had no idea even that he had died. I only knew that you had all returned east. He never was in contact with me again. Which was maybe a small surprise to me. But only small. And not Bernard either, I think, Dr. Rothstein."

Kate shook her head.

"May I ask you when this... happened?"

"Six months after. After we left here. Back in Boston."

Kate looked up finally. After just these few sentences she felt utterly drained, as if there were no blood flowing in her body. But also as if she'd been emptied of pain. There were no tears.

"Is this a thing you would like us to...?"

Kate held Lily's eye. Nodded. "I think that's why I'm here."

"What is it that I can help to you?"

"I don't know." Kate spoke hesitatingly, but out of her own mystification rather than any reluctance to unburden herself to Lily. "I just don't know... anything."

"Did he ever speak with you? I mean, in the time just beforehand, the weeks or months? About anything that might give you... a window?"

Kate shook her head. "Even in our early years, our happy years, there were times when he'd go silent, distant. At first it bothered me, always thinking it was something I had said or done, but it wouldn't last long, and he would assure me that it wasn't about me, that it was just his way. After a while we were able to joke about it. I even gave it a name—Wistan-itis. But after we got back from San Francisco, it was... different. He would go off by himself. I mean disappear. Which he'd never done before. Sometimes overnight. Or two. And when he'd return, he wouldn't speak about it. 'Nowhere,' he'd say, when I'd ask where he'd been. Then, I stopped asking where, and finally asked why. 'What makes you do this?' I asked. 'What are you thinking about?' All he said was, 'You don't want to know.' Which only made it worse."

"I must say," Lily responded slowly, softly, choosing her words carefully, "we medical people know very little about these things. Except... that each person is different. Of course, sometimes there are things we can point to. But we really never know why one person... and not another."

Kate took three or four deep breaths.

"I've always looked to myself. To what I may have done. Or not done. His family too, the Jamesons, they always looked to me, as if somehow it *must* have been me, the girl he should never have married. Never at themselves, how they treated him. Always the outsider, they made him. He didn't speak about it, but I know it hurt him. And then when he came back, sent home from the army because he was ill, for them it was a failure. His illness had no name, you see. More than a failure—a disgrace. Which they let him know. But in the end, after he was gone, in their eyes it was all down to me. Only me. Yet no matter how much I search our life together, Jamey and me, over and over and over, I can never find it... his pain."

"I can tell you this," Lily said quietly but firmly, "if you keep looking at yourself, you will get no answer. Because about all we do know for certain... is that it's almost never just one thing."

Kate lowered her head. Was quiet for a few moments. And then tears. Finally, tears. Which were a relief. Lily handed her a table napkin but otherwise let her be.

"The Philippines," Kate said after a bit. "He was a different man when he came back. But he would never speak of it. Not a word. And that was the time when you knew him, Lily. Just after he returned. And so I hope... perhaps..."

"Well, this I will say to you. After my first shock to be hearing from you this... news, I am not all the way surprised."

Kate picked up her head. Leaned slightly across the table, as if that were a way to understand Lily better.

"I saw many soldiers back from that war. Troubled soldiers. I worked at Angel Island, you remember? The camp where many of them were kept. Where I first met Jamey."

"Yes," Kate said, "of course I've thought of this. Of soldiers damaged by battle. Who never recover. But Jamey didn't fight in any battles. He was a doctor."

"But there are... different damages. I said that I am not so much surprised, to hear this terrible news of Jamey. Not because of any wounds I saw. Or that anyone could see. But because of what he told me. Why me? I don't know. Maybe because I am a doctor, as he was. Or because he knew me a little, trusted me, yet still I was outside his life. Who knows? But he spoke to me. Six, seven times. We would walk. Long walks. By the water, after the clinic closed for the night. And he would talk. And talk. Going over it, and over it, and over it. I almost never said a word. But I listened.

"He was far from the only soldier this way, Kate. The army doctors, they gave it a name. 'Disordered Action of the Heart'... I will tell you what I know. What he told me."

～

By the time Jamey arrived in the Philippines, the American war to oust the Spanish as the islands' rulers had turned into a war to replace the Spanish as the islands' rulers. Though the US government certainly didn't call it that. And among soldiers in the field, it was seen as a fight against unwashed, untamed, ungrateful insurgents who simply didn't understand or appreciate liberation by the Americans and the benevolence of their subsequent occupation.

As with almost every other US soldier, Jamey had no clear grasp of what was going on. The Spanish military, erstwhile enemy, was now providing information to American forces about local resistance. Filipino guerillas, on the other hand, who'd been fighting the Spanish for decades and who had joined the Americans to drive the final spike into Spanish rule, were now waging a campaign against their American former partners. All Jamey knew for sure was that, despite Spain's capitulation, US soldiers were still being killed and wounded; immediately upon his arrival in the islands he was thrown into medical work at a military hospital in the countryside north of Manila.

Within a short time, his superiors noted Jamey's fluent-sounding—though in fact fairly rudimentary—spoken Spanish, developed during his many extended stays in Cuba during his childhood and youth. As a result, they moved him from the field hospital to a more forward position, at the edge of a large battle zone, where Filipino prisoners were being held. Jamey was to treat their wounded.

Not just any wounded. Jamey was primarily tasked with seeing to prisoners who had "special value," meaning information the army might find useful. His job was to save their lives so that they could be interrogated, or further interrogated, though initially he had no idea of the army's plans for his patients once he'd treated them. Nor of how they'd come to be injured in the first place.

It was thought by Jamey's superiors that these special prisoners might respond better to interrogation if medical treatment was provided by someone who could converse with them directly, rather than through an interpreter. This despite the fact that, in the minds of his prisoner-patients, Jamey's light skin and obviously North Atlantic accent could only connect his Spanish-speaking with the hated European occupiers who'd just been overthrown. Attunement to the sensibilities of Filipino resisters was not high in the Army's skill set.

The nature of the prisoners' injuries and conditions was often curious to Jamey. There were the prisoners brought to him with the seemingly anomalous combination of bloated bodies and severe abdominal or back injuries; as Jamey treated them, the men expelled copious quantities of water. When Jamey asked what this was about, the soldiers would explain that the prisoners had been pulled from one of the many nearby rivers. How they could have inhaled and swallowed so much water and not drowned was not a question Jamey asked himself. At least, not at first.

Over time, as the damage inflicted on US forces became more substantial and their personal hostility toward the insurgents more virulent, the efforts of the army jailors to shield their doings from the medical staff became more lax, with some particularly ugly treatment of prisoners carried on in the open. Soon Jamey had seen several instances of what the soldiers fetchingly called the water cure. A prisoner was held down by four or five men while another pried open his jaws, another jammed a funnel into his mouth, and yet another poured copious quantities of water into him. After a time, when the body could hold no more liquid, a soldier would punch, knee, riflebutt or even stomp on the prisoner's stomach or back to expel some of the water. So that they could begin again. Hence the abdominal and spinal injuries that Jamey saw accompanying the water bloating. Very few of the many prisoners subjected to "the cure" were brought to Jamey: most were of little or no informational consequence—they were abused just to vent soldiers' rage—and so were not provided with any medical treatment at all.

On several occasions Jamey had also seen the consequences of a different form of water therapy where, as he later learned, a prisoner was held horizontally on a plank, his head tilted back and water poured onto a cloth covering his face so that it entered both his nose and mouth, to mimic the experience of drowning. The position of the head kept most of the water out of the prisoner's stomach, but not out of his lungs. So that the process didn't merely mimic drowning, in fact it *was* drowning. Jamey was initially told that the first of these men he saw had been pulled from the river. He got the same explanation a second time. He didn't bother to ask again.

There were also the beaten men. Horribly beaten. With injuries that were not, Jamey could tell, from a battlefield, no matter how intense hand-to-hand combat might have been. Jamey knew there was vicious maltreatment of prisoners on both sides and tamped down his growing revulsion in order to tend to these prisoners as well as he could. His duty as both doctor and soldier, as he saw it, was to heal, not judge.

This sense of duty finally began to waver with the reappearance of "relapsed" prisoners, and with one prisoner in particular who, he was told, had escaped and been recaptured. It finally collapsed altogether—as did he—with the arrival of the adrenaline.

During his early weeks in the forward battlefield, he would some-times ask to follow up with a prisoner whose wounds had been par-ticularly grievous and whose life he'd managed to save. The response from the soldiers in charge of the prisoners was always the same: the prisoner had been "transferred."

After a month or so, however, a prisoner he'd previously treated reappeared in the medical hut, brought in a second time with water-filled lungs, barely able to breathe. When Jamey told the soldiers who'd brought him that he recognized the prisoner, one of the soldiers replied—after initially showing surprise that anyone would bother to mention the fact—that the prisoner had relapsed. The undisguised absurdity of this response was such that Jamey didn't bother to refute it. But despite his growing reservations about what he was witnessing, he neither spoke to the officers in charge of the camp nor contacted the main field hospital to raise the matter with his superiors in the army medical hierarchy. He just did his duty.

One prisoner appeared three times. Which finally pushed Jamey over the edge.

This prisoner was a Flip-1, Flip being one of a panoply of deroga-tory terms used by US soldiers toward their native allies-turned-adver-saries. The prisoners were rated by their interrogators according to their perceived importance in potentially providing intelligence, descending from Flip-1 through Flip-3. A Flip-1 generated the greatest urgency for Jamey's medical services; Flip-3s rarely got any medical attention at all.

The Flip-1 in question was named Macario Bonifacio. His jailers called him The Professor: he'd been a schoolteacher before joining the guerillas, where he'd risen to a relatively senior position within the resistance. He was a short, balding, fragile-looking man in his forties whose extreme myopia gave him a severe quizzical squint, though Jamey never saw him when the man wasn't in extreme pain, which likely contributed to the facial contortion. The first time he was brought in, his eyeglasses, twisted and cracked almost beyond use, had been slapped cockeyed back onto his bloody, swollen face. Jamey's first act had been to straighten them and replace them gently. Despite his obvious great pain, Bonifacio sighed with relief.

The soldiers never told Jamey specifically what they had inflicted on any particular prisoner—the interrogation tent was in the trees on the other side of the large prisoner stockades, out of view and hearing from the medical hut—but Bonifacio's gasping, gurgling breaths told Jamey that he'd recently undergone a mock drowning, in addition to bloody gashes and bruising on his face, hands and feet. Jamey wanted to give Bonifacio morphine, especially once he began exacerbating the man's pain by treating the wounds, but he didn't risk it because of its possible effect on Bonifacio's lungs and heart, which were under so much stress from the water inside him. So without anesthetic Jamey cleansed and mended the wounds slowly and gingerly, much to the annoyance of the impatient soldiers standing guard. Bonifacio endured the painful treatment stoically but was now even more desperately gasping for breath. Jamey decided he needed to insert a tracheal tube to help him breathe. However, a patient needs to hold still for such a treatment—or be held, which in this circumstance would have seemed another abuse—and the tracheal tube's resemblance to the tubes forced into prisoners' throats during the water cure made it unlikely that Bonifacio would passively accept it. Somehow, though, the gentleness of Jamey's treatment of Bonifacio's wounds, and his quiet reassurances to Bonifacio in Spanish during those ministrations, created a connection between the two men. So that when Jamey showed Bonifacio the tracheal tube and the hand ventilator that attached to it, demonstrating its use on himself, after a moment's hesitation Bonifacio nodded and allowed Jamey to intubate him. It may have saved his life. For the moment.

A week later, they brought in Bonifacio again. This time, rather than his lungs being filled with water from a mock drowning, his body was bloated to what seemed like twice its normal size. And he cried out in pain when the soldiers dropped him unceremoniously onto a cot in the medical hut: Jamey soon discovered that two or three of Bonifacio's ribs were broken, meaning that each breath he took continued the torture. This time Jamey quickly injected morphine, then was able to give him an emetic that helped Bonifacio expel the water.

Jamey finally asked the soldiers what Bonifacio was doing there again. Oh, he escaped, one of the soldiers said. And it got "messy" when they recaptured him in the river.

Jamey ordered the soldiers out of the hut so that Bonifacio could rest a bit without them hovering. As Bonifacio lay there, panting and groaning between bouts of water-vomiting, Jamey began to speak to him, quietly, in his bare-bones Spanish.

"I have heard that you are a teacher."

Bonifacio could not answer but blinked his eyes in a way that Jamey understood to be an affirmation.

"My wife trained to be a teacher," Jamey added after a bit.

Still Bonifacio did not speak.

"But... I led her away from it... I think maybe that was a mistake."

Bonifacio tried to say something. Jamey leaned closer.

"Used to be..." Bonifacio managed.

"Used to be?"

"Used to be... teacher. Not... anymore. School... blown up."

"Oh, you will be again, I am sure," Jamey tried to console.

Bonifacio closed his eyes, struggled with his labored breathing. Jamey thought he might have lost consciousness but when he bent to check, Bonifacio spoke again.

"Your wife..."

Jamey nodded, said, *"Yes."*

"Mine... they burned... in our house... with our children."

The effort to speak made Bonifacio pass out.

Dumbstruck, sickened, Jamey nonetheless managed to strap Bonifacio's ribs while he lay unconscious. Then he let Bonifacio rest, hoping to speak with him again when he woke. But after a few minutes the soldiers came back into the hut, saw that there was no treatment going on, and insisted on taking the prisoner away. Jamey objected, but the soldiers said those were their orders, then another prisoner was brought in, and Jamey had to treat this new patient, and he wasn't sure of his position in the military hierarchy, and he wasn't sure of his duty, and wasn't sure what he thought, or what he should do. He wound up doing nothing, standing aside feebly while the soldiers grabbed Bonifacio, semiconscious and moaning pitiably, and carried him out.

Whether recalling Jamey to the main field hospital was intended to assess his continuing fitness to treat interrogation subjects or was only to introduce him to adrenaline, Jamey never knew.

A high-ranking army doctor had arrived from the US with what he termed an extremely exciting new pharmacologic agent. It was called adrenaline, and it was purely experimental; this doctor had only very limited quantities of the extract—the army had appropriated some of it from civilian scientists whose work it had been closely monitoring—and he didn't know very much about it or how it worked. But work it did, he said. Spectacularly.

The army had recently used the extract in experiments in the US, this doctor told Jamey, and it showed remarkable properties: it reduced swelling, improved heart rate, circulation, breathing, and muscle function, and slowed bleeding. It also stimulated alertness. And even seemed to improve memory. Its military utility seemed limitless, and the army was now trying it in the field. They'd had good success on a few wounded American soldiers, the doctor said, providing them with immediate, significant relief; he waved off Jamey's query as to what, specifically, that relief had been. Now the army wanted to broaden the scientific inquiry by seeing how it worked with Filipino prisoners. The major in charge of interrogations at Jamey's forward camp was also there for this introduction to the extract—Jamey had seen this man at the forward camp and knew who he was, but they'd had no direct contact—and he nodded at the army doctor's directive that it now be used on prisoners. Jamey was not averse to adding something new to his therapeutic arsenal but, nonetheless, asked how using the extract on Filipino prisoners would "broaden" anything. "Well," the doctor said, "these people are biologically different, aren't they?"

This doctor returned with Jamey to the forward camp, to administer the extract to prisoners and to observe its effect. Because of its extremely limited supply, however, he established a protocol that it should be used only on the most important Flip-ıs. For three days the senior doctor waited, but the interrogators brought in no one who fit the profile, and the doctor had to return to Manila and then to the States. So he instructed Jamey on how to use the adrenaline and what physiological responses to it Jamey was supposed to monitor and record. He specially emphasized that because of its limited quantity, the stuff was to be used only on the most important Flip-1 prisoners, as determined by the interrogators. Jamey didn't like the idea of parceling out a treatment on the basis of anything other than medical need, but he decided that the army's logic wasn't entirely invidious—that is, given the limited supply, relief for one human is just as righteous as for any other—and so he raised no objection.

Two days later, a couple of young soldiers brought in Bonifacio again. One eye was bloody and nearly closed. He was bleeding from his ear. And his bare feet were so swollen and multicolored that they looked like some kind of tropical melons. There was no sign of his eyeglasses.

Jamey was stunned to see him back again. A third time. And stunned at his injuries. Though he'd seen other prisoners in similarly dire condition, this somehow felt more brutal, more three-dimensional, perhaps because he knew Bonifacio's name, knew something about him. Had spoken with him about his life. Had even mentioned Kate.

Jamey tried to speak to him now but Bonifacio was delirious and did not respond. So Jamey just softly called his name over and over—"*Senor Bonifacio. Profesor. Profesor Bonifacio*"—as he checked his body, listening to his heart and lungs and cataloguing his myriad injuries. When Bonifacio went completely quiet for a moment, one of the soldiers stepped forward and used his baton to nudge Bonifacio's gargantuan feet; the shock of pain jolted Bonifacio awake.

"What are you doing?!" Jamey barked.

"He needs to stay awake," the guard replied. "No sleep, that's the whole idea."

The major in charge of interrogations stepped into the hut.

"We're losing him," he said to Jamey.

"I don't know," Jamey said, bending to Bonifacio and listening to his heart and breathing. "I don't know his condition yet."

"Well I do. I know these things. He's right on the edge."

"Alright, let me look at him. Let me figure this out."

"No, there's no time. We have him just right. The point when they say things and don't realize. But we might lose him. So give him the juice. The special juice."

"The what?"

"The juice! The 'dren'lin. Now's the perfect time."

Jamey had almost forgotten about the adrenaline. He looked again at Bonifacio and realized that the major was right, they were likely to lose him, and yes, of course, he quickly decided, who should be saved by the magic elixir if not Bonifacio?

He retrieved a vial of the adrenaline from the cool box and prepared an injection. The doctor who'd explained the drug's administration had not wanted to waste any of the precious substance in a demonstration, so Jamey wasn't sure exactly how the material would respond to the injection needle or how much to use. Another look at Bonifacio, though, convinced Jamey not to delay, so he filled the syringe and injected it into Bonifacio's thigh, as the senior doctor had directed.

In less than a minute, Bonifacio began to stir. An eyelid fluttered, his mouth opened for breath, and his limbs shifted slightly. Jamey listened to his chest again and was amazed to hear a stronger heartbeat and deeper respiration. After another minute, Bonifacio opened the one undamaged eye and looked around him. He seemed to register Jamey; Bonifacio kept his gaze on him for several seconds. But then he saw the interrogator and gasped and jerked involuntarily. Jamey put his hands gently on Bonifacio's arm.

"Don't try to move. I've given you some special medicine. It should make you feel better right away."

The interrogator gestured for the two soldiers to move forward. "Sit him up."

"Wait, wait. Leave him be," Jamey interjected.

"Leave him be? Not the point."

He nodded to the soldiers and they pulled Bonifacio to a sitting position.

The major and Jamey both stared at Bonifacio, who was clearly more alert than when they'd brought him in a few minutes before.

"Good, good. This stuff!" the major said. "Amazing. Alright, let's get him back," he said to the soldiers.

"Back?" Jamey interjected.

"Yeah. What did you think?"

"He's in no condition..."

"Yes, he's in *exactly* the condition. Right on the edge. They can't keep track of what they say, and shit slips out."

He nodded to the soldiers who pulled Bonifacio to a standing position. When his massively swollen feet touched the floor, he let out a howl.

Jamey thought of one of the standing orders of military medicine he'd seen—it was included in a handout sheet he'd received during his basic army training, though no one had adverted to it at the time, or since—which said that medical decisions were to be made by the highest-ranking medical officer on site, not by operational officers.

"But he's my patient," he said.

"Not any more he's not... *captain*."

The major's reference to their relative ranks was clear enough. As was his hulking form, and that of his two other soldiers. Jamey didn't know how to respond. Or couldn't decide to. And said nothing more as the soldiers carried Bonifacio out of the hut, followed by the major.

Jamey paced, wondering what he was doing, what he wasn't doing, what he could be doing. After half an hour or so, one of the soldiers who'd transported Bonifacio came rushing into the hut.

"Major says to come. And bring more juice."

"Come? Come where?"

"Our place. Right now."

"What do you mean, your place?"

"Major says now!"

Jamey hesitated.

"Hey, you want to save the guy, don't you?... Captain?"

Jamey grabbed his medical kit and another vial of the adrenaline and followed the soldier out of the hut. They hurried across the wide field that had been cleared of trees and underbrush, past the open stockades where hundreds of Filipino prisoners were kept, and toward a large tent erected fifty yards or so within a dense Eucalyptus grove. Two guards with ready rifles stood outside. Jamey followed the soldier into the tent.

Bonifacio was sitting on a small wooden chair, straps around his legs and torso keeping him upright. The dirt floor around the chair was dark with liquid. The major stood over Bonifacio, speaking to him in Spanish, though Jamey couldn't make out what he was saying. Bonifacio's head, sunk into his chest, jerked upward when the major lightly touched his swollen bare foot, but then immediately sunk down again.

"*No, no, no sleeping, profesor,*" the major said in Spanish and poked the foot again, but this time Bonifacio's head barely raised an inch or two. "*Come on, now, we've got to keep talking, you're doing so well.*"

The major turned while saying "Where the fuck is. . .?" then saw Jamey standing just inside the tent.

"Good, good. The juice, doc."

Jamey stood there, didn't move.

"C'mon man, hop to it!"

"No sleeping?" Jamey said. "Why no sleeping?"

"Why? That's what we do, that's why!"

Jamey remained where he was. Even inched away.

"Look at him," the major changed tack, speaking in a quieter register. "If he goes to sleep, he might not wake up. And you don't want to lose him, do you?. . . Course not. He's your patient, isn't he? So the juice, man, give him the juice. You saw how it brought him back before. So give him a chance. To live."

Like a sleepwalker, Jamey moved forward, knelt down in front of Bonifacio, took his pulse. It was barely detectable.

The major used his boot to stub Bonifacio's foot; Bonifacio's body jerked, but barely.

"C'mon man!" he said to Jamey. "It's his life!"

Jamey's head was spinning. The sight and fetid smell of Bonifacio reached some place in Jamey beyond his medical training, told him that saving Bonifacio's life was not the only thing going on here. But his commitment and instincts for doctoring were strong, so he prepared the adrenaline and forced it into Bonifacio's thigh.

Within a few seconds Bonifacio began to stir. Jamey and the major watched him carefully. After a few more seconds his good eye opened half-way. And he began to mumble.

"Good," the major said.

"*Used to be...*" Jamey could make out some of Bonifacio's words.

"Okay, good work," the major said to Jamey and started to edge him out of the way.

"Wait, wait," Jamey said, and then in Spanish to Bonifacio, leaning closer, "*What are you saying?*"

"*Used to be... a teacher.*"

"*Yes, yes, profesor, you told me. I know.*"

"*And you...*" Bonifacio fixed his eye on Jamey, just inches away, "*used to be... a doctor.*"

Jamey jerked upright. Backed away. Barely heard whatever it was that the major said. Stumbled out of the tent. And somehow found himself again in his own hut.

He was still holding his medical kit; he threw it violently against the wall. Then he turned round and round the hut, trying to locate something to grab onto, to hold, something that would make sense. There was nothing.

Eventually he lay down on his cot. But whether he closed his eyes or opened them, there was Bonifacio's face, inches away, his swollen lips moving.

At some point, one of the guards entered the hut and said something to Jamey about returning to the interrogation tent, about bringing more adrenaline, but Jamey didn't even turn his head to look at him.

Late that night, soldiers found Jamey wandering the camp, outside the prisoners' stockade. As they escorted him back to his hut, they told him that he'd been mumbling in Spanish. When he sat down again on his cot, he found that he was weeping. Someone brought whiskey. He drained a large cupful. Didn't feel it. The major entered soon after.

"Good job, doc. Near the end, we got something. Could be very useful."

It took Jamey some time to respond: "The end?"

"Well, yeah. You knew he was close, right?"

"But... the adrenaline. It... really worked. His heart, his lungs... I heard them."

"Oh. Sure. But it only lasts for an hour or so. A very useful hour. Then it wears off. Didn't you know? Didn't they tell you?"

~

Kate turned round and round her room at the Palace, unconsciously reenacting what Lily had described of Jamey in his hut, one of the last verbal pictures of him that Lily had dredged up from her seared memories of his long talks to her about the Philippines. Kate was struggling now with the image of him weeping. She'd never thought of it before, but even in his desperate final year she'd never seen him cry. Which meant that now, fifteen years later, she was unable to conjure him crying. But that wasn't the full extent of the problem. Which was that she was unable, now, to bring up any image of his face at all.

The night was long.

It had still been early evening when she'd arrived back at the hotel. Lily had ridden with her in the taxi, then gone on to the Dreamland rally on her own. After Lily's recounting of what Jamey had told her, there'd been no need for the two women even to discuss whether Kate would still go to the rally.

Kate's head was swimming. Every speck her of consciousness was now focused on Jamey when for so many years she had forced herself to think of him as little as possible, and she was ill from the sheer intensity of it.

At first she was crushed by the thought of the misery he'd lived and died with, what must have been a nightmare of self-recrimination. When he'd returned from the Philippines, he'd told her nothing, which meant that back then she'd had no reference, no context, by which to enter his experience, to live in the world as he then saw it. Now she was overwhelmed. Not only by a sudden awakening to the horror he'd carried inside him for that final year but also by the memory of her own inability to share and thereby, perhaps, to ease it.

Inability. But also failure? Here it was, once again: the curse of guilt. She'd grown up in the Catholic Church, so guilt was never far beneath the surface. And looking to herself all these years as the source, however unwitting and unknowing, of Jamey's anguish had been obvious, inescapable, since she'd never known for certain of any other cause. Except for his strange, strained relations with his family, about which he also never spoke. And then, when he'd been sent home from the war as "unfit," the Jamesons had focused onto Kate all their resentment at what they saw as Jamey's, and therefore the family's, shame.

The night was very long.

But finally, she reminded herself, there was now an explanation completely beyond and outside of her. Except that she couldn't shake the very first thing Lily had said to her. That there never was just one thing. So if there had been something else, too, was she it? His inability to speak about what tormented him, was that down to her? Now she became wracked by the notion that her own blitheness about their life together—about her new shiny bright life, escaped from Southie—had prevented her from seeing what must have been Jamey's fragility all along and had kept him from sharing it with her. A habit of reticence that became so entrenched in him that he couldn't break it even when, after the Philippines, he'd had such extraordinary need to.

The night was very, very long.

And Maggie. What would she tell Maggie? Now that she'd committed herself to speaking some kind of truth to her about Jamey, and his death. Kate was beginning to see not how much simpler that would be, now that there was something concrete to say, but how much more complicated. Because wouldn't telling Maggie about the Philippines also be a diversion from Kate's own responsibility? Whatever that was?

Then there was her job for Lansing. Yes, the government was technically still neutral about entering the war, Wilson's election promise to stay out of it still formally in place. But in truth, thinking back on the language Lansing had used, and the attitude of the Bureau's men in Washington, wasn't her remit to find out about San Francisco resistance to American entry into the war *when* the US entered, not *if*? And given what she'd learned about Jamey in the last war, how could she be party to preparations for the next?

The night was endless.

26

Labor Councils: "Stay Away"

San Francisco—Fearing a "frame-up," the San Francisco Central Labor Council and the Building Trades Council issued a joint statement today, urging members of all the city's unions to take no action against Saturday's Preparedness Day parade along Market Street, other than to stay away from the area. The Councils' proclamation reads:

"Whereas, because united labor is opposed to the fostering of the war spirit by 'preparedness parades,' an attempt may be made by the enemies of labor to cause a violent disturbance during the parade and charge that disturbance to labor in the hopes of discrediting labor organizations in the eyes of our citizens.

Therefore, in order to forestall any possible frame-up of this character, we hereby caution all union men and women to be

especially careful and make no
other protest than their silent
nonparticipation in the 'preparedness parade.'"

"No protest."

"Silent nonparticipation."

With a mixture of rage and resignation, Blue read the labor councils' pronouncement in the afternoon newspaper. Given the big labor
organizations' recent retreat in the city—the tail-between-the-legs
demise of the longshore strike, the central council's refusal to support
Mooney's United Railroads fight, among others—and their general
lack of vision or enthusiasm for anything beyond slightly thicker wage
packets, Blue wasn't completely surprised that they planned no action
regarding the parade. But a directive for complete passivity seemed
especially craven, even for them.

And what about radical workers? Blue wondered. Where were
they? In particular, what about the variously striped anarchists in
his own neighborhood, almost all of them vitriolically anti-war and
seemingly always ready, one way or another, to hit the streets? Were
they all just sitting on their hands, too? This was what had confounded
the Wobbly Mario Fraschetti, who'd complained to Blue about it the
night before: a seemingly complete abdication by the *Volontá* men,
at least according to those Fraschetti had spoken with, of any protest
against the parade.

If it was true, it would deepen what Blue was already feeling, what
had pushed Mexico to the front of his mind, what he'd said to Meg
the night before: for him, this town—once again—was done. But he
couldn't quite believe it, that nothing was happening about the parade.
So he headed for the *Volontá* rooms to find out for himself.

On his way, he realized that he might run into Genio Forcone
there. Genio, who'd seemed desperate to see him the past few days and
whom he'd been neglecting. In truth, avoiding. But he'd have to see
Genio eventually, he told himself, and now was as good a time as any.
In fact he hoped to see him, because if anyone would be in the streets

349

doing something against the parade, though not necessarily anything well-organized or coherent, it would be Genio.

It was late Friday afternoon, a time when normally the *Volontá* rooms would be starting to fill. But they were nearly empty. At a table in the front room were a few old bachelors for whom the *Volontá* was substitute family and the rooms their card-playing and gossip center, but Blue saw none of the active firebrands. Then he heard voices in the back room and found a small knot of men there gathered around Luigi Parenti, a frequent collaborator with the *Volontá* in street actions though his affinities were Wobbly rather than *anti-organazzitore*. Parenti was explaining that he'd just been let out of jail, arrested two days before for handing out a leaflet calling on people to stop the Preparedness Day parade. He showed Blue one of the leaflets; a small stack of them was on a nearby table. In Italian and English, it called on workers and "free people" to stop the parade "at all costs" but offered no plan and mentioned no specific actions. The leaflet's tactical feebleness was paralleled by a text, mimeographed rather than printed, that was smudged at the bottom and missing its last line.

Blue took a quick look at it, then squinted at Parenti in mock pain.

"*Yeah, yeah, I know,*" Parenti explained. "*I had to do it on the little machine over at the union local. I wanted Treat to print it up for me, but I couldn't find him. Not for three days. Not that girl, either.*"

It took Blue a moment to realize that he meant Meg.

"*No, she doesn't stay there anymore,*" Blue said more firmly than necessary, since it wasn't information likely to be of any interest to this group.

"*So then, what the hell is happening tomorrow?*" Blue continued.

Parenti shook his head, and the others seemed to inch away.

"*Hey, I just got out of jail,*" Parenti said, "*so I don't know. I'm gonna go back over to the local, see if anyone there's got anything going on. If not, maybe tomorrow I'll just come over here. There's bound to be something here. Right?*"

"*No, no,*" jumped in one of the group, a Sicilian named Pepino, a buddy of Genio Forcone. "*If anything bad happens at the parade, where do you think the bulls will come first, to round people up, eh? So no,*" he said definitively, wagging a finger, "*you don't want to be here. Everybody here agrees on it, eh? Get it?*" He addressed this last remark forcefully to Parenti and Blue.

Blue looked around at the four other faces in the group and saw only blank stares.

"*Yeah, that's right, nothing,*" one of the other men finally said, looking back and forth between Parenti and Blue. "*Just to stay away. From the parade. And from here too. That's the way it is, Baldo.*"

Parenti shook his head in dismay, picked up his leaflets, said a perfunctory goodbye and left. The little group disbanded without further talk.

Both surprised and disappointed at the utter lack of energy there, Blue turned to leave but Pepino took his arm and pulled him aside.

"*Where you been, eh?*" he said accusingly. "*Genio's been looking for you for days.*"

"*I know, I know, I just... been tied up, you know? And then I got... distracted.*" Blue pointed to the bandage on his head.

"*Yeah, we heard about that. Real good job of it, Mooney and them other union clowns.*"

"*Hey, least we weren't just sittin' on our asses over here, wanking to pictures of Robin Hood, or whoever the hell's your latest crush...*"

"*Well, if you'd been around, Baldo, you'd know how wrong you are. But it's too late now. So go fuck yourself.*"

∽

The notes were delivered with her tea.

She'd been up all night, buffeted through a torment unleashed by what she'd learned from Lily. She'd managed a bit of sleep in the morning, then finally around midday had fallen into a deeper sleep in an armchair. Now it was late afternoon. She wasn't hungry, and in any case didn't feel up to dressing and going through the cotillion of social graces required when having a meal in one of the hotel's ornate dining rooms, so she ordered tea from room service.

One note came from Alma Spreckels. Several days before, Alma had invited Kate to dinner, that evening, to further discuss Alma's war victims' charity, as well as Alma's brother-in-law Rudolph's anti-Preparedness position and the parade to come the following day. Alma's terse note now said that she was sorry but that she had to cancel the dinner. She and Adolph had been "called away." But she looked forward to seeing Kate upon their return. Given how distracted and sleep-deprived she was, Kate was more relieved than disappointed.

The other note, which had more to digest, was from Mullally. In flowery language reflective of the Southern gentleman that was, for Kate, the most insufferable of his several personae, he deeply regretted having "neglected" her the previous weeks but hoped she'd understand the demands upon him regarding the upcoming Preparedness event. Could she see it in her heart to forgive him, and would she do him the honor of accompanying him for supper Tuesday week? She puzzled for a moment over what exactly "Tuesday week" meant: it was not a locution she was used to. She vaguely remembered hearing it years before from the Anglo-Irish Jamesons but she didn't recall how it worked. Another reminder of how she was out of her depth: she couldn't even tell which day was which. Well, she'd check with Mullally on Monday, she thought, to get it straight. If she decided to see him at all. Which at this point was hard for her to imagine.

The second part of his message got Kate's more immediate attention. Mullally hoped, he wrote, that Kate would experience the glorious spectacle of "true" San Francisco's patriotic splendor by attending "our" great parade, for which he had the honor of serving as grand marshal. He wanted to caution her, however. He was concerned that "radical foreigners" or "worker elements" might mount some disruption to the parade or to the "good citizenry" in attendance, which might prove dangerous or, in any case, create panic among the throngs and thereby cause her distress. If he might be permitted, he concluded, he would suggest that she watch the parade from a secure distance, perhaps a high window of her hotel.

She was surprised at a warning like this from such a supremely confident character. Since the evening before, her preoccupation with Jamey had pushed aside any thoughts of the parade, but thinking on it now she decided that she wanted to go watch it; Lansing's project aside, she wanted to measure for herself the tenor of the city about the war. Especially now. Because of Jamey. But how seriously to take Mullally's caution?

The only person she knew who might have some insight on the matter was Breyer, the Bureau man. Or else perhaps that detective Swanson. But Swanson never seemed available and trying to contact him might mean another encounter with that horrid character at his office who'd mocked her search for Maggie. Breyer or Swanson. Pick your poison.

It was nearly 6:00, but Breyer's assistant picked up the phone, and Breyer came on immediately.

"Oh, I'm glad you're still there."

"Mm, some of us have longer hours than others," Breyer said.

Ah, the same resentful little shit, Kate thought. But bit her tongue.

"Yes, I have no doubt. So I won't take up much of your time."

"I'm at your service, Mrs. Jameson," he said a bit more accommodatingly.

"It's about the parade tomorrow. I think it's important, for my remit, that I see what the turnout is and get a sense of the people involved. So I'd like to watch it from somewhere near the parade's start, where they'll be announcing the participants. But I've received this somewhat disturbing message from Thornwell Mullally, suggesting that there might be some... risk in being too close to the parade itself."

Breyer was silent for a few moments. As if considering how to respond, Kate sensed, more than merely waiting to see if she'd finished.

"I'm wondering what you make of it," she added.

"Well," he started slowly. "It is true that there have been various threats. Quite a number, actually. Postcards have been received by business and government people. Very ominous, threatening messages. But my people have examined them, and they're all in the same hand, in language that's different from what we see from the radicals we know. So it seems likely that they're just from some crackpot. I'd say the real risk is from people who don't bother with warnings. And they're harder to gauge. Even for those of us who... keep track of them."

"I see," Kate said, though, in fact, she didn't see; she couldn't tell whether Breyer was downplaying the danger or confirming it. "Well, in that case, I wonder whether you think there might be some spot..."

"I tell you what. I'm going to be here in the office tomorrow, for the parade. And as you recall, we sit right on Market, overlooking the street. Only a block from the Embarcadero, where the parade starts. With the windows open we'll be able to hear the announcements of who's who. And anyway, I'll recognize most of them. Be able to tell you, even if we can't hear. So perhaps you'd come here to the office... And report to Lansing how helpful I've been."

Kate thought she heard a faint chuckle in that final remark.

"I... I think that would be... fine. What, ah... what time?"

"Well, the parade's set to start at 1:30. But there'll likely be crowds to get through, so you might want to head over here a good bit before that. Oh... but you're just a couple of blocks away. Is that right? Still at the Palace? All... this time?"

A hint of provocation snuck back into his voice. Kate tried not to rise to it.

"Yes, as a matter of fact I am. So, all right then. I'll see you there tomorrow. Your office. Oh, and Mr. Breyer... thank you."

"Ah, well now. We're both on the same side, aren't we."

27

Hot. Even before noon it was miserably hot.

Miserable, that is, for San Franciscans, who are spoiled by the sea breeze and fog that normally rush in off the ocean every summer afternoon and so, notoriously, are unable to cope with heat. Temperatures had soared each of the past three days and there was no sign yet of any cooling. The entire city was holding its breath.

Since her afternoon at the ballpark with Blue, and still more since Lily's revelations about Jamey, Kate had lost interest in cataloguing for Lansing the characters who'd be supporting the day's big Preparedness parade. But if she went ahead and watched the parade from Breyer's office as planned, she might pick up something useful from him about the other side, about opposition to Preparedness among the city's elites. And if she was going to spend that time with Breyer, she didn't want to give him even the slightest added excuse to treat her askance, such as by wearing an outfit that didn't clearly announce itself as well above his pay grade. So she decided to wear some of her best regalia for her afternoon performance at his office— with Breyer, it always felt like performance. Trouble was, she had nothing high-end to wear that wasn't tight at the neck, full in the skirt, and long at the arm and ankle, altogether uncomfortable in the day's heat. So rather than go out early to watch the crowds gather on the Market Street parade route, she waited until the last minute to bathe and get dressed.

Her hotel room didn't overlook the street, so she hadn't had even a glimpse of the scene outside until she made her way through the main lobby and into the brilliant sunlight on Market Street. As her eyes adjusted, she was surprised by the size of the eight- to ten-deep crowd on the pavement. Surprised because as she'd made her way toward the hotel's open front door she'd heard almost no sound coming in from the street. Despite hundreds of people on the pavement in front of the hotel, and a like number directly across Market and on each block up and down the wide avenue as far as she could see, it was strangely quiet: no boisterous calling from one to another in the crowd, no loud or fervid chatter, no excited buzzing. Even the spectators who were holding little American flags on sticks—there was also a blizzard of large flags and bunting covering building facades and smaller flags hanging from poles and from wires strung across the cleared roadway—did so listlessly, limply, without affect. Kate thought back to the baseball game just a few days before, especially to the raucous bleachers, and wondered how similar numbers of people, gathered in the same city for another festive public event, could sound so completely different. After all, this was meant to be a celebration; it wasn't as if it were a funeral.

Many faces in the crowd were tense, Kate thought, betraying not just anticipation but anxiety. As if they were waiting for something other than just the parade. Something expected but unknown. Something they'd like to escape from. True, almost all the spectators were dressed in their Sunday best which, in the unusual heat, might have explained a certain amount of their discomfort, standing out in the midday sun. Still, the dissonance between the size of the crowd and its stillness was curious. Almost eerie.

Kate picked her way along the broad sidewalk, behind the spectators, heading down Market toward Breyer's office. There were families with children, knots of men and others of women, plus larger groups that seemed to have some organizational connection that had brought them together to the parade. Kate passed through one of these groups that had not yet taken up a position next to the roadway; they were twenty-five or thirty young women in their teens and twenties, all wearing nearly identical plain white dresses and gathered around a sign held high on stick by one of their number, which announced "Magnin"—a luxury department store on Union Square. Next to the sign-holder was a tall, hawk-faced older woman in an expensive outfit who was turning her head to and fro, surveying her shop girls with an expression both nervous and severe, and calling out names.

"Where's Jenny?" Kate heard one of the girls say to another. "If she's not here soon, there'll be hell to pay."

"More like *no* pay," the other girl said.

As Kate continued down Market, she noticed a pattern of difference between the people at the front of the crowd, nearest the street, and those who lingered at the rear. At the front tended to be people with the little flags on sticks, including many families with children, almost all of whom appeared to be at least moderately well-off, and some of whom showed a modulated enthusiasm for being there. Whereas at the back Kate encountered several collections not unlike the Magnin girls—some groups of men, some of women, some mixed—who seemed less tailored and turned out than people at the front and who gave the impression of being there out of sufferance rather than preference.

The crowd thickened as Kate neared the parade staging area on the Embarcadero, at the foot of Market. Breyer's office was on the second block up from the Embarcadero, on the other side of Market from Kate. Because of the heavy crowd, plus the parade groups who were collecting themselves on the side streets there, the police were tightly controlling the intersections. Kate had to wait to cross. As she stood back a bit, her attention was drawn to the next intersection down toward the Embarcadero. A lone figure came from the side street there and stopped in front of the first doorway on Market, under a sign that read Ferry Exchange Saloon. He was surrounded by people milling on the sidewalk but he nonetheless caught her eye: he was hatless, which alone made him stand out, and there was a white bandage on the side of his head. Kate wasn't sure, but she thought it was her baseball game companion Blue Cavanaugh. By the time she shifted herself to get another angle, though, he had disappeared.

With all that had gone on with Kate since the afternoon she'd spent with Blue, she hadn't given him much thought. In particular, after his ballpark outbursts and then his abrupt abandoning her, she hadn't even decided whether she'd want to see him again. She didn't consciously answer the question now, but the sharp lines newly etched in her heart and mind about the Philippines war set off a surge of conciliatory feeling toward Blue and his rage—he'd lost his brother in that war, he'd told her—and she found herself heading down the block toward the corner where she'd spotted him.

Halfway down the block she glanced up at the Ferry Building clock tower: 1:00. Which made a decision for her, at least for the moment; she needed to get to Breyer's office before the parade began.

Breyer opened the locked door himself. With his usual practiced blankness, he greeted her and showed her through the empty outer room and into his own office. In front of two wide-open windows over Market Street he'd drawn up two chairs, placed at such an angle that they'd be able to look out onto the parade four stories below yet still partially face each other. He gestured for her to sit.

"Thank you so much for this," Kate began.

"Happy to oblige. And gives me a chance to hear how you're coming along. If... that's something..."

"Yes of course. And perhaps you'll be able to fill in some blank spots for me."

"Whatever I can."

Breyer's mask of equanimity: hearing him, seeing him, Kate had no idea whether he was actually willing to help or was merely mouthing platitudes.

"Not only about the parade people," Kate continued, "but... the people who *aren't* here. Who are *against all* this. Or at least, aren't willing to join it."

"Mm."

Kate waited for some comment from him regarding the city's anti-Preparedness cohort but all he did was turn his head to look at the scene below. She looked too. A cordon of cops on horseback was beginning to form up in the middle of the first block of Market Street; immediately behind them a marching band, maybe two dozen strong, was aligning itself. Her eyes wandered across Market to the saloon on the corner of Steuart Street, the little side street from which Blue had appeared, but there was no sign of him. Down Steuart she could see army veterans, some of them quite old, in a variety of faded, rough-edged uniforms, trying to sort themselves into formations.

"I was meant to go to Dreamland the other night, where the 'anti' side of things was making itself heard, but I... became indisposed."

Breyer turned slightly toward her.

"You're better now, I trust."

"Better?..."

Before Kate could think of what to say, Breyer glanced back out the window.

"Ah, the Grand Marshal," he announced cheerily. "Your friend Mullally."

Kate looked down to see Thornwell Mullally in his Confederate officer's uniform, complete with saber and plumed hat, astride a large, beautiful roan horse in the middle of the street. He was coaxing the horse into a position at the head of and between a twelve-strong, two-line phalanx of mounted police.

"My... friend. Yes, well. Actually, I've been meaning to ask you about him."

Breyer turned his attention to her but said nothing.

"You see, I've been wondering. Mullally's from Irish stock, as I'm sure you know... since he makes a point of it. And in Boston, before I left, there was quite strong resistance to this war on the part of many Irish there. And Irish-descended folk. Because of England, of course. Not wanting to go to war for England. Especially after the Easter rising this spring. What the English did there, in Dublin. Blasting the city. And... the executions. Not to mention all the centuries before that. So how is it that Mullally, who seems to take his Irishness so seriously... How can he be so... eager... about going to war? For the English?"

Breyer looked at her for a few moments before replying.

"Takes... his Irishness... seriously." He repeated her phrase slowly, deliberately, as if measuring each word. "Yes, I suppose he does. But it's... not the only thing he takes seriously." He waited a moment but Kate said nothing while she ranged over his possible meanings.

"Now, these Irish in Boston you mentioned," he continued. "Which, ah, which Irish exactly are those?"

"Sorry?"

"Well, there's Irish. . . and then there's Irish. Wouldn't you say, Mrs. . . Jameson?"

The remark was unsettling. Perhaps he was simply referring to the obvious truth—obvious in San Francisco as it was in Boston—of the differences between the shanty Irish and the successful merchant Irish families like the Jamesons. Or by pronouncing her surname was he more pointedly referring to the Jamesons themselves, whom she ostensibly represented here and whose position lined up with the Mullallys of the world? As opposed to the Careys, her own Paddy family, whom Breyer somehow knew of?

Down on the street someone blew a whistle. The band behind the police horse cordon struck up a marching tune and, to the cheers—somewhat tepid but cheers, nonetheless—of the crowd, Mullally and his police escort started their horses up Market, officially beginning the parade. Kate and Breyer turned to watch, their conversation in any case halted by the blaring music. Across the way on Steuart Street, the old soldiers were now in something of a formation; in the front ranks were a couple of dozen white-haired Civil War veterans, including two in Confederate uniforms. As they shuffled closer to Market, the ranks behind them moved into view. They wore uniforms from the Spanish-American War. Jamey's war.

". . . Mullally. . . Irish. . ."

Kate realized that Breyer was again saying something to her.

". . .but in the end, you don't need to love the English to pick the winning side. Wouldn't you say? . . . Ah," Breyer looked down onto Market again, "Sunny Jim! The people's mayor. Isn't he grand?" The sarcasm was understated but unmistakable.

Mayor James "Sunny Jim" Rolph—in an enormous white Stetson hat, shiny gold cowboy boots and a long frock coat with a bright red camellia in his lapel—now came alongside Breyer's building, the next in line after the first marching band led by Mullally but having allowed it to get a good fifty feet or so ahead, out on its own, giving the impression that the parade actually began with him rather than with Mullally. Directly behind Sunny Jim was a thirty-foot American flag, stretched horizontally and carried by a dozen policemen, six to a side.

Kate glanced again to the other side of Market, to Steuart Street and the war veterans lining up there. As she did, she noticed something moving on the roof of the corner saloon: a man's feet—or was it two men?—behind a large billboard; the sign blocked everything except what could be seen through a small space at its base. Was that Blue up there? she wondered. But why? It could be anyone.

"I've been meaning to ask you," Breyer brought her attention back into the room, "how things are progressing with your hunt."

"Hunt?"

"Your search. Your daughter. Has the Swanson office come up with anything for you?"

Kate had completely forgotten that it was Breyer whom she had first told about looking for Maggie, and who had been the one to recommend Swanson.

"I'm afraid not. After a first meeting it's been impossible to speak with him directly. And his assistants, well, they haven't exactly shown much support. For my... hunt."

"Well, of course, they are awfully busy these days. I just thought, the postcard, perhaps there might be a lead."

Maggie's latest postcard had been forwarded to Kate via Breyer's office. In an envelope sent from Lansing's bureau, addressed to her. An unopened envelope. Or so she'd thought.

Breyer seemed to recognize his mistake right away, but other than a vein pulsing at his temple, he showed no embarrassment. Unless it wasn't a mistake at all but instead just another small provocation.

A marching band, made up mostly of drums and horns, loudly struck up its music in the street below. Behind the band was a large contingent of spit-polished soldiers in tight formation and, in their midst, an enormous wheeled artillery piece. Directly following the soldiers was a regiment of Boy Scouts, each carrying a little flag.

"So, you started to ask me about the Dreamland gathering. The... pacifist types."

"Well, yes. Not all of them, that is. I'm most interested in the ones who have business weight. I mean, Lansing is most interested. I've learned a bit about some of them. The Spreckels clan in particular. Rudolph Spreckels, the banker, I know he was meant to be one of the speakers there, at Dreamland. I've met him. Very strong against the war. And Older, the newspaper man."

"Ah, yes, Older. He's definitely a thorn."

Kate registered the word.

They watched as a contingent of women came next up Market, thirty or forty of them, dressed from head to foot in elaborate white dresses and white hats, many of them with white parasols, all of them carrying tiny American flags and singing what seemed to be "America, the Beautiful." Kate couldn't quite make out the words but was nonetheless drawn to the women's tinny, non-musical voices because, despite the throngs on both sidewalks, once the marching band had passed, the street was otherwise oddly quiet. The women were followed by a hundred or more mostly middle-aged men in business suits and neckties and hats; two men in the lead held the poles of a large sign announcing them as from the Chamber of Commerce. There was a bit of restrained applause.

Kate noticed that the dozen Civil War veterans were now pushed up right to the edge of Market, making ready to enter from Steuart Street. The larger contingent of Spanish War soldiers was right behind them.

"I had an agent there," Breyer turned back to Kate. "At Dreamland. So I can tell you that other than Spreckels… Rudolph, that is… there may have been a few industry men in the audience, I don't know, but none of them got up to speak. It was all labor types. The pacifist ones. And, of course, the socialists."

"Well then, perhaps it wasn't so much for me to have missed out on. Actually, I'm more distressed about a dinner I missed. Last night. I was hoping to get some details there about certain people opposed to the war fever."

"Oh?"

"Yes, Alma Spreckels, she'd invited me to dinner. Not an event, just a private dinner. Where I'd be able to speak with her in confidence, you see. About who else in their circle is resisting all this." Kate turned her head toward the parade. "And who might even sit out war production, if it comes to that, which is what Lansing wants most to know about. Because she and Adolph, they're in the lead. But then, at the last minute, she cancelled. Apparently they went out of town. Maybe just to get away from all the... hullaballoo."

Breyer looked at her but did not immediately respond.

"San Diego," he finally said.

"San Diego?"

"Where they've gone, the Spreckels. San Diego. Coronado."

"I'm sorry, what's Coronado?"

"Oh. I thought you might know. Given your... duties."

He gave the jibe a moment to get under her skin.

"It's the huge island that guards San Diego harbor. I'd say the most strategic piece of land on the entire West Coast of America."

He let that sink in.

"And do you know who owns it? *All* of it? John... and Adolph... Spreckels."

Kate shook her head slightly, understanding that Breyer was stretching this out but not knowing how to get him to the point.

"That is, they own it... until this weekend. That's why they've gone down there... To sell it."

"Oh. Well, that explains it, then. Must be quite a major event. Even for them."

"Indeed. And for the army."

"Army?"

"Yes. The buyers. The Spreckels are selling it to the military. The whole place. For a war plane center, I've heard. And navy base. There's already an airfield there. And the deep harbor port. All set up. Ready for... whatever's coming."

Kate was stunned.

"But... Alma's... war charities," she stammered. "War victims... And this Preparedness noise, she hates it!"

"Well, the noise, maybe."

Kate just stared.

"I heard that the price," Breyer said, "is five... million... dollars."

"And Germany," Kate croaked, "I mean, it's their family homeland. German was Adolph's first language."

"Mm. Language. Did you know that 'million' is the same word in German as it is in English?"

Kate turned away before she could decide exactly what expression was on Breyer's face.

The news raged in her head: the Spreckels' capitulation to—or was it enlistment in?—war preparations. Alma and Adolph had been the center of Kate's search for the other side of Preparedness. A search that had gradually become a hope. And now, suddenly, she felt as if she were falling. As if she'd been suspended on a high wire over an enormous chasm, and the wire had snapped. A wire she never knew she was walking until it was gone.

Needing something to look at out the window, she homed in on the Spanish War soldiers. The Civil War veterans were just turning onto Market. The Spanish War vets were moving up behind and had come to within a few feet of Market when, just to the side of them, against the wall of the saloon...

Two hundred feet away and four stories up, the blast cracked Breyer's windows and nearly knocked Kate off her chair. The roar reverberated through the canyon of stone buildings, deafening. Dense white smoke and grey dust filled the intersection, and for the first few moments after the echoes of the blast, it was perfectly quiet. A man's felt hat, upside down, floated lazily down past Kate's window. As it did, it turned right side up and something fell out. Kate couldn't be sure, but she thought it was an ear.

The smoke slowly cleared, and Kate could begin to make out the carnage: dozens of fallen bodies crumpled all over the intersection, many of them with much of their clothing gone; hats and coats and shoes and flags strewn everywhere; the lower half of a man's leg, lying by itself on the pavement, its shoe still on; a policeman and his horse knocked to the ground in the middle of Market, struggling to rise; at the top of Steuart Street, a dozen Spanish War vets lying in a bloody straggle, as if reenacting a scene from the end of a battle.

Breyer had risen from his seat but now seemed paralyzed, staring out across Market, not moving, not speaking, not looking at Kate.

Slowly, sounds began to rise. Moaning. Howling. Screams of pain. Screams of horror. Screams for help.

People began rushing to the wounded, tending to those they could, covering with jackets those they couldn't, calling for others to lend a hand. Some of the less badly injured were climbing to their feet, looking around, dazed. Several cops stuttered back and forth, unable to decide whether they should tend to the fallen, look for further dangers, or manage the crowd.

Kate saw that while the front ranks of the Spanish War veterans had been hard hit, the bulk of them remained more or less in formation; those who'd been bloodied but not critically injured had picked themselves up and now stood, shaking, where they'd fallen. Within a minute or so, a man in a bygone officer's uniform—the same uniform Jamey had worn—stood at the head of the ragged troops and faced them; Kate could see that the legs of his trousers had been shredded by the blast, the flesh underneath torn and bloody. He straightened himself as best he could and called out to the others.

"Fall. . . *in*! Atten. . . *hut*!" He waited a few beats for the men to gather themselves. "Move. . . *out*!"

The officer started onto Market Street, turning left to join the parade. The other veterans who were on their feet began to move as well, staggering out onto Market behind the officer. Stepping over and around the bodies of their former brothers-in-arms.

28

Baja. Jalisco. Guerrero.

He'd found a freighter. If he could manage to get himself smuggled onboard, its first port of call on the west coast of Baja in Mexico could put him in position to join Villa and his insurrection in Chihuahua, due east. Or he could carry on further south, moving inland from the coast of Guerrero across to Morelos, to seek out Zapata. The caving in of the dock strike had been a humiliation for the local stevedores but a break for Blue: cargo ships were beginning to steam out of San Francisco again.

Billings had given him the names of two people who'd passed through San Francisco earlier in the year and gone south to fight alongside Villa. But considering Billings's starry-eyed unreliability, Blue didn't put much stock in the referral. Not to mention that Villa was now being chased around the northern Mexican deserts and mountains by the US Army, so just finding him could be a long, dusty, maybe fruitless struggle. Also, Villa himself seemed to Blue too much the *bandido*, the wild man, without a set of beliefs. Without a politics. The only things driving Villa, it seemed to Blue, were outrage and audacity. No wonder Billings idolized him.

No, Blue thought, Zapata was a better bet. More deeply, complexly political than Villa. With an organization. And a popular base. But Zapata too was on the run. And while Villa was known to have welcomed foreign fighters, Blue had no idea what Zapata felt about freelance *gringos* who showed up on his doorstep. Not to mention Zapata's *campesino* soldiers. What would they make of Blue, a city-boy *gringo* claiming to offer explosives skills—and what the hell else could Blue offer, that he could box?—and trying to make himself understood speaking Italian?

And this was just part of the riot of doubts banging around Blue's head. But none of it blunted what had by now become a resolve to get out, to head south, as soon as possible. He'd become mildly dispirited about San Francisco almost as soon as he'd returned, and so much so lately that he'd begun to consider seriously what earlier had seemed only fanciful: Billings's notion of going to join the upheaval in Mexico. Then, after the parade bombing, all waffling was over. Before, it had been about departure; now, it was escape.

Knowing that the police would have nothing to tie him directly to the parade bomb didn't diminish his sense that they'd almost certainly come for him. At the very least to roust and pressure him for information about Mooney. Or about some of the *Volontá* crowd. But also, despite the lack of any evidence, it was at least somewhat likely that they'd charge him with the bombing itself. Likely enough for him to get the hell out.

In the hours immediately after the bomb, the special edition newspapers had already howled that "known dynamiters" and "foul anarchists" were no doubt responsible for the outrage; the police chief and district attorney had both used those exact terms. And Blue knew what that meant. Fickert, the DA, had been shoveled into office with a massive financial push from United Railroads. Among his first official acts back then had been to dismiss a prosecution against Mullally's uncle Patrick Calhoun, who'd been charged with bribery and other graft while head of URR before Mullally had taken the company reins. In a word, Fickert was Mullally's man. Such that "known dynamiters" surely meant Tom Mooney, whom Mullally had been trying to nail since the 1913 power strike, and who just weeks before had been immediately accused, by Mullally's man Swanson, of the San Bruno towers bombing. Given Mooney's ongoing efforts against the railroad, Mullally would now surely bring to bear all his resources, including his puppet DA, to tie Mooney to the Market Street horror. Despite the fact that, as far as Blue knew or could imagine, Mooney wouldn't have had anything to do with it.

Blue tried to think through where he stood. He believed he'd escaped attention for his behind-the-scenes work with Mooney in the 1913 strike. But given his recent involvement with Mooney's URR actions, and believing that the city's entire law enforcement apparatus was now likely to focus on Mooney, how long would it take them to come up with Blue? Not to mention the other trajectory of blame, the "foul anarchists": Blue's long association with so many characters in and around the *Volontá* rooms. Then throw in his reputation as an explosives man, despite the fact that his work for the quarries and construction sites and such had been legal and aboveboard, and how much riper a target could he be?

But hang on, he thought. Maybe he hadn't been identified as part of Mooney's railroad strike crew. So that there'd be no obvious reason to connect him to the tower bombing. And, therefore, no reason to look at his explosives background. Or to look at him at all.

Unless, of course, there was a leak. If someone in the know had talked. After all, Swanson had been trying for weeks to bribe people for information. And it seemed that Mullally somehow knew in advance about the rush hour trolley action. Also, enormous rewards were already being offered for information about the parade bombing. Which might include information about the tower bombing as well. Huge pyres of cash that would fuel bonfires of hearsay and perjury. Even betrayal.

Chewing on it, Blue realized—his jaw clenched as it occurred to him—that there was someone already inside Mullally's camp who knew that Blue was involved with Mooney: Elijah. Whose family was badly struggling. Who'd so painfully thrown their big boxing match, three years before, to get a hefty payday. Who was continuing to box, despite the risk of blindness, just to put enough food on the table for his multigeneration household. Whose brother Isaiah had just been locked up for shooting a striking stevedore. Elijah. Whose feelings about Blue were... well, Blue didn't know anymore.

On top of Blue's increasing sense of a need to flee, there was something viscerally appealing to him about the image, however chimerical, of being embraced by Zapatistas deep in the mountains of Mexico. It summoned a feeling—and at this moment, feelings were clearer than thinking—that he recognized from his time in Dublin and London, where he'd felt that he was part of some sort of forward momentum.

Something extreme but ongoing. Something that included him in its collective intensity but within which he could remain slightly different, apart. Which was how he felt most comfortable.

Yes, but wasn't that the crux of Elijah's indictment of him? Always holding himself apart? Not allowing anyone close?

But wait. No one close? He'd just asked Meg to go with him, hadn't he? And meant it. Wanted it keenly. So what about that? Yes, Meg... Where is she?

And what about the other part of the London story? That after a while there, he'd felt too much the outsider. Felt the need to come back to San Francisco. And had come home.

Yeah, and how'd that work out for him...?

But anyway, who makes the rules? About how to live. Elijah has his way; Blue has his own. Aren't there infinite ways to live a life? Isn't that what Blue had always believed? So what was this shit, letting himself think like this, just because of Elijah? Too much thinking altogether. What was he doing to himself? *Madunnuzza!*

He bolted out of bed. It wasn't yet light outside but the seamen's hiring hall opened at 5:00 a.m., and he wanted to get back there as soon as possible to begin trying to find someone to help him get onto that freighter bound for Mexico. Besides, he couldn't wait to get out of the flea-ridden Mission Street flophouse where he'd spent the night after throwing his belongings into a duffel bag and slipping out of the Genova, a week's rent unpaid. It wasn't so much about the money, though he'd likely need all of his little remaining cash to get himself smuggled onto the freighter. It was just that a lot of people knew he was staying at the Genova, and if it turned out that he was high on the cops' dragnet list, as he suspected, he didn't want to spend even one more night there. Nor anywhere else in North Beach: when he'd returned from his first trip to the seamen's hall the evening before, just a few hours after the bombing, he'd already spotted detectives staking out the *Volontá* rooms. And who knew how many others were flooding the neighborhood?

He hefted his duffel, stumbled out onto Mission Street and headed for the waterfront seamen's hall, just a few blocks away.

~

The Sunday morning newspapers reported ten dead and another forty badly wounded.

Kate had been doubly concussed, by the blast itself and by the sights and sounds of its aftermath. All of which had been immediately preceded by the stunning news of the Spreckels' massive land sale to the army, ending the mirage of Alma and Adolph as bastions of some anti-war cadre that Kate had imagined, and slowly come to hope for, among the city's business elite. Moreover, she had to digest this series of shocks while still reeling from the devastation of Lily's revelations about Jamey in the Philippines. It was all too much. And without, it now seemed to her, the counterbalance of hope—faint though it had always been—that she might find Maggie.

So, during the night, she'd decided it was over. Rising from a troubled half-sleep, she'd crafted a letter to Lansing announcing that she believed her project had come to an end and that she should now return to Boston. She'd take the letter to Breyer's office first thing Monday morning, to be sent to Washington in the special courier's pouch. The charade was over. Lansing's Folly.

A bit before noon she headed down to the hotel lobby to see if any of the afternoon papers had come in. As she walked to the lift on her floor, a door opened down the hall; a man appeared on the threshold, still speaking to someone inside. It was the suite, Kate knew, of District Attorney Charles Fickert. His main residence was in a wealthy wooded enclave south of the city, but he maintained rooms at the Palace for convenience, and also to have an official San Francisco residence, which allowed him to hold city office. Mullally had introduced her to Fickert as they'd left the big Preparedness gathering at the hotel, when the Englishwoman Pankhurst had spoken, and since then Fickert had made a point of greeting Kate when occasionally they passed each other in the hotel corridors.

It wasn't Fickert, though, who now drew Kate's attention but the man leaving Fickert's suite: Martin Swanson. The detective who worked for Mullally and who had, at Mullally's request, agreed to take up Kate's quest to find Maggie. But who'd made no contact with her since their first meeting. And from whom Kate no longer expected anything.

She had to pass the two men to get to the lift; she stopped and waited several yards away while they finished their parting words. Fickert closed the door. Swanson turned and noticed her.

"Ah, Mrs. Jameson." He seemed neither surprised nor disconcerted to see her. "I'd almost forgotten you were here."

"Yes, so it seems."

As she spoke, she kept a distance that normal cordiality would have shortened. Coming out of Fickert's rooms, Swanson had pulled on a wide-brimmed slouch hat, which meant that, in the hallway's muted lighting, Kate couldn't see his face clearly enough to tell how he reacted to her barb. If at all.

"I was hoping to have some news from you," she continued. "Or at least a report on your agency's efforts on my behalf... To the extent there have been any."

If Swanson was at all bothered by her insinuation, she couldn't see it: "Yes, well, we've been... fully occupied."

"Mm. Well, whatever you've managed, please send me a bill for your services. I may be leaving San Francisco fairly soon."

"Ah. Finished your business, have you? Your... family's business?"

"Yes, I'm afraid it doesn't seem like the right, ah, climate at the moment. For embarking on new business ventures here. What with all that's gone on."

"Oh, on the contrary, Mrs. Jameson. I'd say the climate has turned... much the better."

Kate stared at him for a moment.

"Well, that seems... curious. But I'll wait for advisement... from the family."

"Yes. And I'd be interested to know what they have to say. But in any case, I'm afraid my operatives won't be able to carry on assisting you with your... personal matter. We're no longer a private agency, you see."

"Oh?"

"Yes. As of last night, we are now deputized to Mr. Fickert here. The bombing, you see. We'll be. . . specially investigating for him. Which, as you can imagine, will take up all of our energies. But as it happens, we have turned up a small bit of something for you. I doubt it amounts to anything, but you can stop by the office to pick up some notes we've made. Or if you prefer, you can wait until we've had a chance to write up a report, and I can send it to you."

Despite Swanson's deathly neutral tone and less than hopeful words, Kate's heart leaped.

"No, no. I'll come by. Absolutely. When is your office open? Tomorrow's Monday, right? Yes, yes it is, Monday. So tomorrow. I'll be there. First thing."

29

The freighter was scheduled to sail Monday noon.

It had taken half the day Sunday for Blue's merchant seaman friend to find someone he knew who'd be on the ship's crew. Then more time, and whiskeys, for him and Blue to convince this crewman—and to negotiate a price—to smuggle Blue onto the ship and to hide and feed him during the long journey.

Blue had just enough money to cover the agreed-upon smuggling fee, but it tapped him out. So he spent the rest of the day and night raising funds, hoping to have at least a little bit in his pocket when the time came to jump ship in Guererro. He didn't know a soul there.

More than just to rustle up money, though, Blue went around to say goodbye. Flaherty's dismay and Elijah's bitterness about Blue's previous dead-of-night departure still rankled; he didn't want to repeat the mistake.

First, he went to Reb Raney's. She immediately understood Blue's post-bombing precariousness and appreciated his idea of joining Zapata, warmly wishing him well on what she called his mission. Reb's partner was a full-time nurse with a regular paycheck, a rarity among Blue's circle, and together she and Reb were able to scrabble together for him the not inconsiderable sum of forty dollars. Flaherty, on the other hand, couldn't make sense of Blue's plan to head for the Mexican hinterlands. But the old-timer was savvy enough to understand that, in the current moment, given Blue's associations—at least the outlines of which Flaherty had a notion of—Blue might want to get out of town for a while, and he sent him off with another ten bucks. Then Blue swung by the IWW Latin local's meeting hall in North Beach, where Mario Fraschetti stayed in a back room. He didn't find Mario, but Luigi Parenti was there and wholly sympathized with Blue's plan to leave, saying he'd go with him if it weren't for his sprawling family there in the city. Parenti took up a collection from several other Wobblies who happened to be there, most of whom had barely two nickels to rub together, and among them they managed to pass another few dollars to Blue.

By the time Blue left the Wobblies' meeting rooms, it was nearly midnight. One place he still hadn't gone to say goodbye was Butchertown. Elijah's. The place he most wanted to go. The one place he knew he couldn't.

Standing outside the Wobblies' rooms, Blue was looking almost directly across Broadway at the Barbary Palace. Where Meg danced.

It wasn't happenstance, that his last stop was on Broadway. He wanted to try once more to see her. To say goodbye, yes, if it had to be that way. But to ask her again to come with him. Since the moment she'd left his room the other night, through the lead-up to the parade and all the following chaos, then his scrambling to find a way to get to Mexico, she'd been drifting between the front and back of his mind. But never very far back. What he wanted was another chance to convince her that she was wrong. About him. That things mattered to him. People mattered. And that his wanting to leave didn't gainsay that.

The outside lights were on at the Palace but as Blue crossed Broadway he couldn't see any lights on inside. Then he remembered that it was Sunday and the dancehalls were all closed. Which meant, he was pleased to realize, that he wouldn't have to wade through a crowd, and wait for Meg's performances to end, before being able to talk with her. But then, since she didn't have to dance that night, would she even be there? She'd been sleeping there, though, she'd told him, so where else would she be now? Unless she'd gone back to Treat's. No, he didn't believe that. Or so much wanted not to believe it that he shook his head to fend off the thought.

He went around to the alleyway side door where he'd gone in before. Listening for a few moments, he heard nothing from inside except a loud growl from the caged big cat coming, he assumed, from the upstairs backstage where he'd seen it the last time. He was about to knock when the door was shoved open, flinging him backwards. The man coming out was the same bouncer-cum-watchman who had manned that door the last time Blue was there.

"Cavanaugh! Jesus, is there some kinda convention goin' on here?"

"What?"

"Well, you got company this time."

"What are you talking about?"

"Her upstairs. That's why you're here, innit? To see her? I mean, the joint's closed, so you ain't here for the show."

"Aye, so I am. Is she here? . . . Wait, what do you mean, I got company?"

"Well, that bo she used to live with."

"Treat?"

"Yeah, that's the one. He's been comin' round lately. Tryin' to get her back, I s'pose. Mostly she won't even see him. But this time I told her he was all agitated up and almost cryin' and shit, and she told me let him in."

"And you just left them up there?"

"What the hell, Cavanaugh? I ain't her minder. And I don't stick round here on Sundays anyways. I just give it a quick check, make sure everything's jake. So help yourself," he stood aside for Blue to enter, "but I got other places to be."

Inside it was pitch black. Blue stopped to let his eyes adjust. Upstairs and to the rear he could hear Treat's voice rising and falling, and with each rise there came a responding growl from the cougar. At one break between the growls and Treat's salvos, Blue faintly made out Meg's voice.

He didn't know what to do. He wasn't about to beat some noble retreat and leave them their privacy; he had no inclination for such niceties, and certainly no time for them now. On the other hand, he didn't want to just barge into their midst, maybe provoking outrage from Meg that would stop her from giving Blue his own hearing with her. So he left his duffel below and noiselessly crept up the open staircase toward the rear backstage where Meg had made her little sleeping corner. When he could just see over the edge of the second floor, he stopped. The caged cougar, a much larger one than he'd seen the last time, turned its head quickly at the sight or smell of Blue's arrival, but neither Meg nor Treat spotted him. Meg was standing against the edge of her cot, as if she'd backed up to it, as far as she could go. Treat stood a couple of feet away from her, pleading, snarling, groaning, nearly sobbing. His words were slurred, his voice rising to a cry and falling to a whisper. He lurched from side to side, struggling to keep his balance. He was seriously drunk.

"He... he might of been part of it."

"What are you saying?"

"People saw him. Down there. The saloon. I... I even saw him. I could put him at the scene!"

"You don't know what you're talking about!"

"Oh, don't I?" His tone turned nasty. "I know a lot more than you think, missy."

"I don't want to hear this!"

"Okay... Okay, I'm sorry. Maybe... maybe he didn't mean it to happen the way it did. To kill all those people. Maybe it went off... before it was supposed to. And not *where* it was supposed to. That... must be it. I *know* that was it. But I saw him. I saw him there."

"Stop! Stop talking about him. Look, you need to understand, Treat. I didn't... move out... because of *him*."

Blue couldn't make out every word, especially of Treat's drunken slurring, but by now he was certain that he was the person they were talking about.

"No, it was *me*, when you left, wasn't it. I know, I know, 'cause of me. 'cause of *me*!" Treat's drunken cry incited a roar from the cougar. At the sudden sound of it Treat started, lurched, lost his balance and staggered toward the cage, which enraged the big cat more; it roared again and charged the bars. Treat straightened himself and moved away.

"But it's different now," he pleaded. "I was so 'fraid. They were going to close me down, Meg. I'd lose the shop. Lose... everything. I couldn't sleep. I wasn't myself, I *swear*."

Meg shook her head in rejection.

"Maybe even jail, they said..."

"They? Who's they? What are you talking about?"

"The postal 'spectors. Swanson brought 'em, make sure I knew he wasn't bluffing."

"Postal?"

"For using the mails, illegal, they said. All the birth control stuff. And... and against the army. Close me down, they said. Take my presses. Put me in jail! This federal bureau guy. Swanson brought him one day. And... and said you, too! Jail for you, too, Meg!"

"What?"

"No, don't worry, it's fixed now. All fixed. They won't bother us anymore. They promised. And look!" Treat reached into his coat and pulled out a large wad of bills, waved them at Meg. "See? They keep their promises. And this is only half of it. The other half's coming, Meg. 'cause... I did my part."

Blue wasn't sure what Treat was saying. But he'd heard enough and clambered up the final couple of stairs.

"What the hell are you talking about, Treat!?"

The lion raged, banged against its cage.

"You!" Treat howled when he recognized Blue. "It's *your* fault. All of this!"

"Fault? What the fuck?!"

"Forcone. He said you'd do the fuses... or timers... I don't know... And look what happened!"

"Forcone? What do you mean, 'Look what happened'? What are you talking about?"

"Was gonna be on the roof, Forcone said. Not the street. It'd go up in the air, over people's heads. Was supposed to be a timer. He didn't know how to do it. But he said *you* would, Cavanaugh, *you'd* do it. So this, this... It's down to you!"

"You piece of shit!" Blue lunged, grabbed him by the shirt and punched him hard across the jaw. Treat staggered and fell. The big cat roared and banged the cage.

Blue jumped on Treat and straddled his chest, held him by the throat.

"I don't know what the fuck you're talking about!" He glanced over at Meg, who had now backed away from both of them.

"Forcone..." Treat managed to sputter through a bloody mouth. "It was all his move. All I did was get him the gear. For a roof! Supposed to be up on a roof! Said you'd set it up for him... You!"

"You're crazy! I haven't even *seen* Genio..." He looked toward Meg but she was now back in the shadows. "This is fucking madness!... What do you mean you got him the gear?"

"Swanson. From Swanson. Told me he'd get me the blasting stuff if I'd set it up with one of the *Volontá*... or anybody. And Forcone, he jumped at it. Didn't even want to know how I got it, the gear. But then... all those people... it wasn't... supposed to happen that way!"

"Yeah, and what about this?" Blue smacked Treat's hand that was still gripping the huge wad of cash. The bills went flying.

"Swanson. He said if I set it up... I'd keep the shop... and even pay me. But I... I didn't want it for me, the money. It was for *her*!" He turned his head toward Meg. "So she could paint... and draw... and... and stay."

"Me? What!?" She rushed at Treat. Blue hit him another sharp blow, then got to his feet in time to grab Meg and hold her back.

"All those people!" she screamed. "Those people dead!"

"Meg, listen," Blue urged. "Let's get out of here. I mean, who knows what else is gonna happen now? Swanson... and... whoever else. It's not safe. I mean, they're *crazy*. But I got a ship. So we can go. Now. This minute. A ship..."

Meg was dazed.

"C'mon, grab some things." He left Treat on the floor and edged Meg over to the trunk next to her cot. "Have you got a bag? Here." He picked up a canvas bag that held her "jungle" dance costumes, scarves, her long-hair wig, and dumped them on the floor. "Put stuff in here. Quick. We gotta go."

Meg looked over at the semiconscious Treat, then back at Blue. Her eyes began to focus, her jaw set: "You and me."

"Yes." And after a moment, he added, "Absolutely."

"Absolutely," she repeated as if the word were a puzzle. "But..."

"Doesn't matter," he cut her off.

"What doesn't matter?"

"I... Look. We gotta get out of here. Mexico. You and me."

She searched Blue's face for a long moment, then looked again at Treat. She said nothing but took the canvas bag from Blue and began stuffing things into it. Blue knelt down and began to pick up the fallen cash.

"No!" Meg barked. "Don't touch it!"

"Listen, we could use it. *Really* use it. And if we leave it here, we're just leaving it for him."

"It's blood money!"

"Only if he's the one who keeps it."

Treat moaned, moved his head, but otherwise remained motionless on the floor. Meg looked at him, shook her head, grabbed a couple of more things to stuff in her bag. Blue went back to picking up the bills.

The big cat let out a sudden roar. Blue turned, heard Meg scream "Look out!" and saw Treat, his face twisted and bloody, coming at him with a pair of scissors. Blue ducked under Treat's wild lunge and hit him in the gut. Treat doubled over but held onto the scissors; Blue grabbed that arm and with his other hand punched him in the face. Treat stumbled backward and crashed into the cage, sliding down against the bars. In a heartbeat, the big cat reached through the bars and brought its claws slashing down across Treat's head and neck.

"Jayzus!" Blue said but just stood there.

Meg rushed over and yelled at the cat, who backed away. Then she grabbed Treat by the feet and dragged him out of the cat's reach.

"My God," she said, looking at the blood flowing from Treat's ugly wounds. "We got to stop that." Though she said 'we,' she didn't look to Blue for help and scrambled over to a small bag next to her cot. She grabbed a bottle, looked around frantically, then pulled the cover off her bed pillow and moved back to Treat. From the bottle she poured liquid over his wounds, then began to tear the pillowcase into strips.

"The sheets!" she said to Blue. "Tear 'em."

Meg used the pillowcase, followed by sheet strips from Blue, to pressure Treat's wounds, then to wrap a makeshift dressing around his neck, where the most blood was flowing.

"You got it," Blue said, looking down at Treat. "Now we got to get out of here."

"No, he needs a hospital."

"Are you crazy? We need to make that boat before daylight. Anyway, you stopped it. He'll survive."

"No I haven't. I just slowed it down. Something's cut inside his neck. If we leave him, he might bleed to death."

"Yeah? And who'd be sorry about that? Think about what he did, so. A fuckin' monster."

"No," she looked down at Treat. "He's. . . a Judas. And a coward. But your friend Genio. What's he?"

She glared at Blue, still keeping the pressure on Treat's neck.

"Okay, look," Blue finally said. "They got a telephone downstairs, yeah?"

"Yeah. Behind the bar."

"You get your stuff. I'll call an ambulance, tell them there's a drunk here who got mauled by the cat. Tell 'em he's bleeding out bad. But then we get out. And we leave him here. All right?"

Meg shook her head. "I've got to keep this pressure on."

"*Madon'!*" Blue looked around. "Okay, after I call, we'll take him downstairs. I'll open the front door. You stay on him down there 'til I spot the ambulance. Then we get out quick, the side door. All right?"

She wavered, then nodded.

"All right," Blue said. "It's gonna be all right."

30

The fog had returned. Dense. Slow. Silencing the streets.

Market Street felt odd to Kate, a simulacrum, a parallel universe from that of two days before. From the parade. From the bomb.

It was 9:00 in the morning. She had waited as long as she could stand it, almost ill with anticipation to see the "bit of something," as Swanson had called it, that his office had turned up in its search for leads about Maggie. She had tried through the night to tamp down her hopes. But it was a losing effort and by morning her heart was racing. She stretched out her breakfast as long as she could—finding it impossible to concentrate on the morning newspapers, their reports on the city's official outrage and on the hunt for the bombers—then gave in, dressed hurriedly and headed out.

The lower end of Market Street was a curious mix of somber quiet and prurient hum. There were people coming and going but fewer than normal, and at a restrained, cautious pace, as if embodying a respect for those who'd died nearby. But as Kate got further along she noticed a number of people chattering and moving rapidly, almost clambering around and through the mindful slow-movers, heading toward the corner of Steuart and Market. When she crossed Market to get to Swanson's office, she could see a ring of gawkers gathered behind the police ropes that still cordoned off the blast site.

The office was swarming. There were so many people bustling about that Kate could barely get in the door, and it took several minutes to get someone's attention. Finally a young underling took a moment to ask what she wanted. He seemed irritated by her request but grudgingly said he'd look into it and asked her to wait outside. She sat on a bench in the corridor for fifteen agonizing minutes before the young man came out, handed her an envelope, said "Here," turned around and disappeared back into the office. Kate couldn't be bothered by the rudeness: she was too anxious to see what Swanson's people had produced to worry about how they perceived her.

In the envelope were two typewritten pages with a list of dates and corresponding comments. There was also a bill for services, with the final amount tallied but then crossed out in pen, a zero written underneath, and next to it a handwritten notation "Professional Courtesy" and the initials MS. Falling out from the midst of the other sheets was the photograph of teenage Maggie in dance costume, which Kate had given to Swanson during her first visit.

On the first page, next to dates beginning several weeks before, there were abbreviated notations including names such as "Molly Jameson" and "Maggie James" and identifiers such as "nurse, Harbor Hosp," "Union Dance Sch," "too old" and "SF whole life." After each of these entries was the word "Closed." These dead ends filled the first page and the top of the second.

The rest of the second page had five entries, with many black marks blotting out text. The first, from three weeks before, had the name "Meg," and the words "dance," then several words covered up with thick black ink and a handwritten notation above the blacked-out part reading "per MS"; these were followed by "short hair" and "not Jameson." Kate's eye scanned down to the next entry, dated a week later, and her heart thundered as she saw the name "Carey." But all of the rest of that notation was blacked out, again with "per MS" hand-noted above.

Next was an entry that simply said "No release, per MS."

Then, next to a date ten days ago, an entry that read, "Now resides Barbary Palace. No longer with..." and then blackening.

The final note was dated July 23, just the day before: "Meg Carey. Boston. Face and type very close, but short hair. Dance & res at Barbary Palace, Broadway," and "OK release per MS."

Kate wondered at all the blackouts, apparently ordered by Swanson—MS—and at the disturbing inference that he'd been sitting on some of this information for weeks. But she was near to bursting at the sight of the name Meg Carey and Boston, and pushed aside her distress about Swanson. She rushed down the stairs and out to the street.

She hailed a taxi and asked to be driven to the Barbary Palace on Broadway; the driver seemed somewhat incredulous that this well-dressed woman would be heading there.

"You... know the Palace ain't gonna be open this hour, don't you?"

"It's not?"

"Lady, it's a dancehall. And it's 10:00 in the morning."

"Oh, well, still..."

"You sure it's the right place?"

"Am I sure? Oh yes sure. Well, not sure, but..." she glanced down at the papers from Swanson's office, still clutched in her hand, and at the photo of Maggie. "Yes, please."

The cabbie had no more chance to argue since they'd already traveled the short distance from Swanson's office up to Broadway.

Kate hadn't had time to imagine what the Barbary Palace was or what it might look like and was taken aback to see the garishly painted, hulking structure plastered with signs and posters and dotted with dormant multicolored lightbulbs. She was also startled to see two policemen hunched in front of the big front double doors. As she got closer, she saw that they were hefting a thick chain up to the door.

"Excuse me."

One of the cops looked up.

"Is there... anyone here?" Kate asked. "I mean, inside?"

"Nope. And you ain't getting a drink here anytime soon. We're closing it down for the time."

"No, I..." Kate's eye was drawn to a huge poster plastered by the side of the entrance. "Amazon Beauty!" was emblazoned across the top and "Performing Nightly" along the bottom. The larger middle section was a bright color picture of a young woman in a scanty leopardskin costume swinging on a vine, some sort of snarling big cat behind her and stretching his claws toward her back. It was a painting not a photograph, but it certainly could have been Maggie.

The cops began to loop the chain through the door handles.

"Well, when will they...?"

"Don't know, lady. Not up to us. We're just meant to lock it up. Owner's got to deal with the city after that. Some kind of trouble 'bout animals." He lifted his eyes to the poster of the Amazon girl and the big cat.

"Well, can you tell me, is the owner about? I mean, is there anyone...?"

The cop rose up and looked Kate over. "So what's, ah, what's your business here, anyway?"

"Oh, I'm just... looking for someone. Who might be... working here."

"Well, ain't nobody here now. We just checked the place... Maybe you oughta get hold of the owner. Schultz. You know him? He just run out of here. Heading for City Hall, he said. I'd check back later if I was you."

"Yes. Yes, I will. Thank you. I... certainly will."

Kate took a long last look at the poster before turning away.

∽

Blue and Meg were holed up in a closet-like alcove, behind a cloth curtain, in an empty storeroom of the freighter. There were no comforts: the storeroom had only shelves and a few boxes; they'd have to make a bed out of the clothes they had in their bags. And, in any case, their crewman smuggler had told them to stay out of sight, squeezed into the alcove, for the first couple of days until he'd learned what the locations and rhythms of the crew would be.

At least they'd made it onto the ship.

After fleeing the Barbary Palace, they'd spent the remaining hours of darkness in an all-night waterfront café where the crewman named Bolski had said he'd rendezvous with Blue to take him on board. Blue put away a couple of whiskeys when he and Meg first arrived at the café, then ate a big fry-up breakfast, realizing that he might not have another real meal for quite some time: Bolski had said that the trip to Guerrero would take about two weeks. Blue also bought provisions, which the café sold to seamen who were about to ship out, and stuffed them into his duffel: Bolski was meant to get him food on board, but Blue wasn't counting on much. Besides, there were now two of them.

Meg had drunk a bit of tea. Nibbled some bread. And said almost nothing. The look in her eyes spoke for her: she was somewhere else.

Given what had happened, and how suddenly, Blue could certainly understand that she'd be stunned, would be trying to digest it all, wouldn't be inclined to her usual quick and pointed remarks. But her almost total silence unnerved him. He'd always had a hard time with silences. Not just that he was at his best when words were the moment's currency but also because he often got the feeling—uncomfortable, unbalancing—that a silence meant something was being left unsaid. And he had no defense against the unspoken.

Bolski had shown up at the café at 5:00 a.m., as promised. But he was furious about Meg. It wasn't part of the deal, he fumed. Sneaking two on board more than doubled the risk. Finding a safe space on the ship to hide two was too much. No way he could get enough food for two. If the crew found a woman on board there's no telling how ugly things could get—Blue half expected a feisty response from Meg about this, but she remained quiet, passive—and Bolski sure as hell wasn't going to protect her. It was off, he was done, Blue could forget the whole thing.

Blue had stuffed into his coat pocket the large wad of bills Treat had brought to the Palace, and he now pulled out several for Bolski to see. He handed the seaman a ten-dollar bill and told him there'd be four more when Blue and Meg were safely on board. Bolski went quiet—fifty dollars was likely more than he'd earn for his entire two-month voyage—and thought for no more than a few moments before saying, "Well, maybe." He told Blue and Meg to wait there while he returned to the ship, but for them to be ready to move quickly. He was back within thirty minutes, and with the thick fog helping to keep visibility low even as the sky began to lighten, he was able to sneak the two of them on board and into the storeroom without anyone noticing that they were not in fact part of the scatter of longshoremen and supply people who were scuttling back and forth between the ship and the pier.

After they'd settled into the alcove, scrunched together on the floor between their two bags, Blue dozed off for a bit. He woke to find Meg leaning over him, holding a piece of cloth and one of the bottles of water they'd brought.

"I just want to clean up that gash again," she said. "It's not looking so good."

At Meg's strong suggestion—when she'd tended to his head wound during the night they'd spent together in his room—Blue had stopped by Lily Bratz's clinic and had the wound reopened, properly cleaned, and stitched up again by the nurse on weekend duty there. But during the struggle with Treat at the dancehall the stitches had come loose and the wound was bleeding again; Meg had noticed it in the café. From his bag Blue had produced a large kerchief—Elijah's bandana—and pressed it to the wound. Now Meg wet the cloth and tended it again.

"Seems you do this a lot for me."

"Twice."

"And... for himself the Judas back there, his neck."

She kept fussing with the gash, didn't look him in the eye.

"I mean, it's... really something, so it is. What you're able..."

"Yeah. It's called 'being useful.'"

Blue was relieved that Meg had emerged from her shell a bit but had no idea what her state of mind was. He realized that he had to be careful what he said: they'd be stuck together in this tiny space for the next couple of weeks, and then... Mexico. Which he knew so little about that he couldn't even form an image of it.

She was quiet while she finished tending to him, finally fashioning the large bandana into a sort-of-bandage that kept pressure on the wound. He thanked her, then they settled back against their respective bags, their heads only two feet apart but, by mutual silent assent, separate from each other.

"So, what will we do there?"

Blue had dozed off and now took a few moments to respond.

"Do?"

"Yeah. Do."

"Well, the money," he tapped his coat where the stash of bills was. "It ought to keep us for quite a long while, being's I've heard how cheap things are down there. By the way." He took the entire wad of cash out of his pocket and wedged it into the top of her bag. "Here."

Meg barely looked at it.

"That's not what I mean. I mean, what will we do with ourselves, once we're there?"

"Well, I was hoping to go inland, find Zapata."

"Yeah, yeah, but Zapata or not, what will we *do*?"

Blue squinted at her across the short dark space between them.

"Well, look at yourself. You got this great healer talent, doncha."

"Great? It's barely basic. And without speaking a word of Spanish? C'mon. Who am I going to help?"

"Ah, I'm sure you can still... But anyways, what about your painting? You can finally paint. All you want."

She frowned: "Painting is what I do to get *away* from the world. But what am I gonna do *in* the world?"

"I... look. We'll figure this out when we get there. Right now, we just got to go."

"And what about you?"

"What about me?"

"What are *you* going to do?"

"Me? What me?"

"I mean, seems mostly you keep to the wings. Except for punching people... and blowing things up."

Blue felt skewered. He didn't like it.

"What is all this? 'Doing things.' You mean like Treat? There's a doer for you."

"No, I mean like... Lily. Or Belle... Ike and Maysie."

"Yeah, well..."

"Things that matter."

"'Matter.' I keep hearing that out of you. It's an awful big idea, innit? So how exactly did you get to decide what matters?"

"Oh, I don't... But at least I ask."

Blue had had enough. First Elijah. Now Meg. Pressing him. About who he was. Why did he have to sit still for this? He knew who he was. Or at least knew enough.

And anyway, what about all he'd done with Mooney the past weeks? With his head split open in the bargain. And what about London? And Dublin? And back here in '13? Not to mention getting Meg out of who knows what nightmare Treat had brought to her door. Jesus fuck! as his old man used to say. His old man. Who'd also. . . gotten out.

Meg seemed exhausted by the effort of their back-and-forth, on top all that had happened since Treat had showed up at the dancehall. She leaned back, closed her eyes. Gratefully, Blue also sunk back into his bag and soon drifted off.

"What would you have done?"

Blue opened his eyes to find Meg peering at him intently. Even through the darkness of the alcove, her eyes shone fiercely.

"This guy Genio. If he'd found you. And asked you to fix up the bomb?"

"What would I. . .?" He shook his head. "You can't think. . ."

She waited a few moments, then said, "That's not really an answer, is it."

He considered before replying. "I have never. . . killed. . . anyone."

"Yeah, but what if he'd come to you and said, 'Just fix it up for me. So's it'll go off on the roof,' or whatever it was Treat was saying how it was supposed to be? I mean, you hate the army, with your brother dying and all. Hate the war. And there would have been this big chance for you, if Genio had found you. Something big. And sure, maybe you know it's a risk, a few people maybe get hurt, but you can control it, you and your fuses and whatnot. Right? At least mostly. And it's worth it, yeah, the risk? I mean, risks, that's what you're about, right? So tell me, Blue. What. . . would you. . . have done?"

"But. . . I *didn't*, did I. I mean, you keep talking about what matters. Well, the way *I* see it, *that's* what matters."

Meg stared at him, searching his eyes in the semidarkness.

"Listen," he said, "I gotta go see Bolski. He wants the rest of his money before we sail. Got to keep him happy."

He reached toward the money but hesitated. Meg kept her eyes on his face. Waiting.

Blue pulled a few bills from the stack, counted forty dollars, and returned the rest to Meg's bag.

"I'll be right back. Shouldn't be long now, when we sail. Meg... we'll be fine."

"We... will be fine." Her voice trailed off.

Blue waited, and when she said nothing more he got up and went to the door, opened it carefully and looked out. He saw no one in the passageway and slipped out, casting a quick glance back at Meg, her long legs sticking out from under the curtain.

He went to the spot under a nearby metal ladder where Bolski had shown him a tarp-covered bin that could serve as one of several emergency hiding places for Blue or Meg outside the storage room. Bolski was waiting there. Blue gave him the money and, with a few pro-visioners and dockers still moving about and providing cover, Bolski took him around that part of the ship, showing him the two nearest heads, which Blue and Meg could sneak to at night; Bolski gave Blue a bucket for use during the day. Then they ducked out of sight behind a bulkhead, and Bolski explained that he'd bring them food and water once a day, though he couldn't say exactly when; he told Blue a signal knock he'd use. Any other noise near the storage room and they'd have to get themselves completely hidden in the alcove, behind the curtain. He also took Blue around to a ladder that led down to the crew's area; Bolski said that if there was an emergency, Blue was to tie something to a hook behind the ladder. Like that bandana, he said, indicating Blue's head bandage. Otherwise, that was it until they reached Ensenada, the freighter's first stop, when they might have a chance to stretch their legs.

When Blue got back to the storage room, his head was full of Bolski's instructions. But he hesitated before going in, realizing that his last exchange with Meg might not be finished. And realizing that if it was still ongoing, he didn't know what he'd say. He also consid-ered that if he was going to be with Meg, lots of exchanges would be ongoing. That if he was going to be with Meg, certain things would have to be different. Not that he himself would have to be different, no, that wasn't going to happen. But maybe some of his ways. How he went about things. If he was to be with Meg.

But as soon as he entered the storeroom, he understood. With just one step inside he could feel that the room was changed. He looked around for a moment, as if something there might give him a different message from what he already knew.

He went over to the alcove. Pulled back the curtain. Her bag was gone, too. Sitting on top of his duffel was the big stack of bills.

~

Kate paced her room. She was certain it was Maggie. It had to be Maggie. The face on the poster, well no, she couldn't be sure. But almost. And Boston, Swanson's notes said. And Carey. It couldn't be a coincidence. But why would Maggie do that, use Carey? Was it a way of hiding? Or just a way to help her feel different? Or was it... not Maggie?

And if it was Maggie, what would Kate say to her? How could she keep from giving Maggie the impression that she'd stalked her here? And more—enormously more—how would she begin to speak to Maggie about Jamey, as she'd promised herself she would do. She'd learned so much from Lily. But there was still such great unknown. And none of what Kate now knew excused her original and perpetual sin: her failure to have spoken of it to Maggie, any of it, before now.

She sat in the room's reading chair. Picked up *Lear*.

When she'd gone to the public library weeks before, to learn about various city characters and to search for information about the Loie Fuller dance troupe, she'd also thought to ask the librarian for things to read. She'd wondered if the librarian knew of any literature that took as its subject a parent's relationship to a child. Not a child's view of a parent or of the adult world. But the crucible that was a parent's endless struggle: how to go about enacting love for a child.

The librarian had been puzzled. Told Kate that she'd give it some thought while Kate was looking through the other materials. And when Kate was ready to leave, the librarian told her that she hadn't been able to come up with anything. Except *King Lear*. And gave Kate a copy to take back to the hotel.

Jamey had introduced Kate to Shakespeare during their brief halcyon days. They'd gone to see *Romeo and Juliet* and *Macbeth* at the old Federal Street Theater. But Kate was unfamiliar with *Lear*. And because she'd never read Shakespeare on the page, she had difficulty parsing the play's language. She'd had a hard time getting through it but, nonetheless, a few days later had found herself picking it up again. And the second time was captivated by it.

Now she picked it up a third time. And searched for one of the play's moments—Lear speaking to Cordelia, the daughter to whom he'd been such a fool—that had moved her greatly. She found it. And opened her notebook. To copy down the words, so that she'd have them to hand. Whenever she might need them.

When thou dost ask me blessing, I'll kneel down,
And ask of thee forgiveness. . .

AUTHOR'S NOTE

This is a work of fiction. Its three main protagonists are entirely a product of the author's imagination. However, many other notable characters and groups in the novel hew closely to the historical record, as do key movements and events.

In the years immediately before US entry into World War I, San Francisco roiled with pitched battles between labor and capital and between the forces of authority—both state and church—and a broad spectrum of working-class antinomians. Some of these struggles are detailed in the novel: sabotage-heavy strikes against the power companies in 1913; a long and violent waterfront strike in 1916; attempts to unionize United Railroads, including the bombing of its electrical towers; and the North Beach neighborhood's birth control free speech "riots" (there were several, one resulting in the prosecution of Joseph Maccario and the rising to his defense by numerous of the city's well-to-do women). At the same time, the Preparedness movement was seeking to push the US into the European war in the face of primarily working-class opposition, leading in the summer of 1916 to the Preparedness Day parade and its bombing.

Among the overlapping radical labor and anarchist milieux of 1916 San Francisco, some of the most extreme characters—including quite a few who advocated "propaganda of the deed" violence—circulated within and around the *Gruppo Anarchico Volontá* in North Beach; that same district's "mixed Latin" labor group was also home to many of the city's most dedicated IWW syndicalist cadres. Tom Mooney, often abetted by his young acolyte Warren Billings, was a major actor in the 1913 strikes against the big power companies and was the driving force behind the 1916 attempt to organize workers at United Railroads. Belle

Lavin's Mission District boardinghouse was a longtime hub of radical activities, as was the vegetarian restaurant on Market Street. The character of Lily Bratz is a composite of several dedicated women physicians of the time, who gave their energies equally to medical care—especially for women—and to various oppositionist political causes.

The novel's characters and machinations from the other end of the sociopolitical spectrum are likewise empirically rooted: Thornwell Mullally of United Railroads; his shadowy henchman, detective Martin Swanson; Charles Fickert, Mullally's handpicked district attorney; Mayor "Sunny Jim" Rolph; the named members of the business elite who created a vigilante Law and Order Committee to physically crush union workers, at the same time beating the drums to send those same workers to fight the war from which their industries would reap fabulous profits; and Adolph Spreckels and his checkered-past spouse Alma, who initially opposed Preparedness but made a stunning *volte-face* by selling Coronado Island to the army. And then there was the British suffragette Emmeline Pankhurst, who became a rabid supporter of Britain's entry into the war, touting "patriotic motherhood" and publicly humiliating young men who did not volunteer to fight, messages she brought on tour with her to the US in 1916.

As for institutions of the state: Secretary of State Robert Lansing did indeed create a secret intelligence bureau called U-1, to operate parallel to the fledgling Federal Bureau of Investigation; and the US Army at San Francisco's sprawling Presidio base, following the mandate of base commander John "Black Jack" Pershing when he left to chase Pancho Villa in Mexico, freely lent its men and facilities to the Preparedness movement in general and to Thornwell Mullally in particular.

A word on the era's US military subjugation of the Philippines. This dark chapter in American imperialism, hidden in the shadows of US "glory" in the Spanish-American War, is much in need of greater public exposure. During its years-long occupation, the US military engaged in systematic torture—including the institution of what's now called waterboarding—as well as the widespread torching of villages and herding of populations into concentration camps, what came to be known in Vietnam as "pacification." Also arising from the horrors of that war was the identification among returning American servicemen of symptoms that are now recognized as post-traumatic stress disorder; one of the names given to the condition was Disordered Action of the Heart.

∼

In one of the crudest, most grotesque frame-ups in American political history, Tom Mooney and Warren Billings were convicted of the Preparedness Day parade bombing. Mooney was sentenced to hang; Billings got life in prison.

The juridical fraud was directed by Martin Swanson, head of security for Thornwell Mullally and United Railroads, and Charles Fickert, the district attorney whose election had been financed by United. Within hours of the bombing, Fickert deputized private detective Swanson to lead the city's official investigation. Swanson immediately narrowed the field of suspects to Mooney and Billings, ignoring all others of whom logic would have demanded investigation: German saboteurs, already active in the region; Mexican avengers responding to the US army's occupation of Veracruz and invasion of northern Mexico; and the sector of rabidly antimilitarist anarchists, of whom San Francisco had many, who espoused "propaganda of the deed." Each of these clusters was known to have engaged in bombings that had intended, or at least callously risked, random deaths. Which Mooney and Billings never had.

The concocted prosecution, and the so-called investigation that followed rather than preceded it, included coached, perjured and likely paid false testimony identifying the two men as having been at the bomb site. It rejected all inconvenient witnesses: the bomb was packed in a suitcase, and at least five people reported a man carrying a case at the scene as dark and swarthy, some said with a large moustache, nothing remotely close to pale, clean-shaven, Irish-stock Mooney and even paler red-haired, freckle-faced Billings. And it suppressed a photograph that definitively showed Mooney a mile away from the scene at the time of the explosion.

Two juries—Mooney and Billings were tried separately—bought the prosecution's case against them. Given the civic hysteria following the bombing, kept aflame by immediate and unrelenting pretrial harping in the press that Mooney and Billings were the guilty parties, the verdicts were not a surprise despite the utter lack of any direct evidence tying the two men to the bomb. The verdicts were even more likely given the trial's "professional jurors": retired or otherwise unemployed men whose financial solvency depended on their pay as jurors in trial after trial, their ongoing inclusion on the jury panels, determined by the presiding judge, being dependent on consistently returning guilty verdicts.

The fabric of the prosecution's case was so flimsy, so riddled with illogic and falsehoods, that it began to fall apart almost as soon as the verdicts were in: witnesses recanted or were shown to have lied; others disappeared; suppressed exculpatory evidence surfaced. A campaign to free the men grew rapidly, with massive support from labor groups across the country and around the world. The outrage was so impressive—and so potentially disruptive on the eve of US entry in the war—that President Woodrow Wilson took the extraordinary step of secretly contacting the governor of California to have Mooney's death sentenced commuted to life imprisonment. Legal defense committees were established to prepare appeals, funds were amassed to hire investigators, and slowly the case against the two men was unraveled.

Slowly. The legal system is set up to hold fast to a criminal conviction even if its entire basis is shown to have depended on assertions that the earth is flat. Despite steadily mounting and eventually overwhelming evidence that the two men had been framed, for years courts and successive state governors repeatedly refused to overturn the convictions. Tom Mooney was finally pardoned from San Quentin prison in 1938; soon after, Warren Billings was released from Folsom prison. They had served over twenty-two years for a crime they did not commit.

~

If Mooney and Billings didn't set off the Preparedness Day bomb, who did?

The matter has never been definitively determined. But decades after the fact, two sources emerged that strongly indicate that the bomb was the work of someone from the *Gruppo Anarchico Volontá* or its penumbra. The first source was Luigi Galleani, an Italian anarchist notorious for his advocacy of individual acts of insurrectionary violence, including assassinations and bombings. Galleani lived for several years in the US and was in frequent contact with people within the orbit of the San Francisco *gruppo*. The US deported Galleani in 1919, and during his deportation interrogations, the transcripts of which surfaced many years later, he was asked about the Preparedness bombing. He replied that he knew "with mathematical certainty" that Mooney had not set off the bomb. Galleani refused to name the actual perpetrators but left no doubt that he knew who they were: Galleani testified that he'd been approached by a San Francisco Italian anarchist to advise on the action but that he'd refused to participate.

Galleani's testimony was corroborated by Paul Avrich, the longtime historian of anarchism in America, who cited personal interviews with undisclosed sources, most likely members of the *gruppo* itself. Given Avrich's reputation as a meticulous historian, the great respect in which he was held by generations of anarchists, and the trust he was afforded by them, there is ample reason to give credence to these sources.

Knowing that someone from the *gruppo* or its environs set off the bomb, however, leaves yet another question: Who else might have been involved? That is, was the bombing prompted or facilitated by a provocateur from the virulent anti-labor forces that at that very moment had mustered an enormous war chest and a huge force of private operatives to crush the momentum that labor had been building in the city over the previous years?

There is certainly an historical basis for the proposition that agents of the industrial barons—Martin Swanson or someone else within the assembled private army—may have participated in or logistically supported the bombing. When, several years before the Preparedness Day bomb, the heads of United Railroads, including Thornwell Mullally's uncle Patrick Calhoun, were awaiting trial for massive corruption involving the city council, the home of the key witness against them was blown apart by a bomb; two United Railroads employees were convicted of attempted murder (miraculously, the witness and his family survived). Also, during regional strikes in 1913 and 1914, undercover agents, including Swanson, repeatedly attempted to entrap union activists—Warren Billings was among those they snared—by planting dynamite, apparently willing to countenance the use of those explosives by those whom they failed to get arrested. And in the weeks leading up to the Preparedness bombing, Swanson had been collaring numerous individuals across the spectrum of San Francisco left radicalism, combining threats with huge offers of cash ($5,000, the equivalent of well over $100,000 today) for anyone who could help connect Tom Mooney to a bombing.

While there is no direct evidence that a provocateur was involved, the bombing certainly redounded greatly to the benefit of big capital. Just as the central labor council had warned before the parade, the standing and power of organized labor suffered a drastic setback when the bombing was blamed on someone (Mooney) identified with unionism. Combined with the wartime suppression of labor rights once the US entered the European fray a few months later, plus the federal government's campaign against radical unionists in general and anarchists and Wobblies in particular—including deportation of many foreign-born radicals—during the war and continuing through the 1920s, the Preparedness Day bombing and the Mooney and Billings convictions set off a long downward spiral for local labor. The bombing also created new fissures in the already fragile relations among traditional labor groups, local Wobblies and variously striped anarchists, making collective action against this anti-labor tide even more difficult. It wasn't until the early 1930s that San Francisco's labor movement returned to its former strength.

∼

Legions of research materials underlie this novel, but some works are especially worthy of note.

The warp and woof of late nineteenth- and early twentieth-century anarchist and Wobbly communities in San Francisco, and particularly in the heavily Italian neighborhood of North Beach, is presented in great detail and with clear-eyed sympathy by Kenyon Zimmer in his remarkable *Immigrants against the State: Yiddish and Italian Anarchists in America.*

An excellent resource for photographs, as well as a range of informative short texts, about San Francisco in the early twentieth century is the community-based online digital history archive FoundSF.org, curated by Chris Carlsson and LisaRuth Elliott.

The byzantine fabrication of the criminal case against Tom Mooney and Warren Billings, as well as the many-years-long struggle to free them, is comprehensively chronicled in Richard H. Frost's *The Mooney Case* and Curt Gentry's *Frame-Up.* The manifold labor battles of the period are well-documented in *Industrial Relations in the San Francisco Bay Area, 1900–1918,* by Robert Knight.

For a glimpse of the world of radical women physicians of the time, from which the character of Lily Bratz was drawn, and their relations with each other up and down the West Coast, see Michael Helquist's *Marie Equi: Radical Politics and Outlaw Passions.* Those intrigued by the antics of Alma Spreckels can find more in *Big Alma,* by Bernice Scharlach.

As to the Kiddies Scheme and its suppression by the joint efforts of the Catholic Church and the police during the Dublin labor war of 1913, an excellent blow-by-blow account can be found in *Lockout: Dublin 1913,* by Pádraig Yeates. With regard to splits in the British suffragette movement, including the question of support for Britain's entry into World War I, as represented by opposing positions taken by Emmeline Pankhurst and her daughter Sylvia, see Jill Liddington, *The Long Road to Greenham: Feminism and Anti-Militarism in Britain since 1820* and Katherine Connelly, *Sylvia Pankhurst: Suffragette, Socialist and Scourge of Empire.*

Despite its near total absence from American public consciousness, the US's war and occupation in the Philippines has been the subject of considerable academic and journalistic attention. Among the most comprehensive studies are *The Blood of Government: Race, Empire, the United States, and the Philippines,* by Paul A. Kramer and

Benevolent Assimilation: The American Conquest of the Philippines, 1899–1903, by Stuart Creighton Miller.

∾

For their insights on various matters with which this novel grapples, I am immensely grateful to Jolle Demmers, Tim Clark, Sasha Lilley, Sameer Mehendale, Franco Moretti, Anne Wagner and Michael Watts. Kenyon Zimmer graciously shared with me some of his immense knowledge and obscure source materials regarding the San Francisco anarchist community. For unstinting critical support and editorial wisdom, I am greatly appreciative of and indebted to Ramsey Kanaan, as well as to all his dedicated colleagues at PM Press. And for their unfailing love and tolerance during the long slog of book-creating, my boundless thanks to Sanjyot and Jesse.

ABOUT THE AUTHOR

Joseph Matthews was born in Boston and raised there and in California. For a number of years, he was a criminal defense lawyer in San Francisco, where he still resides. He is author of the novels *Everyone Has Their Reasons* and *Shades of Resistance*, the story collection *The Lawyer Who Blew Up His Desk*, and the post–September 11 political analysis *Afflicted Powers: Capital and Spectacle in a New Age of War* (with Iain Boal, T.J. Clark, and Michael Watts).

ABOUT PM PRESS

PM Press is an independent, radical publisher of books and media to educate, entertain, and inspire. Founded in 2007 by a small group of people with decades of publishing, media, and organizing experience, PM Press amplifies the voices of radical authors, artists, and activists. Our aim is to deliver bold political ideas and vital stories to all walks of life and arm the dreamers to demand the impossible. We have sold millions of copies of our books, most often one at a time, face to face. We're old enough to know what we're doing and young enough to know what's at stake. Join us to create a better world.

PM Press
PO Box 23912
Oakland, CA 94623
www.pmpress.org

PM Press in Europe
europe@pmpress.org
www.pmpress.org.uk

FRIENDS OF PM PRESS

These are indisputably momentous times—the financial system is melting down globally and the Empire is stumbling. Now more than ever there is a vital need for radical ideas.

In the years since its founding—and on a mere shoestring—PM Press has risen to the formidable challenge of publishing and distributing knowledge and entertainment for the struggles ahead. With over 450 releases to date, we have published an impressive and stimulating array of literature, art, music, politics, and culture. Using every available medium, we've succeeded in connecting those hungry for ideas and information to those putting them into practice.

Friends of PM allows you to directly help impact, amplify, and revitalize the discourse and actions of radical writers, filmmakers, and artists. It provides us with a stable foundation from which we can build upon our early successes and provides a much-needed subsidy for the materials that can't necessarily pay their own way. You can help make that happen—and receive every new title automatically delivered to your door once a month—by joining as a Friend of PM Press. And, we'll throw in a free T-shirt when you sign up.

Here are your options:

- **$30 a month** Get all books and pamphlets plus 50% discount on all webstore purchases

- **$40 a month** Get all PM Press releases (including CDs and DVDs) plus 50% discount on all webstore purchases

- **$100 a month** Superstar—Everything plus PM merchandise, free downloads, and 50% discount on all webstore purchases

For those who can't afford $30 or more a month, we have **Sustainer Rates** at $15, $10, and $5. Sustainers get a free PM Press T-shirt and a 50% discount on all purchases from our website.

Your Visa or Mastercard will be billed once a month, until you tell us to stop. Or until our efforts succeed in bringing the revolution around. Or the financial meltdown of Capital makes plastic redundant. Whichever comes first.

Everyone Has Their Reasons

Joseph Matthews

ISBN: 978-1-62963-094-6
$24.95   528 pages

On November 7, 1938, a small, slight seventeen-year-old Polish-German Jew named Herschel Grynszpan entered the German embassy in Paris and shot dead a consular official. Three days later, in supposed response, Jews across Germany were beaten, imprisoned, and killed, their homes, shops, and synagogues smashed and burned—Kristallnacht, the Night of Broken Glass.

Based on the historical record and told through his "letters" from German prisons, the novel begins in 1936, when fifteen-year-old Herschel flees Germany. Penniless and alone, he makes it to Paris where he lives hand-to-mouth, his shadow existence mixing him with the starving and the wealthy, with hustlers, radicals, and seamy sides of Paris nightlife.

In 1938, the French state rejects refugee status for Herschel and orders him out of the country. With nowhere to go, and now sought by the police, he slips underground in immigrant east Paris.

Soon after, the Nazis round up all Polish Jews in Germany—including Herschel's family—and dump them on the Poland border. Herschel's response is to shoot the German official, then wait calmly for the French police.

June 1940, Herschel is still in prison awaiting trial when the Nazi army nears Paris. He is evacuated south to another jail but escapes into the countryside amid the chaos of millions of French fleeing the invasion. After an incredible month alone on the road, Herschel seeks protection at a prison in the far south of France. Two weeks later the French state hands him to the Gestapo.

The Nazis plan a big show trial, inviting the world press to Berlin for the spectacle, to demonstrate through Herschel that Jews had provoked the war. Except that Herschel throws a last-minute wrench in the plans, bringing the Nazi propaganda machine to a grinding halt. Hitler himself postpones the trial and orders that no decision be made about Herschel's fate until the Führer personally gives an order—one way or another.

"A tragic, gripping Orwellian tale of an orphan turned assassin in pre-World War II Paris. Based on the true story of the Jewish teen Hitler blamed for Kristallnacht, it's a wild ride through the underside of Europe as the storm clouds of the Holocaust gather. Not to be missed!"
—Terry Bisson, Hugo and Nebula award-winning author of *Fire on the Mountain*

Fire on the Mountain

Terry Bisson
with an introduction
by Mumia Abu-Jamal

ISBN: 978-1-60486-087-0
$15.95   208 pages

It's 1959 in socialist Virginia. The Deep South is an
independent Black nation called Nova Africa. The
second Mars expedition is about to touch down on the
red planet. And a pregnant scientist is climbing the Blue
Ridge in search of her great-great grandfather, a teenage slave who fought with
John Brown and Harriet Tubman's guerrilla army.

Long unavailable in the US, published in France as Nova Africa, *Fire on the
Mountain* is the story of what might have happened if John Brown's raid on
Harper's Ferry had succeeded—and the Civil War had been started not by the
slave owners but the abolitionists.

*"History revisioned, turned inside out . . . Bisson's wild and wonderful imagination has
taken some strange turns to arrive at such a destination."*
—Madison Smartt Bell, Anisfield-Wolf Award winner and author of *Devil's Dream*

"You don't forget Bisson's characters, even well after you've finished his books. His Fire
on the Mountain *does for the Civil War what Philip K. Dick's* The Man in the High
Castle *did for World War Two."*
—George Alec Effinger, winner of the Hugo and Nebula awards for *Shrödinger's
Kitten*, and author of the Marîd Audran trilogy.

*"A talent for evoking the joyful, vertiginous experiences of a world at fundamental
turning points."*
—*Publishers Weekly*

"Few works have moved me as deeply, as thoroughly, as Terry Bisson's Fire On The
Mountain *. . . With this single poignant story, Bisson molds a world as sweet as
banana cream pies, and as briny as hot tears."*
—Mumia Abu-Jamal, prisoner and author of *Live From Death Row*, from the
Introduction.

Pictures of a Gone City: Tech and the Dark Side of Prosperity in the San Francisco Bay Area

Richard A. Walker

ISBN: 978-1-62963-510-1
$26.95   480 pages

The San Francisco Bay Area is currently the jewel in the crown of capitalism—the tech capital of the world and a gusher of wealth from the Silicon Gold Rush. It has been generating jobs, spawning new innovation, and spreading ideas that are changing lives everywhere. It boasts of being the Left Coast, the Greenest City, and the best place for workers in the USA. So what could be wrong? It may seem that the Bay Area has the best of it in Trump's America, but there is a dark side of success: overheated bubbles and spectacular crashes; exploding inequality and millions of underpaid workers; a boiling housing crisis, mass displacement, and severe environmental damage; a delusional tech elite and complicity with the worst in American politics.

This sweeping account of the Bay Area in the age of the tech boom covers many bases. It begins with the phenomenal concentration of IT in Greater Silicon Valley, the fabulous economic growth of the bay region and the unbelievable wealth piling up for the 1% and high incomes of Upper Classes—in contrast to the fate of the working class and people of color earning poverty wages and struggling to keep their heads above water. The middle chapters survey the urban scene, including the greatest housing bubble in the United States, a metropolis exploding in every direction, and a geography turned inside out. Lastly, it hits the environmental impact of the boom, the fantastical ideology of Tech World, and the political implications of the tech-led transformation of the bay region.

"With **Pictures of a Gone City**, *California's greatest geographer tells us how the Bay Area has become the global center of hi-tech capitalism. Drawing on a lifetime of research, Richard Walker dismantles the mythology of the New Economy, placing its creativity in a long history of power, work, and struggles for justice.*"
—Jason W. Moore, author of *Capitalism in the Web of Life*

"*San Francisco has battened from its birth on instant wealth, high-tech weaponry, and global commerce, and the present age is little different. Gold, silver, and sleek iPhones—they all glitter in the California sun and are at least as magnetic as the city's spectacular setting, benign climate, and laissez-faire lifestyles. The cast of characters changes, but the hustlers and thought-shapers eternally reign over the city and its hinterland, while in their wake they leave a ruined landscape of exorbitant housing, suburban sprawl, traffic paralysis, and delusional ideas about a market free enough to rob the majority of their freedom. Read all about it here, and weep.*"
—Gray Brechin, author of *Imperial San Francisco: Urban Power, Earthly Ruin*

The Explosion of Deferred Dreams: Musical Renaissance and Social Revolution in San Francisco, 1965-1975

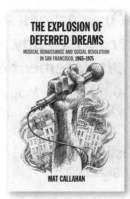

Mat Callahan

ISBN: 978-1-62963-231-5
$22.95   352 pages

As the fiftieth anniversary of the Summer of Love floods the media with debates and celebrations of music, political movements, "flower power," "acid rock," and "hippies", *The Explosion of Deferred Dreams* offers a critical re-examination of the interwoven political and musical happenings in San Francisco in the Sixties. Author, musician, and native San Franciscan Mat Callahan explores the dynamic links between the Black Panthers and Sly and the Family Stone, the United Farm Workers and Santana, the Indian Occupation of Alcatraz and the San Francisco Mime Troupe, and the New Left and the counterculture.

Callahan's meticulous, impassioned arguments both expose and reframe the political and social context for the San Francisco Sound and the vibrant subcultural uprisings with which it is associated. Using dozens of original interviews, primary sources, and personal experiences, the author shows how the intense interplay of artistic and political movements put San Francisco, briefly, in the forefront of a worldwide revolutionary upsurge.

A must-read for any musician, historian, or person who "was there" (or longed to have been), *The Explosion of Deferred Dreams* is substantive and provocative, inviting us to reinvigorate our historical sense-making of an era that assumes a mythic role in the contemporary American zeitgeist.

"Mat Callahan was a red diaper baby lucky to be attending a San Francisco high school during the 'Summer of Love.' He takes a studied approach, but with the eye of a revolutionary, describing the sociopolitical landscape that led to the explosion of popular music (rock, jazz, folk, R&B) coupled with the birth of several diverse radical movements during the golden 1965-1975 age of the Bay Area. Callahan comes at it from every angle imaginable (black power, anti-Vietnam War, the media, the New Left, feminism, sexual revolution—with the voice of authority backed up by interviews with those who lived it."
—Pat Thomas, author of *Listen, Whitey! The Sights and Sounds of Black Power 1965-1975*

Counterpoints: A San Francisco Bay Area Atlas of Displacement & Resistance

Anti-Eviction Mapping Project with a Foreword by Ananya Roy & Chris Carlsson

ISBN: 978-1-62963-828-7
$34.95   320 pages

Counterpoints: A San Francisco Bay Area Atlas of Displacement and Resistance brings together cartography, essays, illustrations, poetry, and more in order to depict gentrification and resistance struggles from across the San Francisco Bay Area and act as a roadmap to counter-hegemonic knowledge making and activism. Compiled by the Anti-Eviction Mapping Project, each chapter reflects different frameworks for understanding the Bay Area's ongoing urban upheaval, including: evictions and root shock, indigenous geographies, health and environmental racism, state violence, transportation and infrastructure, migration and relocation, and speculative futures. By weaving these themes together, *Counterpoints* expands normative urban-studies framings of gentrification to consider more complex, regional, historically grounded, and entangled horizons for understanding the present. Understanding the tech boom and its effects means looking beyond San Francisco's borders to consider the region as a socially, economically, and politically interconnected whole and reckoning with the area's deep history of displacement, going back to its first moments of settler colonialism. *Counterpoints* combines work from within the project with contributions from community partners, from longtime community members who have been fighting multiple waves of racial dispossession to elementary school youth envisioning decolonial futures. In this way, *Counterpoints* is a collaborative, co-created atlas aimed at expanding knowledge on displacement and resistance in the Bay Area with, rather than for or about, those most impacted.

"This collection literally makes visible intersecting lines of structural violence that produce displacement and dispossession, while also tracing creative resistances that are always challenging these processes and building more just futures. As an atlas, Counterpoints: A San Francisco Bay Area Atlas of Displacement and Resistance *is transformative and inspiring—it refuses the knowledge making and representational practices that bind cartography to settler colonialism and racial capitalism, instead developing ethical cartographies and collective praxes for mapping otherwise."*
—Sarah Elwood, professor of geography, University of Washington, author of *Relational Poverty Politics: Forms, Struggles, Possibilitie*s